Getting The Point

Gary Brozenich

Copyright

TABLE OF CONTENT

Chapter 1 1

Chapter 2 12

Chapter 3 22

Chapter 4 34

Chapter 5 44

Chapter 6 53

Chapter 7 60

Chapter 8 77

Chapter 9 89

Chapter 10 100

Chapter 11 111

Chapter 12 125

Chapter 13 142

Chapter 14 154

Chapter 15 166

Chapter 16 180

Chapter 17 193

Chapter 18 209

Chapter 19 220

Chapter 20 236

Chapter 21 255

Chapter 22 268

Chapter 23 274

Chapter 24 286

Chapter 25 300

Chapter 26 314

Chapter 27 325

Chapter 28 340

Chapter 29 354

Chapter 30 365

Chapter 31 371

Chapter 32 379

Chapter 33 388

Chapter 34 397

Chapter 35 413

Chapter 36 424

Chapter 37 439

Chapter 38 450

Chapter 39 465

Chapter 40 478

Chapter 41 491

Chapter 42 504

Chapter 43 521

Chapter 44 536

Chapter 45 558

Chapter 46 577

Chapter 47 588

Chapter 48 608

Chapter 49 621

Chapter 50 638

Chapter 51 675

Chapter 52 687

Chapter 53 697

Chapter 54 715

Chapter 55 740

CHAPTER 1

I do not know exactly when it started, I just remember the smell. We lived in one room with two mud walls and a thatch roof. I was told that the other two walls were built by the French trappers, whoever the hell they were. We had a pot in the corner for night soil that Mother threw into the street each morning, just like everyone else. It all mixed with the dung from the cart animals and any other garbage that was not wanted.

The rats and the wild dogs seemed to live off of it. The smell never left my nose no matter how hard I tried. Father repaired shoes someplace in the center of the hell hole we called The Point.

This was a section of Pittsburgh that was between the main part of the city and the place where the Allegheny River and the Monongahela River meet to form the Ohio River. The entire town is shaped like an arrowhead and we lived in the slums at its point. He made a little less than it took to feed us so he became a pickpocket to add to his income. He was not very good at it so one day, Mother took me by the hand to the town center to say goodbye to him as he walked up the gallows where they hung him. I was ten years old. As we walked home from the hanging she turned to me and said, "I am going to a part of town where women earn their living at the satisfaction of men." "There is no place for you there so you must find your way & quote; I wished I did not know what that meant, but on our streets, there were no secrets and even a very young fellow knew what a whore house was. I did not judge her. Stay alive no matter what was the rule of the streets and now I had a full plate of expectations of my own. I went home to gather my few things and sleep, knowing that the next day I would be thrown into the street. Even the cruelest landlord gave you one night after your father was hanged. I found a small piece of bread and a sliver of cheese wrapped on a semi-clean rag and ate all of it. When the sun rose, I took to the street to find a way to live for one more day.

People suppose that seeking a long term plan would be your first thought, but that is a lot of bull.

Today was my goal. Just survive today. To hell with the future. I walked the streets looking for any way to earn a little food. Unfortunately, the city was crowded with young and old in search of the same thing. As I got closer to the center of town, the smells of frying fish and fresh bread, along with a myriad of cooking, whatever, wafted through the air and my head swooned with the fragrance. My stomach screamed for relief, and I felt feint for want of anything to satisfy my hunger. I begged for work and I pleaded with each vendor for any way to earn just a tiny something to eat, but I was kicked, hit with sticks and driven away each time.

The last stall was occupied by a large man selling hard rolls and, of all things iron hammers. He quoted his price and explained that his wife baked the rolls and he made the hammers. I asked if he had any way for me to earn a little food. His face went red, and he puffed up his chest. He screamed at me to leave while he grabbed a hammer and swung it at me. I scrambled out of the way, picked up a hammer and hit the thumb of his left hand that was resting on the table. He let out a great cry as I grabbed several rolls and ran down the alley. I kept seeing myself up on the very gallows that hung my father for stealing, but damn those rolls were good. I traded one of the rolls for a tall mug of water mixed moonshine. Water in Pittsburgh was deadlier than poison so even children knew to mix it with a halfpenny of alcohol. It was not a great start, but my belly was full and I lived another day. After walking many miles I found a falling stable with just enough of a roof to keep the weather off of me. I curled into a ball and slept. Somehow a little bit of sun light managed to find its way through the clouds of soot that hung like a dirty blanket over the city and found its way through a crack in my roof and right into my face. I could have kept on sleeping, but that darn light just would not leave me alone. I finally gave up and decided to get on with it. I went back to the tumble down shed and did my business before leaving to face the day. I decided to stay away from the food stalls where the hammer and rolls guy worked, assuming that he would remember me. I noticed a small garden patch behind a little cottage that looked inviting so I crawled over the wall that surrounded the garden and proceeded on all fours to see just what was growing. There wasn't much but I managed to gather a bunch of onions before I left the garden running as a big woman with a stout broom came screaming after me as she ran out the cottage door. I found a good spot to avoid people after a long run and decided to sit down and enjoy my onion breakfast. As I sat there eating, I decided to take stock of what I had going for myself. I had a knit hat that was falling apart, a shirt that was my fathers with the sleeves cut off. A pair of my fathers' pants with the legs cut off at his knees and then the ragged bottom halves were sewn over the holes in the rump. I had no socks, but I did have shoes even if they were two different sizes and styles. I held them on with a long rag wrapped around the shoe and around my ankle where I tied it in the front. I was tall for my age, but as skinny as the wild dogs that fought for food in the streets. My hands were big as were my feet and I wished to someday grow into them. My father was a big man and had been able to earn a living as a prizefighter before time and too many punches were not blocked in time leaving their permanent damage to his big frame. His hands were a mess which explains why he was such a poor pickpocket. He did teach me the way to survive in the prize ring and I added to that the tools of street fighting taught to me by the older toughs in the city. Those lessons were brief and painful, but I soon learned to give as good as I got and they left me alone. I guess I had every reason in the world to just give up, but there were so many kids in the Point in the same shape that I was in that it seemed foolish to feel sorry for myself, especially since I always figured that I would make out no matter what. As I was walking down another alley filled with trash, I saw a big kid crawling backward from a window. He was pulling a large sack with him as his feet hit the ground running. I heard a scream from inside the house, and then I turned to see a

Copper running toward me, shouting, "Stop, thief." He was looking right at me so I decided that my best move was a fast escape. I took off after the crook with the sack and I put on my best imitation of a racehorse. That copper would never catch me, but I wanted the crook that caused my current problem more than anything else. It did not take long for me to begin to catch up to him. As I got near him I told him to keep running and to follow me. I do not know why, but he did just that. I turned down several alleys and cut offs with him close on my heels, and then I hit a big wooden fence with my shoulder and it swung open like a gate. He followed me in, and I quickly pushed the eight-foot section of the fence back in place. I put my finger to my lips to keep him quiet. After a while, we heard the Copper and one of his friends running past us down the alley. They sounded like a couple of winded buffalo; as they passed. It was all I could do to keep from laughing out loud. I pulled on his shirt and directed him to a big dead bush alongside a building. I pulled back the bush and revealed an opening that went under the building to an old stone-lined room. I lit a candle that was sitting on a table and went back to pull the bush back in place. I turned and sat down next to him. He was twice my size and a few years older. He stuck out his hand and said, "Hi, I am Toby and I thank you for the help. Half of what I got is yours."; Well, how could I be angry with such a generous offer even if I had no idea what was in the sack? I shook his hand and said, I am Kile and I sure hope there is food in that sack; Toby got a wide grin on his face as he pulled out a loaf of still warm bread, a round of cheese, half a dried sausage and a knife to cut with. I noticed that the sack was still half full but Toby suggested that we eat first and then look at the rest of his treasure. After nothing but onions for breakfast, I was more than happy to sit and eat like a king. I could not remember eating so well. After a while Toby pulled out a bottle of gin from his coat pocket. I went to the back of the room and brought a jug of water and two glasses. We both smiled and decided we might just be the luckiest kids in all of Pittsburgh. With full bellies (for the first time that I can remember) and a little bit of a gin buzz we sat back and decided to empty the sack. Toby said anything else was just thrown in because it was within easy reach. As it turned out he had taken a hand full of silverware and several silver cups that had been in the process of being polished. Much to our surprise there was also a large suet pudding and a bag of raisins. We were in heaven with the pudding, but Toby was almost too afraid to touch the silver. He looked at me and said that he only went in to take food. He had never taken anything of value before. He suggested we wait until after dark and then throw the silver in the river. I looked at him and became very serious. Taking things of great value was not to be laughed at so I moved close to him, looked him right in the eyes and got hysterical laughing. I fell onto my side and could not stop even to catch my breath. Finally, I got control of myself and explained that my father was hung two days ago for stealing a man's silk hanky. "They will hang us for just the bread, let alone the pudding. When Toby realized what I said he too started to laugh and before long we were both rolling on the ground.

After we settled down he said maybe we should take back the pudding and we started laughing all over again. The good news was that we looked just like a thousand other street orphans so there was no need to worry about being identified. With our bellies full we both decided to take a nap. When we woke up it was getting close to dark. Toby asked me what we should do with the silver. I told him to bring it along and follow me. We wondered deeper and deeper into the back alleys of the city to a place where not even the coppers would venture after dark. Toby was scared but I just smiled at him and told him to stay close to me. I finally stopped at a brass door on the side of the big workhouse where people went when there was nothing else left. Most died within a few weeks, some lasted a little longer. I banged on the door and a voice on the other side bellowed,"; Go away, there is no more room today."; I yelled back, "; Open the damn door or I will sell your sister to old McCloud" The door opened and a man bigger than the door itself stepped out. He looked at me and smiled while waving us into the building.

"What do you have?" he asked. He saw the troubled look on Toby's face and said, "I take it you two just met." Everyone in these streets calls the boy Getsit because whatever you need he gets it." We showed him the silver and he was impressed. It was a little above my usual trade goods. He asked what we wanted and I told him to arrange for us to eat regular at the local stalls and Molly's Pub for two weeks. Before I could say another word he said "Don't," and put out his hand. I said, "Not so fast, we also need two fine blades and a change of clothes, including shoes and socks." He hesitated for just a moment and then put out his hand again. I grabbed his hand and before he let go he added one more thing."You do business only with me and no one else."; I smiled and said," Done and done." Thus began my new career.

CHAPTER 2

Toby kept looking at me with a blank stare as we left the workhouse. I finally stopped and looked back at him and said, "What is wrong with you?"

It was not until then that I realized just how big he was. He towered over me and he weighed as much as a man. I could not tell how old he was, but it suddenly dawned on me that this big fellow had been taking orders from a ten-year-old kid. I was so accustomed to being on my own that taking charge was just the natural thing for me to do. Toby just smiled and said, "What do we do next Getts?" I liked the sound of that name so I decided Getts it would be from now on.

"We go to Molly's Pub and eat to our hearts content", I told him and I took off down the alley with my new friend in tow. When we got to the pub we walked to the back and sat at a table in the far corner. I looked over at Toby who still held onto his big smile and I could see he had a lot of questions to ask. "OK, I said just tell me what is on your mind." He started to talk very fast and I had to put my hand up to slow him down. "One question at a time", I said.

"How will Molly know about the deal you made, he asked? I explained that everyone in the neighborhood would know by now.

It is just how it is. "Why did we get no money?" he asked "And how do we know he will stick to the deal?" "In the first place there is very little real money in this whole section of the city". "It is too dangerous for the likes of us to carry any if we had it.' "He would never cheat us because no one would ever do business with him if he did." "The best thing is that no one will be crazy enough to steal from us because it would be like stealing from our new partner and he is like a king here and he and his men will be watching our back," I said. At that point Molly ambled over to our table, pulled me up out of my chair and squeezed me so hard I thought I might burst.

Then she kissed my cheek, sat me back down and said, "Sorry about your Dad, he was an OK guy but a bad pickpocket." No need to order, I have cheese, bread, a roast duck, and mugs of ale on the way.

I reached in the sack and took out the suet pudding and the raisins. I gave them to Molly and asked her to join us for dessert.

A little tear forced its way into the corner of her eye and she said, "You are the sweetest of boys and I will remember this forever."

She turned her head and shouted over to the bar, "Bart please come here". Now everyone in this part of town knew that Bart was a known thief, and a killer. He was the best man with a knife in the city and no one crossed him. When he got to the table Molly explained to him that our friend owed the two of us each a blade and she wanted him to make sure we got something special. Bart told us to stand up and after taking our measure he grinned, shook his head and walked away.

Molly winked at us and said in a very low tone, "I wonder what he will come up with?", and she walked back to the bar. The food began to arrive and we felt like two kings at a feast. While we were eating Toby asked about the man called Bart. Now Bart did not look like much, he was petite and skinny. He dressed in an old shirt and torn pants with a big black cloak that went from his neck to the floor. He walked kind of crab like with a sideways gate. His feet never seemed to leave the floor and you never saw his hands beneath the cloak. My father once told me that when you did see his hands, it would be the last vision you would have on this earth. I told Toby about how Bart made a living and his face got as red as blood. "This back alley part of town is full of all kinds of characters just trying to survive the best they can." "There is a stringent code here that we leave each other to our own needs and only strangers are fair game." I explained to him. Toby said, "I am a stranger here". Not any more you are not primarily with your new partners. I said to Toby the basics of our situation and told him that I liked him but he could leave if he wanted.

He explained to me that he had no place to go. He was only 15 years old, but he had a long way to grow to catch up to his father. They were from Scotland and they came to Pittsburgh before he was born in search of work as a blacksmith.

What work he found paid little and was dangerous, but they managed to get by. A year ago his mother took sick from the foul air in the city and died. A week ago his father was working on a horse no one else would touch when the horse broke from his halter and kicked his father in the head. His father did not recover and Toby was put into the street to fend for himself. When I saw him coming out of that window he was holding the only food he had had in days. I guess it was a sad story, but to tell the truth I did not care. We all had heartbreaking stories, but that did nothing to get you through the next day. I put my hand out and Toby shook it with that big smile plastered on his face. He said to me," So what do we do next?"

I suggested that we finish our food, have pudding with Molly and then go get some sleep. "Where ", he asked, "At the building where we hid out earlier?"

"No,No,No," I told him. "We never go to the same place twice in a row." I explained that when the time came I would show him.

We sat in the pub and had a grand old time. I never saw anyone that could eat as much as Toby. I thought to myself that the food might be the best part of our bargain. Molly came over when the place started to slow down and brought the suet pudding and a hot sauce she made from the raisins to pour over it. It was great and she seemed to enjoy it more than we did.I was glad because she was a good friend to have. Molly was about five foot two with bright red hair and she was what we would call plump, not quite fat but real huggable. She was kind to everyone, but she took no trouble from anyone. Her pub was about thirty foot square with a bar running down the left wall as you walked in. There were many tables scattered around the room with a rather large table in the far corner. The entire room was dark, but the floors and walls were scrubbed clean. We always sat at the corner table.

When we could eat or drink no more I said it was time to leave. Molly pulled me aside and told me to return in the morning and she and Bart would have clothes and our blades for us. As we walked out the door I told Toby what Molly said to me.

We took our time weaving down one ally and another.

We laughed and relived the crazy day we had so far. When we hit a street with a gas light high on a pole I stopped and checked in all directions to make sure no one was around, then I grabbed Toby and pushed him through a window I had just opened on the side of a big building.

When we were inside I pulled a heavy black blanket over the window, struck a Lucifer and lit a candle sitting on an old table. There was no door and no other window in the room. It was about three meters square and besides the table the only other furniture was a couple of poorly put together pallets on the floor.

"How did you find this place and why is there no door?" he asked.

"The outside wall was collapsing so the owner of the building paid my father to fix it." "My old man just put two new walls further into the building for support which left this hidden room". "The owner would never come to this part of the city so he was content that the building did not fall and his rents would continue to come in." "Dad and I used this place to keep our goods in until I could sell them to our new partner." We also knew it would be a good place to hide out." " I know you are wondering how a ten year old kid could

be doing what I do, especially since you came from where you did, but it is different here." "You either take to the streets or the streets take you"

"I was four when dad had me working the streets and selling our wares, and frankly I love it and would not want to do anything else." "People here respect each other for what we can do and age has little to do with it." Dad was a poor pickpocket, but I am one of the best." " I can put my right hand out and ask a lady for a little change and when she bends down my left hand ends up with her earring in it." "Everyone steals a little, even the King has no problem overtaxing the poor." " The rule is, "Do not get greedy."

"Take a little, but never take too much." "If you had taken all their silver today there would be an outrage and the Coppers would not rest until you were caught, but no one feels sorry for someone that loses a few pieces especially when they have so much."

Toby sat on one of the pallets with his head in his hands and said, "There is so much I do not know, how will I ever get by?" I explained to him that he needed to relax because we were partners and I would show him the how and the way of the streets. I also explained that with our new partner our game had changed big time. "We did not just agree to sell him anything we got, we agreed to provide him with a steady lot of goods." That is why I asked for the blades although I doubt we will ever need them". "Everyone here now knows of our bargain. They will show us a new respect as long as we earn it, but people from other parts of the slums will need to know that taking from us will be dangerous because Bart has provided us with the blades." "Now let's get some sleep and visit Molly in the morning."

Chapter 3

Sleep was hard to find. I laid on the pallet and looked at the ceiling and my head swirled. Life was easy with just me to think of. The haze of the night and the smells, oh God, would they ever go away, were upon me like a blanket with hands of death around my throat. I needed to think and I needed to gather the strength that would lead me and poor Toby through another day. Life grabbed the night fog and pushed it into a black halo that smothered the room with expectation. I grinned, and I knew that I would figure it out. I said, "Screw it, and went to sleep.

A small streak of light managed to get through the corner of the filthy blanket over the window.

It was just enough to let me know that the new day had arrived, and we had things to do and people to see. We worked our way back out the window when I was sure the alley was clear and started toward Molly's Pub, but first we had to visit the food stales for our breakfast. We got fruit and bread and cheese along with a jug of apple cider, a meat pie and a dried apple tart. We sat under a tree and began to devour the food as only two young boys can. A couple of other boys came over to us as we were eating. They looked to be my age or just a little bit older. When I asked what they wanted beside something to eat, they told me that they heard that Toby and I were in business and they wanted to know if we needed any help. Those two were just as dirty and ragged as I was and I recognized them from the area. Because I worked for my Dad I never had time to run the streets with other kids so I never had any friends of my own. I asked what they could do and was told they would do whatever I asked and what ever I taught them. I stood up and said, "Good answer." "Help yourself to the food and meet us here again before dark." They helped themselves to the food as Toby and I walked away sharing the tart. Toby stayed close and said very little. We were soon working our way through the back alleys to my part of town and the only place I felt safe. By the time we got to Molly's it was close to noon .I took an extra long route that covered places Toby had never seen before.

I explained to him that I would do that each time so that when we went to the Pub he would learn every bit of this part of Pittsburgh. We went into the pub and right to our table in the back of the room.

Molly came out with a big smile on her face and took us each by the hand and led us into a back room. I was never aware that there was a back room let alone a kitchen and a bedroom. I should have known that Molly had to have someplace to stay, but these rooms were clean and very friendly. She even had a newspaper picture hanging on the wall.

When we entered the room I saw two tubs of steaming hot water and a pile of towels. Molly said, "Strip out of those rags and get into the water" Much as I hated it I was well aware that crossing Molly was not a good idea. We shucked our rags and got into the water as quickly as we could.

Toby seemed to be quite pleased, but I had never had a complete bath before and I did not like the idea. She gave us each a long handle brush and a bar of soap and said, "Start scrubbing and if you miss anything I will scrub you all over again myself." She also explained that we were not to leave the tub until she returned.

About an hour later Molly came back, handed me a large towel and told me to sit on the stool next to her. She wrapped another towel around my neck, took out a comb and a straight razor and began to cut my hair. She kept working until her face lit up with a satisfied smirk and said, "Now that is just grand." "OK Toby you are next." "When she was finished with us both she went to a big trunk and handed us each new clothes. Now they were not really new, but they were pretty damn close and more amicable than anything I ever had.

She told us to put on the shoes, socks, long johns and pants and wait. Well I have to tell you that even only half dressed I felt like an uptown dandy. I never knew clothes could feel this good on your skin, and there was not so much as a hint of a flea or a louse in them. A little while later Bart came in and shut the door behind him. He told Toby to face away from him and when he did he hit Toby in the back right between his shoulders. Toby lost his breath and staggered. Bart now told him to throw his shoulders back and stand tall. He warned Toby that if he ever saw him standing hunched over he would hit him twice as hard.

Well I don't mind telling that old Toby stood as tall and straight as the Queens guards. He towered over me and Bart both.

Bart smiled and patted Toby's broad shoulder. At that point he took out a very long knife sharpened on both sides. He slid it into a sheath and then proceeded to wrap a thin harness around Toby's arms and let the knife hang down Toby's back. The handle of the blade was just below the top of the back of Toby's neck.

Bart said ", Let me see you get it out". Toby had the long blade out in an instant. My God, he was big and that long blade made him look like the devil come to call. Bart said," Stand up tall and no one will ever know it is there." Toby grinned and slid the blade back. Bart threw a shirt and a long wool coat to him and Toby put them on.

Bart was right, the blade was hidden entirely.
Bart looked at me and grinned. He told me to hold out my left arm. From somewhere under his cloak he took out a very thin dagger. He put it on the table and proceeded to belt a funny looking rig onto the inside of my lower left arm. He put the dagger into the contraption with a snap The point of the blade came just to my wrist.

He folded my left hand away from my wrist and told me to push the button with my right hand.

When I did the dagger shot out into my hand with about six inches of blade beyond my grip on the handle. He then pushed the button again and the dagger returned to my forearm. I picked up my shirt and cloak and put them on.

Bart grabbed us both by the neck and held us against the wall. He said, Never show anyone your weapons or I will take them back". "If you ever take them out use them." Do not threaten and do not hesitate." "Stab fast, stab deep, and leave no witnesses." At that he left

What the hell did I get us into was stuck way in the front of my mind. An instant later Molly came in. She gathered up our old rags and told us she would clean them because we would want to use them in the future when we needed to fit in. Whoever would believe such well groomed boys like us were those dirty alley rats that were playing the streets. We went back to our table in the Pub and sat down. I noticed that I was so caught up in my thinking that I had not realized that Toby seldom talked. I asked him if he had any questions and he finally spoke up. "When Molly was cutting my hair she explained to me that my job is to watch your back and keep you safe".

"She assured me that you would take care of everything else." I spend my energy watching and being prepared, not talking." I do have one question though, "What is our partner's name at the workhouse?" I said," His name is Billy but in our part of town they call him Birdshot because he carries a long thin leather tube full of lead birdshot used in a shotgun." "It weighs about fifteen pounds and when he swings it what ever it hits is as good as dead." " Molly uses him sometimes to break up fights at the Pub."

"He mostly just needs to show up and the fight ends, but if it does not he ends it quickly."

As I told these things to Toby I realized what a crazy world he must think we live in. It is, I thought, but it is mine and I love it. Here I can be somebody just because I know the streets and I give respect where it is deserved. We sat there for a bit longer and we ordered some food. After we ate I told Toby we had better go meet the two boys we spoke to earlier.

When we got to the tree where we had left them they were waiting for us. I pointed to the taller boy and said, "You are number one and your friend is number two. We will have no names that we can give to the Coppers and that is how it will be." They both stood there grinning until I asked them what was so funny. They looked at each other and One said," We are a little surprised at how you two look." I would have never recognized either one of you now that you are all dressed up and wow are you clean." Toby and I had forgotten just how much we had changed. "Starting tomorrow your first job is to watch the food stalls and keep the street snatchers away." "If they give you trouble just motion to Toby and we will take care of it." I never needed to tell Toby the what and why of what I did and that was just the way I wanted it. I had two weeks of food and protection paid for and I planned to use every second of it.

The next day we went to the market, got a few things from the food vendors and then sat under our tree to watch. One and Two patrolled the area and moved any would be thieves away. As I expected, it did not take long before a much older boy showed up and I knew he was a thief in search of a free breakfast. I had to give it to One and Two.

They walked right up to him and told him to move along. He grabbed One by his shirt and prepared to hit him with his fist. Before he could swing Toby had his arm bent back and we were taking him into the alley. While Toby held him and came close to breaking his arm I explained that these stalls were under our protection and if we saw him here again we would break his arm. I was surprised at his response. He said " I have to eat too." "Can't we work together?" I told him to wait. I went to a stall got some food and came back. I gave him the food and told him to meet me here tomorrow morning under the big tree.

Everyone in the stalls saw what was happening and at the end of the day I went to each one of them and explained that for a few pennies a week their stalls would be free of theft. They could even leave their merchandise unattended and it would be there when they got back. No one even hesitated. They each dug into their pockets and produced the money I had requested. I divided the money into three piles. I gave a third to One and Two, Toby and I took a third and the rest I put away for Birdshot. One and Two were so excited they could not talk.

They had never had any real money before. I told them to watch the stalls until the vendors went home. The first thing they did was buy food from the stalls which pleased the vendors no end. Toby and I went straight to the workhouse.

Birdshot was waiting for us at his open door with a big smile on his face. He knew about our new business already. Toby could not believe it. I was not surprised. He asked us to sit at his table, but before we did, I handed him his money. He hugged us both, but Toby got a hug followed by a pounding on his back and a handshake for the way he took care of the older boy that morning. He told us to go see Molly because Bart was asking for us. I intended to go right to the Pub anyway and ask her to hold our money.

Blades or no blades, I do not want to carry money. Before we left he said he had a job for us if we wanted it. He explained that a nearby warehouse had a problem with constant break- i n s. They need someone to watch it especially at night. I knew that building well because I had removed an item or two from it in the past myself.

The owner was not local which made him fair game. I thought it was funny to get paid for not robbing, but I saw a good opportunity here. I knew that building well. The second floor was empty except for a few walled off rooms and a big iron wood stove. I told Birdshot to tell the owner I would move into the second floor to make sure it was protected, and he and I would split the fee 60/40 with Toby and I getting the 40%. He thought the arrangement was perfect and he shook his head. "Now you have a place to live in addition to the money."If you keep this up, you will own the whole damn city, and I will retire to the shore, said Birdshot. It was now time to go see Molly.

Chapter 4

We made our way through the alleys to Molly's. I took a new route for Toby to learn that went through very narrow passages crammed with drunks, beggars and ladies trying to ply a trade that they had long lost the looks it required.

Because we were dressed so well, people were pulling at us and begging for money or at least a drink. Every time someone got close to me Toby was quick to move them on. Sometimes with a little more force than I expected. I looked at him kind of funny like and he said, "Just doing my job." When we finally got to the Pub I was fully aware that going through that part of town dressed as we were was a mistake not to be repeated. I felt like it was not fair to the poor fools that lived there. Dressed as we were there was no way they could know that we were one of their own.

We entered the pub and went right to our table. Molly soon joined us and sat down after giving us each a hug. I told her we had a little cash and she said, "So I heard." God, there were no secrets in these back alleys. I told Molly that the money belonged to Toby and me equally and she could take 10% for keeping it safe for us. She looked around the room to be sure no one could hear her and then she said, "I will do you one better." "I will put your money on the street at high interest and I will only take 25% of what it earns " There is so little cash around that it will grow fast." In one of those rare moments Toby spoke up. "What if people do not pay you back?" he asked. That question brought a laugh from both Molly and me. I explained to Toby that they always pay or there will be no more loans to anyone. Others in need will collect for us just to make sure that loans are there in the future. What we did not know was that Birdshot would add our money to others so that large combined sums could be put out in high interest loans. Molly told us to wait for Bart because he had told her to keep us here. We ordered food and sat back to wait on Bart. It did not take him long to show up.

Bart looked over to our table and motioned for us to follow him into the back room. We quickly got up and joined him. After we all sat at the table in the back room, he asked us how many street kids we could get to help us with a small job. I told him at least two more that worked for us now and probably one more by tomorrow. He thought a moment and said that that was perfect. He explained that in a few days he had a job to do and what he needed was look outs to warn him if there was any one around to interfere with his work. He said we would be paid well and he would take care of Birdshots cut himself. It will be a late night job and Molly will tell us exactly when. We all got up and Toby and I went back to our dinner in the main room.

When we sat down Toby said, "Wow, everything happens so fast that I feel like I am just hanging on." I told him that in these alleys you are either in or you are not. Toby then said," Why are you sharing with me as equals?" "I could never do any of this with out you."

"As time goes on I will depend on you more and more, "I said. "I do not need any less than a partner at my side." "Hell, I am only ten years old." "They will take my orders because they need me now, but they will also do it because they will not want to face you." "They saw the look on your face when you grabbed that big kid this morning, and you are still growing." Sooner or later the word will get out about that big blade on your back and that will only add to your threat." " I believe we need each other equally for different reasons." "You can be sure that Bart knows and appreciates that".

We finished eating and then I told Toby to follow me because we had a building to look at. Before we could leave Molly stopped us and told us that Birdshot had made the deal on the warehouse and the money was better than we thought. Well, we had a home, a crew and a steady income . I must admit that I was a little bit blown away, but I knew better than to think about it. I told myself than when it is good or when it is bad, just keep going and don't think about it. So that is what I did. When we got to the building, it was locked so I took out my picking tools and unlocked it like I had done many times before. The main floor was packed with merchandise. It seemed strange to be here to protect rather that steal. I found a kerosene lamp and lit it. The place was bigger than I remembered. In the center was a stair case and a bull rope operated freight elevator. We quickly climbed the steps to the top floor. The place was perfect. There was room for two dozen people to live, windows, and the big stove to keep us warm. The roof was solid and the walls were made of brick. I told Toby to pick a room for himself and one for me. The rest of the space would be for the crew. We went back down so we could walk around the building and check for any possible unprotected openings. When we went out the door two boys I would guess to be about 16 were waiting for us. Toby immediately got between them and me. The larger of the two took a swing at Toby and got a fist to the throat for his trouble. Before the other one could move Toby was on him like the dirt on his clothes.

They both put up their hands in submission. I asked them what they wanted and they told me they thought we were burglarizing the place and they wanted to cut in on our profits. I explained that this building was under our protection and anyone that bothered it would answer to us and our partners. The big one finally got his voice back and said, "You must be the guys working with Birdshot." "I am real sorry about this, hell we were going to ask if we could join you, but we did not know who you were." "We were looking for two alley rats that looked and dressed like us." "Again with the clothes," I thought. We might have to get back to our old rags just to be recognized. I took them back into the building and showed them the second floor. I called them Three and Four and Toby explained the reason. I explained that we would open the door most nights at seven to let everyone in and unless they had a better place to live this could be their home. They were thrilled and said they would be here at seven, but I stopped them. "No ", I said, "You will stay here and guard the place until we get back.' " If anything happens that you cannot handle go directly to Molly's Pub and tell her, she will know what to do." The smaller of the two said we should not worry because everyone knows them and when he explains who they work for that will end it. There are no secrets in these alleys.

We went back to Molly's and to our table. Molly brought over a crock of cider and some cheese . She sat with us for a while and we talked about how fast things were happening. She told us just to keep the rules we learned in these alleys. Pay your dues, never cheat the locals and never snitch. Do that and you will be OK. She did not see Bart come up behind her. She was startled when he added, "Leave no witnesses." Bart sat down with us and began to describe the job we were to do.

He had made a map of sorts and it had marking points that only our people would understand such as a broken wagon wheel where a wagon broke down and it was completely robbed before the owner got back with help. At each point, he wanted a boy stationed and hidden. Each boy was to have two large stones. If there was anyone coming the boy is to smack the rocks together several times. The sound of that crack will carry far in the damp night air. Toby and I are to be stationed close to the house Bart will be in and to warn him if we hear the sound of the rocks. No one else will have reason to pay any attention to that sound. Slate and stone shingles are often falling off a roof to the cobble stone streets. The job was in a wealthy part of town so we had to stay out of sight because we obviously did not belong there and our presence would be quickly noted.

We are to be in position no later than two in the night and not to move until Bart tells us. Bart told us to sleep well because the job was tomorrow night. He also warned us to memorize the map and then destroy it. He also warned that only Toby and I were to know anything other than where to hide and to crack the rocks in case of danger. He said, "You two are in it as deep as I am so I need not worry about you, but the others could be a witness if they know too much and I leave no witness." With that he left like a ghost gliding over the floor.

Toby said to me, "How does he move like that?" "It's like his feet never touch the floor, and you never see his arms and legs under that big cloak." I told Toby that some people think he is a ghost and some think he is the angel of death. I think they are both right but mostly I try not to think about it. Molly came back to our table and sat with us for a while. She said Birdshot gave her this to give to us and handed me a small leather draw string pouch. When I opened it I could not believe how much money was in it. Now folks on the better part of town may not have been impressed, but it sure looked like a fortune to me.

I took six coins out and handed it back to Molly to put with the rest. She smiled and said that at this rate we would be the richest young men in the alleys. When she left I kept two coins and gave the other four to Toby. I told him to pay Three and Four each one when we got back, keep one, and give the other to Five if he showed up tomorrow. I had been thinking about Bart's plan and decided I wanted a sixth look out a block or two from the job sight. He would watch for Coppers specifically and make sure they did not patrol in our direction. We went back to the warehouse we now called home to find Two and Three waiting for us with Four and Five.

They quickly explained that they knew each other and they had been looking for Four and Five when they saw them outside the building. Well, that sure made it easy. I unlocked the building, and we all went upstairs. Here we are with a warm, dry home that is not only safe, but it is legal, and we are getting paid to be here. We explained everything and told them to get some sleep because tomorrow was going to be a long day and night. We all curled up on the floor and went to sleep.

Chapter 5

The soft rain did a rat-a-tat on the windows and I could feel the fog and mist as it crawled down the alley and formed a fuzzy moat around the building. I woke up slowly and realized that I had slept safely for the first time I could remember. I looked around and everyone but One and Two were not asleep on the floor. I was pleased to assume that they were on their way to protect the stalls. I got Three and Four up and went to Toby's room to get him, but he was awake waiting for me. I told Four to stay and watch the building while the three of us went to the market. I told him that Three would bring him back something to eat. At that point we left for the market. The rain was a pain, but this was Pittsburgh and being damp was part of life. When we got to the market we were met with smiles and words of welcome by all the vendors. Birdshot was paying for our food and we were protecting the people from kids just like us. I noticed the man that sold hammers and rolls and he waved me over to his stall. He had a big smile on his face and a bandage on his thumb.

He gave me a big hug and a roll and said that we must talk. I sat next to him and listened. He explained that his wife also sold their goods but at a different market. Since we were protecting this one, the thieves had moved on to the market where she worked. He wondered if I could help them. He told me the location and I agreed to check it out. I ate the roll as I went to the big tree. Our new friend that we would call Five was waiting for me. I asked Toby to get food and then I talked to Five.

I asked if he had a place to stay and he said he did not. I told him he could live with us and he could not believe it. I explained the whole set up to him and asked him to stick with Toby and me for the rest of the day because we had a job to do tonight. He was more than willing and we all shared the food that Toby brought. You must understand that a warm safe place to sleep and food in your belly was a new thing for all of us and it was a welcome and cherished change in our lives. After we ate Toby, Five and I went to the market the rolls and hammer guy spoke about.

When we got there it was crazy. For every three customers there was a thief looking to score. The merchants looked as if the world was coming down on their heads. The worst was a little old man and his tiny wife trying to sell straw sleeping pallets. Two men were pushing them around and threatening them. Before I could say a thing Toby had knocked one of them to the ground with a wicked fist to his jaw and Five was sitting on the others chest and pummeling his face with fist after fist.

I walked over and had Toby and Five hold them up. I explained that these stalls were under our protection. They looked at me and asked if I was the kid with Billy Birdshot. I suggested that they ask him.

They threw up their hands and said no thanks, we will just figure that you are and then they ran. I thought about recruiting them but I decided I was better off with the Alley Rats. We approached each vendor and they did not hesitate to become part of our program. The first thing I did was to buy a dozen pallets for our home. I paid the man and split the rest for Birdshot's share. I gave Five the two coins in my pocket and told him to meet us back at the warehouse by seven. He was to stay and protect the stalls until they closed. I figured we needed another person to help Five in the future, but he would do for now. We hung around for an hour or two to make sure everything was under control and then we made our way to Molly's. By the time we got there half the day was gone and we were pushing into the afternoon.

Toby and I went to our usual table and sat down. My head was spinning trying to keep everything strait. I told Toby we should eat and try to sleep so that we would be alert for tonight. Molly came over and sat with us. She said that she heard we had another market to protect. How the hell did things travel so fast? I gave her our share of the money to put with the rest.

We ordered food and she said, "Oh by the way, my man went to get the pallets and they will be at the warehouse shortly." "No charge of course." When she brought the food I asked her why no charge and she explained that she was doing very well with our cash on the street. It was funny but I had no concept of money because I had never had any. I just gave her what I had and I never even counted it.

Toby and I ate and talked for a bit. His eyes were forever watching everything around us and I was beginning to realize just how lucky I was that we found each other. Suddenly Toby exploded from the chair and had hold of a short but ruggedly built young fellow about 15 years old.

He threw him to the floor and removed a jack knife from a leather holder on his belt.

The young man asked Toby to take it easy because he was just looking for a job. Toby stood him up and he said to me that he was a friend of the guy we called Five. Five told him where to find us, and he was sorry about the jack knife. He explained that he always carried it and did not even think it would cause a problem.

I Told Toby to let him go. I motioned for him to sit. There was cheese and bread on the table and I told him to help himself. It is funny how soon you forget what it is like to know hunger, but watching him eat brought it all back. I swore to myself that I would never be hungry again no matter what. When he finally slowed down I said OK, you are now called Six and you work with Five.

.Put the rest of the cheese in your pocket and go help your friend at the market. Tell him I said to bring you to the warehouse at about seven. Toby excused himself to go out back to the outhouse. Molly came over to the table and sat down.

She said she had a gift from Bart and handed me a railroad watch. She explained that Bart hated anyone that was late for an appointment. I never had anything so beautiful in my life. I did not know how to thank

Bart. Sure I had lifted many watches in the street but never a real railroad watch.

Molly said I was not to mention it to Bart, just be on time every time. Just then Bart entered the Pub, glided to the back room and was gone without even looking at us.

Molly explained that everyone knew he had a job today and everyone knew not to bother him. She said, "Don't worry because he will be his same old terrifying self tomorrow."

We looked at each other and broke out laughing.

Toby came back and asked us what was so funny.

I started to say Bart, but Toby put up his hand to stop me. Toby said, "Never mind, there is nothing funny that starts with Bart." Molly and looked at each other and again we started to laugh.

Toby and I left and went back home to sleep. We did make one stop at the work house and gave Billy his cut. He smiled and said, "You two boys are turning out to be everything I had hopped for,' I will be up very late tonight in case you need me, Just bang on the door with the usual pass word." "I am proud of you boys", he said. We went home after that and when we were sure everything was OK went up to our rooms. Our old clothes were waiting on our pallets for us.

They were clean, but there were so many stains that you would never know from looking at them. My only dread was the old shoes held on with rags, but they were part of the image that allowed us to blend in. I told Toby we would have to take soot from the stove to cover our hands and face, and put on the old caps Molly had provided. We laid down and tried to sleep, but it took a while.

Before I knew, it was seven o'clock and I could hear the rest of the boys coming in. They were laughing and teasing one another.

I got up to meet them and was surprised to see them carrying baskets of food. Five said that the vendors were so grateful that they loaded him up with their left over food. "I told them they did not have to do that but they were sure business would pick up from now on and they wanted to express their thanks', said Five. I looked at them and said, "This beats the hell out of robbing them." Everyone thought that was funny and we all sat on the floor to eat together.

CHAPTER 6

I told everyone to try to sleep or at least rest. I explained that anyone that fell asleep on the job was out and that our partners would be given their name. I did not have to explain further. We were all from the alleys except for Toby and the rules were simple, take a job, do the job, or face the consequences.

At 1:30 I got everyone around the lantern and showed them where they were to be on guard. I told them about the rocks and made sure they knew to listen for a signal and to pass on the information to me. When I finished Five and Six asked me what they should do. I told Five to stay and guard the warehouse. He is also to watch for any of us returning and to let us in. I asked Six how good he was at tracking someone and he grinned and said, "I am the best Getts." "No one has ever caught me." I told him to hide between the police patrol station and follow any Copper that walked our way. "If you think he is getting to close, do something to take his attention away from us."

Five said he understood and we all left except for
Four.

By one AM we were all in position. The night was
very quiet. Toby and I were close to the house where
Bart was doing the job, but we could hear nothing.
Time past very slowly and then we heard police whistles
blowing some where many blocks away. There was no
other sound and no one moved. Suddenly there was a
shadow moving next to me and a hand quickly covered
my mouth. Bart whispered in my ear that it was him
and that I should relax. Toby never saw or heard him. I
leaned over to Toby and told him that Bart was there.
He was as surprised as I was. Bart motioned for us to
follow him and we went into the house behind him. He
gently closed the door and told us in a soft voice to go
into the master bedroom and take anything we saw of
value and put it in the two black sacks he handed to us.
We quickly went into the room and began filling the
sacks. There was jewelry and silver picture frames, and
all sorts of fine leather goods. We gathered it all quickly

and returned to the living room. Bart stuffed several pieces of silver into our sacks and handed me a small leather bag. He said the money was for us to share. The sacks belong to Toby and me. Then he turned with a smirk on his face and said," Not a bad nights work." "Tell the others to go back to the warehouse and then go strait to Birdshot with the sacks." "Remember that I will be paying him his share, but, he said with a wink, do not argue with his price." "He will still take out 10%, which is only fare."

I moved so fast from that house that I thought my heart would burst. We told the boys to find Five and go back to the warehouse quickly and quietly. After that, Toby and I took off for our back alleys.

I felt as though we would never leave that fancy neighborhood. When we were at last on our own turf, we stopped and took a breather.

Even the smell was a welcome relief because we could relax at least a little. No one was ever in our alleys at night unless they belonged there or they had a death wish. When we got to the work house, Billy was waiting for us at the door. He quickly waved us in and locked the door. We put the sacks down on the table and he poured us each a large mug of ale. It tasted great, and we were not aware of how dry we were from running the way we did. Billy dumped the sacks onto the table and said, "Holy mother of the church, what a haul." "I would be tempted to cheat you, but old Bart will want to know what I paid and I don't like upsetting him if you know what I mean." At that he laughed, but not to be merry, but to calm himself down. He went into a back room and after a while he returned with a large leather bag. He began to count out more coins than I ever knew existed. He said, "You boys are among the richest in the whole of these alleys." Molly is waiting for you so take this money and go straight to her pub." We did just that and Molly was waiting for us. She ushered us inside and then to her back room. I handed her the money and she was so shocked that she could not talk.

"I asked," Is it a great deal?' She at last got her voice and explained that it was. She explained that perhaps we should deal directly with Birdshot with this kind of money. I said, "No, I trust you and your 25% of the interest is my insurance that the money is safe."

Molly got a smile and a tear in her eye as she came over and gave each of us a hug. I asked her why we were allowed to take the stuff and she explained that Bart wanted it to look like a robbery that went bad. She handed us a big sack of food and a jug of cider. She told us to take it with us to feed the boys when we got back. As we left the Pub Toby said to me, "Just a few days ago I was hungry and alone, now I have money, friends and a home." I do not think I will ever understand." I told him to do what I do and don't think about it.

When we got back to the building the boys we're waiting and so excited that they could not keep still. We locked up and went to the second floor. When we laid out the food they were all relieved because they were all very hungry. I took the leather bag out from Bart and opened it on the table.

Their eyes were glued to the coins. There was more in the bag than I had thought. I pulled two thirds away and divided the rest between them. It was more money that they had ever seen let alone had to put into their pockets. They asked me what Toby and I did with our money since we seemed to never have any on us and they were afraid to carry money on them. I explained that we gave it to a loan shark to put on the street. They all pushed the coins back to me and asked if I would do the same with theirs. I agreed and explained that Molly at the pub would have an accounting for each of them when ever they wanted it. The word is security. That is what they felt and I understood because I felt it too.

We were young and had nothing stupid like liquor to spend the money on.

I asked what the police whistles and all the racket was and Five piped up with his shoulders back and a big smile on his face. You told me to watch for the Coppers and to do something to keep them away, so when I saw one coming your way I just ran over a couple of more blocks and kicked in a door to the bakery. The baker was starting up his ovens and he came out screaming for the police." "By the time they got there I was back in my original position with no one the wiser" We all got a laugh out of that and I told them what a good job they had done.

I waited, but no one asked what we were guarding. I was pleased because it was enough that Toby and I knew and they all understood that that is a question they can never ask.

Chapter 7

The morning came with a soft light flowing through the second floor windows. I could hear the mill whistles sounding out for a change of shift. In ten minutes they would change again and each worker must be at his post. It was 7:50 AM. and time for me to get up, but not quite yet.

The room Toby had chosen for me had a large steel framed widow.

The black soot from the steel mills up and down the three rivers had been cleaned away by me for the umpteenth time. I laid there and contemplated the last days. I knew I had been smart and I knew I had been lucky. I felt like I had been adopted by all my partners and I guess that was not to far from the truth. I was making everyone money, but my respect for them was the best part. It was too late for me to be judging anyone and I certainly would never let others judge me. We were all just trying to get by the best we could, at least that is what I had convinced myself. What difference did it make any how? Today was another day to survive and Toby was standing at my door just in case I had forgotten. We had washed up and put on our new clothes before we left. After checking the boys and making our rounds to the stalls we decided to walk around the better part of town, which meant leaving the Point and going east past Market Square. I had never been in this part of town during the day except to pick up a few items from unsuspecting passers-by. We spent the entire day walking the streets and looking at how other people lived. I have to admit that I never paid any attention to them in the past.

There were shops of all kinds and tradesmen for every want and need.

River pilots sat together outside pubs and talked of sand bars and pirates that still plagued the long trip to New Orleans.

Business men in fancy suits huddled under roofs to protect them from the black soot from the steel mills and coke works. There was a constant movement of men and wagons taking goods here and there and of course the huge beer wagons with their teams of draft horses. The best thing was the street sweepers that were kept busy removing the manure. I would have to ask Molly about the garbage and the human waste that was missing, much to my relief. Late in the day we went back to the point and to Molly's Pub.

Toby and I went in and to our regular table. Molly came over with a big smile and a crock of cider.

She sat with us and we told her about our day. She explained the garbage pickup and the sewer system in the rest of the city. I asked her why we did not have such things here in the Point and she smiled and told me that no one cared about this part of town and no one would come here to work if they did. I asked her what was available and she said there were water lines and sewer lines right out front leading to the rivers, but it was very expensive to hook up. She said that she was saving up to buy the building next door for a hotel to add to her pub. I asked her if she was close to having enough and she frowned before answering that she was a long way from it. I asked her if I could afford it and she said that and a whole lot more. I thought for a moment and then looked at her and said, "How would you like to have a partner?" She became very quiet. After thinking on it for a while she said, "I will have two requirements." "First the hotel and pub must be neat and clean and fit for decent folks even if it is here in the alleys, and second you must let me teach you to read and to handle numbers on paper." "I will not be here forever and I need to know you will be able to take over if anything happens to me."

I liked the idea of learning those things, and so I put out my hand. She shook it and then Toby put out his. I said, "Done and done."

Construction started right away on the pub. All of the surfaces were plastered and fine gas lights adorned the walls and a chandelier hung down from the center of the ceiling. A toilet and sink was installed in a new room off the back with a six foot steel urinal on the far wall. All of the floors were tiled and Molly's apartment was made into a bright home for her to live in.

We opened an archway to enter the building next door and we converted the building into twelve sleeping rooms and six bathrooms. The entire outside of the structures were painted red with black and gold trim. We also added two suites above the old pub, one for special guests and one for Toby and me.

As the years past I thought of those days often and realized what a wonderful miracle it had all been for a young boy and his big friend. Our five partners now had places of there own to guard and people working for them. They were still religious about bringing any money or items of value to me to take to Billy after I took my share.

We pretty much controlled every business in the city from the stand point of keeping away the bad guys and we collected enough that I felt obligated to donate monthly to the well being of the coppers from the Chief down. My first donation came as a surprise to them, but with each passing month our relationship got closer and closer.

One day I was introduced to the Mayor, can you imagine that?

He shook my hand and handed me a piece of paper. On the paper was a large number. He explained to me that that was the number of votes he needed from the area of the Point and that they had decided Molly's Pub would be the one and only polling place in the point. I along with Toby, were the judges of elections for that area and the party wound make sure we were compensated for our efforts. Now I admit that I know very little about elections and I have never been old enough to vote so when I explained it all to Molly she could not believe it.

She told me that the mayor had just made me and Toby in charge of this whole section of the city.

She said that if we delivered that vote we would control everything here. I asked her what that included and she said to wait until after the election and then ask the mayor.

One of the advantages of being young and naïve is that you do not know enough to be afraid of things you do not understand. Well, it seemed that I had two weeks to get all of the voters ready for the big day. The problem was that I did not think there were that many voters in the Point.

While Toby and I were sitting at Molly's trying to figure the whole thing out, Billy Birdshot walked in and came over to us with a big box. He had a smile on his face that would light up a room. He put the box on the table and pulled me out of the chair in a great bear hug. "Well, he said, "Her are all the ballots, and all the voter registration forms for the big election. "We are already about half way there to the number you need" He sat down quite pleased with himself and grabbed our crock of ale and took a big swig. I looked at him and said, "The election is not for two weeks and this polling place is not even open."

Billy pounded the table and held his side in laughter. "They have their schedule and we have ours." "This is the first time any of us has had a chance to be part of their system and I am grateful to you and I will do my part," said Billy.

I asked him how in the hell did he get all those votes and he explained that everyone in the work house was happy to get a day off to vote and so was everyone connected to his various enterprises including the keepers and the poor souls at the prison along with their guests.. "Now" he said ,"When the word gets out that the good people will not have to go thirsty for want of money while they wait to vote, you can expect to easily get the balance of the votes needed and take your place with the Swells of the community." He had spoken so loud that everyone in the pub sent up a beg cheer. Billy was quite drunk so I ordered more ale and plenty of food.

Over the years we had developed a special bond of which I was proud. I knew the fear he held in the hearts of others, but there was none of that between us. We held a level of trust and respect for one another that only people from the street can understand. People feared him and to some extent they really feared Toby.

Toby was now over 6 foot 8 inches tall and his shoulders were as wide as an ax handle. He weighs in at 265 lbs. and in those days he was considered a giant. It was not abnormal for him to pick up three drunks at a time and toss them out of the pub. Toby pulled that knife only on a few occasions and the results were deadly for anyone that put him in that position. He was basically shy and he had a very hard time dealing with all the young girls that were constantly throwing themselves at him. He was quiet by nature and apparently very handsome. I never teased him and most people just smiled and left him alone. He still had the Scottish lilt to his speech the result of learning to talk from his parents and perhaps that just added to his appeal. We were partners in everything and we were becoming financially comfortable to say the least. One evening as we sat at our table alone he asked me if we could discuss something. I said yes of course and he thought for a while and said," We have done very well." " We have fine clothes for every day of the week and many left over." "Our boots are hand made and soft and we bath every day," Molly keeps our hair neat and we smell nice all the time." "We know how to read and do numbers, you even study things like great writers and geometry." "You can talk to even the mayor and you no longer sound like an alley rat." "What do we have to do to fit in on the east side of the city where we had that walk long ago?"

Leave it to Toby to put his finger on the one thing that was missing in our life. We were young enough to make the transition to respectability but we were only known for our power in the rackets and only in the slums of the Point. I told Toby that tomorrow we were going to take a little boat ride. "Where to", he asked. I told him we were going over the Allegheny River to the town of Old Allegheny. Old Allegheny was on the

North Side of Pittsburgh separated by the river to the east and the Ohio River to the west. It was a small and growing addition to the city. Some Germans had settled there and a family had a bar restaurant that served great German food and beer called Max and Irma's. I had never been there, but it had a fine reputation.

I was fortunate in that I looked much older than I was. At seventeen, most people thought I was at least 20 or 22. I was just short of 6 foot and 180 pounds. My hair was black with a touch of auburn and I wore it pulled back and tied. I never wore a hat even though it was the style. Some said I was vain but the truth is a hat could hamper your ability to see all around you. I learned early never to take any chances. Toby and I had rooms at the hotel we owned with Molly. We shared a bath and had a toilet which still amazed me after all the years without houses. We had gas lights and a gas heating grate to keep us warm. The hotel, the pub and the big second floor we built on the pub were all outfitted the same way.

People in the Point thought it was a miracle and Molly had to stop the patrons from flushing the toilet all the time just to watch the water go down. I had decided that after the election I would talk to the mayor about cleaning up the pocket of streets around our buildings. Toby and I got on the ferry to cross the river early in the morning.

I held the big brass rail and recognized the spin of the rushing water from the Monongahela River as it met the Allegheny and swelled to form the great Ohio River.

Three shades of brown and blue and green water all joined in a frantic escape to find the Mississippi. Even with the never ending smoke stacks it was still beautiful, and I understood for the first time that I was watching the growth of our industrial country. All around me thousands of workers were building and creating. The big paddle wheel boats pushed endless barges loaded with coal and iron ore to the mills while others took away the finished product of rolled steel, glass, and even aluminum from father up the Allegheny. It all seemed endless and the little town of Old

Allegheny was just starting to feel the pressure of growth. We got off the ferry and started to walk toward the main part of town. When we got to Max and Irma's we went in to eat. The place was like walking into old Germany. We sat down and a waitress with a full skirt and a top that made you want to never quit looking at what was there and what was showing. She was blond and pretty as a picture. She took our orders for two mugs of beer and swished away from the table. Toby was glued to her every move. In a short while she returned with two enormous mugs full to the top with a very dark liquid we assumed was beer. We tasted it with caution and proclaimed that it was delicious. She was very pleased with our reaction. She said her name was Annah and we asked her to order food for us because we knew nothing of German food. She seemed pleased and after a half hour she returned with a huge platter of food. We started to dig in and I must confess that it was wonderful. We ate and ate as only two young men can and when we finished it all Annah came back to the table with a man with a very large girth and a big white apron wrapped around his middle. "See Papa", she said. "I told you they would eat it all" The large man looked at us and said, "I see, but you did not describe the very large young fellow to me." Annah and her father laughed and her father had to hold his belly because it shook so much. "I love to see young men who enjoy my food".

We both praised the food and the wonderful restaurant. Annah left and quickly returned with more of the dark beer.

Her father said, "Oh please forgive me for being so rude." "I am Max and you already know my daughter." What brings you to Old Allegheny?" I told him that we were interested in investing in this side of the river. I explained that we had several interests in Pittsburgh proper and we wished to expand. He was very surprised and wondered how two so young could do so well. I explained that we had a large group of investors that worked with us. This seemed to satisfy him and it was kind of close to the truth. He suggested that I visit the few small shops and ask around. I paid the bill and noticed that Toby handed a very large tip to Annah and held on to her hand for a rather long time. She was red in the face, but she did not pull away. When we walked out of the dining room and into the bar area with Annah going before us, a big riverboat man reached out and grabbed Annah by the arm. He said, "Give us a kiss sweet thing and I will take good care of you." His friends all laughed and Annah complained that he was hurting her. Max started over and the big boatmen said for him to stay out of this. Toby grabbed the empty hand of the river boat man and began to squeeze. Everyone got quiet as you could hear the bones in his hand breaking.

The man quickly let go of Annah and held his hand in great pain. Toby took out a roll of money which he now carried all the time, peeled off a substantial amount and put it in the river man's pocket. "Get this poor man to a doctor he said with little or no emotion and the group ushered him out the door. Toby then put some more money on the bar and said he was sorry for interrupting their good time and instructed the bar tender to give everyone a drink on him.

I just shook my head. This was a first. I had expected Toby to carry the man outside and beat him to a pulp.

Max came over and thanked Toby for what he had done explaining that those men have become a constant problem. Toby said that he doubted they would come back and I thought especially when they find out who we are. Toby then said very softly to Max, "May I have permission to call on your daughter?" Max got a big smile and said, "Ask her." If she is willing then I agree." We all turned to Annah and she just stood there shaking her head yes. Toby said, "I will be back tomorrow.", and we went outside. It was the first time I had seen that side of the big guy that was like a brother to me and I liked it a great deal.

His happiness meant more to me than anything. He was just standing there grinning ear to ear and waiting for me to say something. I shook his hand and said, "It is time you had someone in your life beside me." "I like the idea and I like her."

Chapter 8

There was a mist in the air that we called a spitting rain and it ran down the outside of the window over my copper bathtub. It reminded me of the waterfalls I read about in the many books that were piled all over our rooms. I had never seen one, but I promised myself that one day I would, especially the one due north of us called Niagara that I once saw a painting of. It looked wonderful. I could hear Toby moving around and I knew he was anxious about this being election day. All of the places selling liquor had to close so Molly hung the polling sign over the door and closed the bar. To make up for it we moved several kegs of whiskey outside in the street and followed our friends in New York with a hose in the top of each one to eliminate the need for glasses that would get broken or stolen. Each voter got to suck as much through the hose as he could in one breath just to quench his thirst before voting. The ballots were very confusing and few of our people could read so we just filled them out for them and all they had to do was state their name and make their mark.

It also kept the line moving faster which pleased everyone. It was amazing the number of twins we had in the Point. When I accused someone of having voted already I was informed it was his twin brother. By the time we closed the poll and counted the votes we had exceeded the Mayors number by a very large amount. Molly looked at me and said, "Don't you think you are overdoing it?" "Well", I said, "It seems to me that we good citizens of these filthy alleyways now have the power to just about decide any election." "It will take a while for those pompous bastards to figure it out, but when they do we should have at least a little to say about the governing of our great city." Molly shook her head and said, "You mean you will have something to say." "I should have known that you would never let yourself become one of their flunkies." Like a ghost Bart appeared behind Molly and said, "My boy is way too smart for those fools, I knew from the start he would bend this to our advantage." I said, "If they accept these results then they are stuck with them and we become very important in any election,".

Bart then asked me to go with him to the back room to talk.

When we sat down he said that he heard we had an interest in the North Side, or Old Allegheny as it was sometimes called. He explained that he knew me better than anyone on earth and he knew I was looking to enter the other world of the upper class. He knew everyone with money and power in the city and he knew that they were all bigger crooks than either he or I. "In three days I want you to visit a man called Harper." "He is an attorney with an office on Market Square". "All you are to say is that Mr. Bart sent you and then listen to what he tells you." "Tomorrow you are to take a large sum of money to the Keystone Bank on the North Side and make a deposit." "The money will be given to you by the mayor and the chief of police at exactly 9:00 AM tomorrow in the Mayors office. Do not count it and say nothing. Just turn and leave. Go right to the bank and ask for Walter and hand him the money. From now on I want you to deposit half of every dime you make in that account until I tell you differently.

In two days I will need six of your men from the operation across town. Tell Five to do what I tell him. He is smart and he will know what to do. Never ask him about this. It is very important that you know nothing.

It always amazes me that the "Real " citizens never understand how it all works. There is a language of the streets and there are simple rules like when someone you trust tells you to ask no questions you immediately forget about the whole thing and there is no such thing as curious thoughts. It is done, who gives a shit. It ain't about you so move on with your thinking. The next day Toby and I went to see the Mayor at his office. He was half kicked and feeling no pain. He hugged me and Toby and explained what great guys we were and how the city was at our feet. I told him we would be back in a few days to discuss the future and he said, "Oh yes, yes we must do that." The Chief of Police came over shook our hands and gave us each a fat envelope. We left and walked down to the river.

I told Toby to put the money in a local bank. I also told him to start to put half of everything in the bank also.

He was surprised. He asked," Why the change?"
I explained that we were on our way to being upstanding citizens and he must be prosperous to marry Annah. He turned as red as a beet. I looked at him and explained that we were about to become so big that I needed a partner with a good family and a solid reputation. I explained that no brother could be closer or more loved than he was to me so do the right thing and follow my lead. We hugged each other and he headed for town as I went to the ferry for the north side.

For some reason the ferry was broken down so I had to hire a man in a row boat to take me over. He was a filthy mess and he smelled of sweat and whiskey.

He had one big tooth in the front of his mouth and it was black. About fifty yards from the bank he pulled out a pistol and pointed it at me. He told me to give him all my money. I asked him if he knew who I was but he just said, "Yes, a fancy dressed high bob that cares not for a poor man and his boat." I reached out with the bag and pushed against his chest. When he tried to get it I hit the button with my right hand and the blade shot out and into his heart. I had never used it before. I pulled back quickly and wiped it off on his pant leg. He looked at me and said, "You have killed me." I grabbed his shirt collar and his right pant leg and threw him out of the boat. I rowed the boat to shore and got out. I looked at the body as it slowly sunk into the Allegheny and said, "Good by ". Then I walked to the bank.

When I entered the bank I asked for Walter and a tall slender man with dark hair and a suit that belonged only on a man like him glided over to me and said, "I presume you are the honorable Mr. Getts.

I quickly bowed my head and said, "At your service." and tipped with my head. Now, I had wanted to do that a thousand times since I first saw it done, but damn that was as smooth as it gets. I followed him to a back room that was private. He pulled out a portfolio of papers and laid them on the desk. He directed me to sign a series of papers and then sat back. He asked, "What would you like to deposit today?" I handed him the bag of money and he counted it in front of me. I was surprised at how little it was. He did a deposit slip and handed it to me for my signature. When I looked at the amount of the deposit it was ten times the money in the bag.

When he saw my surprise he leaned over his desk and explained that the rest of the deposit had been delivered earlier. Walter excused himself and left the room. When he returned he handed me a bank savings book and pointed to the number that represented my total worth. The number was staggering. He said," Friends have seen to your future." I would be proud if from now on you would refer all financial matters to me" Your legal representative and I work together often.

I waited the three days and then I went to see Mr. Harper. I went into his office in the Frick building on the fifth floor and as soon as I entered the secretary said, "You must be Mr. Getts." "Please go on in." I walked in and Harper pointed to a large leather chair and asked me to sit. "We have had a terrible loss", he said and I am at liberty to reveal it to you because of our close associates." There is a large Brown Stone house in Old Allegheny than has recently come available because of the sad death of its owner." "All of the interested parties are out of the area and it has fallen to me to dispose of his property including all of the interior furnishings." If you will just sign these papers the property is yours and I will deal with Walter at your bank. I knew a setup when I saw one and when I looked at the price it was as ridiculous as it could be. I took the pen and thanked him for his service. When I was through signing he handed me the keys and asked one further thing. "The butler and manservant has been there for a long time and it has been suggested by your friends that you keep him on".

His salary along with all other expenses will be taken care of by Walter at the bank. "It would be my pleasure and honor if you would consider me and my office as your personal legal representative in all matters," said Mr. Harper.

I shook his hand again and explained that I too was honored and that I would have need of him in the very near future.

I picked up Toby on my way out of the office and we went down the stairs. We went to the dock and got on the north side ferry. I had the address of the house, but I knew which one it was because Bart had me set up three of his men around it two nights ago. I explained to Toby what had happened. I further explained that I was going to live there from now on, but we would keep the rooms at Molly's for when we were in town. I also suggested that he see my attorney and arrange to buy a house out of the city. I told him Old Allegheny was fine and Annah would be close to family.

We went to the door of my house and before I could get out my key the door opened and the man I assumed was the butler/manservant did a small bow and said in perfect English, "Welcome home sir, I have prepared for you and I hope all suits you." I thought Toby was going to fall over. I do not know how to describe what we saw. The place was gigantic and every room had thick rugs from the Orient and mahogany furniture covered in silks and leather with carved marble tables and Paintings on every wall. One room was a library and every wall up to the 16 foot ceilings was packed with books. Leather chairs and couches worn to a perfect softness were scattered throughout the room. There was the smell of good cigars and soft brandy. Along the wall was a bar stocked with every kind of spirits you could imagine. I could see myself sitting here and holding every book on the shelves. James, the butler spoke up and said," Why don't you two sit a while and I will bring a snack and perhaps a glass of wine." You have one of the finest wine cellars in the state." "Will you allow me to choose a special vintage"? I told him yes and he said, "Wonderful because I already have one open to breath in anticipation of your arrival." He poured the wine into two fine crystal glasses and then excused himself. Toby and I just looked at each other without knowing whether to cry or run like hell before reality set in and we were thrown out.

A few moments later James returned with a tray of fruit and cheeses.

He sat it down and left explaining that we were to call if we needed anything else.

Toby asked," Do you really own all of this." I said yes and it is all paid for. We decided to sit and enjoy ourselves before we took in the other floors of the house. Toby made it plain that this was too much and he could never live here. I was secretly thrilled and I saw myself as having no problem adjusting. I have read hundreds of books and I knew just how this was all to be lived. I said to Toby that we have come a very long way and this was not the time to stop. I further explained that I would have Atty. Harper find him a suitable house on the North Side close by. I asked him about how he and Annah were getting along and he explained that they were much in love and very happy. I told him that it would suit our plans if he married and the sooner the better.

I told him that I wanted to expand our operation. He just rolled his eyes and smiled. We toured the rest of the house and it was fit for a king. I asked Toby to meet me at Molly's first thing in the morning and we had two things to do.

Chapter 9

I lay in a bed that was softer than a cloud. I had slept in a rainbow trance that filled my being with contentment. I laid there for a while trying to convince myself that this was not a dream. Like a ghost James appeared and explained that my bath was prepared and as soon as I finished he requested that I dry off, put on the robe and return to the master suite. I did just that and after a luxurious bath with French soap, towels that felt like cotton balls and a feeling like I was about to wake up smelling the stink of the Point because all of this had to be a dream, I returned to James.

He had a small table set with a spectacular array of breakfast foods and fruits. I looked up at James from my chair and said, "Surely you must know that all of this may be wonderful, but it is all very new and strange to me". "I don't know if I can adjust let alone figure out how I have come to deserve it." He was silent for a moment as though deep in thought and then he said, "Who are we to decide what is deserved and what is not?" " A king is born and so is a boy in a shack." "Neither had a thing to do with their situation but one lives in luxury and one in poverty." "Throughout history kingdoms have fallen and poor men have risen to power." "Try not to think about what you do or do not deserve, but rather concentrate on using your talents to the fullest and who knows, perhaps you too will become a king in your own heart." "Kingdoms are not about castles, they are about happiness and satisfaction."

While I ate my breakfast and thought about what he said, James made the bed and began to set out clothes for me to wear. All of the clothes were new. They spoke of money, or as they say in the Point, "They look like cash", but they were plain in color and were a simple cut that did not stand out or look flashy. James explained that he took the trouble to give my measurements to his friend who would continue to make my clothes if I approved. He also laid out the knife for my forearm and assured me that the clothes were adapted to conceal it. It seemed like once again someone had stepped in to help direct my path.

I thought back to when Toby and I took the first bag of goods to Billy and exchanged it all for food and a change of clothes. We have come so far, but we were still simple at heart and only really looking for the same thing, but it appears our tastes have been elevated. I also wondered what the poor bastard that used to live here had done to deserve a visit from Bart. I knew many things and knowing the system was certainly one of them. I actually had no real interest in the facts about the previous owner and figured that if I needed to know Bart would see that I was informed. Well, I thought it is time for me to meet Toby at the Pub.

People looked at me when I entered the Point and many wished me a good day. I was happy to smile and return their good wishes. These are my people and all the fancy clothes in the world could not change that. I knew that we would always have a common history and understanding and I never wanted to lose that. Everyone

I had met so far from the "better" part of town had turned out to be a bigger thief than the people they looked down on.

When I went into the Pub Molly and Toby were both waiting at the table.

Molly gave me a hug and Toby just smiled and shook his head. Toby had obviously filled Molly in on my new home and she was beaming. "Who would have dreamed that my two boys could come so far," she said. I filled my mug with ale and held it out. I said," To we three and those friends that are not present." We all clicked mugs together and downed the ale.

"Now, I said it is good that we are together but I need Billy here too." Molly called a boy over and ordered him to fetch Billy Birdshot.

He looked frightened but Molly told him to just tell Billy who was waiting for him here at the pub. It was mid-morning so the place was empty when Billy walked in. He pulled out a chair and filled a mug with ale. I asked everyone to hear me out before asking any questions and they all nodded in agreement. I explained that the only one missing was Bart but he is to share in everything we do. I thanked them and expressed my good luck and deep affection for them all. I explained that even though our partnership was based on a mutual need and benefit it had become more to me. Molly had a hanky to her eyes and even Billy had a glisten in his eyes. I further explained that the Mayor had made a very big mistake by accepting the votes and registering them with the city. They now confirm that we have control of enough votes to swing any election. The votes we turned in way exceeded the number he gave me and I knew his ego would not let him throw out the excess votes so he could claim a landslide victory. I believe it is now time to collect on this new advantage. Questions?

"Son of a bitch", Billy said. "Remind me never to get you angry with me".

Toby said, " I know you too well to think that you have not thought all of this through and already have a plan, so what is it"?

Molly was still too busy with the hanky to speak. "OK", I said here is phase one." I have had a friend researching the city budget and it seems there is a large amount of money earmarked for improving the Point, but those of us who are here know that money gets lost way before it arrives. All of that money will now go to Allegheny Contracting for the greater good of the point. Sewers and street sweepers will be hired to get the stink out of the alleys. The workhouse will be improved and food kitchens will be set up to feed the needy. A new director of the poor will be appointed at a good salary paid for by the city. The new company will have a president and a secretary-treasurer. The stockholders will be paid their legal dividends twice a year. All building of any kind in the point will go out for legal bids and Allegheny Contracting will somehow always win. No one could say a word. They just sat there with their mouths open.

Toby will be the president of Allegheny Contracting, Billy will be the Director of the Poor. Molly will be the secretary treasurer and we will all be share holders including Bart and the Mayor's wife. Off duty police will be hired to protect construction sites, and all our men will share in the side profits from the purchasing of material and equipment. Bart and I will see to any problems that come up and I now have a very fine attorney to handle all our legal matters. He will receive a monthly retainer paid for with proceeds from our other ventures with cash only.

You would have thought that the room had been infiltrated by ghosts. They were so quiet that I was a little afraid that I had gone too far. I decided to wait them out and I just quietly sat in my chair. Finally Billy spoke up very quietly, almost at a whisper. He leaned over the table and said," I do not know how you will pull this off, but I believe you will and all of our lives will be better." " Thank you and whatever you need I will be there for you." Everyone expressed feelings that were the same.

I told Toby to follow me to the Mayor's office. I kissed Molly, and I told Billy I would see him later on a matter of great importance. Toby and I left to go see the Mayor. When we entered his office I was told that he was to busy to see me and that the earliest opening was in two weeks. I leaned over her desk with a smile on my face and whispered to her to tell that fat son of a bitch to open the door or my very large friend would kick it in along with most of the Mayor's ribs. She went white and opened the door a crack and announced that we were coming in. I pushed her out of the way and Toby and I entered. Toby closed the door. The Mayor was sitting on his chair and the chief of police was on the couch with a large glass of whiskey. I smiled and said to the Mayor who was sitting with a frown on his big fat face, " Hear me you fat shit ," " If you ever try to treat me like the fools that come here to kiss your ass, an election will be the least of your problems." " Get that flunky secretary in here to take notes while I explain to you the future." "If you listen and smile I will make you richer than you ever dreamed," "If you give me a hard time you will never win another election". "Now get out and go to lunch while I explain the whole thing to the Chief of Police. The mayor got up, put on his coat and left. I laid out the whole plan for the chief and I explained that this was just the beginning. I told him that I needed people like him that could think and I needed people that understood that all of their dreams could come true if they just got on board our train. I turned to Toby and told him to give the chief $500.00 which was more than he got paid for six months of work. Toby pealed it off and handed it to the Chief.

The chief was speechless. I explained that for every dollar we paid his men for off duty work he would get fifty cents. I also told him that his son would become an investor in our future projects.

He said that he was on our train and anything he could do for us was just a request away. Before he left he turned and said, "You are a smart young man." The Mayor is a fool but me and my men now belong to you."

I decided it would be fun to sit in the Mayors chair so I perched myself there while Toby strutted around the room. It was all we could do to keep from falling on the floor laughing. I told Toby that sitting in the chair made me feel fat and I figured it was time to leave. There was a beautiful bronze figure of a running greyhound on the table by the door. I told Toby to take it as a reminder of the day we took over city hall.

With that we left and returned to Molly's. When we got there Billy was still there and he was eating lunch. When we joined them, Toby explained that he was starving. They were both anxious to hear how it went with the Mayor. Toby almost choked when he told how I explained that he would kick the Mayors ribs in if they did not open his door. He further added that the

Chief of Police said that he and his men now belonged to me. Molly left to order more food and Billy just shook his head.

CHAPTER 10

I sat at the table while everyone was eating and my mind shut out all the sounds around me. The smells of the point kept closing in on me like an angry dog that will not let go of your pant leg. I hated it and I was determined to get rid of it, but I still loved it because like everything in the Point it was mine and it bespoke of everything that made us so different and it was the glue that held us together. All my fancy clothes and all the material things on earth would never take me away from the soul of these alleys. I would never trust others the way I trusted the people here. There was a cat outside sitting on the window sill trying to catch a fly that was going up and down the inside of the glass.

The cat could play that game forever, but he will never catch the fly because he was on the outside. I was like the fly protected by the glass barrier that separated us from them. I will buzz around and make you crazy but you will never catch me because you do not how we think on this side of the glass.

Like a puff of smoke blown away by a sudden breeze my thoughts were interrupted and the silence was replaced with the voice of Billy calling for my attention.

I snapped out of my silent world and heard Billy ask me just what it was I needed him for this afternoon. "First things first", I said. "Toby, I have two questions, first did you ask that ladies father if you could marry his daughter, and second did you buy a house yet"? Toby got as red as a beet and tried to talk but no words would come out. Molly got a big smile on her face and said that she had better answer that question for him before he trips over his tongue.

He did ask her to marry him in front of her father and everyone is thrilled. She also explained that Annah and father are looking for a house even as we speak. I explained to Toby that we would keep our residence here in the hotel, but his house has to be in Old Allegheny. Toby just shook his head yes and that was that. Molly took me aside and explained that Annah's father was just keeping his head above water because of a ridiculous loan he had with some crook on the north side. Annah confided in Toby because she did not want her father to try to pay for a big wedding he could not afford. I asked Billy if he knew the loan shark and Billy said he knew him and he hated him for being a cheat.

I was quiet for a moment before I explained to Toby that he should inform Annah that he was sure it would all work out fine about her father's loan.

I then waved to Billy as I got up and asked him to come with me.

Billy and I took the ferry to the north side and walked up to a building a block from Max and Irma's. It was a three story brick structure that was as big as the entire block. The only occupant was a small book store on the right front corner. The building was a fort by construction and was originally used as an armory for the army. Billy was dying to ask questions, but I held my finger to my lips for silence. We went into the book store and the little bell over the door alerted the fellow

that owned the store that we were there. His face went

into a big smile as he came and gave me a hug. "My

dear friend and my best customer is here again.' "I

have two more rare books that were just brought in

this morning." "I put them away for you as you have

instructed." I introduced him to Billy and then I

instructed him to explain how he happened to be in

the book business. The man's name was Ben and he

looked at the floor and let out a great sigh before

speaking. He explained that in Paris he owned and

operated the biggest pawn shop in the city. He had

come from a long line of experts in rare books and

jewelry although they ventured into fine silver,

dinnerware, furniture and just about anything of value.

"My father, bless his sole, did some business with a

gentleman that had trouble showing receipts for his

merchandise and when a certain diamond broach

turned up in our shop the police and the countess that

owned the broach found out and someone had to take

the fall, or the whole business was over." "I left a note

for the police confessing and hopped a ship for America." "The little money I had got me here and allowed me to open this simple bookstore," said Ben

At this point Billy had caught on to my thoughts and he was excited. I explained to Ben that I owned the entire building and that the upper floors were to house the offices of Allegheny Contracting and Billy and I thought the entire first floor would make a wonderful pawn shop. Furthermore, we had many items to be put in the store on consignment and many contacts that would be happy to consign estate property contents to the store. All we needed was a well-trained person to run the place at a salary plus commission of 10%.

Ben put out his hand and thanked both of us and asked when we could start. I told him that Billy would work out all those details with him. After we left, Billy, was beside himself with excitement. I told him that the front would be for untraceable items and the back would be for our special clients who could keep their mouths shut. I looked at Billy and said," This is no joke."

You are going to have an important job and title in town so I need you to be an upstanding Keeper of the Poor and a citizen." "All of your dealings will have to be delivered here," I said. "We will work with every attorney in town to handle their estate auctions at a cash thank-you for their trouble."

Now let's go see this loan shark that is screwing Toby's father in law to be. It is no secret that Billy Birdshot was an enforcer of the first class, so taking him to transfer his interests to Ben and helping me with this crook at the same time was perfect, and Toby was kept out of it. Down by the river there was a filthy little tavern that looked like it was falling down. Billy explained that the shark called Angel owned the place and he sat there all day drinking and doing business. He was a pig and the place was a pig pen. We went inside and I walked up to Angel and asked him kindly to back off my good friend Max. He jumped out of the chair and swung a knife at my face. I moved before the blade could hit me and hit the button as my knife shot out and entered his throat.

Behind me two of his men tried to jump Billy but when they got in range the long leather tube of bird shot took first one and then the other alongside their heads with deadly effect. When Billy turned to me I had already cleaned my blade on Angel and returned it to my sleeve. Billy asked what happened to Angel and I said I think he committed suicide. On the way out I pushed over a barrel of whiskey and threw a lit match on it.

The place went up in seconds with the bodies inside. I told Billy that our little town did not need that kind of trash talking about and the building was an eye sore. We stopped at Max and Irma's and said hello to Max and Annah. We ordered two of the dark beers because I wanted Billy to try it. I explained that Billy worked for the city and he and Toby and I did some minor business on the side.

We were not there very long when a man ran in and announced that Angel and his thugs were dead, and the tavern burned down. The story is that the three had a fight and killed each other before accidentally setting the place on fire. I asked Max if Angel was a friend and he said hell no. After that we all shook hands and Billy and I left. As we were leaving I saw the look on Annah's face and she seemed to suspect something. I thought the idea was cute, I really did not care.

When we left I told Billy to go see Ben and work out the details. I explained that I was going home and that I would see him tomorrow. James met me at the door and took my coat. I was tired and I was hungry, but first I wanted to sit down and have a little of the scotch that James was teaching me to appreciate. When I walked into the den I was surprised to see Bart sitting on one of the big leather chairs with his hand around a crystal glass of that very scotch. He pointed to a glass on the table and said "I took the liberty of pouring one for you when I heard you come in the door. He rose to his feet and put out his hand. I ignored the hand and gave him a big hug. He was very surprised, but I think he was pleased. I said that I have so much to tell you." He laughed out loud and said, "You mean about killing Angel or the story about calling the mayor a fat shit and throwing him out of his own office or is it the pawn shop with Ben and Billy." There was nothing for me to say. I thought, "How could I forget that there are no secrets in the alleys of the Point, and never any from Bart."

Finally, Bart broke the silence and said, "How do you like the house?" I told him it was like a dream and I would never be able to thank him enough. I also begged him to live here with me. He grinned and said, " Follow me." It was my first time in the basement and I was surprised to see row after row of wine bottles from all over the world. In the back was a wall of scotch and cognac with at least 200 bottles on display. Bart walked up to the wall and slid his knife into a small crack. When he removed it the entire wall swung in like a great door. On the other side was a beautiful living area with a bedroom and a bath off of it. The furnishings were as fine as those in the upper floors, but the artwork on the walls was magnificent. Bart motioned for me to sit. He explained that these rooms were his and the artwork was worth a fortune. He explained further that the wine and the spirits represented years of collecting and the next phase of my education was about to begin. We would dine together each evening and he and James would teach me perfect manners and a perfect appreciation for fine foods. Next would be the world of wine, spirits, and most of all fine art. He explained that I was to become a mystery person in society. I would belong to nothing and yet I would be known by everyone. My extensive reading must continue and James would introduce me to music. Both he and James were accomplished pianists which explained the concert grand piano upstairs. He told me he was pleased with my placement of all our people and especially the pawn shop that James and the other service people in the great houses would use to buy and sell when the boss was short of funds. It seemed that every move I made was somehow orchestrated by Bart and I never even knew it. My lesson in fine art began right away as Bart showed the different styles of the artists and what they were called and why. He touched each brush stroke with the love of a father admiring the beauty in his child. He told me he wanted me to feel the painting as much as I could. He told me to look closely and imagine the artists' thoughts and emotions that went with each stroke. He explained that when I could do that I would be able to differentiate between artists and their periods of work. His motions and his voice made me fall in love with each work we looked at. So much to learn.

CHAPTER 11

The night wind blew hard against the tall window while the trees waved their great branches as if to say good-by to all the day time creatures that were away from the streets and alley ways that they protected all day from the sun. The musty smell of old leather and yellowing pages filled my senses as I studied the book propped on my lap. My mind was captivated by the words as they spoke to me from each page and allowed me to enter the world created by the writer and for just a little length of time, escape to another place. My world had become so greatly expanded with the introduction of music and art and literature that I felt somehow, like my soul was a cup that would never be filled even though I was compelled to keep trying to fill it with experience and knowledge. It seemed like a moment later that the sun light exploded into my bed chamber and forced my eyes open. I did not remember when I fell asleep, but as usual there was a book at my side in the bed.

Where had all the time gone? So much had changed since I discovered that my mentor, Bart, was a sometimes resident of my house. I was only twenty years old, but I looked closer to thirty and Bart had become my great teacher and friend.

He had his own entrance and exit through a tunnel out of the basement that came up in an old carriage house a short way from here. He spent most of his time away but when he was home I shared every moment in the pleasure of his guidance and company. He and James no longer spoke English in the house. They had informed me that French and or Spanish would only be spoken in our home so I would have to learn them. It turned out that I had a natural ability to learn to think in other languages so I was able to master them in a short period of time. I also picked up German from being around Max and his wife Irma when they were speaking to their friends. I was easily recognized by people in the city and in Old Allegheny. Toby and Annah had a grand wedding and they were settled in a large brick house on a large lot not far from the tavern her parents owned. The money from the city kept pouring into Allegheny Contracting for the betterment of the Point, and Toby proved to be a fine director of any kind of construction as you can imagine; no one ever argued with the giant Scotsman. He was soon getting construction jobs of every kind including houses. Architects loved working with him especially because the material and crews were never late to the job sight and Toby was a fanatic for keeping his construction schedule.

The Pawn Shop was growing by leaps and bounds. Ben also added a loan business to fill in the void left by our old friend Angel. A while back I decided that our little village needed a police department.

I donated the far end of the old armory to the village for a rent of one dollar a year. Toby fixed it up and even added a small jail cell. I suggested to the police chief in Pittsburgh that his son move to the north side and run for office. The young man followed the suggestion and was duly elected by a unanimous vote since no one ran against him.

I still spent time at Molly's where I met with my men now named One through Nine. We settled problems, divided the income and looked for new ventures for profit. I insisted that they each buy up income property and put aside substantial profits in legitimate bank accounts. At first they were reluctant but as they saw their illegal black money turn white through the profits from rents and as the equity in their property went up as they improved them, they soon understood and became independent business men in their own right. The best part was that they never forgot how they got there and as they got married and started families they easily moved into the better parts of town while keeping their standing in the Point.

One day after our meeting Four, whose real name was John, asked me to have lunch with him and meet one of his new friends.

I agreed and we went to a fine restaurant in Market Square in the center of the city. We were taken to a private table in the back which always happened as soon as I entered any restaurant. The owner came immediately to the table with two glasses and a bottle of his best wine. I suggested that we would need a third glass as we were waiting for a friend and he quickly produced a third glass. He asked me to let him know when we were ready to eat and he left us alone. Shortly afterwards a large man that was obviously a boat captain by his dress spotted John and came back to our table.

We poured him a glass and John introduced Mike Staiger to me. He gave my name as Getts because that is the only name anyone ever knew. Mike started to speak, but he had great difficulty with English. When I spoke to him in German and suggested he do the same the relief and surprise on his face were great. He explained that he owned a Paddle Wheeler that ran from here to St Louis and back. It seemed he had a brother who owned a large pawn business there that was very much like the one Ben was running. The problem he explained, was that much of his merchandise was too easily identified by the local patrons and he needed an outlet in another place distant from St. Louis. I explained that we too had such a problem and perhaps we could be of service to one another especially since we had ready access to transportation between the two cities. I suggested he bring some of the merchandise and a representative from his brothers' shop to visit Ben on his next return trip. I even promised him a great German feast when they got here. We stood and shook hands as I said in German, done and done. I asked him when he would be leaving and he said in two days. I asked him to stay at Molly's Inn when they got back so I could arrange the meeting and he agreed.

With that he left the restaurant. I looked at John and said that he would share in every transaction. He looked at me and said, "How did you ever bring us so far?"

I just smiled and told him that I would order for the both of us since the fish here was the best.

After lunch, I went back to Molly's and sat alone at my table. She soon joined me and said that our people were so spread out with different jobs that I needed someone to watch my back the way Toby had done. I had been so busy that I did not think of it, and my reputation was such that few people came within several feet of me. She said that Bart had a friend he wanted me to meet. I thought, "Bart, always Bart." She gave a signal and a small man who moved like Bart came to the table. He explained that he would drive my new surrey, accompany me where ever I went and wait for me each morning at my front door. His expenses were already guaranteed by my banker and no one would ever bother me. "Well," I thought, Bart to the rescue again. He got up and moved back to his table. I explained to Molly about the river captain and then I just slumped in my chair and finished my ale. When I was done I decided to check on things at Allegheny Contracting. When I got there every one was out on the job. I knew how much Toby loved his work so I tried to stay out of his way. I stopped and told Ben about Captain Staiger and then I went to Max and Irma's to get a mug of beer. The place was packed but Irma came running out of the kitchen when she heard my voice with the biggest baby I had ever seen. She was beaming and kept saying, say hello to your Godfather. The little boy was beautiful and I knew he was the apple of everyone's eye. His smile could light up a room and I knew that Toby and I would spoil him rotten if we could ever get him away from his Grandmother. I held him for a while and loved every second of it but he soon began to squirm for his Grandma and I surrendered him to her.

During this entire time, I noticed that my new friend was never very far away from me. Well, I thought that was his job. I decided to go home and my new friend followed me very closely.

When I got to the door I wished him a good night and said I was in until morning. He doffed his cap and left as soon as I closed the door. I never even got his name.

When I went into the parlor I had the pleasure of seeing Bart sitting there sipping scotch. He smiled and handed a glass of the same to me. He waited as I took a drink and I said, "Single malt, northern islands, aged no more than ten years." Bart smiled and said, "I tried to slip one in on you since you know I never drink scotch that is aged less than twenty-five years."

I told him that he is the teacher and how I can help him if he is so talented.

We both sat down and Bart called for James. He instructed James to take away the scotch and return with fresh glasses and a proper bottle. I asked him about my new friend and Bart explained that he found him in New York where he was guarding a Russian member of the royal family. He explained that his name is Sasha and he became available when one of the royal ladies was found to be too fond of him. He is a Cossack and a fierce fighter with fists or any weapon. He wants to stay in America so he agreed to work for you. He speaks some English but he is most comfortable with Russian or French, the language of all European royalty.

Well, I said, I guess I will try to learn Russian

We spoke of many things as we sat together. Bart explained that he was very comfortable with Five and in the future Five would take my place in dealing with the others and covering all of Bart's late night enterprises. I would, of course be informed of their every move. He emphasized that the added guard that led the police away the night we kicked in the bakery door was brilliant and he wanted my input on every job. I thanked him and he handed me a beautiful envelope that came from city hall and the Mayor's office. He explained that it had been delivered today by the police chief since he is the only one with this address. In addition to everything else the Chief and many of his men were doing so well that they were all building new houses.

Since they were not supposed to have the money they were spending they were paying Toby in cash for most of the construction costs, and since he had to pay the suppliers in cash to cover the paper trail the cheap little homes began to compete with the finest houses in their neighborhoods.

The suppliers soon began to use their new found cash to either have Toby do extensive work for them or they sent their wives to shop the back rooms of our pawn shop. It appeared that no matter how much we spent the money always seemed to find its way back to us. Well. I finally opened the beautiful envelope. The Mayor was throwing a very formal ball to celebrate his victory.

Bart explained that everyone of means or importance would be there. It was also my informal entrance into society. He handed me a box of calling cards and a gold card case with a beautiful G on it. The cards had the name Getts on it in 20 carat gold in Black silk covered board paper. At the bottom of the card in small print it said, "Contact Harper Esquire" and gave his address.

When Bart saw the questioning look on my face he said, "Let those stuck up bastard's figure that one out." "No one gets to you without proper screening from your attorney." "Harper will refer their questions to your new secretary Mona at the Allegheny Contracting building where you now have an office that you will never be in." All of your mail will go there and Sasha will see that you get it hand delivered. You can never go to that building again. Any business meetings will be conducted at Molly's where we control the streets, alleys and everything else. You will never meet with more than one person at a time so all discussions will be your word against theirs."

"You are entering a whole new world of our relationship and I could not be prouder of you." "We are truly just beginning."

I responded that that was fine as long as I was informed of every detail of our operations. "I never want to lose my contact with the streets and alleys of the point." "I am too much a part of it and no matter what kind of a picture I paint to the rest, I am still an alley rat and I like it," I said.

Bart looked at me and said, "That is why you are where you are and I will never let you lose that edge." We sat and enjoyed each other's company for the rest of the evening and then I went to bed with visions of the ball and how I could possibly fit in. Hell, I had no idea just what a ball was, but I could dance, pick fine wine discuss literature, and evaluate any painting and artist of our time or in the past. I spoke several languages played the piano, and I could describe the great cities of Europe as if I had been there. Bart taught me to memorize faces and names in a matter of seconds and the Mayor sure as hell knew who I was so I guess I was as ready as I could possibly be. I thought about it for a few seconds more and said to myself, "Screw it" and fell asleep.

Chapter 12

The walls of our home were thick with four courses of interlocking bricks. The windows had wood shutters inside and out. The sounds of the world had little chance of getting in so the sounds of the house itself were distinct and by this time a deep part of my everyday life.

I lay in the soft bed with dreams of the kind that come and go like flash memories that you are aware will fade away as soon as your eyes open. Wide plank boards on the floor creak and the clock at the foot of the stairs tick, tick, ticks toward the next excuse to call out with a chime. Wonderful smells of coffee and breakfast meat sneak up the stairs and tantalize your senses until you can take it no more and stretch your arms toward the heavens and kick away the blankets.

James stood in the doorway and signaled that my bath was ready. It seemed like just yesterday I had my first real bath at Molly's and my first experience with soft clothes free of any fleas and lice. "Never forget where you have come from", I said to myself, and remember that you are no better than the alley rat you once were." "You just got luckier".

I was well aware that arrogance is for fools. It is like trying to hide behind a window pane, it just makes you look stupid. When I finished my bath and began to eat breakfast, James and I spoke of the ball and what I needed to do to prepare. I explained that I wanted to take a closed cab and horse over the ferry to the Point and to Molly's Pub. I want to have a drink with her before I go to the ball as a sort of thank-you and to let my people know that I will be representing them.

"It is important to me that I arrive from the point", I said, "because that is where I am from, and I am proud of it."

James thought it was a fine idea and he asked to go with me and wait at Molly's for my return after the ball. James laid out clothes for me that I had never seen before. He explained that the tailor had been very excited about making the clothes for the ball and that he assured that no one there would be as well dressed.

He was very familiar with the work all the tailors were doing in preparation for tonight and he wanted me to look the finest. I asked James to see that he got a special thanks. The clothes were beautiful and the fit was perfect. As we left the house James handed me a cane with a silver handle and a new black silk cape lined in gold lamb's wool. It had a large hood that spilled out over my shoulders. I felt ready to face anything so we opened the door to leave. Sasha was waiting with the cab pulled by a beautiful pair of black stallions. It was obvious that he had a great control of horses or he would never risk two great stallions together. Sasha opened the door and James and I got in. I said, "To Molly's" and we were off.

On the ride James and I switched back and forth from French to Spanish with a touch of German thrown in just for fun. He wanted to make sure I was ready for any language thrown at me. After a while, I spoke to him at length in Russian. I was trying to surprise him, but he answered back in Russian also and we had a great laugh. At last the cab pulled out in front of Molly's Pub. Sasha halted the horses with a command in Russian. The sight of us caught the attention of everyone in the area and I wished a good day to them all. When they realized who I was a little cheer was made by the crowd. We went inside where Molly was waiting with her arm hooked in the arm of Captain Staiger. She rushed over and gave me a great hug. Then she stepped back and did a little walk around me as though an inspection was required. When she was done, I pulled her close and whispered in her ear that later on, I wanted all of the details concerning Captain Staiger and her. She blushed and shook her head yes. We all sat down for a drink and Molly explained how pleased she was along with all the street people that I came to them first.

Suddenly the door burst open and Billy came in. He took a long look at me and smiled as he said that I looked grand. We all sat and had a great time chatting until it was time for me to leave. As we headed for the door Billy stopped and said," I have a present for you for all that you have done for me and it is waiting outside." When I opened the door I could not believe my eyes. The cab was gone and in its place the great stallions were hitched to a shiny black closed cab trimmed in gold with a shield painted in red with a gold G in beautiful script on the doors. The black horses were trimmed out in gold and red braid on their bridles and all of the harnesses. Sasha got down to open the door. He was all in black with gold trim. On the front of his black coat was a red shield to match those on the doors. He was wearing the big black fur hat of a Cossack with a black fur tail down the right side held tight by a red shield with a gold G in the middle. Sasha looked as proud as he could be. He also wore a long red cape trimmed in gold. All in all the sight was spectacular and I did not realize it was for me until Sasha opened the door with a bow

I entered the cab and sat back as I heard a whip crack and Sasha called to the horses. We took off to the cheers of the people, my people, and I vowed to never forget them for their pride given to one of their own. I decided that this cab would be kept in the Point and any trip in it would begin here. Sasha sped through the streets until we entered Market Square where he slowed down to make a trip around the square to show off how the stallions pranced in perfect time with their heads held high and the bells on their collars chiming. I was glad to stay hidden in the cab for this was Sasha's time to show off and he was not disappointed as the crowds watched a true master control those beautiful horses. When it was time to head away from the square he stopped and with all eyes on him he cracked the whip three times above the heads of the horses and they stood up on their hind legs and seemed to wave their hooves at the people before they settled to the ground and took off at a trot to the cheers of the crowd.

My only regret was that I had not been able to see the spectacle. When we pulled up in a line of horses and liveries of all kinds in front of the court house I began to think about all the people and friends I now had.

I thought about my mother and remembered her raspy voice as she told me goodbye.

It was less than two weeks later that Molly told me she had died. I now realized just how tiny and delicate she was. Her hair was as black as coal with a shine to it like one of those fancy fur coats. She had a beautiful smile and she was forever singing songs from Ireland that she learned as a young girl. You would have thought that we were rich the way our little shack rang with the sounds of her beautiful voice, and I guess in some ways we were. She knew how to escape our surroundings with music. Of all my wishes having her here with me right now was my greatest.

"Who knows", I thought, maybe she was here. Religion was something I found way too creepy to even think about let alone try to understand.

There were several coaches in line before us, so Sasha held the horses until all the others had pulled up and discharged their passengers.

There was a good one hundred yards between us and the exit portico. Sasha hollered out a command in Russian and the horses began to prance in place. They were like two dancing beautiful beasts. A moment later he gave out another command and a single crack of his whip. Without missing a step the horses moved forward at a very slow high stepping march. Everyone was glued to the magnificent spectacle as the cab moved up to the portico. When Sasha called for a halt the steps to the building were crowded with people that had come out to see the show.

With great flare Sasha climbed down from his seat and stood stiff as a soldier as he opened my door. I could hear whispering in the crowd, wondering who was in the coach. As I stepped out Sasha tipped his head slightly in a salute. I smiled and nodded my head to everyone I passed on my way to the entrance.

The Mayor and a lady I presumed to be his wife were waiting inside to greet the guests as they arrived. When the Mayor introduced me to his wife I was shocked.

Although several years older than me, she was quite beautiful and she had that wonderful aura of intelligence and grace that her husband was greatly lacking. She smiled and became even more attractive. I bowed and kissed the back of her hand. I said in French that I was truly delighted to meet one of our business partners.

She responded in perfect French that she was honored. The Mayor looked at us and said, "Don't encourage her with all that silly foreign stuff." "She talks to our help like that and I never know a damn thing they are saying." The lady looked me in the eye and said, "Exactly," again in perfect French. I gave a slight bow again and moved on into the room. I could feel all eyes on me as they tried to figure out just who this stranger was. A waiter stopped by and I took a glass of champagne. I was enjoying the sights of so many beautiful women when I was rescued from my thoughts by the Chief of Police and his lovely wife. Introductions were made and I found his wife to be good company. She asked about her son and his new position on the North Side and I assured her that he was doing an excellent job and she could be very proud of him. The time passed pleasantly as the city elite were announced into the room. The Mellons, the Fricks, Carnegie, and the Brainard family from the glass business were all introduced with much whispering among the crowd as if royalty had finally graced us with their appearance. A moment later the orchestra began to play and everyone relaxed a little. As I turned to look at the orchestra, I saw Kathleen, the Mayors wife, coming toward me. She gently grabbed my arm and pulled me to the dance floor. She told me, still in French, than she and everyone else in the building were dying to find out all about me. I explained that my name was Getts and that alone was what everyone called me. "I am an investor in businesses and real estate, and I have the honor of working with her husband judging elections in the Point," I explained. "So you're the one that threw the election for my husband," she said. "And what is this about me being a business partner"? I explained that I had a minor roll in Allegheny Contracting and that the Mayor had invested in it also in her name.

She said," Well then, How am I doing?"

The company has become a great success and your part of it has grown along with it, I explained. I suggested that she speak to the president, Toby if she had any questions. I told her that his offices were in Old Allegheny. She smiled and commented on what a fine dancer I was before pulling me off the dance floor and taking me around to meet "all the right people". It seemed that the more we climbed the social ladder, the more we spoke in French. I decided that the more money you had, the more you wanted to act like the Europeans.

As the evening progressed Kathleen found it necessary to surrender me to the crowd so she could attend to the other guests. I did not mind since there was no end to the beautiful young women that came to my aid. I was a curiosity and I tried to dance with as many ladies as I could.

There was one lady in particular that seemed to be hiding alone in the corner except for frequent visits from her mother.

She was short and very square of build. She was not ugly, but she certainly was plain. At one point I overheard her mother speaking to her in German, telling her not to be so sad, that things have a way of working out for young ladies. I walked over to her and bowed. I asked her in German if she would be so kind to dance with me. She seemed to light up even though I could tell she was nervous. As it turned out, she was a wonderful dance partner and as I tried to do every dance move I had been taught, she responded with grace as though we had danced together for years. I insisted that she stay on the floor with me as the orchestra played on. Finally, a young man came over and cut in. I whispered in her ear, "To all flowers a season, be patient", and then I gave him her hand after I placed a small kiss on it and they danced away.

Someone handed me a glass of champagne and when I turned, I saw a very large man with a great mustache and side whiskers. He spoke to me in German and said, "I am Hans and the girl you danced with is my daughter." She is only fourteen and very shy." You have turned this evening into something special for her and I and her mother are very grateful. I told him his daughter was delightful and the honor was mine. He handed me his card and said, "Come see me at my brewery, so we can talk. I took out my card case and told him it would be my pleasure and gave him my card. After seeing me pull out my shiny card case it seemed everyone felt the need to have one. I believe I met everyone who was anyone that evening and as the evening progressed I made a point of dancing with all the older women much to the relief of their tired husbands.

I had great fun and the best part was that no one knew any more about me at the end of the evening than they did at the beginning, although the stories seemed to travel endlessly from lady to lady especially the rich matrons who insisted they had the inside information. By god Bart was a genius in his planning. Kathleen came to me for the last dance of the evening and insisted on walking me to my coach. It seemed everyone was waiting to see Sasha and the horses. When I got to the portico, there were no coaches in sight. Then I heard a whip crack and the two stallions high stepped down the street and up to the portico. I turned and said good night to Kathleen and she said '" I wished I had seen the show your driver put on earlier, everyone that did could not stop talking about it". I could not help myself when I said please wait here and perhaps my horses would like to wave goodbye to you.

Whispers quickly spread through the crowd and soon the portico was full of people. When Sasha opened my door I asked him if perhaps the horses would like to circle the driveway and wave good- by. His face was beaming as he climbed to the top of the coach. He called out his commands and the horses began a dance step as we pulled away. With a crack of the whip they went into a perfect trot in unison.

As we rounded the bend to return he called out again and the horses did a perfect high slow walk to the front of the crowd.

When he passed Kathleen he whistled and the horses slowly backed up until they were facing her. He cracked the whip three times and the stallions rose upon their hind legs and once again pawed the air as though waving goodbye. While the horses were still on their rear legs, Sasha stood up, bowed and cracked the whip. The horses exited at a full gallop to the applause of the people under the portico. We retraced our route back into the Point and stopped in front of Molly's. I explained to Sasha that the coach was to remain in the Point. I also gave him a great hug that only a Russian could appreciate and told him he was the greatest of horse handlers and that the entire city was talking about him and his beautiful stallions.

When I went into the Pub everyone was waiting. The place smelled of the most wonderful food. Molly said that those big hitters never served good food and I realized that in the thrill of the evening I had paid no attention to the fact that there was very little to eat and I was starving. I got a hug from Toby and a kiss from his wife. I tried to recap the evening, but I had to admit that Sasha stole the entire show with the horses.

The women wanted to know about the gowns and the men wanted to know who all I had met. Standing quietly in the corner was Bart. I walked over to him and said," Why don't you ask Bart?" and then I hugged him and whispered thank you in his ear.

He pulled me aside with a questioning look on his face and I explained that every server, waitress, bartender and coachman knew who I was.

"There is only one person with that much power and it is you", I said. He gave me one of his rare smiles and hugged me back while whispering in my ear, "You are learning". The rest of the evening was wonderful and again it reinforced my love of these people and this place. My last thoughts were of Hans and what tomorrow would bring.

CHAPTER 13

The sound of the piano was like the heart of my life as the notes reverberated through the rooms and the halls and moved every fiber of my existence in a swirl of dreamy euphoria that settled back onto me and kept my hands and fingers working the keys to keep the feeling alive. "How had my mentors been so successful in taking the music from my heart to my hands and then to the piano?" James and Bart were astonished when they heard my heart capture their lessons like a starving man to a banquet. The piano was not an instrument but rather an extension of me. The vibrations of the keys were the pulses of my heart and I could stay at the keyboard forever. But alas, that could never be because I belonged to the streets and the alleys of the Point and they were an unforgiving lover that held tight to me never to completely let go. Perhaps the time would come when I could share them both with one another, but not now.

James stood in the doorway and said it was time for me to go to my meeting with Hans.

Sasha was waiting outside with the old cab. I put on my coat and left the house. We took the ferry to the city and then traveled north through the Strip District where all the food came into the city. We soon reached the front of the great brewery. Sasha locked the brake on the cab and led the way to the door to the offices. We entered and I asked for Hans. A young man said "You must be Getts, and he waved me down the hall to a private office.

I told Sasha to wait outside the door.

When he saw me, Hans left his desk and came over to vigorously shake my hand. He said over and over how pleased he was to see me. I asked him simply what I could do for him.

He asked me to sit and listen to his problem.

He explained that many of his wagons of beer were being stopped and forced to either pay a very high toll or the men would smash the kegs and often hurt the drivers very badly. He had gone to the police, but the Chief told him he did not have enough men to help him out.

The Chief suggested that he talk to me.

I sat silently for a long time and then Hans asked me if he could pay for my help. I told him my accountant would go over his books and if they proved to be a good investment, I would buy 20% of his company at an amount he agreed to. In the meantime, I would look into this problem he was having and see what I could do. Hans just sat there in shock. He asked me why I would invest in a company with so much trouble and I explained that I liked to invest in the future. "You will be completely in charge of your company.", I said I will only be available to help you when you need me or to ask for advice on matters to grow the company." If you are agreeable, then we can move forward. He said that he could not see how he could lose so we shook hands and I left. I told Sasha to take me to Molly's as soon as possible.

When we got to Molly's I sent for Billy Birdshot. He was there very quickly. I explained the problem at the brewery and asked him what he knew about it. He said it was a group from the Strip District that was trying to take over the whole town.

I asked why this was the first time I heard of it and he said they stayed out of the Point so he ignored them.

I tried to remain calm when I said to him, "They stay away now but soon they will get greedy and want it all." "Who is in charge and where do I find him?" Billy said that a guy named Sullivan ran the gang and they had about four others. He said they hung out at a bar called Smitty"s. I told him to find Toby and Five and bring them here. When he left Molly came over to sit with me. She looked worried and asked me if I needed to get involved in this problem directly. I told her I was an Alley Rat and all the soap could not wash that away.

I also explained that everyone needed to know that, or they might forget who they were really dealing with. It took about an hour for Billy, Five and Toby to show up. We all got in the coach and Sasha took us to a spot about a block away from Smitty's. When we got there, five watched the door as Billy, Toby, Sasha and I walked in. We walked over to a big table and I said, "Are you Sullivan?" He said, "piss off" and I hit the button and pushed my blade into his throat. Before anyone could move, Billy, Toby and Sasha dispensed with the rest. Sasha then went to the bar and asked the old man if he was Smitty. He said he was and Toby handed him a roll of money and asked him if he knew what they were fighting over when they killed each other. Smitty said it was probably a woman. We all agreed and on my way out the door, I told him we only drink Steel City beer made by our good friend Hans.

When we got back to Molly's, Five and Toby left. Billy said he would keep me informed from now on and he left too. Molly came over and sat down with me as Sasha took his usual place in the corner by the door.

Molly brought us a crock of ale. It was ice cold and it felt good on my throat.

I told Molly to buy a good piano for the bar out of my money and then I asked about Captain Mike. She explained that they were in love and as soon as he could sell his boat they were going to get married and run the Pub together. I asked if he was around and she said he was in the kitchen.

She explained that he loved to cook. I asked her to get him and she left. A moment later, they returned. I asked them to sit. I asked if he had a man to run his boat and he said he did. I told him to see Walter at my bank and he would pay him for the boat. I also told him to tell his man that he would get a 25% share of all the profits, but I needed a complete list of everything needed to make the boat the fastest on the rivers. I also wanted at least two more boats if they were available. Poor old Captain Mike did not know what to say. Finally, he asked what kind of cargo I would carry. I told him I was now in the brewery business and there was a hell of a lot of little towns between here and St. Louis with thirsty people. We would haul and wholesale beer along with anything else we could carry. Hell, there was enough moonshine made in the point to raise the river three feet. The good captain nodded his agreement. I also told him to have Walter send the papers to Harper since it was Allegheny Contracting that would own the boats.

When I finally got home, Bart was waiting for me in the library. He had a fine glass of scotch in his hand and one for me.

He looked at me and said, "You have had a busy day." "Beer, boats, and bar fights". "Why did you do it yourself?" "I looked at him and said, "We are what we are, and everyone needs to know it". What happened today will last a very long time in the minds of anyone that decides to bother us",

"I do not just give orders; I must lead the way". Bart looked at me and said, "Exactly".

It was not long before a messenger came to the door. He was from the police chief. It was addressed to no one and the note simply said, "A certain beer maker wanted a visit as soon as possible."

Bart looked at me and said, "It appears that you are in the beer business."

I asked James to have Sasha bring the coach and when I finished my scotch, I left for the brewery.

I entered the brewery offices and was escorted directly to Hans. As usual, Sasha was not far behind. Hans shook my hand with vigor and asked me to sit. He said he had a story to tell me. When his trucks returned today from their deliveries they told him that they were not only left alone, but they were treated special. They also said the many other tavern owners stopped them and gave them orders explaining that they wished to do business with us from now on.

They even got orders from some of the hotels in the city. It seems that a gang of thieves had a falling out and killed each other. He looked at me and said," I don't suppose you know anything about that, do you?" I looked him right in the eye and said, "A good friend and business partner just purchased a large paddle wheel boat and he will soon need one thousand kegs. Eight hundred of them will be filled with Steel City beer and two hundred need to be empty. His first trip will be north up the Allegheny where he will stop along the way to sell your beer. Once he reaches Ford City, he will exchange the empty barrels for barrels full of their fine Golden Wedding whiskey. He will also load as much lumber on the boat as he can haul from the sawmills in Freeport to be used in our construction company. They will unload the lumber in Old Allegheny and continue down the Ohio, selling the barrels until they are all sold. The price will increase the further they travel, so the smart distributors will bring their wagons north to get the best deal.

We hope to have another boat that will do the same thing down the Monongahela River into West Virginia, where we hope to pick up a load of their fine mountain dew along with more lumber to feed our ever-growing construction business. "I hope that answers your question because that is all I know about hauling beer, " I said. At that point Hans handed me an envelope. He explained that I now owned 20% of his brewery and I was a very welcome partner. We stood and shook hands while his brewmaster brought us each a mug of Steel City Beer to finalize the deal.

When I left the brewery I had Sasha go north following the Allegheny River until we came to the little town of Verona where there was a man with a crew that made barrels. I went in and finding the owner I asked if we could talk. He said why not since he had very little to do. When I asked him what the problem was, he explained that the big manufacturers undercut him on every bid to drive him out of business. I asked what a fair price was and he told me. I asked what he was going to do and he said he was going to close up. He said he needed money just to pay off his creditors. When he told me how much, I doubled the amount and told him to see Walter at my bank and he would give it to him for a 40% interest in the company.

He told me I must be crazy because the whole company was not worth a few dollars. I took an order sheet from his desk and wrote out an order for 1000 barrels to be constructed as soon as possible for Steel City Beer. I told him to see Hans at the brewery tomorrow and he would have the paperwork ready. Then he could see my banker for the money. I stood, shook his hand and left him standing in shock. I told Sasha to take me back to the brewery. When I went to see Hans, I explained that we now owned 40% of Verona Barrel Works and they would start work right away on our 1000 barrels. He asked me how I knew he was worried about having enough barrels and I said my accountant made a note of your lack of inventory. Now, we will never have a problem and our boats will make sure our new partner gets all the lumber he needs. When I left Hans was still shaking his head. I stopped on my way out to make sure he got the paperwork from Harper, our new attorney, before our new partner arrived. When I got back in the coach I told Sasha to head for home.

It was a long day, and I had had enough. James met at the door, took my coat and told me that there was a package for me in the library. When I opened the package there was a roll of money and a shot glass that said Smitty's on it. I knew it was a message from Bart. Never leave a witness was his final law of the street and Smitty was surely dead. James handed me a drink, and I went to the piano to escape into the music. It was a fitting ending to a day begun in the sounds of the piano.

CHAPTER 14

It was six AM and I was sitting at the piano in Molly's Pub. My fingers were talking to the beautiful instrument and it was grabbing my soul like a fist at my throat. I was sipping on a clear moon shine and falling in love with the idea of Chopin as the notes played with the swimming brain in my head. I was alone because it was so early, and everyone was afraid to come near me in this euphoric trance that the piano and I were sharing. Sasha was at his usual table, but he did not count because he was always there. When I looked out the window I saw that a crowd had gathered outside to hear the music. I realized that Chopin was the magician and the piano and I was just his means of delivery. It humbled me to think that the great composer had allowed me to deliver his miracles to these people. I opened the door and beckoned them in. I would play for them and I would tell them that this music was for them. I believed then and I believe now that truly great music was for the people of the streets because only they were capable of riding the notes above the stink and the poverty they lived in. I played on and on and no one moved. I spoke of the notes and the meaning of a tortured mind that wrote them so that the real people, my people, could listen and cry. I played the Blue Danube and suggested that they close their eyes and dance with me to spin and spin until we were lost in the beauty of movement. I played for a very long time until my hands could stand it no more. Finally, Molly came and held me close to her. The Pub was packed with people and the rich smell of sweat and dirt surrounded me and I got up and kissed each person as they looked up at me with tears in their eyes. I told them that they were special and that I would come back to play only for them.

They slowly left the Pub and when they were all gone, Molly held me again and said, "I will never understand your heart." "You can deal out swift and terrible cruelty and then create a beautiful time of peace to the lowest of the low as though they were your children." I looked up into her beautiful brown eyes and said," They are my children."

I had ended up at the Pub after a night of difficult sleep. I had Sasha bring me over and I let myself in with the key I always carried. Molly had become accustomed to my arrivals at all hours of the day or night.

The beautiful piano she found was a perfect upright with great sound. Everyone knew it was mine and no one went near it. I had so many irons in the fire that I was very thankful for the quality of the friends I had and their dedication to their tasks. Toby was running Allegheny Contracting and also the new boats.

Big Dave, the new captain, turned out to be the perfect man to handle the newly rebuilt boat and his crew responded to his every command. He and Toby were perfect together although they terrified children by their size when they walked down the street. Dave was almost as big as Toby. Hans and his new partner in the barrel business were quickly becoming great friends. My original crew was still maintaining order in the stalls.

Molly and Mike were prosperous in the hotel business and we added a large dining room that served great food. Ben had built an enormous business at the pawn shop, and Billy was cleaning up the Point and setting up food kitchens to feed the needy in his new role as Keeper Of The Poor. It may seem crazy, but I still wanted to continue to build as long as I did not have to manage the things I built.

Molly came down with her husband Mike and said they enjoyed the morning music. They both went to the kitchen and began to cook breakfast, but before anything else she brought me a big mug of coffee. I decided it was time I visited Billy. I knew he was busy with all his duties including running the workhouse and moving product over to Ben, but I had an idea. When I banged on the door Billy opened it right away. He threw his arms around me and said that he never expected to see me here again. We went in and sat down. I looked around and said, Just what the hell do all these people work at in this enormous structure?"

Billy explained that they made wicker baskets and furniture. It does not pay much, but they stay busy. I asked how often anyone ever came down to inspect the place and he told me never in the twelve years he has been running the place. I said, "What do you say we make this a profitable business that pays these poor people a little money, and we make a little ourselves?"

Billy thought that sounded great. I told Billy there were some folks from a place way up the river called Tionesta that were bringing moonshine to the market in small jugs to sell. It was not very much so everyone left them alone. "I think they should be arrested and you should save them and bring them here.

They might be interested in making their product right here in this building. Gallon jugs could be fitted into wicker baskets and barrels could be filled for sales downriver. We could try a product I heard of from a West Virginia family. They put peach peels and seeds into the mash to make the product brown and to add a slightly different taste. I never tried it, but they said it was sold out every fall when they had the peaches.

Billy loved the idea and said he would arrange everything with the Chief. I reminded him that the workers were to be treated well and paid. I had no interest in slave labor. I suggested that if the new people were interested, they tell us what they would need to produce in quantity. I wasn't looking for great quality, but I wanted a safe product to sell. We now had three boats, although one was smaller than the other two.

It was, however, very fast and it had a wonderful secret. The boat had four big guns hidden in the hull that could be put into action at a moment's notice. One in the bow, one in the stern and one on each side to cover anything afloat. I pictured this boat taking whiskey to New Orleans and returning full of cane sugar to make the shine. I told Billy to start working with those guys as soon as he could and let me know what they needed.

I never had a problem with illegal liquor because it was the only thing the average and the poor could afford to give them a little escape from their everyday lives. There were also opium dens and other drugs, but they stole your soul and left nothing. Even a drunk eventually sobered up. At least, that was how I saw it. I decided to go home to get ready for the dinner party I was invited to that evening. In the years since the ball I found myself having dinner at many of the finest homes in the city. It was interesting how little they knew about me and how much they made up my "true Identity" in the back parlors and clubs they all seemed to belong to. Kathleen, the Mayor's wife, loved all the gossip, especially since the Mayor had filled her in on the truth. She felt like she was a close associate with the privilege of inside knowledge. She was always at the dinners and parties I attended and each time she would find a moment to take me aside and share the latest word about just who I was.

It was a harmless game that she enjoyed very much and I had fun dropping hints whenever I could. She told me one evening that the latest was that I was a man bewitched by a woman from an eastern European royal family and even though my father was a Russian Duke, alas, I was a bastard son and rejected by her family and forced to leave the country. That evening, as the party wound down, I asked if I might try their beautiful piano. Now, no one was aware that I played the piano, so it sparked great curiosity among the group as I walked to the beautiful instrument in the corner of the hall. I sat down and began to play a series of pieces from some of the Great Russian composers. Everyone seemed to be captivated, so I turned to them and said in Russian that I would continue with their blessing. I then acted as though I had caught myself and apologized in English and repeated the question. They asked me please to continue, so I started a series of old gypsy music that spoke of great loss and sorrow as only gypsy music can. As I got deeper and deeper into the sound from the piano, I described the words to the songs and I soon had an audience dabbing the corners of their eyes with the kind of silk hankies I used to steal when I was a kid on the street. The place grew very quiet, so I turned and said, "Enough of the past", and I played a lively piece to bring the party back to life. I exited the piano to an enthusiastic applause.

Katherine brought me a glass of scotch and whispered in my ear that I was a devil and every lady in the city would be swooning over the poor, dejected Russian lover.

When I was leaving the party Katherine came to me and asked if I would take her home in my coach. She explained that the Mayor had hoped to come later and take her home, but he often got detained. I, along with everyone else in the city, knew that the mayor was detained by a large bottle and a determined lady of the evening. I, of course, agreed and we left together. It never came to my mind that this would begin another chapter in the gossip of the elite. I frankly did not give a damn. I thought Katherine could handle it and what could be said about me? We took her home and she asked me to escort her to the door since the butler did not appear to be around.

We walked into the front room and I helped her off with her cape. After that she turned to me and kissed me full on the mouth. She smelled like fresh flowers and her lips were as soft as down. I never even considered pulling away. As I have said before, she was beautiful. As I held her tight to me she leaned her head back and said," We both know that nothing can come of this, but tonight, I will save a poor, dejected Russian lover". "Tell your driver to come in and wait by the fire while he helps himself at the bar." "I will be upstairs waiting for your return." Later that evening, before I left, Katherine said that she was going to refine all of my bedroom talents to make any woman that had been with me never forget the experience.

She also told me that it was time for her to find me a proper wife. We both smiled, but I could tell by the look on her face that she was quite serious.

When I got home, Bart was waiting for me in the library. He held his glass up as a salute and said, "The mayor's wife is a good choice for now because she will teach you much without any designs on your future." This time even I could not believe it. How the hell did he know so soon?

I just looked at him and shook my head. "What?" he said. "I think an older woman is perfect and thank goodness she is beautiful." I sat down with him and accepted a glass of scotch. I told him I needed a secretary to keep all of the business dealings in order. I explained that there were too many details to keep in line in my head and that I would never write things down in my own hand. We thought about it and Bart said he had the perfect person. A client of his had a terrible problem with an abusive employer that held an indiscretion over his head. I solved the problem, but now the poor fellow is out of work. The client is a genius with details and numbers, but no one wants to hire him because of the incident with his former employer. "I can guarantee that he is totally trustworthy and if you pay him right, he will dedicate himself to your every endeavor." "That sounds perfect," I said. "When can I meet him?" He has an appointment with you at Molly's at two this afternoon. "Why do I even try?' I said. You are forever way ahead of me."

Chapter 15

Often, dreams follow the path of reality when they draw you into their embrace and divorce your thoughts from the everyday world.

Perhaps the Native Americans are right in their belief that the other world speaks to us through our dreams. I awoke having had the wonderful experience of continuing the real life of being with Katherine, which blended into a dream that continued the experience. As I looked around my bedroom, I had to focus on the fact that this was reality. I was helped by the sound of James speaking and the breakfast smells coming up the staircase. "My God", I thought, "It cannot ever get better than this", but of course, time would prove me to be wrong.

Several days passed before I got word from Billy that the two unsuspecting men from Tionesta had been arrested and then released by the chief into his custody. He met me at Molly's and was waiting at my table when I got there. He seemed very excited as he described everything that he had learned about our potential partners. It seems that they came from a large mountain family that makes and sells liquor all over the northwest area of Pennsylvania. They have never been able to break into any of the larger cities.

They currently are able to produce about 100 gallons a week, but they can never get enough sugar or gallon containers for even that. He further explained that they could set up enough stills in the workhouse to produce at least 1000 gallons a week, but again, sugar and gallon jugs were the problem.

I had told Billy that the only whiskey we would sell in barrels would be the Golden Wedding, so I liked the idea of selling this product only in gallon jugs.

I instructed Billy to start making the baskets for the gallon containers and buy whatever these guys needed to set up the stills. I also told him to have Big Dave meet me here as soon as possible.

I saw the boat at the dock, so I knew he was there. During this entire discussion, I noticed a small man in a dark suit and thick glasses sitting on the other side of the room, taking notes in a small black ledger. I summoned him to my table and I said, "I presume you are Simon, my new secretary." He tipped his little black hat and said, "At your service." I said, "Give me your little book," and he said, "Absolutely". I opened the book and soon discovered that the book was written in code. I had no idea what it said. Simon explained that the notes were taken in his personal code and that he would teach it to me and no one else. He also explained that he was hard of hearing and that he could read lips from a great distance. I thought about all of this and decided that I liked it very much. I said to him that we would do well as long as he stayed loyal. He thought that was hilarious because Bart was his mentor, and Bart's rules were simple: absolute loyalty or death. I told Simon that he was to stay close to me at all times. The door opened and Big Dave came in. He walked over to me and asked what I needed. I asked if the boat was ready and he said it was always ready. I told him we were going up the Allegheny to Glassmier.

It was a short trip, but the glass plants on the north side of the river were forever in need of customers. We docked the boat and walked to the offices of Glenshaw Glass. We went in and I said to the president, "Do you know who I am?" He shook his head yes. I explained that I needed him to begin production of at least 1000 clear glass one-gallon jugs. I want the bottoms to be round so that they cannot stand up. He looked at me like I was crazy and explained that they would be worthless for any other use. I smiled and said, "Exactly." It would take our wicker baskets to make them useful for anything else and wicker had a very short shelf life. I told him to contact my banker and prepare for many more orders. "One down and one to go," I thought as I turned to Big Dave and told him to get his boat and my quick little gunboat ready to go south to load up with sugar. He just grinned and I knew the devil I had hired to run the boats was deep inside his heart and hell awaited anyone that tried to stop us. I thought about sending a message to Bart, but then I just smiled and figured he would know before we left. "That was Bart."

I cannot tell you how happy I was to go off on another adventure. I was quickly becoming bored with life as the boss and I looked forward to sailing with Big Dave as a member of his crew.

He, Simon and I left on the boat and headed for the Ohio River and south. We stopped at Old Allegheny to pick up clothes for Simon and me and a load of Whiskey and beer from one of my new warehouses.

As we got near the point, I switched my things and those of Simon to the little gunboat. We were soon on our way toward the Mississippi.

This was my first long boat trip and I was very excited. Captain Keys of the gunboat and his crew were anxious to show off the boat and how they could handle it.

As we cruised down the Ohio we were soon hailed from the bank by a group of men driving several wagons. As we pulled close to shore they explained that they knew our price policy and they wanted to be the first to buy. I just grinned as Captain Keys pulled us upriver a few yards from the main paddle wheeler. One of the men on shore hollered, "What is Mad Jimmy doing with the smaller boat?" I looked around to see who "Mad Jimmy" was and noticed Captain Keys moving to the edge of the boat. "Watch your mouth and pay attention", he said. With a brief but loud command, the bow gun and the two side guns were quickly hoisted into their locking decks and just as quickly fired. Trees were obliterated in seconds on both sides of the river. Everyone on shore was shocked into silence. "We be traveling along to guard our sister ship, the Jane Carroll, and the next half-ass wagon jockey that calls me Mad will see just how mad I can be," said Captain Keys, and then he let out a laugh that boomed down the river. "Give those fine lads a bottle of our best Golden to sample as they drive home," directed Captain Keys, I owe them that much for trying to see how high I could make them jump".

After we offloaded some of our product we were again under way. We were traveling with the current, so we were moving quite fast. I asked Capt. Keys why he showed off the cannons, and he explained to me that the story would spread very quickly and the river scum would think twice about trying to steal our cargo. "We will be a long time on these rivers and it is a far piece to New Orleans, much can happen and we will be tested for certain before we are done." At that, he hollered some orders to the crew and moved away. One of the crew remained standing near me and I heard him whisper to himself," To hell with the cannons, damn few men will want to tangle with Mad Jimmy". Now, it was obvious the Captain was a man of exceptional strength. I watched him remove his shirt and pull the barrels of beer onto the boat while we were loading.

I doubt the good Lord packed more muscle on any human being than was solid on the frame of Captain Keys. He was also as quick as a cat and never showed any emotion, but a brief look into his eyes was enough warning for anyone. I asked the sailor where the name Mad Jimmy came from. He explained that it was not what you would think. The Captain almost never got angry, and he could remain calm in the worst of circumstances even when all else were in a panic, but let anyone abuse a woman or a child or even an animal, and the good captain went mad. There was no way and no one to stop him. "I have seen the biggest and the toughest men on the docks either back away from him or be pounded into the dirt."

"Many sailors had to leave the business because of permanent injuries after a roundabout with our captain," said the sailor. I was finding out that rivers like the Point had their own rules and people to be aware of. I asked the tall sailor his name and he replied that he was Andy. and he pointed to another sailor close to the bow and said that the one there with the mop of black curly hair was my older brother Bob and to his right, the blond fellow with the grin on his face is my younger brother Ray.

We signed on together because Captain Keys is a distant cousin and he got us out of a small problem we were having."

With that being said, Andy moved on to his duties.

The rest of the day was pure pleasure as the current moved us swiftly down the Ohio and the sun hung high in the cloudless sky and the warm rays danced on the water all around the boat. It was a soothing feeling of peace that I was experiencing for the first time in my life. I soon understood why so many men took to a life on the water. My dreamy peace was interrupted when Simon touched my shoulder and explained that the Captain wished me to meet him for dinner in his cabin.

I understood that the captain did not eat with the crew and since it was no secret that I owned these boats, though indirectly, I was not surprised at the invitation. Simon and I went to his cabin and I was pleased to see a bottle of single malt scotch waiting for me on the table.

Simon sat off to the side to take notes as was his job. I had become accustomed to stopping, often in mid-thought, to request Simon send a letter or a note to someone with instructions from me. He never failed to follow through with my request which he considered a command. Captain Keys was wonderful company. He spoke at length about his wife Sandy and all the babies and grandbabies.

He was a man deserving of pride who could only take pride in those he loved. We enjoyed the scotch, followed by a very special fish dinner that included caviar as a side. The Captain was a man who took pride in learning anything and everything. Halfway through the evening, I asked him about the three brothers I had seen on deck. This brought a hearty laugh from him. He explained that they were three rogues of the first class.

He could not stop smiling as he described them to me. He said that they were the sons of a man from Croatia in Eastern Europe. From a very young age, they were put to work feeding a furnace in a steel mill along with their father and uncle. Now, the father and uncle had a reputation for clearing out taverns just for the fun of it, so when they started to take the three boys with them, you can imagine the result. Andy is the tall one and the middle child. He is also very intelligent and not easily pushed into a brawl. He also hates to lose, so he quickly develops a skill with either knife or sword, but the twenty-inch knife he carries at all times is his weapon of choice. Therefore most people are content to let him sit at the bar unmolested while the rest of the family are fighting. Bob is the oldest, and no boxer or street fighter born can match him pound for pound. He also enjoys a good brawl. Ray, the youngest, is the crazy one and the one to be most feared. He is equally skilled with a knife, sword, club, or pistol. If he thinks for even a moment that his brothers are in danger, he will unleash a terrible wrath on anyone around him.

He can pull out guns and knives faster than you can imagine.

One of the men at the steel mill tried to attack his brother Andy from behind for a reason still unknown when Raymond saw him and went after him. Within moments, the man was in pieces on the floor. I happened to be at the mill picking up a load of steel when it happened. I saw the whole thing.

I walked over, picked up the dead man and chucked him into the furnace. I turned to the brothers, told them my name, and asked if they needed a job to come see me. Bart had informed me about the new boat and the job I was to do. He also mentioned your name, which by this time carried a great deal of weight and I thought we could use three good men.

The next day, the brothers came to see me. They said that their father and uncle suggested they leave the mill before things got out of hand. They also said that there might be an arrest warrant out for them. I explained the job on the boat and asked if they wanted it. They were thrilled at the prospect of working outside and eagerly agreed.

I told them that the case against them was closed and there would be no further problems. They seemed not to believe it, so I looked hard at them and explained that we were beyond that silly nonsense, but tavern fights and stupid brawls were in their past, and if they did what they were told to do, their future was secure. "Just do not ever screw with me," I said. "We work for very powerful people who just want to make money as quietly as possible." Now they are here and hopefully, they understand why.

When I left his cabin and started out for a walk around the deck, I noticed a shadow coming toward me. I instantly put my back against the outer cabin wall to prepare for anything. When a large man appeared out of the shadow, I noticed a knife in his hand, but before he could move an inch closer, his face took on a strange look and his breath seemed to burst from his mouth. A moment later, I saw his body lift off the deck and then cascade over the side and into the river. It was then that I saw Sasha smile at me and say,

"Did you think you could go away without me?" I started to ask how he sneaked onto the boat, and then I just looked at him and said, "Bart."

He shook his head yes.

CHAPTER 16

As the boat churned through the water and the deck lights on both the boats reflected off the ripples, I felt my mind wonder like the wake that followed behind the paddle wheels of our boats. As they inched toward the shore growing ever smaller the peace slowly engulfed me and I relaxed. The ever-groaning engines took on a simple pace that coordinated with the waves of our wake as they both disappeared up river.

I thought about my father and wished he were here to enjoy a little calm in his life, but I knew his story was already written before he was born, for him and thousands of others from the alleys of the Point. I was the exception and I decided to carry as many Alley Rats away with me as I could. A mother dead of too much and not enough and a father hanged for a silk scarf. This was the poetry of my birth and a story of the Point. Songs were written about such sad tales, but those of us who lived them stopped crying early on because it did no good. You cannot eat tears. You can only survive today and begin tomorrow again. I realized that at this time I had only one fear and that was poverty. I would never have enough to send that fear to the depths of hell where it belonged. A man had tried to take my life tonight and yet it did not bother me because he was floating in the river and I was still here. Some one wins and some one loses. It is just another law of the Alleys of the Point. This law I understood and this law was simple. I knew that Bart wanted me to have the fruits of his labor and I was determined to live the life he could not. I was aware that there were more permanent decisions for me to make and carry out on my own in the future but as long as they fell with in the rules I lived by, I would never regret them.

Then Sasha came to my mind. I guess I was foolish to think that Sasha would ever allow himself to be very far away from me, but I was to caught up in the excitement of the trip to notice his absence. He had been stalking the man that had been stalking me and that was his job so I decided to just let it pass. I heard footsteps behind me and so I turned to see Captain Keys approaching. "You live an interesting life", he said. "Do these things happen to you often?" "I am sure they do, I said, but I am seldom aware of it because it is taken care of quickly." "In the Point murder is a common event, and I am a son of those streets and alleys." "No one can touch you unless they get rid of me, and no one can get to me and live", I said. Unfortunately there will always be fools that will try if the money is enough." I stepped very close to the Captain as though to whisper in his ear and then I pushed him aside, hit my left wrist and plunged the blade into the fool behind the Captain who was holding a blade of his own. I heard Sasha behind the man as he threw him overboard say," You know damn well that is my job." "What would our friend say if he heard this story?" I pulled the Captain to his feet and asked if he cared to share a bottle of scotch with me. His face was blank and he just shook his head yes. We proceeded to my cabin. Now the Captain was a fighter and no man to fool with, but the idea of a professional killer was new to him. I explained that the two men were sent for me and he need never worry about such things. He seemed shocked by my calm behavior, so I explained that over was over and now it meant nothing. "Whoever hired those two is probably dead by now. "I said. "They are from the Point and there are no secrets from me in the Point ". He asked how I knew they were from the Point and I said, "Their smell". "I could smell that man before he even got close to you, so there was never any real danger, just an inconvenience." "Sasha is never far away and he is the real danger, but not to us".

Captain Keys asked me how I could live like this and I explained that it is a way of life that all of us from the Point understand. We finished the better part of the bottle of scotch and then decided that it was time for rest.

The next morning I saw the three brothers talking together at the bow of the boat. I approached them and asked if they would speak with me. Andy spoke for them all when he said "go ahead." I told them that if they stayed out of trouble and protected my boat and the captain that I would see that they got a sizable bonus at the end of every trip. I also said that I might have work for them when they were in port.

Andy asked me what sizable meant and I said, "Double your take for the whole trip." Andy said, "Is it true that you control City Hall and all the police in Pittsburgh?" I said to him, "I cannot answer that because I do not know all the police in Pittsburgh." That seemed to bring out a great deal of laughing from all three of them. "OK ", he said, "We are with you." I wondered how surprised they would be when they realized that the job I had for them was working with and keeping an eye on Toby. Toby loved the construction work he was doing and he was becoming a solid citizen and a church going father to his growing family. I was slowly removing him from the darker side of my business to allow him the freedom to live in peace. My fear is that someone will try to get to me through him so I needed to know that he was protected. I would always be in the thick of my work because I made the decisions.

Toby was the brother I wanted the best for and after all he was not from the Point.

As we traveled south I was curious to see the number of wagons that waved us to the water's edge to buy our beer and whiskey. It seemed that they liked the discount they got for buying early. The two captains asked me to meet them on shore the next time we stopped and I agreed. Later that day we pulled into a small settlement with a substantial loading dock.

There were buyers there for our products and they had questions about future trips. They wanted to know if we would be making more frequent trips and if we could bring other products like dried hard wood planking. The city of St Louis was growing both in size and in wealth so the demand for oak, maple and other wood for flooring and furniture in the wealthier homes was growing with it.

It seemed that trade was a bigger option than I had thought. Later, I met with the two captains over dinner.

They explained that the sugar we wanted was not available in St Louis. The growers were afraid to ply the Mississippi because of the pirates.

We would have to go almost to New Orleans to get the load we needed. While I was thinking about that, I asked them their ideas concerning the questions we were asked. Big Dave spoke first, suggesting that we either bring the Willy Z, my third boat that was usually on the Monongahela River, or we push a barge

or two down and back. Captain Keys preferred the barge idea because it would be difficult to keep three boats together. I asked how much lumber a barge could hold and they said more than enough if we made our trips every month.

The sugar was the problem because it would lengthen the trip by at least a few weeks. I hated to lose all that trade so I needed to find an answer. I suggested that we push the heavy lumber down river to

St Louis in the barge, dock it there and then go south to get the sugar when the boats were empty. I also asked them to think of something light to bring back in the barge. As it turned out the answer was simple. We would just return with the empty beer and whiskey kegs to be used again or sold, all loaded on the barge.

The Jane Carol would stay in St. Louis to sell their contents, load the barge after the lumber was sold and then purchase products to fill the Jane Carol. In the mean time Captain Keys and I would take the Surprise south to get the sugar. The fast little boat would make the trip in a third of the time.

At last we got to St Louis and tied up. The city was unreal with so much commerce going on in every inch of the docks. The traffic in the streets was elbow to horse carriage with a level of excitement that pulled me in and I wanted to be part of it with all my heart. Vendors were everywhere and people dressed from tailor made to buckskin were deep in barter everywhere. I thought to myself, "This is truly the center of commerce in our country. Our men left the boats as soon as they were released to sample the available entertainment in the saloons along the river. Big Dave, Captain Keys and I went to the heart of the city to check into their finest hotel.

We stayed at the "Pride of St. Louis" hotel and the moment I walked into the lobby I knew the place was properly named. The combination of French décor the Americans desire to make everything big was enough to make you want to just stop and stare. Beautiful silk covered furniture and large tapestries on the walls were embellished by paintings, sculptures, and other works of art perfectly stationed in every available space. It was truly palatial. Big Dave said that since Keys and I would only be there for one night he wanted me to see this beautiful hotel. When we were escorted to our rooms I was just as pleased with the beautiful quarters as I was with the rest of the Hotel. I made myself a drink at the bar in the room and waited while my few things were put away by the bell boy. When I was alone

I sat on a down-filled chair, sipped my scotch, and just wondered when all of this would end because it was too wonderful to last. After about an hour of enjoying the peace of my surroundings I heard a soft wrap at my door, and an envelope was slid under my door. I opened the note and discovered that it was a simple invitation to dinner in one hour with Captain Keys. Captain Dave sent his apologies and explained that he would be meeting with merchants and could not attend. I took my time finishing my scotch and washed up before changing my clothes. Since we were to meet in the bar, I did not mind getting there early to see what kind of a bar this place would provide. I walked down to the lobby and asked directions to the bar. It turned out that the bar was just around the corner from the lobby. As I entered the bar I was over come by the opulent décor. I never saw so much leather and brass in one place in my life. The floors were marble and the bar itself was at least 100 feet long. I placed my foot on the brass rail and ordered a drink. The bartender expressed that they carried more that twelve single malt types of scotch, but only two were aged over twenty-five years. I chose the one I was most familiar with and the bartender smiled and said, "Very good Sir, very, very good indeed." As I sipped my drink I was approached by a man of about 28 who came to me and asked, "Would you happen to be a man called Getts." I was a little bit surprised because he spoke to me in French with a slight accent that I could not recognize.

I answered his question and asked him what he wanted. He asked me to meet him at the Surprise when I was finished eating. He further explained that he wished only to be of service and he knew Captain Keys. He handed me his card.

There was nothing on the card but a drawing of a sailing ship. After that he left. As I was studying the picture on the card, Captain Keys came up next to me and said, "I wonder what they want with you?" "So you do know the owner of the card and what it means," I asked? "Oh yes", he said and so do most of the people that work on this river". He suggested we go to our table in the dining room and talk over dinner. The food was wonderful and the service was as expected, great. During the meal Keys explained that the man I met was one of five French Creole's common to the lower Mississippi. The five of them work together all the time and if you hired one then you hired all five. They come from a long line of famous pirates like Jean Lafitte and they are excellent gunners with any kind of cannon. The picture on their card is of Lafitte's ship. They are top sailors in addition to the guns. "My guess is that they heard about the guns and the speed of the Surprise and like the idea of terrorizing any would be pirate on the river", said Captain Keys. I mentioned that it would be a lot of crew for that boat and Keys agreed. I also asked how he would feel about having the Frenchmen as a permanent crew and he surprised me by saying that it would complete the boat and he would love to have them. He asked about the three brothers and I explained that I had other plans for them. Now all I had to do was convince everyone that they would be happy with the changes.

Chapter 17

While I changed in my room before meeting the Creole's, I settled into a large silk covered chair and tried to relax. The distant sound of boat whistles blended with the sounds of metal horse shoes on the cobblestone streets and the wash of a thousand voices that tried to push those sounds away. Every few seconds a whip cracked over the heads of the teams of laboring draft animals or a church bell vibrated over it all to call to those who were believers. The whole sound was the music of life moving and growing to some unknown potential that only some historian would explain many years from now. I could easily close my eyes and drift away to the past and remember where I came from. I could feel the dirty cloths of my childhood and picture every room I had ever been in down to the smallest detail. It is a strange thing that I recall in mental pictures of people, and places cataloged in their time period. I remember every detail and when something changes I am instantly aware of it. I was forced to leave these thoughts by a light rap at my door. A voice on the other side stated that Captain Keys was waiting in the hotel lobby.

I joined the good captain and we began our walk down to the boat. As we walked we spoke of the voyage ahead and he was quick to note that the trip was full of peril and not to be taken lightly. He further explained that the five Creoles knew something of the danger or they would not be so willing to make the trip. I was surprised, but he further stated that our five new friends lived for this kind of adventure. They probably already knew more about the Surprise than we did. This truly was a new world for me and I realized that I must become someone in a learning mode to survive.

"More lessons," I thought and it came to me that this was what I enjoyed most. We met the five Creoles at the boat where they were waiting.

Before we boarded the boat I told them that we needed to talk. I said that all that was mine was sacred and I tolerated nothing less than loyalty. They all laughed and the one who always spoke for them said," I am Jacque and I am the oldest." " I speak for us all and we know who you are and we know who Captain Keys is." "We work for you and no one else if we come to an agreement before we board the boat." I asked him what they wanted and he said, "We want a fair wage and we want control of the guns with no fools telling us what to do." I told him that was not good enough. I told him that they would get a good wage and a percentage of the profits from each trip. I also explained that they could control the guns as long as they accomplished the wishes of Captain Keys. They all agreed and we went on board where we all shook hands. We were on board only a few seconds when there was a call from the dock asking about loading a crate.

Jacque told them to wait as he swung the loading crane over the side and told them to attach the crate. In very little time the five Frenchmen hauled the crate on board. They quickly opened it and showed me a short, squat mortar with a stack of ammunition. Jacque explained that it was a present from the five of them and that it would complete our arsenal of power. I knew nothing of mortars so Captain Keys explained with a broad grin on his face that a good crew with such a weapon could drop a bomb into the back pocket of a sailor two hundred yards away. The five Creoles smiled and Jacque said," Aye, Aye, Captain and that would be us."

We now had four cannons and the mortar on board with a crew trained to use them. Jacque also informed us that our sugar was held by their family and they waited for us to come and pick it up. I asked him why they did not just bring it to St. Louis and the five of them found that very funny. I asked again and Jacque explained that they wanted to watch as we blew the hell out of the pirate boats. His whole family thought it would be great fun to watch and Jacque promised them a great show. I turned to Captain Keys and said, "You were right, they all are crazy." This brought on an even bigger round of laughter.

I took Captain Keys aside and told him that I had invested a fortune in this boat and I wanted to see just how fast it would go and how it would handle. This brought a big smile to his face and I saw my first sign of the name "Crazy Keys". I thought to myself, "The whole crew is crazy."

Keys went to the wheel house and called below for full power. The Surprise was different from the other two boats not just in size, but where the bigger boats had a big paddle wheel at the back of the boat, the surprise had two smaller wheels, one on each side. Captain Keys hollered for everyone to hang on when the boilers reached maximum steam and he shifted the boat into all ahead. The big paddles dug into the water and the boat lurched ahead with a jolt that threw the entire crew backwards, hanging on to whatever was near. We moved off into the main stream and picked up the current where we took off like a shot. The smile on the

Captain's face was so wide that I swear it pushed his ears back and out of site. Before we had gone less than a mile the Captain reversed the left paddle wheel and spun the boat to a complete reverse. He reset the left paddle and we were going back up the river in a flash.

This time he reversed the right paddle wheel and spun the boat around the opposite way and we were charging down the river again and picking up speed. The boat went faster and faster until I became concerned that we might hit a sand bar and then suddenly Captain reversed both paddle wheels and we came to a stop. He kept the wheels moving just enough to compensate for the current so we stood perfectly in place in the middle of the river.

The entire crew began to holler and clap their hands. I ran to the wheel house and put my arm over the captains' shoulder and said, "By all the saints, that was quite a show." "You and this boat are a marvel." He just continued to grin as he put the boat back into a normal progression down the river. There were places along the river where Keys was able to speed up so we were having very good time. This area was all new to me so I stayed in the wheel house and Captain Keys pointed out land marks and potential dangers to the boat along the way. I found it all fascinating and I pestered him with questions. He was very patient with me and I assumed he thought that as the owner I needed to understand the perils the boat captains had to overcome. My respect for him and all the captains grew as we maneuvered our way down river. After just two days travel we pulled into a small dock to take on more wood for the boilers. Captain Keys instructed the crew to stack the wood all around the railing of the boat except where the cannons would be mounted.

While the work was going on I questioned the Captain about the placement of the wood. He explained that we were making incredible time and we would be loading sugar tomorrow. He further explained that he expected the pirates to attack before we loaded. "They will not want the sugar ruined," he said. The wood would serve as more protection for the crew. After the wood was loaded and the provider was paid, the Creoles brought up a long thin box from below decks.

We all watched as they opened the crate and took out several very long rifles. There was one for each member of the crew. Sean proceeded to load one of the rifles turned to the Captain and said, " Do you see that big buzzard sitting at the top of that tree about two hundred yards from here." The Captain shook his head yes and Sean quickly shouldered the rifle and fired. The buzzard fell dead from the tree and the crew just stood with their mouths open.

All I could think of was how lethal these crazy Frenchmen were.

Sean explained that these rifles were for parting shots after the battle.

He explained that if used to soon they would just scare off the pirates and they would find another way to attack, but if used as the enemy ran away they would give the pirates something to remember. This was a war that I knew nothing about, but I could not wait to learn.

That evening, I spoke to Captain Keys as we had our evening meal. I could tell that he was tight with the excitement of the battle to come. I asked him what he thought would happen and I emphasized that I knew the difference between confidence and arrogance. He said that the enormous amount of money spent on the Surprise had been a burden to him. He needed to prove that it was a good investment. He explained that no matter how hard he tried to explain the significance of this boat, only a show of its potential would ever justify its worth. He told me that tomorrow the pirates would come and tomorrow Mr. Getts and his shipping would be the bench mark for all safety on the Mississippi. We will be able to charge just about any price to escort boats traveling on the river, and by all the saints I will strike vengeance on the lowly bastards that have tried to cripple honest commerce. I did not know the story behind that statement, but I later learned that Captain Keys had lost a brother to the river pirates several years before. I explained that I was just one of the investors in the boats, but he cut me off and said, "You cannot hide behind that story on these waters." "You are here and you are known to be a fighter and a dangerous man." "Those are the things that we admire, and those are the things that make men like me and my crew glad to serve you and the things you wish to obtain."

"Prepare for tomorrow and stay with me in the wheelhouse so we can put your killing machine to good use", he said.

I laid on my bunk for most of the night looking at the ceiling and wondering what it would be like. I had never witnessed the type of battle we were about to make. Yes, I had read about all kinds of battles even those that take place on water, but this was different, I will be a participant.

I must have fallen asleep because there was a rap at my door that woke me up. I dressed quickly and went to the wheel house. Captain Jim was waiting for me. His steward brought us a pot coffee with warm bread and cheese. Jim told me to eat because we had a long day ahead of us.

It was a beautiful morning with a clear sky and the soft beat of the engines as we made our way through the water like a knife sliding through the soft icing of a tall cake. The shore line was alive with birds and small animals that watched us go by as though we did not matter. They were probably right. Captain Keys turned to me and said, "When we turn that bend ahead to our port side, it will start." "That is a wide place in the river and there are two creeks that enter from either side of the Mississippi." "They will attack us from the front and eventually from the rear, while the main force will be divided between our two sides." "They will have shooters on the banks, but they will be a problem for a very short time." The deck of the surprise was alive with men preparing the cannons and passing out rifles, swords and ammunition. I was given two pistols and a sword. The attitude of the men was totally unexpected. They acted like we were going to a party. The Creoles were singing in French and the crazy Maletic brothers were laughing and teasing one another. The Captain explained to me that he had met with the crew and they each knew their job and they looked forward to showing off their ability. The Captain said, "There has never been a boat and a crew like this on the Mississippi and our men are anxious to show that river trash just what we can do."

Time seemed to crawl along but finally we entered the bend. I found that I too was more excited than afraid. When we turned the bend and the river opened up ahead of us, I heard one of the crew say aloud "Oh shit, now they are really in for it." The Captain's face was white with anger and as I followed his eyes I saw the pole sticking out of the water. There was a sign on top that said "For Crazy Jim" and below it there was a little boy tied to the pole. Rifles instantly started firing from the shore at the helpless child. I dropped my pistols and ran to the front of the boat and dove into the water. When I got to the boy I hit the button on my wrist and cut him down. A rope was thrown over the side with a big loop in it that I pulled over my head and the crew pulled me up onto the boat. The boy was in shock and he had been shot in the side, but he looked to be fine enough for now. As I took him below I heard the Captain calling the crew to stations. As I laid the boy in my bed and bandaged his side I felt the boat shudder followed by the booms of the cannons. I ran to the wheelhouse in time to hear the Captain say "Take that you filthy pigs". As I looked at the shore on both sides of the river I realized that no one along those banks could be alive. Our guns had fired three rounds of grape shot so quickly that I thought they had only fired once. The accuracy of the gunners and the forward motion of the boat caused a killing field along the banks of some two hundred yards.

While I stood there with my mouth open I heard our enraged Captain shout out, "Here they come." I scanned the river in all four directions and all I could see were boats of every size and shape and canoes bristling with men and guns. The problem was the distance. We had to let them get close enough to hit with our canons, but by then their force would be to close to stop all of them. The Captain got a crazy look on his face as the entire crew seemed to be looking up at him. I heard someone speaking in French say, "Now you will see why they call him Crazy Keys." "The safe thing to do is to wait for them to get in range but I'll bet a years pay he will not do that. With the steam in the boilers full up, the Captain threw the throttles full ahead and we charged the boats ahead of us and pulled away from the others. When we reached the boats he locked the left paddle wheel and the boat crashed broadside into the nearest enemy craft and our cannons finished off the rest. When we completed the turn and were heading up river he opened up both wheels and charged into the mass of boats behind us. Bullets were flying all around us and our guns were doing their best to stop the endless fire. The wheelhouse was shattered and it was a miracle that the Captain survived. I was shooting one of the long rifles and trying to hit as many of the men steering the small boats as I could. The Captain shouted, "Prepare for a circle of fire." I had no idea what that was, but the crew must have as they cheered as loud as they could. The Surprise charged into the middle of the remaining boats and canoes at full speed as they began to close in on us. The Captain locked the right paddle wheel so quickly that our boat began to spin clock wise. All four cannons and every gun on board was firing non stop as our boat kept on spinning. The devastation to those small boats was near total. With every turn of our boat the grape shot ripped into men and boats leaving both dead in the water. Finally the Captain stopped the Surprise and we went after the few retreating pirates. The long rifles did the job on all but a few of the retreating pirates. Captain Keys drove our boat slowly down the river.

Everyone was silent the entire time waiting to see what came next. We could see the escaping pirates climbing a steep mountain side to a fort at the very top. Captain Keys said, "Prepare the mortar"

We watched as the last of the pirates entered the fort. Captain Keys leaned over the remaining piece of railing and looked down at the crew. There was blood running down his face from a cut on his head and his left arm was hanging at his side covered in blood. He said, "By God I want you bloody Frenchmen to blow that den of trash strait to hell." They worked that mortar like a fine Swiss clock until there was nothing left of the fort but burning timber. "Now" the captain said, "Where the hell is my sugar?"

Chapter 18

The engines rumbled and the boat plied the water like a fish with a full belly. I sat in my cabin with my hand on the head of the sleeping little boy. I had checked his wound and it appeared to be minor. I smelled of sweat and gunpowder and I felt the letdown after experiencing the terror of battle. I thought of Bart and I remembered the silver flask in my pocket. It was filled with a special scotch that was over one hundred fifty years old. It was part of Bart's private stock and he made me promise to never share it. It had a ruby cast to it and the taste was as soft as a kitten. I took a little sip of it when I ever thought of Bart.

It was as though he was whispering to my mind that it was time for a little taste.

I often had thoughts where I could swear Bart was talking to my mind. Maybe he was. What did it matter?

I looked out the small porthole and the surface of the water was covered with a blanket of black cotton. The black powder from all the guns had settled and it awaited the wind to carry it away. I kept stroking the boys head until he opened his eyes. He looked up at me and said, "What happened after that man tied me to that pole?" I explained that there had been a battle and that he had a miner wound, but he was safe now.

He curled up close to me and I asked him his name and age. He said that he was six years old and that his name was Dale and they did not give him a last name yet. I asked him who "they" was and he said the people at the orphanage. He went on to say that he had spent his whole life in an orphanage just north of New Orleans and he had escaped over a year ago and was working his way north. I asked him," Why", and he took off his shirt and I saw the scars from a whip. Some of them were years old. He explained that he had been living with the pirates because he had nowhere else to go and they fed him some times. I told him that I too was an orphan and He could come with me if he wanted. I further said that I had a special place where he might want to live, but it would be his choice. We went up on deck where everyone was busy putting the boat back into good order. The Captain was taking us into the dock to get the sugar, but it looked like we may be delayed.

There were over a hundred people on the beach. There were big pots of beans and rice cooking alongside of fish stew and a massive whole pig roasting over a fire. Loaves of hot bread were piled up in baskets everywhere, and there were the biggest bottles of wine I had ever seen. They were sitting on swivel brackets that allowed them to be tilted forward to pour. The music was glorious with homemade instruments and fiddles, guitars, and something they called a squeeze box. Everyone was dancing and eating. When we got to the dock I grabbed Dale and we ran to join the celebration. I swear that that little kid could eat more than Toby. There were whole fried crabs that tasted like heaven and burned like hell. The only way to survive was to keep drinking anything. Thanks to barrels of cider I was saved. Finally, Jacque from the boat came over and explained that all of these people were his relatives and there were hundreds more that lived back in the swamp. He told of how the pirates were cruel to his people and they stole anything of value they could find and that is why we are getting such a welcome party. He said that we should enjoy ourselves because his family would load the boat.

As I sat and chatted, sometimes in English, sometimes in French I noticed a very old woman across from me and looking right at me.

When she caught my eye she motioned for me to come to her. Rather than risk any offence I went and sat on the ground in front of her as she instructed.

The music stopped and everyone got very quiet as she placed her open hand on my head. Up close she looked to be at least 100 years old. She had big loop earrings that had stretched her ear lobes from their weight until the loops were laying on her tiny shoulders. Most of her teeth were gone and her skin was wrinkled, but her eyes had a twinkle and a spark like that of a child. I was mesmerized. She ran her fingers all over my face and head. At one point she very gently touched my right ear and said to me," You are one who is chosen, you are soon to be a Red Gate as I once was." " Continue to honor it as you have so far" Then she kissed me on each cheek and said," no one heard my words but you, and no one should know of it but you and me and him."

Then she cackled like a crazy old witch and demanded music. Again, the party was in full swing.

When I got back to Dale he said nothing, but he pointed to my right ear.

I reached up and felt something on the ear lobe. I went over to a tree where someone had mounted a small mirror for shaving and looked at my reflection.

The ear was pierced and a small gold nugget was attached on the front of the lobe. It had to be the old lady, but how did she do it? One of the men came over and saw what I was looking at and got a big smile on his face. He said," It appears that grandma has found another one." I asked what he was talking about and he explained that all of these people and many more are direct descendants of hers. "No one has lived long enough to tell us her age." " Two or three times in my lifetime I have heard of her putting a gold nugget in a person's ear but I am seventy three and this is the first time I have seen it." "It must mean something or it is just an old witch's trick to keep us interested in her."

Dale stayed close to me all evening and even though I asked the crew to see if anyone knew him, no one seemed to know a thing. The day was getting late and we were all tired after the high from the battle wore off. I could see that Captain Keys had a large crew loading the boat so I took Dale on board and to my cabin. I hooked up a hammock and placed him in it. He was instantly asleep. The cook had checked his wound and felt it was minor. I took a pull on my flask and went up on deck. They were just finishing loading the sugar. It was twice as much as we had expected and the extra was a thank-you from the growers for getting rid of the pirates.

Captain Keys said he wanted all on board with in an hour. He did not need much of a crew to begin the slow trip up the Mississippi so all of the men hustled back on board. We had some daylight left and he wanted to get away from the party before it became a three day event. The boilers were coming up to steam and the repairs were sufficient for the trip to St. Louis. With in the hour the crew was on board and we were in motion.

It took a little longer going north against the current especially with the added weight from the sugar. I found that I was anxious to get home. It was a great adventure, but I decided I was not meant for life on the water. I could not keep from thinking about Dale. He had to be a tough little boy to have endured the beatings and to go off on his own into an unknown territory.

I thought about Molly and I wondered if she would like the idea of having a boy of her own. Toby and I were like sons to her, but we still had memories of our real mothers. This little boy would be hers and the Captain alone. I guess if it did not work out I would keep him with me.

The trip up the river passed without any problems and we caught up with the Jane Carol just as we entered the Ohio. When the two boats pulled into a dock to refuel, I thanked Captain Keys and explained that Dale and I would be transferring our things to the other boat. I further explained that I did not want to be any part of his welcome home. I also asked him to hold the boat a day so we would get to Pittsburgh ahead of him. He liked the idea because he wanted to do final repairs on the Surprise before getting home. He told me that Bob, Andy, and Ray were excellent carpenters and even their finish work was superb. This fit in with my plan for them perfectly. I approached the three men and told them to meet me at Molly's Pub when they got in and I would have their bonus money.

We arrived at Pittsburgh without fanfare and Dale and I went to Molly's right away. I explained to Dale what I wanted for him including summer work with Captain Keys. He was very nervous and he asked what would happen to him if Molly did not want him. How could I explain to this young orphan that that could never happen? Molly was the flame that lit every candle of love and caring that existed. Just to ease his mind I told him that in the event he was not wanted there, he would come to live with me. When we entered the pub I heard a scream of delight from the kitchen as Molly and the Captain came running out. Molly kept shouting," Dale is here, Dale is here".

"Oh Captain" she said as she approached Dale, "We have a son and look how handsome he is." With that she pulled Dale off the floor in a great hug.

She kept holding him with his little face buried in her ample cleavage and his feet dangling far off the floor. The Captain was beaming and trying to rub the little boy on his back. Molly finally put him down and said, "You must be hungry, I have been cooking for days waiting for you" Molly then gave me a hug and she ran to the kitchen. I explained to Dale that he better get used to being hugged because Molly is full of them. Dale, the Captain and I went to my usual table and sat down. The Captain explained that they knew all about the pirates and what happened with Dale. He looked at Dale and said, "Molly and I have been waiting for days to see you." We will be good parents if you will have us." "We first fell in love with the idea of you and after seeing you we are in love even more."

"This is about as long a speech as you will ever hear from me unless it is about boats and ships. " "The choice is yours, but if you will have us your name will be Dale Staiger from now on." "You can call me Captain, Dad, father or anything you want and it will be fine with me but if you want us and you can find it in your heart to call Molly Mom it would mean the world to both of us." I knew Molly was hiding in the kitchen terrified that the boy would not want them. She and the Captain had planned to give Dale an opportunity to decide on his own. Dale would have a future, a family and security, but most of all he will have a last name. I was afraid for Dale even though he and I had talked about these things many times on the boat.

We waited for what seemed a very long time before Dale looked up and said that the term Captain had come to mean a great deal to him during our trip. He could not imagine a name that meant more respect.

He looked at the Captain and said with a big grin, "If it is OK with you father I will call you Captain." With tears flowing all around, even at the other tables, Dale looked toward the kitchen and hollered, "Mommy we are about to starve out here."

CHAPTER 19

There was no sound except the beat of my heart and the tick, tick, tick, of the big clock in the hall. I scrunched down into the leather chair as deeply as I could and pulled the woolen afghan up to my neck. The smell of the leather and the woolen blanked were like a tonic transporting me home.

My scotch was on the marble top table next to me and the glow of the gas fire was dancing up the walls in concert with the flickering of the flames.

It felt like I had been away for an eternity and I promised myself I would never abandon my home for such a long time again. How could I be so desperate for this grand old house when not so long ago I was living on the streets?

I could only surmise that the old house and I had adopted one another as I assumed the house had adopted Bart.

I knew there was much celebrating when the Surprise docked. I also knew that all the sugar was taken by Billy Birdshot and the people at the workhouse. Dale was trying not to smother under the attention of his new Mom and Dad, and I was free for tonight. I had to meet Toby and the three brothers at Molly's in the morning, and the wonderful book next to my drink did not care if I remembered it or not. This was truly peace and contentment.

I do not know how long I lingered in that state of euphoria before James appeared and told me my bed was turned down and my night clothes were laid out. I slowly abandoned the chair and climbed the stairs to my bed. I changed quickly and crawled under the covers and snuggled into the pillows. I thought to myself that this was all I would ever desire, but what did I know?

Sleep came quickly and I was soon awake, dressed and on my way to Molly's. It was good to see Toby again. He was seated at our table with the three

Maletic brothers. I had hoped they would all get there early and get to know one another. I sat down with my back to the corner in my usual chair and Molly brought over coffee.

I said "Good Morning Mother Molly" and she put a handkerchief to her eyes and ran back to the kitchen saying, "Darn you boys, you always make me cry." She then stopped, ran back to the table and hugged me before again heading for the safety of her kitchen. Toby and I just laughed.

I greeted each of them and gave Toby a big bear hug. Toby explained that I had just missed Dale and the Captain on their way to go fishing. That too brought a smile to my face. I handed Toby three pokes of money and told him to give it to the three brothers. I explained that they would never do business with me again. "We did honest work together and you have been given an honest bonus," I said. "If Toby agrees you will have a job with him for as long as you want it."

"Captain Keys said you are all fine carpenters and Toby owns the biggest construction company in Pittsburgh."

Toby stated that he needed the help and they were welcome. At that point I asked them to wait while I spoke to Toby alone in the kitchen.

I noticed that Simon was taking notes in his book. I had told him earlier to stay and write down everything he heard after I left. Molly left the kitchen and went over and sat with the brothers. While she was going to their table Bart came in and made his way to the kitchen, followed by Billy Birdshot.

The brothers looked at Molly and Ray asked," Do you know who those two men are?" She looked at Ray and said, "They are as close to Getts as you boys are to each other." That is a good thing to remember." "Your job", she said, "is to work hard but most importantly you are to protect Toby at all times. "If you agree you will be given a place to live in Old Allegheny close to Toby and his family.'

You will have a cook and all your expenses will be taken care of in addition to your salary from the company." If you are smart you will invest as much of your money as you can with our people.

I am the secretary treasurer of Allegheny Contracting and I will gladly handle your investments for 25% of the profit only. As you meet other members of our group you will understand more clearly what you are being offered. This is not a seasonal job and people who walk out after working for us are handled by one of the two men now meeting in my kitchen." Ray said, "Holy mother of the church, I had no idea just who Getts really is." Molly said, "It does not matter because you will most likely never speak with him again." The three brothers looked at each other and then to Molly before they said together, "You have a deal" They put out their hands and with each shake Molly said, "Done and done." "You start to work as soon as Toby leaves his meeting" "Enjoy your breakfast while you wait." Andy asked if he could ask one more question and Molly agreed. "Who are the weird little guy and the big burly one sitting by the door?"

"The little guy is none of your affair and the big guy is always with Getts and he is just as lethal as the two in the kitchen if not more so"

Bobby said, "It will be nice to tell our parents that we got jobs as carpenters right here in the city especially with a company like Allegheny Contracting."

They all decided that the other part of the job was best kept secret between them. Ray said, "From what I know about Toby and what I have just seen of his size, I cannot imagine anyone trying to hurt him." Bobby said, "If there are people crazy enough to go after Getts like those two on the boat, then anything is possible." While the brothers were enjoying their coffee, the meeting in the kitchen had been moved to the luxurious parlor in Molly's apartment. It seems the captain had been collecting beautiful things from all over the world when he was working at sea and he surprised Molly with them after they finished their home.

Naturally Bart took over explaining all the pieces to a delighted Getts and a somewhat bored Toby.

Finally they sat down to bring Getts up to speed on what had happened while he was away. Toby went first explaining that when the Willie Z unloaded her freight in the Point he sent it up to Glassmier to get the bottles. Birdshot went along to make sure they fit in the baskets he had designed. The baskets looked like an old ladies purse with big round wooden handles woven into each side that came together at the top so they could be carried with one hand. They worked perfectly. The gallon bottles were delivered and many of them were sold to our partners up the Allegheny River in Tionesta. They have slowly introduced them for sale in Market Square and they are a big hit. Our share of the profits paid for the entire load of jugs. All the local taverns have put in orders for more, and the street sales are sold out within an hour. "Our construction business is growing every day and One through Nine on the Street are all doing well and I spend half my time building them houses and remodeling apartment buildings for them. Ben has the Pawn business roaring now that the "well to do" know that they get private showings in the back part of the building and quick loans when they need them with no publicity. Ben also has a great deal of money on the street at high interest. So far it has not been a problem, but some of the once very rich are getting in too far. They never seem to understand the game. They borrow

$1000.00 for thirty days at 20% interest and when they cannot pay it all, Ben insists that they pay either all of it or just the $200.00. They are thrilled and hand over the $200.00.

He then mentions that the interest is 25% for the next thirty days and they smile and walk out. For the next five months he collects the $250.00 because they have long forgotten the original loan. After six months the payback amount goes to $2000.00 and $100.00 a week interest paid weekly. At this point our $1000.00 has earned $1450.00. Over the next six months, we will earn $2,600.00 more and the outstanding debt will be $3000.00. In one year our $1000.00 loan has earned $4050.00 and the debt pay off is $3000.00. Six months later the poor jerk will have paid $6650.00 with a balance of $4000.00 and interest of $150.00 a week. We currently have several people in that situation and a few are not going to make it without help.

I told Toby we would work it out with Ben and if that was all then he could pick up his new men and show them their new home. I also asked him not to argue about the added protection because I needed to know he was safe. We hugged and he left. I told him I would see him and the kids this weekend as he walked out the door.

I turned to Billy Birdshot and said," OK, fill me in on your activity while I was gone." Billy explained that the stills were up and they started with what sugar they could beg, borrow and steal. He further explained that the mountain people were having a great time and their families wanted to know if they could just buy all their liquor from us at a discount so they could get out of the dangerous business of making it deep in the mountains. They would haul in their own boats if we could get it as far north as Franklin. I told him that I loved the idea, but to let me think on it. If we did it right we could bottle the whiskey from West Virginia for northern sales and sell our product here and down river. I would need another boat and Captain.

I told Billy that I wanted his people paid a living wage out of the profits. He started to laugh. I asked what was so funny and he said, "You realize that when we start that people will be fighting for jobs in a place that was once thought of as a death sentence." I looked at him and said," Hell, the whole Point has been a death sentence for anyone born here for generations, just ask my mother." "I do not give a damn how much confusion it creates, just do as I say" Even Bart was shocked, for I had never barked orders at anyone before.

I stopped and took a deep breath before saying, "Forgive me Billy, you and Bart and Molly have been more than family to me and I can never pay you back enough."

Billy grabbed my shoulders and looked me in the eyes and said, "We are your family and we are proud of it," "Your passion to save the people of the point is a good thing and you never have to say your sorry for it." I looked at him and said," I never want to hear of a hungry man being hanged for a silk scarf again".

Billy went on to say that the work house had toilets and a new thing called a shower that worked better than a bath. The place was free of rats and lice and all the clothes were washed clean every week. Anyone that did not cooperate was made to leave and no one wanted that. Also the food kitchens were working fine and ending the need to steal from the venders.

He said, I do not know where all this heading, but I sure am proud to be Keeper of the Poor now that it means something". I told Billy thank you and hugged him and then he left Bart and I alone.

Bart looked at me and said "You have had quite an adventure." "I will bet you are glad to be home." What do you say we go home, enjoy a fire and a touch of out best scotch while you tell me about Grandma and the cute little earing you are sporting?" I looked at him and said, "Why don't you tell me about grandma and this crazy earing that I cannot seem to remove?" We went out, kissed Molly and had Sasha take us home. Bart and I got home and sat in our favorite places with scotch in hand. I had asked him about the old lady and he had yet to answer. I also asked about the red gate she told me about. Finally he looked at me and said that he had met the old woman many years ago during a trip to New Orleans. She had pretty much told him the same thing, but he never got an ear ring. He was not sure how long ago it was, but it was awhile.

He said that the Red Gate was an old ritual performed by some of the swamp people to welcome new members into their secret society of would be witches and such. He suggested I forget about it for now and he would fill me in on any other information he learned in the future.

He then asked about the battle we had because he wanted my take on it. He had of course been filled in on those events by Captain Keys and others.

I recounted the entire trip to him with great detail including the two attempts on my life. When I was finished he explained what had happened here. "While you were gone", he said, "I learned that the little group of thugs that hung out at Smitty's was larger than those you disposed of." "It seems that they were also working with an old friend of yours called Angel and they were not happy to hear that you were also responsible for closing his business." "My sources informed me of the two fools they sent to kill you on the boat, but I knew you and Sasha would take care of them." "These men are aligned with some men with serious money interests here in the city." "I have not made a move

because I want to be sure just who these people are."
"Thugs are for hire by the dozens so if this is a serious
threat we will need to cut off the snakes head or heads
as the case might be." It is obvious that my once
contact with the street, Billy Birdshot, is too busy with
his various enterprises to notice what is happening
around him." I never thought he would take to
responsibility the way he has, but I am proud of him
and I am proud of you for recognizing his abilities.'
'Our friend Ben has a deep knowledge of everything
going on because of his business clients." "It seems
that he is also buying and selling information about the
financial position of his various clients." "Of course all
of it has to come to me first and you and I will
determine what is for sale and what is not." "What is
your plan for business here in the city?",he asked.

I did not have to think about it for very long because
it is no secret to me exactly what I want our enterprises
to be. I explained that we have a small interest in a
beer maker, a barrelmaker, some liquor manufacturing,

construction, and shipping besides the work we do with Ben which seems to never end. We help companies like Glenshaw Glass and Golden Wedding by being good customers. Our mountain friends will now be able to spend the manpower to go after business in Erie and other places in the northwest. We make a profit from the product, but it is their business. Our boat, the Surprise, has done a great service to all shipping on the rivers, but we have never tried to go after any of their shipping and we will not now.

I would expect a fee for escorting any of their boats.

The picture I am trying to paint is one where we are miner players in many things and we provide a service like on the rivers, in the stalls in the city, keeping warehouses safe, and creating a whole new group of paying customers for goods and services that were too poor before we employed them. Watch and see the development in the Point when the people there have a little money to spend. I expect to begin building shops and restaurant sites to be rented to small businesses that would have never considered opening in the Point. We are going to have strict fire and building codes.

Anyone who does not like we will buy out. Those who cannot afford to improve will get low interest loans from the city. I want to pull Toby away from getting all the city projects so he can concentrate on building the houses he loves. We will buy twenty percent of some of the smaller builders and see that they start winning contract bids. The list is endless, but in each case we will be a minor player until we are needed to handle those jobs that only we know how to handle.

Bart just smiled and asked just how long I expected all of this to take. I told him I did not expect to live long enough to see it all happen, but we would try to set the wheels in motion while we were here. He looked at me, raised his glass of our beloved scotch and said, "We shall see, we shall see" and we touched our glasses with a chime only the finest crystal can make and downed our drinks.

Chapter 20

I was walking down the tree line streets of Old Allegheny and thinking about Toby and his three children.' They were not two years apart, 2 months old Mary, two years old Molly and the only boy, Max was just past three. He told me he had to slow down, but I had a feeling Annah would make that decision. He was my brother and to see him so happy meant everything to me. It was time to remove him from any part of my business that would put him in danger. I wanted him to be safe, after all, he was not from the Point.

The breeze pushed the leaves on the trees around and a quaking aspen growled at me with every motion of its branches. Every so often a buckeye fell like a giant chestnut and banged off a metal roof, while apple trees were buzzing with bees and huckleberry trees were staining everything purple including me if I was not careful.

This place was so different from the Point, but perhaps if we planted some trees it would help the

Point look more like this. That sounds like another task for the future. I loved walking alone even though I knew Sasha was not far behind. I entered the pawnshop to the sound of the original bell he always had over the door.

The place was huge with employees running everywhere. A young woman started toward me only to be intercepted by my old friend Ben. He quickly explained to her that I was one of the partners and she walked away after giving me a cute smile. Ben rolled his eyes.

"So", I said, "How is business?"

Ben had a smile from ear to ear as he motioned me into his office. I looked around as he shut the door and said," What a dump". He motioned me to another door that required him to take out a key to unlock and pushed it open and waved me in. This office was beautiful and very much an impressive place. He explained that the other office is for dealing with most clients so when he tells them how poor he is and how he can only afford to give them so little for their jewelry, he looks the part. This office is for special clients that are too dumb to know that the broach they inherited is worth three times what he is paying. That item goes to St. Louis and our partner, there to be sold. He started to go on about how honored he was to see me and I cut off with a wave of my hand. I told him I needed the names of large boat owners and quality construction companies that were in financial trouble. I wanted good honest people who got into trouble through no fault of their own, or because they ended up owning a business they knew nothing about.

Ben thought for a moment and then said I have a boat owner that is in way over his head to us for a loan he took. He inherited the boat which I had inspected and it is worth a great deal, but the way he pays he owes us twenty times what he borrowed and there is no way out for him. I asked Ben what the boat was worth and what was owed. Ben said the boat was worth twenty thousand dollars, and the man owed the same from an original loan of two thousand dollars. Tell him you have a client that will pay off his debt and give him five thousand more. Ben asked me why do that when we could just take the boat.

I looked at Ben and said I want him to have the option to think I am buying the boat from you and you are being nice and passing on the profit. Ben said, "He will never believe I gave up that much profit". I told Ben that I did not give a damn what he believes.

"One of my companies will make the purchase and I will never be in this building again, so you will never get the opportunity to argue with me again:, I said. "I came here for information, not advise." Ben turned red and seemed to panic. I put up my hand and said, "Don't worry, it is not you." "It is just that I have returned to a great deal of work and I am a little tired." On that note I left. As I was walking out I realized that I have spent very little time with Ben or he would know that I hate being second guessed.

I stopped in at Max and Irma's after leaving Ben and by luck Toby was there. We sat down to eat lunch at a private table in the back and I asked about the children. That discussion was good for at least an hour. It was great to be with him again. I explained that he should see Ben and get the names of potential construction companies that are in trouble and we can buy a percentage of them and move some of the city contracts over to them and away from his company. I further explained that this would allow him to concentrate on houses and specialty construction.

He liked the idea and said that we were doing too much city work and it was becoming obvious. He also said that he could guess what companies Ben would suggest and he was well aware of their potential. I told him to do the background work and I would have Harper handle the negotiations. With that said our food came via a new cute little waitress.

I gave Toby a playful look and he held up his hands and said, "Oh no", one waitress in more than I can handle." We both got a good laugh out of that.

It was such a pleasure to sit with my dear friend and talk about everyday things and exciting business like the building of a beautiful home that when he brought up the people that were taking over the business that Angel and Smitty's gang had I cut him off. I leaned close to him and said, "You are no longer part of any of that." "You are living a life that would have made your parents proud and it allows me to escape sometimes from mine." Toby explained that they rebuilt the bar and there are two of them there talking about collecting Angels old debts. I was suddenly furious. I became very quiet and I asked if the Maletic brothers were around. Toby explained that they were probably waiting for him at the bar because he was seldom out of their site.

I told Toby to stay where he was. He looked at me and said that he more than anyone knew that look on my face and he wanted to be with me for whatever I was about to do. I explained to him that he could never be part of this work again. "Your wife, your family, and I need you to be the citizen you are especially here in Old Allegheny", I said, and then I left. When I got to the bar I told Ray and Bob to come with me and for Andy to stay with Toby. Sasha joined us as we walked out and the four of us went to see this new tavern. It turned out to look like a new pig pen on its way to being another dump. I left Bob to watch the door and the three of us went in.

There were two huge filthy men sitting on stools at the bar. I walked over and asked if they were the new men taking over for Angel. The bigger of the two said," Yes we are and if you owed him money than you owe it to me." I said, "You mean like Max at the tavern?" He said, "Exactly and we will be dealing with that fat bastard very soon." I looked at Sasha and faster than lightning he was on the big ape and cutting him into pieces. When I turned around Ray was already grinning and pounding the other one. I told Ray to step out as I touched the button and my knife shot out and into the windpipe of the man Ray had been hitting. I cleaned and returned the blade while Sasha threw whiskey all over the new wooden walls. We walked back to the tavern as the place went up in flames. There was no one around when we left. I credit that to the look on Bob's face. No one would want to cross him or be a witness .

Back at the tavern I thanked Ray and Bob for their help and I left. I was told later that Ray especially was surprised at what had happened. He told Toby that he never saw anyone so calm before what I was about to do. Toby told him never to underestimate me or anyone else from the Point. He explained that we live by a different set of rules and what just happened would mean nothing to me. I, of course, agreed with Toby's statements and I still do not understand how others think. All we did was remove a couple of rats that threatened our beautiful town.

After that I had Sasha take me to Molly's. Bart was waiting there for me. He motioned me to the back table and had Molly get us a mug of ale. I drank it straight down. The cold liquid felt wonderful on my throat. When I sat the mug down Bart said, "I see you have had a busy day." "Are you going to the strip next to remove a few more?"

Lord above, he always knew everything first. I looked at Bart and said, "I will have nothing and no one interfere with Toby or the North Side" "My patience does not go past the city of Pittsburgh." Bart laughed and said that lucky for me he knows who the money and power behind the dear departed is.

He told me that he suspected for some time, but it was not until the chief of police had his son bring a message to the house that he could be sure. "Well Bart", I said "Are you planning to tell me or not?"

"It seems our dear Mayor is not satisfied with the newfound wealth you have provided him." "He wants to feel like he has power too." "The police chief is so happy with what has been done for his family that he offered to kill the Mayor himself." "He is furious with the mayor for getting into things that might ruin all that has been accomplished." "How do you like that?"

I must admit that I never saw that one coming. This was a whole new problem. Getting rid of the mayor was easy, but new elections and all that other mess was more than I wanted at this point. Bart then informed me that the Mayor is leaving for a few days. He was quickly told about what happened on the North Side and he told the Chief he would be leaving town.

"I took the liberty of having a note sent to the Mayors wife that you would be dropping by this evening," Bart said with a grin. "I think you can use the distraction."

I would have argued, but that is exactly what I had in mind when he said the Mayor was leaving town. He is always one step ahead of me.

I went home with Bart and the two of us sat and enjoyed our scotch as I waited to see Katherine.

We talked for quite a while about books and art until Bart told me he had a present for me.

I was very curious as to what it could be. He reached behind one of the couches and lifted a large canvas wrapped in cloth. When he pulled off the cover I was speechless. It was a beautiful oil painting I had admired from his collection.

It was done by an artist Bart described as a Dutch Master and I knew it was priceless, but it was more than that to me. It was the first gift anyone had ever given me and I did not know how to respond. "You need say nothing", Bart said, "I can see on your face the thoughts going through your mind.

I gently set the painting down and hugged Bart for a very long time until James came and handed me a message from Molly. It said that there was a boat owner waiting for me at the Pub. Bart said he had just the place to hang the painting and that he would take care of it while I was gone. Sasha was waiting out front and we went directly to Molly's.

I went into the pub and back to my table.

Molly brought bread and cheese and a crock of ale. She gave me a hug and motioned for the man in at another table to come over. She explained that the young man was the son of an old friend of the captains.

The friend had died and the older brother that was groomed to take over the boat was killed in the same accident.

The young mans name was John and he knew nothing of boats. With that Molly left and I motioned for John to sit. I asked him what he was trained to do if anything. He responded that first of all he was very nervous and very upset to have to go through all this and he begged my patience. I told him to take his time and have a glass of ale. He took a couple of drinks and seemed to settle down.

He told me he tried to keep up the boat business, but no one would help him with finances. He ended up borrowing from a pawn shop on the North Side, but he did not understand how it all worked. His $2000.00

loan soon became a $20,000.00 Loan and he has paid back close to $ 10,000.00 and still owes the twenty. Again I told him to relax. Molly told me you might be able to help. Captain Staiger and my father were close friends and I have no where to turn. Again I asked him what he was trained to do and he explained that he was a professional chief, and that he had trained in Paris, France for the last eleven years. I looked at him and started speaking to him in French. His face lit up and we spoke at length about food and wine and I found he even had an eye for art which we spoke about for at least an hour.

I finally realized how far off the subject we had come.

Just then the Captain came in with little Dale in tow. Dale quickly ran to the kitchen to show his mom the fish they had caught. I asked the Captain to sit and he shook hands with John. I asked the Captain about the boat and he said it was an excellent craft and that John's father and brother never stopped fixing it up. I then asked him to get Molly. Dale was content with his cookies and milk in the kitchen so the four of us could talk Of course Simon was at another table taking notes. I asked Molly if the old theater down the street was still vacant at which point.

Simon walked over and whispered in my ear that I bought that building months ago along with every other building on each side of the street. I looked up at him and said," I did?". Simon quickly flipped back through the pages of his notes and said, " Oh yes, it says right here that you gave those instructions some time ago and I forwarded the request to the proper people.

I made a mental note to check on what else I had instructed him to do. Simon returned to his table and I went back to the discussion. Molly was trying not to laugh out loud. I said, "I guess that is why I need a secretary" Poor John was totally confused.

I looked at John and said that if we all agree, I will pay off your debt and give you an additional

$5000.00 for the boat." You and my brother Toby will look at the old theater and see of it can be remodeled into a spectacular French restaurant with a stage for entertainment like those in Paris that I have read about." "You will own 25% of the business including the building from the beginning. Molly and the Captain will own another 10% and the rest will be held in one of our companies. You will get a salary in addition to your percent of the profits. The Captain will help me with the boat which I happen to need and Dale will own 10% of the boat and 5% of the restaurant both to be held for him by one of our companies. Molly will get you in touch with Toby and I want you to spare no expense in making this place the grandest in the city. I turned to Simon and asked if we owned that big warehouse behind the theater and he said that we did. I told John that I wanted Toby to make an enclosed walkway from it to the restaurant so people could depart their cabs inside the warehouse and enter the restaurant unseen.

If everyone agrees our people will take care of the contracts and the money. Simon looked at me and shook his head yes. I explained that I was going to my apartment to relax, take a bath, and change clothes before I went to another meeting. Everyone just sat there with their mouth open except Molly who was smiling. Molly asked if she could speak to me later upstairs and I agreed' After I left John said to the Captain, "Is he serious?" He explained that I am always serious and that this is how I do everything.

He further told him that these plans have probably been in the back of my mind for a long time just waiting for a chance to fulfill them. John asked what he could do to show his appreciation. Molly explained that he could create a great restaurant. " She said," You do not understand how much he loves the Point and what he has done to make it better for the people that live here." He asked if I had any family and Molly said the Point hung his father and killed his mother, now we are lucky to be his family."

I thought to myself as I sat in my apartment that this has been a busy day. I had a big glass of scotch as I heard a rap at the door. I told Molly to come in since I knew she was the only one with access to the second floor. She swished into the room and sat in the chair next to me. I poured a glass of scotch and handed it to her. She said, I shouldn't and we both laughed as she took a big swallow. She turned to me and said, "Damn, if you don't drink the smoothest of scotch." I pulled her close and kissed her cheek and told her that my mother would be proud to know her.

She said, "Darn you, you can always make me cry and the magic hanky was wiping her eyes." I asked her what she wanted and she explained that she had known me since I was a boy and I never asked very much but I always gave everything. "When will you do something for yourself?" I asked what she meant and she said, "I want you to have a wife and children like Toby to come home to and to take care of you the way you take care of all of us." "I am not alone, look around at all those poor souls from the work house that are buying houses and living like real human beings because of you. Billy Birdshot tells them all that you are the cause of their new found quality of life." "Bless him for being a man of principal and putting the credit where it belongs". We are all of us aware of what you have done. At this point a word against you can get a man killed here in the Point.

I had no idea what had been going on. I did not know what to say. I hung my head and heard Molly say, "Go have a good time with Katherine tonight but think about what I have said and take it to heart." I got up and held her close to me and said, "The night my mother left me I knew that her courage and love would never be duplicated by another, but since meeting you my only regret is that I was too young to save her so that she could know the magic and wonder of you." Molly ran from the room sobbing. Well, I thought, I handled that poorly.

I filled the tub with water and slowly lowered my body into it. With scotch in one hand and a book in the other I began to reach for the bliss of the occasion.

CHAPTER 21

Clip, clop, went the sound of the horses on the cobblestones and my mind began to melt away into the soft light of the setting sun. It was a long day and I was having trouble staying awake no matter how much I looked forward to seeing Katherine. Sasha opened my door and said he would wait for me as usual in the parlor after he tended the horses. When I walked in the door she was waiting for me dressed in what I can only describe the most material I had ever seen that hid absolutely nothing about her body. I had to blink twice to believe it. My god but she was beautiful. She looked at my eyes and said, " This will never do." She led me up the winding staircase and into her bedroom. I laid on the bed as she went to the adjoining room and began to fill what I later learned was an enormous bath. I must have dozed off because she woke me by rubbing my face with the soft edges of her gown.

When I opened my eyes she untied the top of the gown and as it fell to the floor she used her finger to indicate I was to follow. It was then that I realized that I too was naked.

The sun came screaming through the window like the room was on fire.

It turned the inside of my eyelids crimson and suggested that it was time to get up. At first I was confused because I had never spent the night here, but I soon became aware that I was entangled with the most beautiful long legs and arms I had ever had the pleasure to wake up with. Her hair was covering the pillow that her face was buried in.

I looked down her spine at still another beautiful sight. I reached down and gently swatted her on the rump. Her head came up slowly and she said, "It appears that we slept in, so if you do not want my domestic help to discover what they probably already know, dress quickly and we will meet downstairs.

I could not help but laugh as I followed her instructions and joined Sasha in the parlor. He explained that the horses were hitched and ready out under the portico.

Not too much later Katherine came into the room looking like she had taken hours getting dressed and carrying a tray of coffee and sweet treats. She suggested that Sasha help himself and please wait with the horses.

We sat back and talked as her hired help began to infiltrate the house and take command. Our coffee was replenished and a tray of breakfast foods was placed on a table between us. A similar tray was taken out to Sasha by a very pretty maid that looked like she too had a busy evening. Katherine said that we had two things to discuss. She first explained that she was quite aware of what that fool of a husband of hers was trying to do and she wanted to know how I planned to handle it.

Second she handed me an invitation to a ball at the home of certain beer maker here in the city. She assumed that I would get the same invitation.

I sat back a moment and said, " If you are worried whether a certain Mayor will be alive to attend the ball then you can put it out of your mind. I have little doubt that his health will be hampered in any way." "As to the fool that has designs on my business activity, here again he will be dealt with along with his friends. "These are matters that I know very little of and they do not concern us."

Katherine grinned and said, "You mean like the two fools in the shack on the North Side yesterday?" My husband ran around the house screaming like his hair was on fire yesterday, terrified that he was the next to die and then he left to get to his mistress." I just shrugged my shoulders and said that I too had heard the rumors about the men over in Old Allegheny.

She just looked at me and rolled her eyes. I kissed her cheek and said that I would see her at the ball. She said that she would try to save me a dance. I asked Sasha to stop at a local tattoo parlor down in the Point.

When we got there I asked the owner if he remembered the crest on my other cab and he quickly drew it for me. I then asked if he would like to make some serious money for a few hours of work. He was extremely willing. The cost of a large tattoo of my crest was about two dollars so I offered to pay him fifty. He quickly agreed.

Next I told Sasha to go to an address on the other side of town by the Strip District. I happened to know of a certain mistress that lived there and entertained our dear Mayor in her lovely home. We parked about a block up the street from her house and Sasha went to the front door and rang for the maid. When the maid came to the door he told her to get her mistress and be very quiet about it. He handed her ten dollars. Shortly the lady of the house appeared and Sasha handed her one hundred dollars and asked where the mayor was. He assured her that he would not harm him. She explained to Sasha that he was passed out drunk on the couch.

Sasha came and got us and we took the tattoo artist into the house. The whole thing was just too perfect. Sasha stood over the mayor with a blackjack, just a short version of Billy's birdshot tube, just in case the mayor woke up, and the artist went to work. He finished in less than two hours because he said the client was so cooperative.

The lady and I had a delightful conversation about all the thugs that had been hanging around the Mayor. She wanted them out of her life and away from her home. I assured her that we were in agreement on that. I suggested as we went to inspect the work of art that she begin drinking heavily so that when our friend woke up she could claim that she had also passed out and knew nothing. We tried our best when we saw it not to laugh, but the whole thing was so funny that we were required to leave the room so we did not wake him up. The tattoo was quite beautiful in red and black and gold, but it looked so out of place on his enormous belly.

On the way out I got a kiss on the cheek and Sasha gave her another hundred. We took the artist back to his place and Sasha followed him in and gave him another fifty. The best part is, he was from the Point and he would never speak of what he did.

When we got to Molly's I went in to find Bart waiting at my table. On my way to him I handed Simon the list of thugs working for the mayor and instructed him to copy it into his ledger which I was finally able to read. I went over and sat down with Bart. He said, "You have had a busy morning". "You have to tell me just what you tattooed on the Mayor". I guess I should not be surprised that he knew about it, but I was happy he did not know everything.

When I told him about the large crest on that fat belly he came as close to laughing as I have ever seen.

He said, "Where do you come up with these things?" I explained that I did not want to hurt the poor slob but I wanted him to have a reminder that we can get to him when ever we please. "Now I need to get this list to the Chief of Police so he can rid the city of the rest of the trash," I said. Bart suggested that I leave the list with him and he would see that it was delivered to the proper people.

Within a week I was informed that a rail car load of bodies was unloaded somewhere along the tracks in Kentucky. They were found under a load of limestone shipped from Pittsburgh. I thought it was inventive if not interesting.

When I returned home after being with Bart I found my invitation to the ball given by Hans at Steel City Beer. It was a long time since I had seen him and years since I had seen his family. I looked forward to what I expected to be a fun evening with Katherine. Later that day, I returned to Moly's where I met with Toby, and Billy B. Billy asked that we shorten his nickname now that he was a serious member of society. I thought it was kind of silly, but if it made him feel better, what was the harm. Toby told me about two young construction companies that were having trouble making a living. He said their men were solid and their equipment was adequate. I told him to offer enough money to get them on their feet and cover any debts they might have for 25% of their business.

I told him to further explain that Allegheny Contracting was at capacity and that he would move business to them now and help them with bids in the future.

If they agree, send them to Harper and then to Walter for the money. Let them know that Crimson Investments would be buying into their companies and its banker and its attorney would handle them in the future to safe guard the investment and to add a level of sophistication to their companies. I further said that Harper had set up the new company a few months ago and that we were all investors.

Next I spoke to Billy B and asked him to tell Ben about the boat and to throw away any paperwork he had on the loan. I suggested he explain that there was a personal relationship with the owner and that the matter was settled. I do not want any further contact with John who will be our new partner in a restaurant and nightclub. Billy agreed and asked about the new boat. I informed him that as soon as we found a captain it would begin to haul our product north to the friends in the mountains. I suggested a 45% discount from retail for a price.

Billy B felt they would be very happy for that price since we were able to make the shine so much cheaper than they could in the mountains.

This would enable them to continue at the same rate of profit with no involvement in the distilling. I told him to expect shipments to begin next week. I also asked him to have them arrange for us to purchase hardwood lumber to fill the boat for the return trip.

Again I spoke to Toby and asked about the old theater and the warehouse behind it. His face lit up like a little kid. He told me that the buildings were in excellent shape and he was already gutting the old interior of the theater although he wanted to keep as much of the of opulence it once had for the character. He suggested that we keep this as the worst kept secret in the city to get peoples curiosity up. He mentioned that John had many friends in the entertainment business and that a new thing called Burlesque was becoming popular in the eastern cities as well as Europe. I explained that it was up to John to arrange those things, but Bart and I wanted to approve the menu and taste the food before it was offered. We would also arrange for the wine. The beer and liquor was obvious.

While we were talking, the Captain came in with his little shadow in tow. Dale was filling out. I guess it was either that or burst from all the food Molly was stuffing in him. I asked them to join us, but Dale said he had to see his mother first.

The Captain explained that cookies had something to do with that decision. The captain said that he had good news. A good friend of his and an excellent riverboat captain was in town and stopped by to see if there were any prospects for work that he knew of. The man was named Howard and he wanted to work shorter trips. After many years of going to New Orleans and back Howard explained to him that he wanted to spend more time with his family. I told the Captain to give him the same deal we gave the other three, salary plus 25%of profits if he can begin next week. Captain Mike was sure he would take it especially when he saw the boat.

I turned to Billy B. and said, "There you are, you and your friends are in business."

Billy looked at me and said, "Does everything always work out for you the way you want?" I explained that everything works out if you plan for it and you grab opportunity each time you see it.'

When Billy and Toby left, Dale burst out of the kitchen, ran to our table, and gave me a big hug. He said, "Hi Uncle Getts, I think the Captain and I are just about the best fishermen in the Point." I could do nothing but smile. Next, Molly came with cheese and bread, smoked fish and a jug of ale. She also had a big hug for me. "You know", I said, I could get use to this whole family thing".

The Captain shut his eyes and said, "Oh No". Molly lit up and began to tell me how Toby had babies and she had a little boy and it was about time for me to start a family of my own. "Now", she said, "I have been thinking of a long list of fine young ladies that you should consider before making up your mind." "Remember that you are quite a catch and there is no reason for you not to be choosy about it." At this point the Captain was just shaking his head and groaning to himself. I quickly got up, gave Molly a big hug and ran out the door.

CHAPTER 22

The smell was still there just not quite so strong. It threw its arms around me and carried me back like a maple leaf floating on a soft breeze.

I could feel my mother's arms around me and I could hear my father's gruff old voice teasing her for coddling her only child. I cannot say that we were happy, but there were moments when I thought it was wonderful and I think they did too. I was sitting on the dirt floor of the little hovel we had called home. It appears that times had changed in the Point and no one wanted to live in this pathetic old hut. I remembered special times like when we had enough to eat and we would sit around thinking that we were the luckiest of people because of a full belly if only for a little while. Toby's son asked me once if I liked being a little boy because he was having so much fun in his own life.

It was not such a strange question, it was just that I have no memory of a time when I was not hustling to stay alive another day. The rule of the streets was simple then. Parents did what they could and after that you were on your own.

I had walked and walked throughout the Point after I left Molly's in such a rush. Somehow as my thoughts drifted I ended up here and it pulled me in. I remembered my father and me looking over the results of our day in the street picking the pockets of those people, the ones that had everything. He would say that they would hardly miss what would help us through another day so how could we be doing wrong? I never thought of it as wrong, I was just helping myself to what they had too much of. I was just getting my share any way I knew how. Then I flashed back to that last day. I had seen many hangings, but this time it was my father. He did not have anything to say to me as he walked up to the gallows. It was as though it was an ending that he always expected and it finally had come.

My mother held my hand and she did not have any more tears to shed in this world. The Point and life had drained the moisture from her eyes and left a shell of what was once a beautiful young girl. It seems as though everyone in the Point tried to live life as fully and as fast as they could before fate cut it short. I called it fate, but it really was reality. Girls started having babies as soon as nature allowed it and most men were on their own before they were old enough to get them pregnant. Few people made it past the age of thirty and those that did had few teeth if any and they passed easily for fifty. Too much too fast was an early death sentence, but when they looked at the result of growing older, who would want It?

I looked up at my father as the rope was put around his neck and I remember how badly I felt that I did not have the money to pay the hangman to make it quick. He could adjust the drop so that your death came fast as your drop ended. For that you had to pay and I had no money. The rest like my father would be left to kick and strangle until at last it was over. I was grateful when the time came and the trap door was open that his very size caused his neck to snap and he did not suffer long. One simple blessing in a place and time when there were so few. My father was twenty nine. These were the thoughts that kept me going in my quest to make things better. I decided to buy up this whole area and turn it into decent living spaces. When I finally emerged from the hut Sasha was standing guard outside the doorway. If he thought what I did was strange, he would never say, but I often felt that he understood.

It was getting late so I told him to take me home so that I could get some rest before leaving for the ball that night. As I rode home I realized that it must have been Molly talking about me having a family that directed me back to that place. That place and those times were the anchor that held me to the reality of life no matter what successes I might achieve. That was the real me and I would never be able to let go of it, nor did

I want to.

272

PART TWO

CHAPTER 23

I could hear the waves hitting the side of the ferry as we crossed the Allegheny River. We moved slowly with the current constantly pushing us toward the Ohio River. The big paddle on the back of the ferry churned the brown water into a curtain of bubbles that drifted downstream. The ferry was painted red, white and blue and a huge American Flag flew over the Captains deck house. This was a time when the city and surrounding area was flooded with people from all over the world. Even in this filth and working conditions that were not that far from the slavery we had fought to end just a generation ago, there was a pride in being here. There was a pride in being an American, even if you had yet to learn the language. This country was on its way up while the rest of the world lay dormant. The new arrivals knew it best because they had begged, borrowed and stole their way here. They would endure whatever so that their children would have better. Pittsburgh was the center of industry as witnessed by the never-ending trains and boats that carried the goods to all places in every direction of the compass.

Below the clouds of smoke and greasy soot was a twenty four hour hustle of men and equipment that created the foundation for the construction of a great country. Iron, steel, cement, glass, aluminum, tool and die, oil and innovation poured from every foot of space along the three rivers and the Point was central to it all and I was central to the Point.

I was twenty-four, a little over six foot, with thick black hair and a neatly trimmed mustache. I wore no jewelry except the little nugget in my ear. My clothes were tailor made and I had at least thirty pairs of handmade boots. My hair was tied in the back and it hung down past my shoulders. I weighed just short of two hundred pounds and I had the build of a prize fighter just like my father.

I was trained with sword and gun beside my fists by the best available. I knew about books, art, math, and I was considered an accomplished pianist. I was fluent in English, French, German, Russian, Spanish and most of the Baltic languages. My financial interests spanned most of the business in the city, and I was buying stock in most of the growing new industries while keeping a sufficient cash reserve. I considered myself the luckiest of men and I was going to a ball tonight thrown by one of my partners in the beer business.

For one of the few times in my life I wondered just what was next.

I never lost my lust for adventure and I anticipated each day with excitement.

When I got home I poured a glass of the ruby scotch and sat in my big leather chair. James brought me a snack and suggested I take a bath and rest before leaving for the ball. I agreed to do just that as soon as I finished my drink. I ate most of the food and then climbed the stairs to my bath. It felt like heaven as I slid into the hot water. I could not stay in the water long for fear of falling asleep so I got out, dried off and climbed into the bed. In moments I was asleep.

Apparently enough time had passed because James woke me up and suggested that it was time to dress for the ball. I felt refreshed and began to put on the new clothes he had laid out for me. I had a suit of fine black wool, with gold trim and a gold silk shirt with a red silk scarf. My boots were black and they had a high shine on them. I was one of the few people that wore boots all of the time, but I could never get comfortable with the low shoes that were popular. If I were honest with myself I would admit that I never wanted anything that was in the street to get close to my skin ever again.

James was going along as far as Molly's where I would change the horses to the other carriage and travel to the ball from there. We always enjoyed riding together and testing each other's language skills. I never quite matched his ability to change from one language to another in the middle of a sentence. James was not what you would call tall, but his perfect posture and the way he presented himself gave the illusion of a much bigger man. He had a solid build and thick brown hair that he kept short.

I guessed that he was in his mid to late thirties, but he never seemed to get any older and he moved like a young athlete.

He was always dressed formally and when we went out he wore a large hooded cape, but on his head he had a wide-brimmed black hat with the brim turned down all the way around. I also noted that he had the ability to move with that misty angled gate just like Bart did. He was a natural-born teacher and he never missed an opportunity to take on that role.

Whenever he saw that I had finished a book, he would find reasons to quiz me on the finer points the author had been trying to make. He made a point of doing it when he thought I would be the least prepared.

It was like a game and we both enjoyed it a great deal.

At last we were at Molly's and we entered the pub. Bart, Simon, and Molly's family were waiting and naturally Molly gave me a full inspection before giving me a hug and telling me how proud she was as she blotted a tear from her eye with her scarf.

Bart came to me and said that the mayor was going to the ball and he could not wait to hear how that would go. He had that evil little twinkle in his eye and all I could do is smile and tell him what a devil he was.

Molly had set our table with a light snack and everyone was enjoying it and each other until Sasha came in and said the horses were changed and we should leave. After hugs all around I got in the coach and we left. There was a large crowd waiting for Sasha to put on a show with the horses and he did not let them down as we rode through the Point and into Market Square which he rounded twice before leaving for the Strip District and up the hill to the large home of Hans the brewer. The Strip District is an area along the Allegheny River just north of the city proper.

Trapped between the river and the rail tracks are a series of warehouses where food from all over is unloaded. There are also a few stores selling imported small items like cookware. When the loading docks are no longer in use for the day some enterprising owners allow the public to come and buy their products on the docks. Some even take the fish and other products they prepare before sale and cook them right there so they are available to the public fresh and hot. I predict that someday this area will be a destination for people living here and those visiting.

Sasha made a great showing during the ride through the Strip and the horses were applauded all along the way.

All in all it was a pleasant evening and I enjoyed the ride. When we arrived there was a level of expectation as our horses were spotted. Other carriages moved to the side to let Sasha do his thing. Many of the guests were summoned to the front portico to watch our entrance.

I hated the attention, but it was little enough to do for Sasha since he had saved my life on occasion. The pull up the long hill was little work for the stallions and the coach was a thing of beauty and perfection that needed a minimum of effort to move. The horses first went in a synchronized gallop, but at the crest of the hill, Sasha slowed them to a perfect stepping march.

When we got close to the portico he slowed them again to a pacing crawl that hardly moved, then we stopped. He jumped down and opened my door. I escaped the coach and quickly stepped to the front door. When Sasha climbed to his seat atop the coach, the crowd began to applaud.

Sasha stood and gave a deep bow and then gave a command in Russian and the two stallions bowed their heads low and held them there while the clapping increased. Then Sasha cracked the whip twice and they trotted away. I was glad to be out of the limelight. Hans and his wife greeted me right away and escorted me into the ballroom. There were many familiar faces including the Mayor and Katherine.

The house was large by any standards and the huge entry served as the ballroom. The ceiling was at least twenty feet high with an enormous crystal chandelier hanging down in the center. The circular stair was all of twelve feet wide and it began at the back of the room.

There were sculpted crown moldings and decorative carvings along the walls. It was all painted a very light shade of pink that was almost white with ivory and gold accents. It was all very beautiful. A small orchestra was in the far right corner and they were a pleasure to hear. Hans and his wife took me around to make sure everyone knew me. There were many people there that I had never met.

The group was made up of well to do business men and their wives with a few politicians thrown in to show respect, thus the appearance of our beloved Mayor. Cocktails and the finest wine was constantly placed before everyone by a great many waiters.

It was inevitable that I would be brought to face the Mayor and Kathleen and so as we approached them I used every bit of my skill to keep a straight face. Kathleen had a silly grin on her face and it was obvious she was enjoying her husband's discomfort.

As soon as I got within reach, I put out my hand to shake with the Mayor, but before I knew it he had me in a bear hug and he was proclaiming how happy he was to see his dear friend and how glad he was that we were now forever attached toward a glorious future for the city. Kathleen covered her mouth and quickly left before she broke out in a laughing fit. The Mayor then released me and announced that he and I had formed a bond and he was forever my dearest friend. All I could think of was how I should have tattooed the bastard a long time ago. I quickly grabbed a glass of wine and moved on.

I was enjoying myself talking to the various businessmen and listening to what they were working on. These were good people and I was glad to get to meet them. The music played on and many people were dancing. Katherine came over and grabbed my arm. As she did she turned me to face the staircase. I looked up and saw perhaps the most beautiful young woman I had ever seen. Her gown was full to the floor and a very pale green with fine dark green lace trim.

Emeralds hung from her ears and around her perfect white neck. Her hair was a strawberry blond mass of curls pulled up and then behind her ears to cascade down her back. She looked to be about five foot ten inches and her waist was tiny while her dress left just enough to show her bare shoulders and neck. I was captivated as was everyone else in the room. She walked straight toward me but her eyes were looking to my right. I had not noticed that Hans was standing next to me. When she got close enough he kissed her cheek and put his left hand on my shoulder and said, "I believe you remember my daughter from the Mayors Ball.". I could not believe this was the same little girl I danced with that night. She put out her hand and said,

"They are playing a waltz and I believe I owe you a dance."

She gently pulled me onto the dance floor. If I could have seen Kathleen, I would witnessed her holding her hands tightly together with a look of triumph on her face. She said nothing as we danced and danced. I finally took my eyes off her face long enough to whisper in her ear, "To all flowers a season and you truly are the most beautiful of blooms."

CHAPTER 24

My mind swirled with the music and her image bounced from every crystal on the chandelier and some how I was lost in the smell of her perfume and the feel of her in my arms.

But, all things end and the music stopped and the moment passed so I had to return to the here and the now, but I was reluctant to let go of her until I realized that we were alone in the middle of the dance floor and everyone was applauding us. Hans walked over and took her arm while he smiled at me and said," I had forgotten just how well you danced together." I let go of her, bowed and thanked her for a delightful dance. When I turned Kathleen was waiting at my side. She took my arm and escorted me off the floor. By the time we reached the bar I was back in full control, almost.

Katherine looked beautiful in her low cut gown, but for some reason I kept thinking of Hans daughter Rebecca. I guess I was caught somewhere between her beauty and the surprise of how she had grown up. Katherine could not stop smiling as she captured two glasses of wine from a waiter and handed one to me. As we drank the wine I watched Rebecca move to the dance floor with a handsome young man dressed in his finest military uniform. Katherine turned me to face her and said," You had better grab this one before one of these young men takes her away." "What! ", I thought. She now had my full attention. "The lady is quite stunning, but I have no time or desire to grab anyone at this point, and certainly not the young daughter of a business partner." Katherine just grinned, squeezed my arm and kissed me on the cheek. "Whatever you say", she answered.

It was a very nice evening and I danced with many of the guests including Rebecca several more times. Unfortunately, the Mayor stayed for the whole evening and escorted his wife to their home, so Sasha and I returned to Molly's. There was food waiting and Bart, Billy B, Simon, James along with Molly's family all wanted to hear about the evening. I spoke of many things including the growth of the oil business up north and the natural gas wells in the area that were everywhere.

Molly asked mostly about the clothes the ladies were wearing and the house. It was a pleasant evening with friends and once again I realized how important these people were to me. It seemed like the whole world was functioning out there, but we were to be forever with each other in our own little world in the Point. After awhile it was time to go home so Sasha brought the carriage and Bart, James and I left.

When we got home I noticed that Bart and James were very quiet and every so often they looked at one another with a strange gleam in their eyes. It looked more like pity than anything else. When were in the house I changed into more comfortable clothes and joined Bart in the library. He handed me a glass of our favorite scotch. I loved the way the dancing flames of the fire in the fireplace flickered off the crystal glass in my hand. Bart had introduced me to many great single malt brands of scotch, but this was the one we craved the most. I thought it odd that in my thoughts I would think of it as a craving, but I guess that is the point of great food, wines and the like.

I quickly finished the first glass and James was there to refill my glass. Instead of leaving the room, he poured himself a glass and sat down with Bart and me. I was surprised, but I was pleased to have his company too. When we were totally relaxed Bart began to speak. He said he had questions for me and I needed to answer them as honestly as I could. I became very nervous and James explained to me that I should not worry because they thought of me as a son and this talk was about how they felt as parents. I was surprised and pleased at the same time. I said, "It has been so long since I had any parents but in my heart they had assumed the role along with Molly who seemed to mother everyone."

Bart began with these questions which I could only answer no to.

Do you remember being sick? Do you remember having a cut, or a bruise or even a sore since we got together? Have you stumbled or fallen down or ever felt even like that could happen in these last years since we got together? As I said, my answer was no in each case. I asked him, " Why all the questions?" Bart and James rubbed their eyes and the silence seemed to last forever. Finally James said that he had a story to tell me and I needed to listen to the whole thing and say nothing until he was finished.

The most ancient culture in the world was located in present day China. It is one of the few countries that remained basically the same through out all of history. There is not even a name for the country besides China because for all intents and purposes it predates all known experience. Chinese culture and science was ahead of the world for centuries, but they are and have always been a very secret and mysterious people with no desire to have anything to do with the rest of the world. They were students of chemistry, math, and the human body while we were still living in caves. Who else would ever contrive to produce silk from the secretion of a worm? Some of the very early religious cults experimented with the blood system and its effect on the rest of our bodies' They called the heart the "Red Gate" because all life and all blood must pass through what we refer to as heart valves among the more learned men of science. They tried to live on a series of diets to study the effects of them on their blood. One such experiment was a combination of wolf and other animal blood mixed with chemicals unknown to us today that they had developed. The result was a human that could live for extended periods of time on that combination alone. Some of their subjects evolved into the beasts called vampires that are written about in books to scare little children.

They did exist, but they could not recreate themselves and they hid away in places like the mountains in Slovenia and were hunted down and were killed. They were hampered mostly by inability to live in sun light and the fact that they tried to live on human blood alone which in inefficient.

The others found a way to live a normal life and enjoy all things human while extending their life dramatically and being exempt from disease and bodily harm of any type.

They developed formulas that controlled aging. The old lady that gave you that earring is several hundred years old. She allowed her body to age so no one would question her role her as grandmother as the generations died off and she remained. It is a very successful ploy with the people of the swamps where little is questioned. She gave you the nugget because she realized that we knew you and she wanted us to know it.

We can have children as long as we do it before we pass through the Red Gate. There are very few women amongst us because they do not wish to outlive their families. We cannot pass on this gift to anyone in any of our families. Bart and I age one year for every fifty years we live. We have been around for hundreds of years and age very little because we were young like you when we began. Now it is time for you to ask questions.

I was taken aback and I needed time to think. James poured me another drink and believe me I needed it. My first question was to ask why they were telling me this now. Bart explained that they could feel my thoughts and they were aware of my reaction to Rebecca. I am close to going through the Red Gate and I must decide if I want to continue before I am unable to have children and I will undoubtedly outlive a wife.

I asked how I got close to the Red Gate and they said that the ruby colored scotch contains the formula that they have lived on and I have been drinking. I asked how long I will live and they said it is up to me. I currently will live fifty years for every normal year, but that can be increased or decreased. I asked how I explain why I do not age and they said that when the time comes that it is to awkward Bart delivers a body to your home. The coroner who is one of us writes a death certificate and sends it to our funeral parlor and it is buried while you assume a new life and a new identity in another place like the previous owner of this house did. Your current formula is a combination of blood from me, James and a few others. Everything we know and can do you now know and can do like the piano and the languages. We do not fly or turn into bats, but there is one trick we do have.

We always land on our feet and we can control the rate of speed as we fall. I do not recommend that you test it, but it can come in handy. I asked who else was part of this and Bart explained that our lawyer, banker, and various people we do business with are all in our group. The former owner of this house and the house he let us rob were former members that needed to move on. "So you don't kill people." I asked. "Well," he said that is not exactly the truth." "One does need to earn a living."

"When you travel you will find that you can recognize others of our group, and they will recognize you." Bart explained. There are many thousands of us and we must pick our candidates very carefully." " You are the first for me and James in all these hundreds of years", Bart said. I asked, "Why me?" "You showed a natural ability to survive." "You watched your father die and kept on going." "You have a keen mind and a natural ability to see talent in others that draws them to you". "You can kill if needed or in anger without emotion." We live for a very long time and there is no room for self pity or extended sorrow." "Who can live for hundreds of years mourning a lost love?" " That is worse than death."

" If we stop now you will be like everyone else, but if we continue you will soon be one of us and what you can accomplish is beyond belief," said James. "If you can, find happiness in Toby's family and see to all your friends". "You have known from the beginning that the way you live invites death and if they cannot get to you they will go after what and who you love," "Think about it and we will talk again. They both said, "Good night"

I sat alone in the library and listened to the sound of the big clock, while I sipped the scotch with the ruby cast and marveled at what I had been told. I shut my eyes and rolled my thoughts back to a time when I just wanted to stay alive for another day. I wanted to see my father bring home enough for us to eat and I wanted to hear my mothers' voice that was not followed by a spell of painful coughing. I wanted to show them what I had achieved on the street with my skill as a pick-pocket and hoped it would help if for only one more day. I want, I want, I want, I want was the backbone of our existence just like all those around us and now I did not know what I wanted.

I loved seeing Toby with his ever growing family and I loved my special place in it. I never thought about having a wife and a family of my own.

I was just so involved in my life that it never came up. I had loved running the streets and alleys of the Point and having the respect of the people there that really mattered.

Looking back I realized that I was a kid functioning in a world of adults and I was accepted because I could handle it. These two men entered into that world and brought me to a place where I could be offered a never ending world to grow and achieve and continue to do what I loved, but the price was high. The family I have will grow old and die and the death of so many people that I care about would forever be a part of my existence while I went on. I would create a new life and it would start all over again and I would have to watch as they too passed away. Could I endure that? Was I willing to know that I was part of the most privileged while others lived as I had as a child?

I did not know the answers to these questions, but I did remember what my kids on the street that we called One through Nine had told me over and over when we had our meetings. Five, who was older, said it best when he told me, "We have escaped the alleys and the stink of the Point because you have led us to a better life." "We are the first to have nice homes and families that do not know hunger and it was you that brought us here". "You should live forever so you can keep on doing and saving people like us." There was a great cheer from the others at the table from his toast and it embarrassed me, but it swelled my heart. Live forever, what a concept.

I laid my head back into the soft down filled leather of my chair and slid a little forward. The smell of the old books filled the walls except for the small space where the gift, the beautiful Rembrandt, hung just halfway up the wall, mixed with the smoky fragrance of the fire. The gas lights glowed and an orange glaze covered the ceiling interrupted only by the shadows of the dancing flames from the hearth. The scotch oozed down my throat after each sip and tickled my skin the way a cold wind tickled your spine. I now knew what I was drinking and it did not repulse me but rather seemed to bring me closer to Bart and James. I thought about one day adding my blood to a mixture and perhaps bringing another to the front of the Red Gate. I could do everything any other human could do except die young and have children. Was that so great a sacrifice?

I sat there for hours until I finished the decanter of scotch. Sleep, I thought, right now only sleep would do.

CHAPTER 25

Somewhere in the world there is a rainbow, and somewhere there is a shooting star streaking through a glitter filled night. A baby is being born who will one day write great poetry and another will create art that the world will enjoy forever. The hands of a master are carving a violin from what was once a tree and the tusk of an elephant will provide the keys for a piano that will entertain masses of music lovers. Someone invented a machine that can fly and someone else will discover a way to destroy an enemy with terrible consequences.

Most of the inhabitants of the world will not live to see these things, but those that pass the Red Gate will. They will see all this and I can hardly wonder what else. Will mankind cure terrible illnesses, and will he find a way to feed everyone? Will we learn to share or will we continue to pass through times of great greed where all of the money will be kept in the hands of a very few? It seems that we have gone from Tsars and kings to Robber Barons. I cannot even guess who will hold the reins of power next. The questions are simple. Do I want to be there to see all that or do I want to try to lead a full life now and perhaps die surrounded by a loving family?

I keep thinking that I need time to decide such an important question, but I am just fooling myself. I pushed Toby toward a family and I was happy to provide one for Molly, but my true love is building things and finding new opportunities. I enjoy passion and I loved the feel of a beautiful young woman in my arms, but my first love will always be the thrill of challenge. I will forever take chances and make enemies that will do anything to get to me. How could I risk the lives of my family and still be me? I have lived like this since I was a child in the alleys.

I have made no attempt to change these last years and I knew nothing of the Red Gate. There is an Alley Rat inside this body and it will never leave, and I never want it to. I will do whatever is needed to join the members of the Red Gate and I will live on and on until I wish to live no more.

The next morning James pulled open the curtains and let the light in. He informed me that my bath was ready. I smiled and asked him why he continued in this role. He explained that he loved doing it and it suited him. He also said that he has had the same job for hundreds of years and since no one pays any attention to servants, he never has to leave unless he wants to. He mentioned nothing about my decision. After my bath I enjoyed a lavish breakfast and then went to the living room where Bart and James were waiting. I told them that I thought the whole thing through and I realized that I would be a rogue no matter how much society offered me and that was no life for a family man. I realized that I needed to be me because it was my true love, so I wanted the Red Gate.

They both seemed pleased, but not surprised. Bart explained that when you live as long as they have it is easy to accumulate great wealth. "Of course", he said,

"You are well on your way right now, but the trick is to turn it into assets for your new identity when it is necessary." "We will help you with that."

By now my curiosity was getting the best of me so I asked exactly how I would make the change. James said that I will be having an exclusive dinner party here on Saturday night and I would pass through the Red Gate then. I told him that I thought no one was to ever come here and he explained that all of these guests had been here before. Now my curiosity was even more aroused, but I somehow knew better than to ask who these people were. Saturday was just a week away and I liked the anticipation of the event.

I decided to go see Molly and check on the new restaurant. When I got there the Captain was sitting at the corner table with Molly. I walked over and sat with them. The Captain explained that Howard had made his first trip up the Allegheny River to Franklin and the men from Tionesta were thrilled with the cargo. He returned with some of the most beautiful hardwood lumber there is. The profits from the two loads is far more than we expected. So few boats can handle the low draft requirements that far up the river that we are getting requests from merchants for all sorts of goods. The most exciting is the demand for drilling equipment.

There is some railroad hauling now, but the problem comes from offloading the awkward derricks. Our boats are equipped with their own cranes and our men are skilled at handling the weight. We will not replace the rail shipments, but we can land the load anywhere there is a dock and save time and money when they wish to drill in more remote places. Captain Howard is beside himself with excitement at the profit potential.

The oil madness is taking over that entire part of the state.

I told him how pleased I was with their success and suggested that he and Molly continue to monitor the progress. Molly also explained that an old friend of mine stopped by to see me. I asked who and she said

that he told her to tell me the rolls and hammer man.
He also said I should tell you that his thumb is fine
except on cold rainy days. I burst out laughing, I could
not help it. I told them the story of how all those years
ago I had hit his thumb with his own hammer and stolen
his rolls. We all got a laugh out of that. Molly said
that she told him to keep stopping in because sooner
or later I always showed up. I thought about it and
decided I owed him a favor after all these years so I
went to his stall to see him. When I got there two
young alley rats were watching the stalls and moving
would be thieves along. I was greeted by just about
everyone much to my surprise. It had been a long time
since I visited this market and I looked very different
from the boy that first came here.

There were many well wishers, but with Sasha in tow
no one got too close. When I saw the rolls and
hammer guy he ran out from behind the stall toward
me. I signaled Sasha that it was alright and then I

tolerated a big hug. I gently pushed him away and asked what he wanted to see me about.

Before I knew it there were eight or ten of the stall owners grouped in front of me.

The rolls and hammer guy said that his name was Angelo and he was from Italy. He was second generation, and he and his friends had been able to save some money since we started protecting the market. I said, "That is very good and I thank you for telling me."

"No, no, no," he said, "That is not what we want to talk to you about." "We have seen that our old friend Toby has built a series of store fronts with second floor living quarters all up and down both sides of the street by Molly's hotel and tavern". We want to buy them and set up our businesses and homes there." I will open a bakery, and we have a shoemaker, a butcher, an iron worker and even a silver smith plus many more."

I was in shock. I never thought I would have good businessmen who would choose to move into the Point.

I raised my hands for silence as I got hold of my senses. I told them that I was very happy with their proposal and if they would go see Molly I would arrange for each of them to get the space they needed. I said that one of my companies would finance their loan balances at one half normal interest. I was so pleased that I needed to get away before they saw the tear in the corner of my eye. This is what I was meant to do. I went back to see Molly. I told her to set up all the purchases and get the paper work from Harper. I told her the loans would come from Crimson Investments which we were all a part of. She asked me if I would sit and talk with her for a little while. I did not know to interpret the look on her face so I had no idea if I should be worried or not. When we sat down, there was ale and cheese, along with fresh bread and smoked fish on the table. She took a deep breath and let it out slowly before saying to me," Do you know how much money and general wealth I now have?" I thought about it and said," I pay no attention to money," "I never even count any of the money I pass to you from our guys on the street each month." "She said, "I am the wealthiest woman in the Point in terms of cash and property." "I purchased all the property on the street behind our hotel and all the property you did not buy behind the new restaurant."

"Now you tell me that in addition to this fancy French restaurant you are building, I am to be on a street full of new shops." "I would like to take most of the money we have out on the street and start a real bank right here in the Point." "When Toby finishes with the building here I want him to do the same on the other two streets." " I think we can also begin to build row houses for the new employees at the work house." 'There are less and less poor here in the Point with all the construction and other jobs available." "I want to establish a free school for children with promise, both boys and girls." "I hope that someday we will have to build an academy out of town where rich and poor can go and learn together." "Well", she said, "That is all I wanted to tell you."

I did not know what to say. I was so proud of Molly at that point that I could not find words to express it. I told her I would look into what was needed to form a bank and I would talk to Toby about the other construction. I put my arm around her shoulder and said, "Let's go look at this fancy restaurant."

We walked the short distance to the old opera house and before we went in I asked Molly if she had seen any of the renovations. She shook her head no. When I opened the door we were both too stunned to talk. Every detail that once had once been a magnificent theater was restored and perfected beyond the original. The room was huge and the ceiling was a mosaic of stained glass windows and crystal chandeliers. There was a bar running at least 200 feet down the right side made of mahogany and brass. The back bar was also mahogany with beautiful cut glass portraits of working men and women from the Point with a gray blue sky above them and children sitting at their feet.

One little boy was watching the whole thing from a perch all alone in the corner on a warehouse roof. He was dressed in rags and his feet hung over the wall. He had two different shoes on that were many sizes too big so they were kept on with rags that wrapped around the shoes and around his ankles before they were tied. In large faded letters on the building it said GETTS. Molly pulled out her magic scarf and began to cry profusely. I held her for a long time before she got control of herself. When she seemed to be OK we turned and started to walk through the room. Toby met us half way across the expanse and said,

"Well, what do you think?" We both stated how beautiful it was and I expressed my surprise at the size.

Toby grinned at me and said, "Remember the warehouse you owned behind this building?" "Well, it had the exact same ceiling height as the opera house so I just combined the two into one building."

I said that I specifically told him I wanted a private entrance for some customers.

He said, still grinning, "You also owned the warehouse next door to the first so that is now a private entrance and stables for horses." "There is nothing like this place east of the Allegheny's." I gave Toby a great hug and he lifted me off the floor and whispered in my ear, " How do you like the mural Bart had designed and made by some kid called Tiffany?"

"I still remember those shoes and wonder how the hell you could run so fast in them," he said.

Toby gave us a tour, including the kitchen in the back and the beautiful iron gate at the entrance to the new garage. There was red carpeting leading to the rear entrance and a station for a formal guard to operate the gate. The furniture had not arrived, but he showed me renderings that were quite beautiful. He explained that everything was from the Pittsburgh area and even the furniture was being made by local craftsmen and that we would soon be turning out more for the retail market in the other warehouse that we owned. I decided to talk to Simon and find out just how much he had purchased at my request. I asked Toby about what retail market he was speaking of and he said, "I forgot to tell you that we had a big plant on the North Side with 30 or 40 Italian craftsmen making furniture. He explained that he hated to use the beautiful hardwoods for flooring, so he put it the use of very high end furniture. He said that our orders were already ahead of our capacity which meant that the prices had to go up. I began to wonder just what I had created.

On the way out we met John the chef. I asked him when we could open. He said three weeks and the smile on his face was about to divide his head in two. I looked at him with my most serious face and said," Do not make a fool of me." I will pack this place with everyone who is anyone on opening night," "I expect all the help and all the food and all the wine to be perfect," "Not adequate, but perfect."

"Find someone to drill the staff until they are like a unit in the Queens guard." "Do not open until everything is perfect." "Do not screw with me, I am not Toby and I will fry your ass in your own grease before I will let you embarrass me." I thought John was going to faint dead away. It had been too long since we started this project and I did not want him to think this was a silly adventure of a rich young man. "If you do this right, the world will be at your feet and every patron will try to get your attention." "You will be the Chef of the City and I will take pride in having introduced you to them. This is just the beginning and we have far to go.

Molly and I walked back to the Pub. When I sat down we shared a jug of ale. She told me to go home and rest. She said I looked tired.

I kissed her hard on the cheek and told Sasha to take me home.

Chapter 26

The smell of saw dust and fresh paint mixed with stale beer and the aroma of yesterdays cooking. It was still dark out and the world should be asleep. It would be at least an hour before the sun tried to work its way through the haze of mill soot that covered the city like an old worn blanket. I had been playing the piano for longer than I knew, but the music was soft and it allowed me to drift away into that place where nothing mattered but the sound of the piano. I had left the door open and the pub was full of very quiet listeners as was the street outside. Soon the hammers and saws would begin again and all would give up to the noise of construction and new beginnings.

My shoulders were hunched over the piano keys and I was wearing my night shirt stuffed into a pair of trousers. I had left home in the middle of the night with the need to have this music and this place surrounding me. Sasha had the horses and the cab waiting for me when I went out the door. He always seemed to know.

The audience was a mixture of the alley people who were still fighting for another day of life and many others that now occupied the Point with a level of comfort now that so many jobs were available. They had heard the music and came to inspect and then stayed to listen and watch me as I got lost in the warmth of it all. I never stopped playing when one song ended, I just started another.

My soul mingled with the notes and my fingers kept moving without any direction from my mind. This was everything, my sounds, my place, and my people. If I could not hold them all at once in my embrace then I could embrace them with the music. The piano was against an outside wall with the large window next to it. The few gas lights Molly kept on all night blazed and flickered as their reflections jumped up to the ceiling and played with the shadows they created.

Sometimes they moved as though in unison with the music and the people would tilt back their heads and watch the dance. I played on and on and the crowd outside the window grew larger. No one made a sound as they joined me in the rapture that is music, a thing created for the betterment of everyone. As I played I felt a warmth beside me and I could feel the heart beat of another close to me. Dale had his head in my lap and he holding me around my waist.

I could smell his hair and as I looked down I realized that this was as close to being a father as I would ever come. In a way I was sad, but I decided to do what I could to save more children like Dale. I sat up straight and played a lively tune to signal that the concert was over. The people were all smiling as they left the pub and many voiced their appreciation.

Molly scooped little Dale up and told him to go back to bed. She went to the kitchen and began making coffee and breakfast. I moved to my table, and the Captain came over and sat with me. The coffee soon arrived and I told Molly I was sorry about waking them up.

She smiled and explained that this was her time to get up because the men would soon be here to get their breakfast before work. A moment later several young women came in and headed for the kitchen. It seems business was brisk and Molly had finally hired some help to do the work.

Soon I could smell onions frying on the grill. Potato slices and corned beef would be added until there was a huge mound of hash piled high in the corner of the grill. As we sat and talked customers began to wonder in and take their seats. Molly, being Molly, asked me again about settling down and starting a family. The poor Captain just looked up to the ceiling. I smiled at her and said, "You know how I have lived and you are aware of some of the things I have done." "I love who and what I am." "There will always be those trying to get to me and a family of my own creates to easy an opportunity for them." "My family grows with those I meet and with those I learn to care about." "You saw my family a little while ago listening to the piano play." "I know the food kitchens will open soon and the alley people will be fed." "I saw the results of what we have all created in the others wearing decent clothes and having enough to fill them out instead of living the slow death of the work house." "You know that Bart and I will have more enemy problems to remove and you know how we will do it" "There is no place there for a wife and children."

Molly surprised me by not shedding so much as a tear. She had listened closely and she must have understood. She looked at me and said, "I hate the fact that what you have said is true," "I wanted more for you because you have been like my own child." "I watched you take over the Point and I was well aware of what that required, but most of all I watched what you have done to distance yourself from Toby and still you keep three men watching him all the time." "I know what you mean about the people having decent clothes and enough food because I remember when you traded everything you and Toby had for two weeks of food and a change out of the rags you were wearing." "You are right, the Point created you out of necessity, and you are creating the Point." "If you tried to change now they would find a way to kill you because if I have learned anything it is that there will forever be people that cannot abide success in those they see as beneath them." "I guess I got caught up in my own happiness and the feeling of safety we now have in this neighborhood." "We can do that, but you my son must be forever diligent." "There is always talk that all of this will be taken away and I try to ignore it, but we need you and Bart, and Billy B to keep it from happening." "The mayor tried to get to you but he is an old fool." "The next one may not be like him, so do what you must and we will be here for you."

I was pleased to have her understand and I was very pleased when the plates of food arrived. I was starving and breakfast is my favorite meal. The Captain and I dug into the food and Molly, as usual, was happy to see grown men eat. Not much later Toby walked in along with some of his work crew. He looked great and the hard work had put even more muscle on his giant frame, if that is possible.

He came to the table, kissed Molly and gave me a hug that lifted me out of the chair. He said he thought I was getting heavier and stated that it was about time. I asked about Annah and the children and he explained that she was pregnant again. We all laughed and he said that it was not funny. "I am not even sure how many we have any more, at which Molly, the Captain and I really started to laugh. Toby just shrugged his massive shoulders and grinned.

Molly told him there was a cure for that problem and Toby told her that he did not want to know what it was. We all laughed and I realized how very much I loved being with these old friends. I knew I would always be there for them and the Red Gate would make it happen. It was a comforting thought. We all talked while the crews had their breakfast and when they got up to leave Ray came over and asked if we could talk. He said that Bob and Andy would stay with Toby. I told him that was fine and we waited until everyone left. Ray explained that he was the youngest and considered the wildest brother, but the truth was that he had the freedom of the streets because everyone was afraid of his brothers. He further explained that because of this he knew many of the more dangerous people from the other side of the city, especially in the Strip District. He said that the word on the street is that Toby has become a target because his company controls so much business in the city and others want a piece of it.

I asked him if he could name names and he said he could, but someone was behind them with the money and he did not know who it was. I asked if he had told Toby and he said he came to me first because he knew Toby would want to handle it himself and I was specific in my instructions that Toby was to stay out of this type business. I thanked him and told him to give the names and all other information to Simon. I also told

Sasha to give him three hundred dollars. I sent

someone to get Billy B and bring him to the Pub.

When he arrived I asked what he knew about the

people after Toby. He explained that he just became

aware of it and he had men on the street looking for

information. He said that they would stay out of the

Point because everyone here watches any strangers. He

suggested I get Ben involved because Old Allegheny

was where Toby was most vulnerable and Ben had an

ear close to the ground over there. I had no intention

of going to see Ben, but if he knew anything and I have

not been told then there was going to be a problem. It

is not my job to be searching for information, it is there

job to make damn sure I am informed. I was suddenly

very tired and I wanted to go home and put on proper

clothes.

Sasha took me home and when I got there James

was waiting. He insisted I go right to bed and finish

my sleep. I was way too tired to argue with him. After

a nap of several hours I got up and James got my bath ready and laid out my clothes. When I was dressed I went down to the library where Bart was waiting for me. He had a stack of letters from my secretary at the company building. I still have never met her. He told me he had gone through them and other than the usual invitations, there was a long one from Ben at the Pawn Shop. Ben explained that there was talk on the street that Toby had an enemy because of the construction business. He also heard that there was to be a fire at the new restaurant right before opening night.

He had the names of several men involved, but no idea who was behind it all.

He further stated that he had a handle on the financial condition of every contractor now and before Allegheny Contracting, and none of them seemed to be able to be a threat. He felt most were happy that the business was being shared.

I suggested that Simon compare the two lists and see how close they are. It was now after noon and James brought in a tray of food and the three of us sat down to eat and to think about how to handle this. We were well aware that a fire at the restaurant would burn down half the Point before it ended including all the new buildings Toby had created.

CHAPTER 27

I lay in my bed and the quiet was like death, Each tick of the hall clock sounded like a gun going off and each creak of the floor was like the crash of a tree hitting the street. My ears were ringing like I was trapped in a belfry when a call for church services was being sent to the believers. This is to be the day. The dinner is tonight and I will pass through the Red Gate. All of my senses were acute and on edge. I had slept very little and when I did, I dreamed of my parents and we were all together and they had fine clothes and clear skin and I was showing them my home and pointing out the rooms they could have for their very own and then I would wake up and the clock would tick like a gun and I would stare at the room until I fell asleep and dreamed again.

Finally the sun began to come up and the yellow shards of light raced through the windows and stabbed at the room from corner to corner. I laid there waiting for the smells of breakfast food to creep up the steps and the footfall sounds of James echoed from the hall and I heard his voice telling me that my bath was ready. My heart began to slow down and I could feel the calm beginning to cascade over my body. James was standing in the door way and he went through his morning ritual. I gladly left the bed to slide into the warm luxury of my bath. After breakfast I joined Bart and James who were sitting by the fire in the living room.

They were sipping on mugs of hot tea.

Bart explained that the dinner party would begin at six o'clock and guests would arrive any time. He explained that time had little value to our guests because they had so much of it and so all you could do is give a date and hope for the best. I asked how many people he expected and he said any where from ten to two hundred depending how curious everyone was. John from the new restaurant would begin delivering food for the kitchen out back of the house at about two and he would cook it there. "It will be a good time to taste his cooking", James said, and the out door kitchen is as well made for preparation as the finest restaurant in France". I did not know what to say.

James said to me, "Why don't you go visit Molly or someone while we prepare." "Make sure you are back by four to get dressed, I will lay your clothes out."

I seemed to be dismissed so I left and headed for Steel City Brewery. I wanted to check in with Hans to be sure everything was going smoothly with production and shipments.

Sasha took me down through the Strip District and as I looked around I wondered who was plotting against Toby and what was I going to do about it. Ben had yet to gather any more information for me so there was nothing to do but wait. When I got to the brewery I was quickly ushered into Han's office.

He greeted me with a warm hand shake and a great smile. In moments two ice cold drafts of beer were delivered and his door was closed. He said he was glad I was here because he had a very delicate matter to discuss with me.

I told him we were friends and there was nothing we could not discuss.

Hans cleared his throat and he seemed to have a hard time getting started. Finally, he said," You know I admire and trust you very much and when I saw you and my daughter dancing together I started to think." "If you were interested in talking to me about her future I would be proud to discuss it."

A young Captain that you may remember from the ball has been trying to get her attention and I have no problem discouraging him if you would like me to." At that he let out a great sigh and collapsed into one of the overstuffed chairs. I knew this was very important to him so I approached the subject very seriously.

I said, "Hans, you flatter me beyond words and your daughter is as fine a young woman as any man could want." "I admit that I have thought of her many times." "You know who I am and you know how I sometimes have to conduct business to protect my friends and my interests." Unfortunately there is no place safe next to a man like me from those who wish to do me harm." "I will never marry." " It is too dangerous and I would live in constant fear for her safety." "You will be getting an invitation to the opening of our new restaurant." "Why don't I send this young man an invitation for him and a guest from me personally and the four of you can come together?" " I will get a chance to meet him and my intentions will be obvious with no harm done."

I think Hans was relieved.

He began to extol the qualities of the young soldier and his family. I told him I would dance at their wedding. We went over the progress of the business and the barrel company. Everything was in order and doing well. I went to shake his hand before leaving, and he grabbed me in a big hug instead. He said that he knew his business would be safe for his sons and daughter as long as I was around. How long would I be around? Perhaps a great deal longer then he thinks. What a concept to think about, living for centuries. I hope James and Bart will tell me about the past some day and let me experience their lives from so long ago. How were they brought to the Red Gate? Did they ever have a family? So many questions that I found my head was spinning. I told Sasha to take me to the Mayor's house.

When we pulled up in front of his mansion I got out and before I could say a word, the Mayor said, " Sorry, so sorry but I am on my way out and will not be back until tomorrow." "Perhaps Katherine can give something to drink after your long trip." I had no idea what he was talking about, but when I looked up Katherine was standing in the door way and just shaking her head. I asked her what that was all about and she explained that the poor man was terrified of me and when he saw my coach he panicked. She waved to Sasha to come in and she led me up to her bedroom. I thought, "Now this is a good way to pass the afternoon."

When the time came I said good-by to Katherine and Sasha took me home. James was waiting at the door and he ushered me to my room to dress. I could hear the voices of a great many people in the house laughing and talking. Our house was over 2500 square feet on the first floor alone, but it sounded crowded already. We had eleven bedrooms and I could hear doors opening and closing as the sound echoed down the four story staircase. James followed me into my bedroom and pointed to the clothes on the bed. There were white silk stockings and silk black pants. I beautiful blouse with a tight three-inch high embroidered collar and solid gold buttons was next to the bed on a hanger. It was infused with pattern after pattern of silk in every color you could imagine.

Everything was made of silk with pure gold thread stitching. There was a pair of silk slippers and a glass of our scotch on a stand beside the bed. James told me to strip off my clothes and he would dress me. I asked about the clothes and he said. "The People, our People, came from China a very long time ago as I have told you." "The first person to pass through the Red Gate was a very powerful leader of men. He came from the vast lands of Mongolia and conquered all of China. As with all others who entered China. He was pulled into the culture by the time he reached the center of the country.

For all intents and purposes he was Chinese with an incredible ability to lead the Mongols in battle. When he realized how far advanced the people of China were he insisted that all men of learning be brought to him. It is well known that after his death his body was taken out to the vast plains of Mongolia, and buried and his army of thousands rode their horses over the site so that it could never be discovered. What they did not know was that he had discovered the secret of the Red Gate and when he realized that he had conquered the known world and there was nothing left for him to do, he faked his death and he still lives in a temple that honors the old gods high in the mountains of Tibet." "He is often visited by those seeking wisdom." " You have read about him and you know him from history as

Genghis Kahn." "We are all the People and he was the first." "We wear these clothes to honor the Chinese who discovered the formula."

What the hell do you say to respond to that? After James helped me dress he asked me to wait until he also dressed. The clothes were wonderful. I could not believe how comfortable the whole outfit was. James looked like an emperor in his clothes and I was amazed how easily I could move in this most magnificent attire. When we went down stairs the place was full of people all dressed in beautiful Chinese silk. The gas lights bounced off all the clothing and each room was alive with color and voices and happiness.

Everyone moved like Bart and James as though their feet barely touched the floor and there was every race and color from the darkest to the whitest people I had ever seen. I was free to gawk and go from room to room like a kid at the fair taking in all the sites. No one spoke to me or even seemed to look my way. There were hundreds of people throughout the house and I marveled at the difference in their apparent ages from a few that looked to be in their early thirties to some that appeared ancient. Suddenly Bart was at my elbow and he whispered in my ear that these people were all here for me. He explained that they have all followed me from my time on the streets as a child and they were pleased with me as a candidate to become one of the People.

I asked him how they knew about me and he just remarked that I would understand by the end of the night. I asked him why they ignored me and he said that was because I was not yet one of the People. It was all wonderful and it was all confusing. Bart handed me a scotch in a very delicate Chinese cup with no handle and it was so thin that the ruby liquid showed through it. Bart was all dressed in red. Even his slippers were the color of rubies. He looked wonderful and for one of the few times since I had known him he was smiling and working the crowd of people like the finest of hosts at the grandest of banquets.

Suddenly a troupe of men in silk and with jewels on their foreheads entered the house from the back carrying platters of food. Everyone cheered as they began to set the food at stations through out the first floor. There was every dish possible including bowls of caviar, fine breads and every meat from hummingbird to yak. The platters never seemed to stop coming and the aroma of it all was intoxicating. Thank goodness I knew how to use chopsticks for there were no forks and knives. One whole section of the library was devoted to food from Arabia and only fingers were proper for scooping up the delicious dishes.

The whole scene was wonderful and I felt honored to be among them. I was grateful to be ignored because it allowed me to observe them all and feel the love that infiltrated the house.

They were mostly men, but there were several women and some of them were so beautiful that they took my breath away. They wore silk dresses to the floor that held to their bodies and had a slit up the right leg that reached their hip. Just to look at them made my heart jump. The festivities went on for hours and I was having the best of times until I heard the sound of a huge brass gong and everything became silent. Bart came and got me and led me to the front room where there was a low ivory table with a beautiful Chinese bowl with a series of dragons decorating the exterior of it. The bowl was not large, but it was so thin that I could almost see through it. Bart made me kneel in front of the bowl and he told me to watch and remember everything that I witnessed. The house was extremely quiet and I could hear my heart beat. Bart stood with the bowl between me and him. One by one each guest walked between me and the bowl and bowed to Bart. They put out their right hand with the palm up and Bart grabbed the hand and said, "We are the people" and placed his hand on theirs and held it tight, Bart was wearing a large bone ring with a huge ruby on the top and a long silver spike on the bottom. Before he let go each person smiled and said, "For the People".

They then made a fist and drops of blood fell into the bowl. I could only sit and watch the procession. No one looked at me. After a while there were no more people to come to the bowl. Bart took a tiny vase and pulled the stopper. He looked at the crowd and said," Should this human join us or die now? There was a silence that was terrifying and then a low sound from the People said," Red Gate, Red Gate, over and over and Bart put a drop from the tiny vase into he bowl and told me to drink it all. As I held the bowl to my lips the chant, Red Gate, Red Gate got louder until it was all I could hear.

I emptied the bowl and handed it to Bart. I was instantly pulled into the crowd and kissed and hugged with everyone smiling and jumping up and down for joy. Finally James parted the well wishers and everyone became silent. I looked around the room and suddenly I could read their thoughts and understand their language no matter what it was. They were all smiling knowingly and each one wished me well in their minds.

These were the People and I instantly loved each and every one.

Bart motioned for me to sit in a chair he brought over. Each person there walked to me and gave me a greeting. At the very end the old witch from down on the Mississippi came to me and kissed each of my cheeks and touched the gold nugget in my ear.

She said, "Welcome, my son, welcome and thank you for saving the little boy." When she walked away I noticed that the nugget in my ear was gone. The party resumed and everyone wanted to tell me about the new powers I would have. It seems that my strength was increased one hundred times and I could not be sick or cut or shot. While all of this was going on and my mind was swirling I had overlooked a man standing in the corner. He looked so out of place in an outfit belonging to a very long ago army that I was confused. He came to me and I knew in an instant it was my protector, Sasha. He smiled and said that he was the only one who had made war against the great Kahn and survived. Genghis Kahn loved his skills with bow and sword.

He gave him the gift of the Red Gate for his bravery and he was allowed to wear his old uniform as a symbol of his love for the people.

The party went on and on. I was having a wonderful time and I did not want it to ever end, but a few hours before the sun came up we decided it was time to rest. Bart and James came to me and I held them tight. I whispered that I would never forget this gift and then I went to bed.

CHAPTER 28

It was just past dawn when I woke up. My mind was full of excitement and the house was full of talk and laughter. My clothes from the night before were gone and, so I quickly dressed in my normal attire and, skipping my bath, went down the stairs. In my excitement I jumped the last two steps, but instead of landing with a thud at the bottom of the steps, I slowly descended to the floor. As I started to walk toward the living room I noticed that I could hardly feel my feet on the floor and I was gliding the same way Bart and James did. I heard in my mind James saying that they were in the library and that I should join them.

Suddenly, my head was filled with the thoughts of people throughout the house but if I concentrated on only one person then I could just hear them. It was strange and wonderful at the same time.

When I entered the library it was filled with people and food. Everyone was hugging me and again wishing me welcome. Bart explained that most of the People were gone, but he invited anyone to stay if they could. Some had a long way to travel and they were anxious to get to their homes. I filled my plate, got some coffee and found a place to sit down. The room got quiet and Bart said that they wanted to tell me about all the changes that I would now experience. Walter from the bank was first and he explained that in addition to the increase in strength, I would be able to control my rate of descent no matter how far down the distance was and I would always land on my feet. Harper, my attorney, told me that any of the People could contact me in my mind no matter how far away they were and I could do the same to them. Herman, the stock broker explained that any question I had about investments or the current condition of my stock portfolio was available by simply thinking of him saying the word portfolio. Bruce the undertaker told me that we can cross any body of water simply by standing with our feet in the water and thinking about the other side, even an ocean. My dear secretary Simon said that he is not the least bit deaf, as a matter of fact, all the People have extremely fine hearing much like that of a wolf.

He said that he likes the cover that being deaf gives him and he has been responsible for keeping all of the people informed of my progress. Dale, the coroner said that we cannot fly, but because of the strength in our legs we can jump very far, even up the side of a building.

There were many other things like being able to live with out food or water for long periods of time, but at this time my head was spinning from trying to take it all in.

Bart explained that I now had the blood of every one of the People. The group of People that came all represented everyone else and he was very pleased that I had such a fine turn out. He stated that every time someone came through the Red Gate with a representation of all the People, that person would have the strongest powers possible and now that person was me.

He said, "I do not know exactly what that will mean, only time and you will be able to tell us. James said that they would get into the details of the formula later and answer any questions I had.

All I could think of why had this happened to me and how would I ever repay them for what they had given me. As we all sat and talked a woman named Lorraine said," Let's talk about the local problem that we have." Bart explained that anything that was a problem for one of the people was a problem for us all. Bart further said, "We now know that the fire at the restaurant is to occur on the night before we open." "There are to be no less than fifteen thugs there to start the blaze." Everyone in the room got very excited and Lorraine said," Oh, it will be such fun and I can hardly wait for it all to happen," She turned to James and said," Do you remember the night we threw all those Roman soldiers into the Adriatic and how mad that silly Captain got?" James rolled his eyes and said, "There was no we, you and the other two women tossed them so far out into the water that most of them never made it to the shore." "Twenty men were gone forever." "Well," she said, "He should have told them to keep their hands to themselves." "If you had not flirted so much with them they might have left you alone" Bart said," Enough of the past, can we concentrate at the current problem"? Lorraine said, "What problem." "We will wait on the roof and when those fools show up we will ring their necks and toss them in the river." "I do hope John will have a special dessert for us all after and some decent champagne." "I so hate cheap champagne."

Bart looked at me and said, "I hope you are paying attention and you will be ready." Nadene said, "Oh for heavens sake Bart, why are you always so dramatic with the long cloak and mysterious look in your eyes?" "Lorraine is right, it will be good fun." "There are almost thirty of us so how difficult can it be?" "Is there any more French toast left, and please pass the wine." Bart rolled his eyes and explained that drugs and liquor of any kind have no effect on us, unfortunately. James said that all the invitations had been sent out and everyone was excited about the grand opening. Most were curious because they had never been in the Point and they thought it a great adventure. The invitations described the private entrance to those thought in need of it and that only added to their curiosity.

The ladies decided that they wanted me and Sasha to take them to see the restaurant. They also wanted to meet Toby because they had heard he was huge in every way. James looked at Bart and said, "This is going to be a long and interesting visit." At the last second Willivene, who insisted on being called Willy, Kerry and Dagmar all decided to go too. Everyone went to change clothes before we left. It is important to know that these five women appeared to be in their late twenties and each one was more beautiful than the other. I knew that parading around anywhere with them would draw a great deal of attention. I would quickly become the center of gossip in the whole town. After they left the room, I explained my concern to Bart. In less than a second, I heard the five of them screaming in my mind, "We heard that and you will just have to get over it." Bart and James along with everyone else was pointing at me and laughing hysterically. Bart said, "I guess you forgot that we have no secrets," and everyone laughed even harder.

By the time I bathed and changed my clothes the five women were waiting for me in the entry hall and Sasha was out front with the coach. They were all wearing riding clothes with long skirts brought tight to their tiny waist and even tighter jackets that pushed up and out every curve from waist to neck I sheer silk blouse was under the jacket and it left little to the imagination. Each outfit was a different shade of brown or gold and their tall hats were wrapped with a silk scarf of the same color as their skirts. They had tall boots on their feet that also matched the color of their skirt. I had to admit that I thought that they looked absolutely stunning, for which each one turned and thanked me. I turned to Bart and said, "Is there any way to turn this thing off." My comment was followed by another round of laughter. We all squeezed into the coach and Sasha took off to the restaurant. I was thinking about Molly as we neared the Point and they all got excited and said how much they wanted to meet her. This mind reading thing is going to take a great deal of getting used to.

The coach pulled up in front of the restaurant and Sasha jumped down to open the door and pull down the step. I got out first and then turned to offer a hand to the ladies. As they exited everyone on the street stopped and stared at them. I mean everyone from the pickpockets to the shopkeepers wives were dazzled by their splendor. They charged into the building and stopped dead. Even they were shocked by the magnificent structure. Every workman and all the other help were staring as the six of us proceeded through the dining area and went to the bar.

Toby was in heavy work clothes covered with sawdust as he came over to meet us. When they saw my massive friend they screeched out loud and ran to him and wrapped themselves around him like he had fallen into a pit of snakes and that was not to far away from the truth. They held on tight to him as they praised his work. Toby's face looked like an overripe tomato about to burst.

From the back of the room I heard a very loud voice saying, "Excuse me Toby but the children and I are about to leave." Toby managed to free himself from the ladies and make a break for the safety of his wife. She looked beautiful standing there pregnant with what they expected to be twins. At her side were two nurse maids each holding two more children. I quickly got between Annah and the five ladies and introduced them to her. Toby stood behind Annah for safety and the five ladies fussed all over the children which seemed to calm everything down for the moment. Fortunately John showed up and offered to open a bottle of champagne for them to enjoy while he showed them the rest of the building. They all fluttered to the bar while staying very close to John and brushing against him in all the right or perhaps wrong places. Toby decided to stay with Annah until the coast was clear. All I could do is shake my head and remind myself that there was no way to control them.

The five ladies sipped wine and fluttered all through the building with John completely surrounded by them. His face was beet red and he was sweating even though it was cold in the building. They flirted with all the workmen as they passed them and in short disrupted everything. I was frustrated until I heard Bart in my head telling me to relax and let them have their fun. He was saying that the women would be around me for the next hundreds of years when all the others were gone so just enjoy their harmless antics. He was right so I just watched and smiled at them. When they were done with the tour they smothered the poor John in thank-you kisses and I think I saw more than one hand rub the poor man in the most inappropriate places. John just fell into a chair as I led them out the door. All the workmen were cheering John and adding to his discomfort with their comments.

The ladies insisted on going into every shop and fussing over the new owners. When we got to the bakery they sampled everything and proceeded to order box after box of all of it, Angelo was beaming and when he handed Willy a sample of a chocolate tart she grabbed his hand and said to the others, "This is the poor thumb that was damaged by that awful street urchin." They all ran to him and insisted on examining the poor thumb and giving Angelo a kiss on the cheek for being so brave. Angelo could not even talk. Sasha paid the bill and followed us out the door carrying all the boxes.

The street was now packed with curious people and a great many kids from the alleys. The ladies opened all the boxes and handed sweets out to all the children and people. They were the center of attention and I found myself enjoying being with them. We walked across the street and into Molly's Pub.

She was waiting for us and before she could come to me the five of them ran over screaming, "You must be the wonderful mother Molly and we have heard so much about you from our dear Getts that we feel that we have known you forever." At that point poor Dale came out of the kitchen and was quickly scooped up and passed around from one to another while smothering him with kisses and shoving his little face into their ample cleavage.

They kept saying, "Our poor little Dale" as they passed him around. The good news is that Dale was just old enough and savy enough to enjoy it. At the first opportunity Molly rescued Dale and his grinning face and sent him into the kitchen with the Captain.

The girls all decided that they were starving and pleaded for, "Just tons of wonderful home cooking". Molly shook her head and went into the kitchen to order the food. Molly decided that any women with bodies like these five could not eat much, but she ordered enough food for a small army anyway. Kerry turned to me and demanded some of that wonderful Golden Wedding whiskey. I went behind the bar and got two bottles and seven glasses. I motioned for Sasha to join us but he refused so I took him a full glass anyway. We all started drinking and having fun. When Molly came back I got her a glass so she could join us. She watched as the ladies polished off the two bottles and I got two more.

They drank the whiskey like water and of course it did not effect them

When the food arrived we pulled over another table to put all the extra platters on. I sat back and smiled as they demolished all of the food and two more bottles of whiskey. Molly was so shocked she just watched with her mouth open. I told Molly to put it all on my bill, but she just looked at me and said, "If I had not seen it I would never have believed it." "It was a pleasure to watch and it is on the house." At this point the ladies were streaming into the kitchen and smothering the poor Captain for his wonderful cooking. Molly and I decided to rescue him and so we did. I had to promise to take them for ice cream. We went out the door and over to the candy and ice cream shop where they ordered huge bowls of ice cream and several pounds of chocolate.

Finally they said they needed a nap and we should go home. I was truly grateful for the suggestion. We loaded into the coach and headed for home. I was just happy to end this crazy frolic, but the truth was that I enjoyed them very much.

Chapter 29

The five ladies were loud and wild the whole trip home, but when we arrived they ran from the coach and headed for their bedrooms. Bart came out and got in with me. We were to meet with One through Nine back at Molly's. This was not our usual meeting. They had requested it and I could not refuse this very loyal group of partners and friends. Bart had nothing to say so I lay my head back on the stuffed leather seat and closed my eyes. I thought about all the people still at the house and I wondered how far they had all come. Bart answered with thoughts of his own describing how the invitation had been sent out over a year ago and there were people from all over the world that attended. He then asked me in Japanese while speaking out loud how I had enjoyed the ladies. I opened my eyes and answered him also in Japanese. He smiled and I realized that I could speak any of the languages that those who bled a drop of blood into my bowl at the Red Gate could speak. This pretty much included most of the world languages.

When we got to the pub Sasha locked the brake and we went in. All of the men and a few new faces were there. As I looked around the room I tried to picture each of the dirty faced Alley Rats that we started out with. Now they were prosperous young men. I was extremely proud of each and every one of them. As I went around the room we were greeted with hugs and I felt the love of a brother for each of them. I was introduced to the new faces and it turned out that they were the little brothers of some of my original group. I noticed that Toby was not invited, but I said nothing. Molly put a closed sign on the door and locked it. There were fourteen men there all together. Five, who was the oldest, spoke for all of them.

He explained that they were all aware of the threat to the new restaurant, as was just about everyone in the Point. He said that anyone that threatened any part of the Point threatened all of them and everyone that lived here. The word is out in the streets and in the alleys that no stranger is allowed in the Point after dark unless they are with one of us. Anyone else will be dealt with in the old way. Just then there was a knock at the door and Molly heard Billy B's voice so she let him in. Everyone said hello to Billy B and before he sat down he said he knew why we were here and that all of his men and most of the women would be out at night watching. He said, "Heaven pity the poor bastards that the women catch." They feel alive and safe for the first time and when I over hear them talking about what they will do it is down right scary." No one laughed because we all remember these women from when we were Alley Rats and we knew how cruel they could be. Five explained that they would all be carrying blades and they wanted it all handled very quietly and the bodies dumped into a coal barge docked on the Allegheny. I was not surprised that Five had taken over my roll as leader and I was very pleased to see what a good job he was doing.

He then turned to me and explained that only people from the Point would be part of this and that is why Toby was not here. He said, "I do not have to explain to you how much we respect and care about Toby, but he is not from the Point so he cannot be part of it."

"No one from here will ever talk about what is going happen, but many people do not know just who Toby is and we figure that is the way you want it."

"We have already begun patrolling, and there is a reward of a gallon of our finest whiskey to anyone that helps, and you can be sure that the night people living in the alleys want to earn one." "They would slit a throat for just a glass." At that, Five sat down.

I explained that I would be staying here in my apartment over the pub until this was finished. I said," This is the night they are to come since tomorrow we open the restaurant. We will stay close to that building while the rest of you cover the Point. Bart said that he would get a few things from home and join me here. After that Bart had Sasha take him home. Molly, being Molly, began bringing food out from the kitchen and setting plates and things for all of us. I took turns sitting with the different men at the tables and talked about how we all started and they told me about their investments and their wives and children.

No one mentioned that I was not married for they were all aware of the attempts on my life. Molly was having a wonderful time and we were all fussing over Dale. It had turned into a grand reunion and I vowed to find a way to meet all of their families. Some time later Bart and Sasha returned. Everyone wanted to be home and return before dark so the party had to break up.

While we waited there was a meeting down in the strip in the back of a warehouse. A man was standing on a large crate giving orders to a room full of men and one tall dark woman. They were all dressed in dirty street clothes except the woman who was wearing tight black slacks and a black turtle neck sweater that fit close to her and hinted at an exceptional figure. Her hair was as black as her clothes and it cascaded over her shoulders. She wore soft leather boots that were cut away at her knees and they shined like black velvet. Her face was stern yet sculpted to an attractive softness. She stood away from the other men as the man on the crate who was dressed in a beautifully tailored suit, held up five twenty dollar gold pieces and shouted that each one would get an equal reward after their work tonight. There were at least twenty men in the room.

"Tonight at ten you will spread out and enter the Point, each with a can of kerosene and matches," he said to the group. "You will spill your kerosene on the restaurant at your assigned spots, light it and leave as quickly as you can." "We will all meet back here" "There is no way they can die out all those fires before it burns out of control." When you get back I will have your gold waiting." After that speech the men left the room to wait for time to go. The leader walked over to the lady in black and said," Well Lou, what do you think of our plan?" She said to him, "I will love if it works, Sir Robert."

"Please", he said "This is America and I am just Robert here". "I do not mind financing your revenge, but your brother was a thief and a murderer." "You are not even sure Toby is the one that killed him." "He killed him and burned down the bar with him and his friends in it." "He did it to save his wife's father from his debt." "No matter what my brother was to others, he raised me and kept me safe." "I just wish Toby could be in the building when it burns to the ground."

"We should just kill him," she said. Robert got very serious when he responded, "I will have nothing to do with murder." "I will help you with this, but after that it is over."

When Bart returned to the pub he had Kerry and Willy with him. He explained that all the other guests left when they heard we would not need them, but Willy and Kerry insisted on coming even if they just waited here at the pub in case there was more trouble than we could handle. Bart said, "It never hurts to have someone in reserve." By the time it got dark we were watching the outside of the restaurant. One through Nine were scattered through out the Point while Bart, Billy B and I stayed close to the building with several of Billy B's men and a few women. At nine thirty a young alley rat in tattered clothes came up to me and said, "They are coming now." They are scattered around the Square and waiting, but they are anxious and they will not wait much longer." I asked him who he was and he said, "Billy Birdshot is my father". "I am called Little Bill and I am responsible for this section of the Point." He then turned and ran off into the dark. I looked at Billy B and said, "I am anxious to meet your wife." His face got red and he stuttered a little when he spoke. He said, "Well there isn't exactly a wife, you see, but I am responsible for a few wee ones here and about." One of his men spoke up and said, "A few!" "You have enough brats to start a small army and those are just the ones I know about." "What can I say except that the good Lord has decided I should go forth and multiply like it says somewhere in the scriptures, so who am I to argue with him?" With that said we all had a good laugh.

At ten a small army of thugs entered the Point from all directions. Some stayed on the main roadways while the rest began to work there way through the dark narrow alleys. Within a few moments the sounds of men in their last moments before death could be heard drowning in their own blood as unseen blades magically appeared from doorways and slashed at their throats. A few ladies of the night stood in the road and when the intruders got close, they raised up their skirts to expose themselves while they flirted. With their attention fixed on the view, death came in the form fine steel wire looped over their heads and pulled tight around their throats. Two women each took a wire wrapped handle and slowly pulled while the wire cut through each neck, bringing a slow death. Soon, a beer wagon with two draft horses made its way slowly through the Point. Body after body was thrown in the back.

Only two men got with in a block of the restaurant and they were brought alive to me.

I asked if they knew who I was and they said that they did. Then Bart got close up to them and said, "Do you know who I am?"

One man was so scared that he wet his pants. The other managed to croak out that he knew him. Billy Birdshot had his leather tube out and he hit the first man in his right knee. The man went to the ground. I told the second man that he had one second to tell me who was behind this and why before I let Billy ruin their legs. He did not hesitate. He explained that an Englishman named Sir Robert was supplying the gold for a woman named Lou the always dressed in black. The woman had a brother that ran a dump of a bar in Old Allegheny, but his real business was loan sharking. Toby's father in law owed money to this guy and Toby killed him and burned down the bar. Billy B and I looked at each other and laughed. I grabbed this fool and said, "Where can I find this Lou and her English friend?" He told where they were to meet after the fires were set. I explained to the two of them that the Point was no place for strangers and they should turn and run away as quickly as possible. I knew they would never leave the Point alive. The blood was up in the people and the gallon jugs of whiskey were distributed to just about everyone.

I turned to Bart and said that perhaps we should gather Willy and Kerry and visit a certain warehouse in the Strip. He thought that it would make the ladies very happy.

CHAPTER 30

I was such a small part of the events of the evening
that I hardly remember what all happened. It seemed
to begin when we were leaving the Point and the beer
wagon pulled up in front of the pub. The wagon was
loaded with the bodies of the would-be arsonists and
there was a troupe of people following and feeling the
effects of the whiskey bottles they were carrying. They
insisted that we listen to their stories of revenge
against the intruders. It seems that the majority were
captured by the local men and then turned over to the
women. The women were convinced that they were
about to lose what little they had and like a mother
bear protecting her cubs, they responded with a
viciousness known only to those that live in a sub
culture of anger and resentment. There were other
stories, but I tried to just shake my head and not listen.
I guess I had been away from the alleys too long to
take the brutality in stride. They spoke of torture and
death as though they had been to a party and that was

part of the entertainment. The good thing was that the bodies would be loaded into the barge and floated down the Ohio River for several miles before the barge would be sunk. Anything the carp and the catfish did not eat would float far to the south where no one would care. The people of the Point would never speak of it to anyone outside of our streets so it would be as though it never happened.

The four of us loaded into the coach and Sasha took us to the warehouse in the Strip District. He parked a block away and we walked quietly to the building. It was an extremely large warehouse with great access to the river and the railway. The building was brick and two stories high, but when we looked in the window it was obvious from the second floor lights that the small office area made up the entire of the second floor. The whole thing was built for stacking product high. There was a staircase leading up to the office. The outer door had been left open to leave access for the men when they returned. We walked in the door after searching the entire outside of the building and finding no one on guard. We moved as quietly as only the People can and made our way up the stairs. We could hear a woman we assumed was Lou screaming at Sir William. She wanted to know what was taking so long for the flames to be torching the Point, and he kept saying that she needed to be patient. The office was small, no more than twenty feet square. There was a large window that looked down into the warehouse floor some thirty feet below. In one corner was a small wood stove with an old roll top desk next to it. There were several more wooden chairs in the room and everything was covered in a thick layer of dust. The only other thing in the room was an old safe with the door hanging open. We walked into the room and Willy and Kerry grabbed the woman while Sasha took care of Sir Robert.

I explained that their men would not be returning tonight or ever for that matter. Lou spat at me and said that she would still get to Toby some how. I took a deep breath and blew it out slowly. I told her that her brother Angel was the lowest piece of slime I had ever met. I said," He was a pimp, a murderer, a thief and just about the worst that mankind had to endure." "He slashed at me with a knife and I slit his throat and burned down that eye sore of a building. Her eyes were spitting fire and all I could think of was how beautiful she was and I wondered what it would be like to hold her close. "Toby had nothing to do with it. He never even knew it was happening." I turned to Sir Robert and asked him how he became part of all of this. He smiled and said, "I came to America for the excitement and I found the beautiful Lou in need of assistance." "It all appeared to have the prospect of great adventure so I agreed to finance her vengeance and help her with the planning. I told him to put the money to be paid to the men on the desk along with any other money he had on him. He did as I instructed and got a big smile on his face. He said, This is what I love about you people." Everything can be solved with money." "If that is not sufficient then I might agree to add a little more to it from my bank."

I asked him if he considered how many women and children might have died if the fire spread, he just said, "Do you mean that trash that huddles in the filth of the Point?" "Surely proper people do not care what happens to those people." I nodded to Sasha and he threw Sir Robert through the window and onto the cement floor below. We heard the thud when he landed and we could detect him moaning.

I turned to Lou who looked like she was in shock. Kerry loosened her grip on the trembling woman and Lou just looked at me and tried to talk. I felt a touch of pity for her until she pulled the pistol from her pocket, shot me in the heart, grabbed the bag of money and ran down the stairs and out the door. I looked at my coat with the hole in it and at the bullet lying on the floor and said," James will never be able to fix this." We all started laughing and we were having a hard time stopping until we heard a loud moan from

Sir Robert. Kerry skipped to the stairs, floated down to the floor, snapped Sir Roberts royal neck and then threw him from the door way into the Allegheny River. We all decided to go back to the new restaurant and sample the wine. Sasha cracked the whip, made the horses wave good by and we left assuming that Lou was long gone from the scene of my murder. In the coach I asked Bart to remind me to have Simon arrange to purchase this warehouse and any other buildings in the area that are available. I said," I think it is time we have an interest in the Strip District.

Chapter 31

There are things that come to you in every possible form and It is up to each individual to grasp the opportunity posed by their presence. There are waves of scents like those that hover over a steaming soup or a fine wine that is learning to breathe as it swirls in the glass beneath your nose. The musk of a woman as her soft skin meets yours or roses floating their powers on a light summer breeze. Of course, there is touch, like your finger jumping back from a thorn or that same finger curled into the fur of a loving pet.

Music can march you off to war cradle your mind as you read a book or help you glide over the floor as you gaze at the most beautiful of creatures in your arms. The light of the sun can dazzle your eyes or a candle can add the mood of a room full of romantic intent. All of these things and the multitude more live in your being and beg to be appreciated.

A large fire roared in its stone castle, throwing much needed heat into the room. The scent of a fine bisque mixed with the deep aroma of superb wine from France and caviar cradled on crackers with just enough shaved onion and chopped egg to enhance the pleasure of each bite. The best part was the reminder of a boy who once stood on this very spot dressed in rags. I could not help but look up at the mosaic on the wall and remember those days and realize that no matter how much my life changed, that boy and all his fears would forever be inside me. The restaurant was beautiful and everything was ready for tomorrow. Of course John was a nervous wreck and the employees were running around checking everything again and again while Willy, Kerry, Bart, Sasha and I were having a wonderful time eating drinking and trying to drive poor John crazy.

Bart finally decided that we should leave them to their work and return home.

We loaded into the coach and headed for home. While Sasha took care of the horses we sent the ladies off to bed and James brought three glasses of our ruby scotch into the library and we three sat back to enjoy our drinks as the fire crackled in a language all its own and filled the room with warmth. Bart decided to take this time to explain to me how the formula works. He explained that all of the People had a small silver flask that contained a concentrated amount of all of the blood and chemicals from the very beginning. Thousands of years ago the Chinese developed the formula and added quantities of blood from all the necessary sources to create a final potent mixture. It was then dried into a powder and stored in air tight containers. Over the centuries we have all added our mixed blood that represents everyone who contributes to the drink at the Red Gate. It takes less than a grain of the original dried formula with a drop of our blood to make several hundred gallons like what we are drinking. James and I prefer to mix it in barrels of scotch, while others mix it with wine or water. How much and how often you consume the potent drink determines how quickly you will age. We have set ours at twenty years for every one year you age so in one hundred years, you will be five years older. You can adjust it to whatever you want as time goes on. Many of the people like to stay in the mid-thirties. Years ago men died in their forties. Now, they easily live to their mid-fifties. "Who knows what it will be like in a few hundred years. We allow very few people to enter the Red Gate.

How many of the People come to add their blood determines just how powerful the new member will be. "You will have more powers than any before because of all who came here for you." I know what we can do, but only time will reveal what you can do. Reading minds, crossing water, and being impervious to pain and bodily damage you already know about. "Your massive increase in strength allows you to jump very high and far, and we all can control our rate of decent, but we must wait and see what else will come."

I looked at them and said, "I can see perfectly in the dark, and I can feel the presence of any other person or animal up to several miles away if I concentrate"

" I can distinguish different smells by simply sniffing the air and I can read the mind of everyone, even those that are not of the People."

"All this came to me tonight while we guarded the restaurant", I said. "I must constantly filter all of these powers to keep my sanity or my head would spin from all the voices." "It gets easier with each passing moment." James and Bart were not surprised that the new abilities had come so quickly. They also stated that there may be more, but they might take time to develop. I thought about all of that and I was surprised that it all seemed so natural and I felt so normal. I asked them if anyone ever decided to die and James said that it happens all the time. "Many of us fall in love and after a while we cannot stand the mental torture of watching the person we love grow old and die", James explained. "If you give up the formula entirely, you will eventually die, but it will still take a long time." "The old witch down on the Mississippi stopped taking it years ago and she just seems to age without ever facing death." "The truth is there are still many things we do not fully understand."

We spent the rest of the evening talking about many things and basically enjoying the company of each other. I finally decided it was time for me to sleep, so I bid them both a good night and went to my room. As I lay in bed, I could not stop thinking about Lou and wondering what she was like under better circumstances. There was just something about her that I could not put my finger on, but I felt like I had met her before. I knew I wanted to rest before tomorrow and the opening of the restaurant. We had sent out invitations to just about everyone that was anyone in the area and a great many of our friends including all of my men. I wanted this place to be a center for everyone.

A place where people from all over the city would be able to meet and hopefully get to know each other.

Everything tomorrow would be free so I was wishing that everyone would attend. I made sure through Toby that all of the ladies would have the money to dress for the occasion and not feel awkward around any of the other guests. We hired some of the finest dress makers in the city to make their gowns and the pawn shop supplied jewelry to dazzle even the wealthiest that attend. I lay in my bed and thought of all these things until the feeling came to me as the smell of fine leather entered my nose. I could feel the presence of another person in the house that did not belong.

I could hear the footsteps as they tried to move as softly as a cat and I knew that the person was coming for me. Time seemed to stop as the feeling became stronger and the person came nearer to my bedroom. The motion stopped just outside my door and paused for what seemed forever before I saw the door handle turn very slowly and the door open just enough to allow a slim person to enter my room. Everything was pitch black, but my night vision allowed me to see the intruder easily. I noticed a knife in the right as it was slowly raised to plunge into my chest.

I stayed perfectly still and I did not make a sound as the knife began its descent.

Chapter 32

How fast can time move on? My assassin moved with the speed of a snail going up a hill of ice. I had to admire the stealth it took to get this far, although I found it hard to believe that the killer had gone undetected. What should I do? I guess I decided to wait and see just what this was all about before I reacted.

I could see the person perfectly, but there was just enough haze to keep me from total recognition. There are times in life when what happens now does not matter. Perhaps my current abilities made that even more realistic, but I still lay there with a clear head, and my curiosity was far out weighing any fear I might have felt. I looked up at the knife held high above and waited for the downward stroke and then I caught the scent of a woman, but not just any woman. I heard her say in her deep, sultry voice as she fell on top of me, "I know you are one of the People and I know I cannot harm you." I said, Then why the knife?" She laughed warmly in my ear and whispered, "You mean this candle in my right hand?" She then said, "Damn you, I should never have looked into your eyes." "My great-grandmother's grandmother told me after she put the nugget in your ear that if I met you again, I would never want to leave you." I was there on the Mississippi when you spoke to her." " I watched you take that boy with you and I tried to hate you, but the more I tried, Damn you." She threw herself onto me and our lips met and I felt the warmth of her body against me and I knew that those thoughts I had about holding her were nowhere near as wonderful as the real thing. I held her close and said, "Lou, are you sure this is what you want?

She said, "I know all about the People and I know all about you and I do not have a choice." "Just because we live down in the swamps does not mean we are stupid." "Grandma has let out just enough information over the many years to allow us to figure it out." She stepped out of the bed and took off her leather and then crawled under the covers and held me close.

The sun came up and once again the house filled with the sounds and smells of breakfast. I could hear Kerry and Willy talking loud and with great excitement down in the dining room.

James, as usual, was standing there trying hard not to act like he knew there were two of us in the bed when he said the bath is ready, and clothes have been laid out. "Perhaps you would join us in the dining room for breakfast?" he said. Lou ran to the bath without caring that James was there.

She was laughing as she plopped into the water with a sigh. She turned to me and said, "Come on, Getts, there is plenty of room for two." James rolled his eyes and I just shook my head and joined her at the spacious tub. There were my usual clothes laid out and I was pleased to see beautiful clothes also set out for Lou. She touched each piece of clothing and held them to her nose to smell. Her face was alive with pleasure as she began to dress. I told her I would meet her down stairs in the dining room, and I gave her privacy. A little while later, she came down the steps. I must say that she was the most beautiful woman I had ever seen. The dress and her hair cascading over her shoulders were like magic. Willy and Kerry screamed with delight and ran to usher her into the room.

For the next two hours I could not get a word in no matter how hard I tried. They told her that they heard her come into the house and they knew who she was and they knew her grandma and they were so excited that she found my room and on and on and on until my head began to hurt. They explained that they had trunks full of gowns and that she just had to go to the grand opening tonight as my escort. While they talked, the three of them stuffed their faces with food until they got up and ran up the steps making more noise than a room full of children. I just sat there with nothing to say. Finally, Bart asked me if I slept well and then he and James broke out in a fit of laughter.

I spent the afternoon at the restaurant, making sure everything was in order. When I was content, I went to see Molly. She was sitting at my table with a grin on her face. She said, "So, how was your night?"

I looked at her and said, "How in the hell do you know about my night?"

She smiled and said, "There are no secrets in the Point." I shook my head and thought, "I may have to move to the moon to get a little privacy." We talked about the restaurant and all of the excitement surrounding the event coming that evening.

Molly told me the Captain had a new uniform made and she had a gown made by one of the best dress makers in the city. She reached over and hugged me and said, "Who would have ever thought that I would be going to a great formal event in a big fancy place, and that place would be right here in the Point." "It is all because of you." "You could have left and joined the rich people, but instead, you never left us and you made a life here so much better." I told her that it never entered my thinking that I could leave the Point. "You cannot ever give up who you are." "Arrogance is for fools, and no one gains by running and hiding behind success." "All that changes is your ability to be honest with yourself." "I like the story about the boat that was anchored in the current where a huge river emptied into the ocean. They were dying of thirst and did not have the strength to row that last distance to the shore. When they saw a man standing on the shore, they shouted to him that they had died for want of fresh water. He shouted back, "Cast down your buckets where you are." It seems that the fresh water current was so strong that it reached out into the ocean, where they were anchored. "Too many people die of thirst before looking at the opportunities right where they are," I said. "I do not allow people to judge me and so I do not judge them."

Dale and the Captain arrived and Dale ran to me and gave me a hug. He explained that the Captain had taken him to see the new restaurant and had told him that he was one of the owners. Dale was very excited about the whole thing especially since the Captain said they would take him there for his birthday.

Dale sat with me while his parents went to check things in the kitchen.

He pulled his chair very close to me and said he wanted to ask me a question if it was alright with me. I agreed and so he said," Captain said that the boy in the picture on the wall was you." He told me that my Mom knew you when you were little and you really looked like that." "Is it true?"

I explained that not only was it true, but his mother took care of me in those days and helped me get by. I said, "That is why I always think of Molly as a mother to me."

He asked me about my real parents and I told him that I was an orphan just like him.

He thought about that for awhile and looked up at me with a big smile on his face and said, "I think that kind of makes you and me brothers since we have the same Mom." I grabbed him held him tight and whispered in his ear, "You are my little brother now and you always will be." I let him go and he ran into the kitchen yelling, "Mommy, Mommy, guess what, Getts is my big brother and I now have a mom and a dad and a brother." Molly burst from the kitchen and saw me sitting with a grin on my face and a tear in my eye and I said, "I told him you knew me as a child and I thought of you as a mother and he decided that made us brothers since we had the same mother." It makes sense to me so I guess you have adopted both of us." That was too much for Molly so she ran back to the kitchen with tears in her eyes.

The door to the pub opened at that point and Toby came walking in. I swear he was taller and more muscular than ever. The hard work was keeping him in good shape no matter how much his wife fed him. He yelled toward the kitchen, "Mother Molly, what does a hungry child have to do to get some food around here?" I lowered my head and said to myself, "Oh no, here we go again." When I looked up Dale was running out of the kitchen and jumping into Toby's arms.

CHAPTER 33

I walked the back alleys of the Point and my senses were attacked by the old smells, the ones I forever remember no matter where I went. My mind began to spin with the wonder of change and the feeling of happiness at the possibility of more and better for these people.

I was dressed very well for this part of town, especially in the back alleys but there was a change. Instead of beggars pulling at me and thieves checking me out, people came up to me and said things like, "Evening Getts, how are you," I remember you as a little snip of a lad running in these very alleys." I asked them to wait for me there until I returned. I ran to the work house and told several of the men there to fill a wagon with food and several gallons of our whiskey and follow me. In moments, the wagon was full and I returned to the alley. There was a crowd there and they were excited with the banquet. I stuffed a piece of bread in my mouth and grabbed a gallon jug to wash it down. I said, "Now, here is the company I love the most, and I promise you I will do this often because all of you are in my blood and all of you are those that I trust." I past the jug around and we all shared stories of the past. One of the men asked if I still had any skill as a pick pocket. I told him I was not sure and then handed him the contents of his back pocket. Everyone cheered and then checked their own pockets as the women all laughed. I told them I hated to leave, but I also told them to watch for the closing of the restaurant tonight because all of the excess food would be served in the warehouse behind the restaurant to all of my friends.

I walked back to the pub and got Sasha. I asked him to take me home so we could get dressed for the opening of the restaurant. I wanted to stop by and check on John, but I decided he had enough to do without me adding to his panic.

When we arrived at the house, the place was in an uproar of ladies, liquor, and lace. James met us at the door with a sad look of defeat on his face and explained that the three of them had been driving him crazy all day. I asked about Bart and he said he was hiding in his secluded rooms in the basement. I looked at Sasha and said that if we did not have to leave in an hour or two I would take my things and hide out in my rooms at Molly's. I made my way to my room and began to fill the tub. I fell on the bed and waited for the tub to fill. Shortly, I heard the water being shut off and I thanked my stars for James, who I assumed had shut off the water. I stripped and went to the bath, only to find Lou waiting for me in the tub.

What can I say, she is beautiful and I am human, I think, and so I joined her. We made very, very sure we were both clean all over. Suddenly, as I laiy exhausted in the tub, she jumped out of the tub and took off down the hall, shouting that she had to get dressed. James was standing just outside my room when she ran past, totally naked, and kissed James on the cheek as she continued up the staircase. James just shook his head.

These are the times when the earth quits spinning and the stars are frozen in the sky. The air is laden with all the smells that leave the trees and the grass and all of the manmade pollution that beat your senses into submission. I think I could have just lain in the warm water forever, but like all good and wonderful things, reality took over and I decided to get dressed. I went to the window and looked up to the stars and felt the impact of a universe pushing down on my head and wanting recognition. We are here it demanded and you are nothing beneath the vastness unless you can come to an understanding of the reality of life. The reality of life was much a mystery as long as I knew nothing of time, and how can I who have lived so little, understand time? I will continue on and hopefully, life will answer my needs.

James had a beautiful suit made for me. I enjoyed putting it on and feeling the soft texture of the wool and linen cloth. My boots were soft with a high shine and my silk shirt was a very pale yellow. I went down to the library to meet James and Bart who had just poured three glasses of our favorite scotch. James closed the door to baffle the sounds of the three ladies on the upper floors. I told them about my afternoon and the good time I had with the people in the alley. They made no comment and I realized that there was something going unsaid. I asked what was wrong and Bart said that they had lived a very long time and they agreed with all I was doing for the people in the Point. He further explained that it has been their experience that some of the people will come to resent my success and interpret the things I do as showing off and looking down on them. I was shocked by the very idea that I could be so misinterpreted and I said, "Surely no one will take my efforts that way."

They said nothing and suddenly the ladies were pounding on the door and demanding that we come out and see how lovely they looked.

Lovely is a poor evaluation of how they looked.

Willy was in yellow with a full gown to the floor and a low-cut front lined with fine Irish lace. Her tiny waist appeared even smaller by a wide ribbon as black as her hair that girdled her waist and then flowed down the back of the gown. She had pearls around her neck and a pearl ring on each hand that wore an elbow length blank glove. A long string of white and black pearls hung from each of her ears, and she was ready to dazzle everyone at the restaurant. Kerry was in deep red silk with the identical dress pattern. There were rubies around her neck, and a ruby ring on each hand that dazzled above her elbow length gloves. Her waist was wrapped in a gold ribbon that trailed down the back of the gown and from her ears was a series of gold nuggets and rubies. Lou also had on a gown of the same pattern, except it was silver and the lace in the deep cut from her neck was white with small diamonds sprinkled in it. Around her waist was a gold band that encircled it and streamed down the back of the gown. She wore diamonds around her neck and more diamonds dangled from her ears. Her raven hair cascaded over her shoulders and strings of diamonds were woven into the thickness of her curls as they lay on her shoulders. I looked at the three of them and I was speechless. Thank goodness Bart was there because James was as speechless as I was.

Bart walked slowly around the three women and finally said, "The three of you have the beauty that was the dream of every woman who graced the halls of Paris, Rome and St. Petersburg." "I have been in all of these places, including Versailles, and all of those women are put to shame by your beauty." Everything got quiet as the ladies realized that Bart spoke the truth from the heart. " We will wait for another hour before we leave because I want to walk into the room full of people in your company and for the first time in hundreds of years see the faces stair at me with envy,"

James and I were both taken aback and Willy got a special look on her face as she reached over and took Bart's hand. It was then that I noticed the yellow tie around his neck and a huge pearl ring on his hand. He was standing very erect and I realized how tall he was for the first time. I was now about six foot two and Bart was at least six foot. His hair was oiled and combed back into a neat yellow ribbon before it hung down his back. He had a neat thin line of hair over his upper lip and trimmed sideburns sculpted to a point that barely touched the hair over his upper lip.

He had startling gray eyes that had a rim of gold around them and damn, was he handsome. There was a small patch of black hair centered just below his lower lip and his teeth were as white as snow as he smiled at Willy. To see Bart smile was a treat in and of itself and I was pleased beyond words to witness it. He looked like the dashing men in my history books. I could see him leading a cavalry charge or standing like an oak tree as he delivered the telling shot at a duel. There was nothing of my old teacher in this picture and I realized that this man was the real Bart that had been hidden inside his cloak and wide brimmed hat. I could picture him standing in full uniform of the army of the Tsar with a Borzoi beside him and a fire crackling in a hug hearth at his back. Yes, I am sure he was in St Petersburg gracing those magnificent palaces and dancing with all the beautiful women. As these thoughts entered my head I was surprised to see the very pictures of Bart as he sent them to me from his own memory.

I thought, "These are the pictures and dreams that they all must let me explore.

CHAPTER 34

It was a night full of fragrance from the perfume that
swirled inside the coach as we traveled over the Allegheny
River, to the outside smells of the industries in the
Pittsburgh area.

The horses were high-stepping and the crowds of
people were lining the streets. We could feel the
excitement and I could read the thoughts of the people as
they watched the parade. They were pointing out each
coach and guessing who was in it. They had turned it
into a game and we were all part of it. When the coach
pulled up in front, our crest gave us away and we could
hear the sounds of the crowd as they called out for Getts.
I was proud and I was embarrassed at the same time. I
waved to those I knew and they cheered even louder. I
could hear them saying that I was one of their own and
didn't have a dandy coach and horses. The gas lights were
ablaze in front of the building and the place was
crowded with beautiful women in every color of gown
imaginable. We could see people milling about with

glasses of fine wine and one eye on the front door to see who was brazen enough to ignore the more private entrance through the back warehouse and subject themselves to the scrutiny of everyone when they entered off the main street. James, Bart and I exited the coach from the side opposite the restaurant and then waited in front of the restaurant doors for Sasha to help each lady from the coach interior. We made such a spectacle that the crowd grew quiet and all were waiting to see just who was coming. As Sasha took Kerry's hand to assist her step down, he turned and handed it to James. There was a gasp from the crowd as they walked into the room.

Next, he gave Willy's hand to Bart who was beaming with delight as he glided into the room with the beautiful Willy on his arm. I will never know, but I would bet that no one in the entire hall recognized him. He stood so strait and so tall with his flashing white teeth framed in his trimmed facial hair that I hardly knew who he was. I, of course, was last and since everyone knew me and no one had any idea if I even had an escort, all eyes were on the side of the coach as Lou made her exit. I walked to her and Sasha gave me her hand. I made a slight bow and turned her toward the entrance as we walked to the door. We moved slowly to the entrance and we were stopped just inside the door. John was waiting there for me and he looked magnificent in his black suit, high collar silk shirt and bright red tie.

He turned to the crowd of people, gave a slight bow and said in a loud voice, "I give you our dear friend and your host for the evening, Getts and his lovely escort, Miss. Lou." There was much clapping and even a cheer here and there and then we were swarmed with people shaking my hand as the ladies pulled Lou away to try to find out just who she was and did she had anything to do with my royal problems in eastern Europe.

The orchestra began to play the Blue Danube in my honor. Somehow, John had found out that it was one of my favorite pieces. I turned and Bart, always Bart, was bowing to me. I worked my way through the crowd and grabbed Lou, who was delighted with the attention she was getting, and escorted her onto the dance floor. We glided to the music and she was so damn beautiful and the building was so elegant, and the food smelled of heaven, and then my eyes focused on the mosaic on the wall and I saw myself in rags with those big shoes and the dirt on my face and I could dance no more. I pulled Lou close to me and I kissed her firmly on the mouth. I was astonished to realize that the orchestra had stopped playing and everyone had followed my line of sight to the boy on the wall. The room was very quiet and I did not know what to do. I was frozen in the middle of the dance floor. Only about half of the people there understood that that little boy was me and first and foremost of them all was Molly. She looked beautiful with her red hair and white skin packed into the mint green gown and covered in dark green emeralds. She walked to us and said in a loud voice, "I believe this might just be our dance." She turned to Lou and said, "Do you mind if I cut in?" The Captain took Lou in his arms, Molly pointed to the orchestra to begin and we danced away to the music as a great many others joined us on the dance floor. I thought to myself, "How many times had she saved me?" As we danced, I regained my composure and I held Molly tight. I whispered in her ear, "If I had seen you dressed like this before, the Captain would have never had a chance." She just smiled and said, "How do I thank you for all you have given me?" "You brought me the Captain and my son, and you made me rich. "Now you allowed me to have an evening like this where I am not just some tavern maid, but a lady dressed in a gown with precious stones at my throat and fingers." "People here come up to me and treat me with respect, even the Mayor and his wife."

"You have allowed so many of us to grow to a place we never dreamed of." "Look at your men and their families all around the room." "You made sure they were dressed properly right down to the jewelry so they would not be made to feel out of place." "How do we thank you?"

I just smiled at her and said, "That little dirty and hungry boy on the wall is still inside this man." "You fed me when I was starving and you guided me when I was lost." "Even tonight, it was you, my mother, that saved me again." "How do I ever thank you?" Well, I should have known where this was going.

Molly started to cry, and I shouted out that this crowd needed more wine. I got a great cheer from everyone and just then a dozen waiters appeared with trays of wine and trays of snacks. I surrendered Molly to the Captain and he handed Katherine to me. God only knew where Lou was. She was beautiful and as always and I must admit that it was all I could do to look at her and not slowly peel that gown from her body in my mind. She made several comments about Lou and I just smiled and asked about the Mayor. She explained that he was here and having a great time. He apparently was convinced that all was forgiven and he and his tattoo were both in my good graces. The truth was that I was glad for him. At the end of the dance I dropped my right hand a little lower down her back than what was proper and squeezed her against me and said that I missed her.

The bar was open and the food stations were taken away.

Suddenly, tables were being placed all around the room and chairs were put around the tables and a parade of waiters were setting all the tables with dinnerware. John stood on the stage that had housed the orchestra and announced that everyone should be seated so they could serve the dinner and begin the entertainment. Everyone took a seat and I made sure Lou saved a seat next to her for me. I wanted to go around the room and greet everyone. It was wonderful to get to meet the wives of my men and I asked each one about their children. It was easy to complement the ladies on their appearance because they truly did look lovely. I kept thinking about what a bunch of dirty little Alley Rats we were and how proud we all were to have been able to grow and change. I visited everyone, but my oldest friends were special. When I went to the table where Hans and his wife and daughter Rebecca were sitting I was quickly greeted by a young man resplendent in his military uniform and a smile as wide as his face.

He stood, gave a slight bow and thrust out his hand. While he was pumping my arm up and down he thanked me over and over for the unexpected invitation he received. Everyone at the table was smiling and Rebecca had a red face. Hans rose to his feet and introduced his soon to be son-in-law to me. "His name is Greg and he comes from a fine family," Hans explained. I told him he was a lucky man and I suggested that if he were looking for employment after the army he should contact me.

When I moved on I noticed a very well dressed Billy B sitting at a table with a lovely and quite buxom lady. Next to him was Simon sitting with an attractive woman of about his age. When I got to the table Billy B jumped up and grabbed me in a bear hug. He proceeded to lift me off my feet and shake me like a rag doll. Everyone was laughing and all I could think of was, "He will never change and for that I am glad." When he finally put me down, he introduced me to his lady and when she made a slight bow I wondered if perhaps they ran out of material when they were making the top of her gown. Billy B could not stop smiling. He told me that they were engaged and I wished them well. Simon stood and I shook his hand while he introduced his wife.

I made a point of thanking him for the substantial achievement he had made at the business and I made sure his wife was aware of my gratitude.

Simon was beaming.

I visited all of the ships captains and commented on their uniforms, and their lovely wives. I saw my attorney, the banker, my broker, and I made a fuss over the Mayor and the police chief and his son. I saved

Toby for last. When I got to his table he stood up and we hugged one another. I guess we each had a tear or two that we could not hide because Annah and her parents were all a little emotional too. Toby and I just looked at each other and Toby said, " I made sure there would be a suet pudding with raisin sauce for dessert."

We both started to laugh just like the two little kids that sat in that stinking hole so very long ago.

It was an inside joke that Toby promised to explain some time later. When I got back to my table the first course had just arrived.

Each place setting had a card that explained what each course would be and what wine would be served with it. All of the finest and wealthiest families were hear and John wanted to make sure they went away impressed with the food and the presentation. During dinner there was entertainment on the stage. There were several song and dance acts plus a comedian and a magician. Between acts the orchestra played and everyone enjoyed glass after glass from the never ending parade of wine waiters. When the seven courses finally ended, the men were invited to the bar for brandy and cigars while the ladies were introduced to the Ladies lounge which was Toby's special project. There was a huge sitting room with mirrors and stools for adjusting hair and makeup. Beyond that was a series of ten small rooms each with a toilet and a sink with hot and cold water.

The fixtures all came from France and the wallpaper was beautiful.

There were four women in uniforms working the area passing out towels, soaps, and tending to the needs of the ladies. The male rooms were similar, but simple and more masculine. According to James and Bart there was nothing like it even in Europe.

The evening was perfect and I danced with just about every woman in the room. I tried to dance with Lou as much as possible, but the competition was strong and she was having the time of her life so I just let her have fun.

I made a point of spending time with some of the older women that represented the more powerful names in the city. It was great fun to answer their questions with just enough information to keep the roomers about me alive and I even started a few more just for fun. One of the ladies asked if I missed Eastern Europe. I said, "Alas the pain of those times is something I try to bury in these fine mountains around us." "I can never return so I must move on." I laid my head on her shoulder and she said, "My dear, dear boy we ladies of influence must find you a lovely creature worthy of making you forget." She patted my head and said, "Would that I was just a few years younger and I would take on the task myself." I said to her, "I am sure that we speak of a very few years," and she blushed. Toby came up to me and said if I spread around anymore bullshit he would have to get the street sweepers in to clean up. I asked him how many children he had now and he said seven with the twins. I rolled my eyes and he said," Tell me about it, I can barely keep count myself." We both wanted to talk about how all of this had begun, but somehow, neither one of us knew how to start, so we just left it unsaid at least for now. Toby knew why I stayed away from him and he understood. I knew he was grateful and he knew that he was to live for me a life I could not have. He was my friend and my brother and I would protect him and his family from harm forever.

When the ladies returned the orchestra had just started up. They began with a very lively polka and I went to the table that Billy B was sitting at and I asked his lady for a dance. She smiled with a showing of beautiful white teeth and grabbed my hand like a steel vice. We hit the dance floor and I must admit she was light as a feather on her feet. I swung her round and round as we circled the dance floor and I wondered just how she kept her ample breasts from exiting her gown. I hooted and yelled like the folks from the old country and the orchestra joined in on the enthusiasm to the delight of all the dancers.

When the dance ended I gave her a big kiss on the cheek and thanked her for a delightful dance. She smiled and we went back to her table. Billy B was grinning like a chipmunk with a peanut. He said, "How did you like having a real woman in your arms?" I gave him a deep bow and said, "You are forever my teacher." I turned to his Lady and said, " Should you become tired of this much older man, feel free to call on me." She was obviously pleased with the compliment and so was my dear friend Billy.

As the evening slowed down from all the food and drink I finally got to spend a little time with Lou and the rest of my friends. Lou and I danced a few slow sets and we felt the allure of our earlier times together. I explained that Sasha would take them all home and return for me because I wanted to help set up the food for the street people as I had promised.

All of the guests were leaving and there was an atmosphere of satisfaction that told me we were a hit with the local establishment. The Mayor tried to thank me but he was so drunk that talking was an exercise beyond his ability. When the back warehouse was empty I began the task of setting up tables and chairs for everyone to enjoy the same fare we gave to the first party. I even had the orchestra set up in the warehouse to play for them. I was more excited to spend time with the street people that I was with the first group. It began all so innocently with people coming and sitting down to enjoy the food. I made sure there was plenty of wine and everything else. A dozen tough looking men showed up and their leader said, "You can kiss my arse. Getts you lousy piece of shit." "We do not need your leftovers."

They began turning over the tables and all of the people ran away. Again he looked at me and said," The Point belongs to me and I will kill any of your men that interfere with me." I walked up to him and smiled as I said, "If you screw with we you are dead." He laughed and stabbed me with a knife he had hidden in his sleeve. I just stood there as he realized that the knife had no effect on me. I then picked him up by the throat and threw him at least twenty feet into the wall of the warehouse. He did not die, but he did not forget the experience, I walked to him and told him to leave the Point and never come back. When I got home I was confronted by Bart who told me it was time I took a trip. He suggested I take Lou home to the lower Mississippi on our next boat to leave.

I was so angry that I knew I needed to get away so I agreed. When I got to my room I could smell the sweet scent of Lou's perfume. She looked at me and said, "Time to come to bed."

Chapter 35

The sound of the engine and the smell of the churning water was an introduction to the peace of escape. We left the Ohio River and entered the Mississippi and all the frustration melted away. I kept remembering the words of advice from Bart, "Take the lovely lady and leave for a spell." "I am here and all will be taken care of while you are gone. " Lou needs to be back home and you need to see more of the country if you are going to be here for the next god only knows how many years." "You cannot confine your thinking to this place when someday you will have to leave." It was hard to think about leaving, but I was aware that it would happen someday. Bart and I could communicate through our thoughts so I would always be in the loop. Lou was standing next to me and we were both enjoying the smells and colors of early fall. We knew we would arrive at the lower Mississippi in time for a slight cooling off.

Lou looked at me and explained that the old witch they all called Grandma wanted to see me when we got to her home. I was anxious to talk to her because I assumed she had some answers to my questions. I thought of her and my mind wanted to know so many things. She answered me in my mind that she was busy and I should not bother her until we got there. Boy, was all of this a new experience!

We stopped many times along the way to sell our barrels to wagon freighters. When I spoke to them they said they were taking the product west where the markets were better. I told them that was great and asked if we could help. They said their markup was much higher when they traveled west and what they needed was more whiskey on a more regular basis. I asked them where they needed it most and they explained that Columbus, Ohio was the ideal place. They gave me a place to telegraph them and I said I would look into shipping gallon jugs to Columbus by rail. The explained that it was the gallon jugs that they wanted most. Simon wrote it all down. After they left I thought of Bart and told him the details of the conversation. He informed me that he would take care of it. Because of the work house we could make the whiskey cheaper than anyone and the more we sold out of state the better.

This whole way of communicating was new and strange to me, but as I became accustomed to it I realized what an incredible advantage the People have. I also found out that it did not always work if the other person was strong enough to keep you out of their head. I knew Lou was hiding something from me, but I was always blocked from reading her thoughts by her very strong will. We made the trip a voyage of romance even though neither one of us expected it to last. I was amazed at how much she knew about the People. She spoke of it freely and I wondered why it was allowed, so I came right out and asked her. She said, "The people of the lower Mississippi know a great many things, but because we are viewed by the world as a cross between a dozen religions with witchcraft and voodoo thrown in, no one knows what is real and what is invented." "It is a convenience and a problem at the same time." It allows us to live apart yet we are seldom taken seriously." "I know what I know because you cannot keep anything secret in a society as isolated as we are. " "Many of my people never leave the swamps, and they live on boats their entire lives." "We are a mixture of white, black and Indian blood that has co- mingled for so long that no one is sure just what we are and frankly, none of us care." "We speak a blend of French from the trappers, local Indian with a dash of color from run away slaves and a spot of English." " The language is beautiful as you will see when you get to my home."

Damn it, I was falling in love because she was all the things that I was with a touch of Southern charm. I grabbed her and kissed her as though I would never see her again. When I finally let her go a cheer went out from the crew and I just kissed her again. She looked at me and said, "Help!" and I kissed her again.

Sometimes the reality of a situation is just dumb and you have to let the heart take over. The next days were wonderful and I pretended that they would never end. Everything smelled like her and everything I touched reminded me of her, and I did not want to be awake or asleep unless she was near. Every time I thought of Bart he was laughing and yet he made no comment.

When we reached the dock where she was to go home I left the boat with her. Within a few seconds there were two hundred plus people on the beach. The food was cooking and everyone was happy to see us. We were like one person in two bodies and the swamp people seemed to know it. I never felt so surrounded by family love in my life. People came up to us and kissed us and talked as though we had always been there. We ate, we drank, and we danced to music that was so full of life that I was transported to this place and this time as though I had been there all of my life. Lou never left my side until late in the evening when she took me by the hand and we walked over to the old lady they all called grandma. I kissed her cheek and she took my face in her hands and kissed me on the mouth and said to Lou, "Leave us."

She pulled me into her little shelter of branches and pine boughs and we both sat on the ground. She had a wonderful toothless smile on her face as she said, "I need you to listen and not to interrupt." "You are now the most powerful member off the People because you have the blood of all of us. This has never happened before in all these hundreds of years." I am the longest living one of us on this side of the world."

"For some damn reason I do not die no matter how hard I try." Lou is no blood kin of mine." These crazy Swampers have been sleeping with everyone for so long that they have no idea who is and who is not related. "You are here because Lou is to pass through the Red Gate and we only need your blood to make it happen because you have the blood of everyone." "The feelings you have are real and they are a result of our planning." "We need parents to those that come next and we all feel you two are perfect to fulfill the role." "In time you may tire of each other and need to separate, but you will always come back to one another because you are less apart than you are when you are joined." I know some of your questions and I will try to answer them."

"Lou will never be as powerful as you are because the drink you had was a combination of all the strongest of us on this earth." "She will, however, be second only to you." "Now, ask me your questions."

"Are we vampires, I asked? She cackled and said, "Hell yes you fool." "Do not listed to the other idiots, the blood drinkers did not die out, we just improved on our needs." " You may still get the urge to bite into a soft white or brown neck , but drinking their blood is more like a treat than a meal" " I still do it every ten years or so, but it is very messy." "The original vampires are treated as poor relatives even though many of us still exist." "What about the idea that we can turn into bats and wolves and even a mist?" "That comes under the heading of bullshit." "Some of the original blood did come from wolves which is where the werewolf thing came from, but so far none of us has been able to become a wolf." "One of the reasons we are so excited about you is if it can happen then you are the one who will have that power." "We have no idea what the concentration you have ingested will create."

"You must try to never fight the feelings that come on to you." "They are natural and they are important." "We all believe that the future of the People rests with you and Lou." "All of the rules we have had to live with may not pertain to the two of you, but only time will tell." "Come back here tonight at midnight and we will take Lou through the Red Gate." "There will only be the three of us, but you will hear the voices of all the rest in your head." "Send Lou to me now and come back at midnight."

I did as she said and then I joined the festivities on the shore. There was plenty to drink and food everywhere. Off to one side was a group of women dressed in long ragged gowns of many colors. They carried rattles that seemed to be made from human bones and their faces were painted bright red with black streaks from their foreheads down through their cleavage. On the other side of the crowd was a group of men naked to the waist. Their upper bodies were painted black with red streaks from their foreheads down to their waist. Each one was holding a human skull that they were drinking rum out of. There was the sound of drums in the background and the children were crying out in a loud high pitched shrill. Two women came up to me and pulled me to the bonfire in the middle of the crowd. They pushed me to my knees and pulled off my shirt. They began to paint my upper body half red and half black and then they stood me up. At that point I felt a strange power coming into my body. I raised my hands to the sky and they removed the rest of my clothes. Two men came and threw blue paint on me from the waist down. The children and the drums got louder and the women and the men began to make a loud whistling sound. I could feel the power pulsating through my body and the flames of the fire grew taller. Many men and women ran past me and slashed my body with their razor sharp knives and nothing happened except the power in me increased until I shouted out to the sky and threw my head back and shouted again. My eyes rolled back in my head and everything got very quiet.

My body felt like a feather and when I looked over the crown I realized that I was hovering far above them. I lowered my hands and slowly drifted back to earth.

I looked over and the old woman was motioning for me to come. Lou was sitting on the ground in a silk robe. I put on the bone ring that was handed to me and punched the silver needle into my hand. The old witch did the same and we pressed our blood into the bowl. A drop of the potion was added and Lou brought the bowl to her mouth and drank. The old witch took her hand and gave it to me. The voices of all of the People were shouting their happiness into my mind, and when we left the hut everyone was dancing and drinking. We celebrated until dawn and then we went to a special hut that they had prepared for us.

Chapter 36

The sun was forcing shafts of light through the roof

and sides of the little hut we were in. There was the dank

smell of the water from the swamp that surrounded us.

The night calls of strange birds and serious frogs was

gone, replaced by the sounds of the day traveling

creatures. Far off I could hear fishermen speaking in the

beautiful language of the people of the lower Mississippi.

Lou was still sleeping in my arms and I moved slowly to

allow her to sleep as I went outside to take care of my

morning necessities.

I went to the waters' edge to wash off the colors

from the ceremony the night before. I was still naked

so I just jumped off the boat dock into the water. The

paint dissolved into the brown of the river and I

climbed back up on the dock. I was alone and only the

dying embers in the fires were a reminder of the night

before. I watched an alligator glide over the river, and

a blue heron waited until the last second to take flight

and escape the hungry predator. I could hear the

thoughts of the disappointed alligator as he swam away.

I turned toward the thick jungle of trees and plants in the swamp and with little concentration I could understand all the thoughts of the predators as they slinked through the brush. A bobcat came out of the weeds and sat next to me on the dock. I scratched the fur behind his ears and he purred like a kitten as he climbed up on my lap. I could smell the blood in the fur around his mouth and he signaled my mind that he had had a successful hunt in the night. He told me that the predators were all made aware of me last night as I hovered above the fire and they were glad to have a human to talk to. Lou appeared from the hut and walked to me. She was aware of the big bobcat but said nothing. He tried to communicate with her, but it did not work. He turned to me and indicated his disappointment, and then walked back into the swamp.

Lou kissed me and asked if I planned to dress in the near future. I smiled and threw her into the river. I then joined her and we reveled in the cool water. She asked me about the bobcat and I told her about my ability to communicate with all the predators, and I suggested she give it some time because I was just finding all of my powers. The great alligator began to move slowly toward us and Lou became afraid. I laughed and said, "He could not hurt you no matter how hard he tried and I know why he is coming to us." When the big alligator got close to me he slowed almost to a stop and rolled over.

He had asked for a belly rub and after scratching the bobcat I felt that I could not turn him down, so he floated on his back and I rubbed his belly.

He rolled over, sent me a thankful thought and swam away. Lou just shook her head. We crawled up onto the dock, laid out until we were dry and then got dressed. About an hour later our boat pulled in and tied up to the dock.

They had picked up a load of sugar down river, but it was not enough to justify the trip so I suggested we head for New Orleans and see what we could find to haul home. I also wanted to stop at the orphanage that Dale came from and check out the conditions.

We got onto the boat and headed south. When we came to a small town just north of New Orleans I had the boat drop Lou and I off. We got directions to the orphanage from a few people in the street and we walked up the long hill to the old wooden building on top. I knocked on the door and a nasty old woman of about three hundred pounds opened the door and blocked the entrance. I politely asked her if we could come in and she said we should get the hell away before she had us thrown down the hill. I made a slight bow and grabbed the enormous leather belt that was holding up her filthy work pants and heaved her off the porch and into a rather large thorn bush. While she screamed we went inside and locked the door. A very tall fat man grabbed me by the front of my shirt and lifted me off the floor. I reached down and grabbed him between the legs and began to squeeze. He put me back on my feet and I escorted him to the door while keeping a tight grip on his crotch and then threw him in the same bush with the obese lady.

Lou and I went into the kitchen and inspected the stock of food. There was little enough to keep a flock of birds alive.

In the corner was a locked cabinet. I ripped the lock off and discovered a horde of dried, smoked and canned foods of every kind. We bellowed for all the children to come to the kitchen. There were about twenty children that came to us all dressed in rags. We fired up the stove and began to cook all the food that was there.

I went out to the porch while the children were eating and spoke to the two people that I had thrown out. They began to protest until I grabbed them both by the throat and lifted them off the ground. I explained that if I ever saw them again I would kill them and feed them to the gators. To prove my point I took them to the edge of the river and called to the gators in my mind. In moments there were a dozen gators at the rivers' edge. The smallest was at least fourteen feet long. I dropped the two and they ran for town. I thanked the gators and they swam away.

In about thirty seconds another fat man came waddling up the hill. He was pointing at me and shouting, "Just who do you think you are to abuse the two god fearing people that run this fine home?" I grabbed him by the ear and pulled him into the kitchen. I told the boys to remove their shirts and I made him look at the scars from the whip. He said that he was the Mayor and that he had no idea that this was going on. I explained to him that these children were in his town and they were his responsibility.

I then asked him if he knew about the boat named Surprise.

He said that if I meant the one that blew up all the pirates then he did.

I said, "I own that boat and if I ever hear of anyone harming these children again I would do to his town what I did to the pirate fort." I asked who might run this place properly and he thought for awhile before saying that there was a new preacher and his wife in town but they had no church and no money. I asked if he had a bank and he said yes. I told him to get the preacher and his wife along with the banker and come right back.

We kept feeding the children and soon the Mayor was back with the preacher, his wife, and a fat banker. I told the young couple that they would get a salary from me and a budget to run this place if they wanted to do it. The wife burst into tears and said it was her dream to operate a good home for children. I turned to the banker and asked who owned the building. He said that the bank did. I asked him how much he wanted for it and before he answered I warned him that I wound not tolerate a crook.

His number was a little high, but I agreed to pay it. I told him I would be depositing a large some of money in his bank and that my people would wire the money and my crew would be here with the rest to rebuild the home. I told him to establish a line of credit based on the deposit at all the stores in the town because the children would need food, clothes and material for the school we would be building. I turned to the Preachers wife and instructed her to hire a cook and several servants to clean and help in the kitchen.

I thought for a moment of Bart and he said that he was on it and Toby wound have a crew coming south on the next boat along with building material and Harper to handle all of the papers.

I told the Mayor and the banker that Crimson Investments would by buying this place and that we would look into other local investments. I said, "The Jane Carrol would be here to pick me up later and we would put the first of the money in his bank today." "The balance will arrive with my construction crew on the Surprise in a few days." The Mayor asked if we would be stopping here on a regular bases and I explained that we would if we had a good reason. "We have access to sugar and cotton among other things that we desperately need a market for." he said. I asked when he could have it here and he said by tomorrow. "If the price is right, we will buy it all," I told him. I left Lou and the new managers to inspect the children and begin a list of their needs while I walked down to the river. It was not long before the Jane Carrol pulled up to the small dock. Captain Dave came to the rail and said he could find no more goods to transport. I told him to anchor and leave the ship because I might have what he needs. When he and I walked into town I introduced him to the banker and the Mayor and suggested they go have a drink and talk business. I also told him to make a deposit in the bank to cover my new investment.

We carried bank drafts on the boats for purchases so it should not be a problem.

When they walked away I went to the general store and spoke to the owner. I asked him about business and he looked like his world had come to an end.

We sat at a small table and I could read his thoughts. The poor man was desperate and there appeared to be no good news in site.

He told me he had borrowed money from the bank to keep going, but the note was due and he could not pay it. I knew from his thoughts that he owed two thousand dollars. I asked if he was married and he said his wife and two boys all lived and worked with him in the store. I told him to get them. He asked me, "Why?" and I smiled and asked him to just do it. When we were all together I told him that I would like to buy twenty percent of his store for four thousand dollars, but he had to pay off the bank and agree to let me help him with the store. His family would all get a salary and we would split the profits with eighty percent going to him. He looked at me like I was crazy and asked me again, "Why?" I explained that my company often invested in good people and his family looked to be just that. I told him that we just bought the orphanage and we would be in need of new beds, sheets. Towels, clothes for the kids and stock for the kitchen. We would purchase it all from him if we had a deal. We shook hands all around and just then the Captain and the Banker walked in.

Big Dave was smiling. He explained that the town would build us a big dock for future business and that he just purchased all their sugar and cotton.

I asked what he thought of this place a stop and he loved the idea. He said that the bigger boats and cities had shut these people out on purpose and we do not need their other business so the little town of River Bend would be ours. We asked Tom and Linda where they got their supplies and they said by freight wagon and the prices were high because they had no choice. Big Dave said they should give him their list and we would bring it to them at a much lower price for their store. I said, "You mean our store because Crimson Investments just bought a piece of this place. Tom turned to the banker and said, "We will be able to pay off the loan when we settle up."

I told him we would pay it now on good faith so he would not have to worry anymore and the papers could be signed in a few days when our attorney got here. In the mean time I asked banker Boudreau if we could talk in his office and so he and I left. When we were seated in his comfortable leather chairs and drinking his fine bourbon I told him I wanted to buy forty percent of his bank. Before he could protest I put my hand up and explained that our business was growing rapidly and we needed two banks. We need a bank here on the southern Mississippi to deposit our profits in and we need a bank in Pittsburgh to service a small community. I assure you we will pay a very fair amount for our share of this bank and you will get a no risk part ownership in the Pittsburgh bank as a bonus. Our deposits should triple your current assets and this town will grow increasing the value even more.

I suggest that you speak to anyone of influence in Pittsburgh about me and you will get a positive response. I opened my gold case and gave him several of my cards. If you agree, you can work it out with my attorney when he arrives. I left the bank and went up the hill to the orphanage. Lou was busy and they already had hired several ladies to help clean and scrub the building and the kids. There was a line of wash tubs down the hall each with a child screaming from the pain of the soap and brush. The preacher and his wife were sent to the general store to buy whatever shoes and clothes they might have. The whole place smelled like soap and chicken soup. I looked over the entire building and decided it mostly needed paint and indoor plumbing. The kitchen needed new stoves and pots and pans. I decided to send them down from St. Louis to the new store on our return trip.

The town did not have a real school so I decided to build one next door. This was an ideal location for us. It would be a safe place for our suppliers to bring their products, and a good place for our boats to stop and refuel. I decided we would need a warehouse and a nice hotel eventually.

I wanted to take the long way along the river to walk back to the boat. It was thick with trees and the smell of the river was mixed with the musty smells of heavy ground cover.

It was pleasant until I was stopped by the fat man and his wife that I had thrown out of the orphanage. There were five riverboat men with them and they looked like they had spent most of their lives in the worst dives along the river. They smelled of cheap whiskey and sweat and I doubt if any of them had been introduced to soap in a very long time.

Three of them had knives and the other two had wooden clubs. The woman told me that these five were her brothers and they were here to get rid of me. I grabbed the first one by the hand that held his knife and I squeezed until we could hear his bones being crushed. The others ran at me and I just moved aside in an instant, grabbed one of the clubs and broke it over the back of his head. The other three were just looking at me and one of them said, "Who the hell are you?"

I told him that people call me Getts. He turned to his sister and said, "Crazy Captain Keys and the French cannon fighters work for him." "He is the one that killed all of the pirates." "Are you out of your mind?" "The woman with him has more family and witches down here in the swamps that you could kill in ten life times." He turned to me and asked, "What do you want me to do with my sister and the idiot she married?" I told him to make sure they go away and never come back because the next time I will not be so nice. He looked at me and said, "Yes Sir."

I gave them a roll of money and told them to see a doctor about the hand and have a drink on Getts with the rest.

When I got to the boat the Captain asked where I had been and I said, "Just meeting the locals."

CHAPTER 37

I laid in my bunk listening to the water splash against the side of the boat. The slight rocking convinced me that there was something to all the cradles and rocking chairs that many people started and ended life in. I had the porthole open and the soft breeze brought in the smells of the river and the heavy growth along the banks.

There was also the sweet scent of blossoms that seem to be never ending as you move further south down the river. It was very early and the sun was just peeking over the trees. They call this time of gray haze before full sun the wolf dawn, but I do not know why.

Perhaps some time I will be able to ask a wolf and find out. Now there is a concept that I never expected to think about. The Captain was up on the deck and I could hear his thoughts. He was pleased to have a full cargo to take to market and he was wondering how I knew where to make all of the investments and when to do it. I decided to dress and join him. Perhaps I could put his mind to rest. When I got up on deck one of the men from the galley came over and handed me a cup of coffee. I took a sip and it was delicious. I said so to the captain and he explained that the beans came from South America and they were the best in the world. I asked how he got them and he said he had friends at the Maxwell House Hotel in New Orleans and they got them from ships coming north. I smiled at him and said I think we will be making a trip to New Orleans. I further said that opportunity comes to the door of all of us, but to win you have to let it in. Sometimes you can create the opportunity like we are doing here at River Bend. Other times it is just reacting to an idea that comes into your mind.

The thing I know about the north is that there will never be enough beer and whiskey to satisfy the need. Until just now I never thought about coffee.

But not just regular coffee, but a product that tastes like this.

The Captain looked at me and shook his head.

He said, "I think that I am beginning to understand you."

I asked him how well he knew the people at the Maxwell House, and he said well enough, but Jim on the Surprise was very good friends with the owners and the crazy French gunners just might be relatives. I decided to have the Jane Carol loaded and gone as soon as ready. I told the Captain that I would wait for the Surprise and take it to New Orleans and speak to the coffee merchants there. I left the Captain shaking his head and went up the small hill to the orphanage. When I got there the place was wild with activity.

Breakfast was being served at a huge table in the clean dining room and the older children were doing the serving. The preacher was directing activities and the kitchen was alive as the breakfast pots and pans were scrubbed clean and prepared to start cooking lunch. There were three men talking to Lou and two more men I could see out back busy with another project. A couple of them looked familiar, but I could not place them. Finally Lou saw me and called me over. We stepped outside and joined the other two men. When I saw the thick bandages on the hand of the one man I knew these were the brothers of the lady I threw out of here. Lou explained that they came looking for work and they also told her who they were and what they had tried to do. She had told them to go clean themselves up before she would consider giving them work. The men were all very contrite and told me they had been loggers until the work ran out. They wanted to have honest work if at all possible.

They were clean and shaved and to tell the truth I was impressed. Lou told me they were building a chicken coop and a pig pen for the orphanage.

They were also going to cut fire wood. I agreed and added that they should start stacking fire wood for our boats to refuel down at the dock that the town was going to build. I also suggested that they watch for my construction crew coming in on the next boat and I would speak for them "We have a lot of building to do here in town and if you prove yourselves we can keep you working," I said. They were very agreeable and before I could say another word, they went to work.

Lou and I went for a walk and I told her about the coffee and how I was going to New Orleans to speak to the people down there. She thought for a moment and then said, "I am pretty sure we have several relatives working at the coffee warehouses and I know we have some at the Maxwell House." "Why don't I go with you and I can show you the sights of a truly special city."

I liked the idea and looked forward to spending time with her.

It was strange how our relationship seemed to work. I do not know if it was love, but we were drawn together like the animals that mate for life, except we would never have children and life was a very long time. We felt a strong peace between us and a joint sense of responsibility toward others, both the People and everyone else. Perhaps that is why we were chosen. Lou asked me about Grandma and she wanted to know how she was sure that the two of them were not related. I told her that the woman they all called grandma was several hundred years old before she came to the lower Mississippi,

She married a trapper that had eleven children and no wife. It seems that his wife died along with child number twelve due to a difficult birth. The trapper was a good man and in desperate need. Grandma wanted to experience a family so she gave up the formula and expected to die with her new family. No one knows why she keeps aging but never dies, but she loves her enormous family even though none of them know they have no blood relationship.

We assume that one day she will pass, but no one can even guess when. In the mean time she is very happy to be surrounded by so much family and to have the special love and attention they give her. Lou was very pleased with the story and she felt that it made the woman even more wonderful than before. She said, "She gave up everything to become a mother and a grandmother to all of those children. She even gave up her ability to live and never grow old for the love of the trapper." " How can that sacrifice ever be looked upon with anything other than love and respect?" I agreed with her and stated how much I wanted to know the stories of the other People. I feel there are many wonderful tales of their time with others over the centuries. I guess that is why I am writing about all of this so others will know of my experience.

We heard the whistle from the Jane Carroll warning all that it was about to depart. We waved to the boat as the paddle wheel began to churn up the water. Captain Dave pulled on the great whistle again as he waved back. With in a few days the Surprise would be landing and we would be off to another city. I was excited, but I was also a little home sick for Pittsburgh. Oh well, I had all the time in the world. We walked back to the orphanage and I was surprised at how much work the five brothers had accomplished and I told them so. Ramon, who turned out to be the oldest brother, explained that a few of the older boys staying there insisted on helping and that they were very good with their hands. He asked if they could have permission to teach them the use of tools.

He said that their father was a skilled wood carver and finisher and all five of them were trained to build fine stair cases and moldings for homes and commercial buildings. I said, "I thought you were wood cutters?" He explained that they were when there was no demand for their talents and they did not want to leave the area where they grew up. I knew that the demand for fancy houses in Pittsburgh was growing and I knew we had been bringing hard woods to St.

Louis for the same reason so the idea that we had skilled people right here where we also had young men to apprentice was too good an opportunity to pass up. I asked them to be patient for a few days. The work at the orphanage went on and the time went by quickly until we heard the whistle from the Surprise announcing that is was pulling into the partially built new dock. Lou and I hurried down to the river to see who all was on the boat.

The first one off the boat was Harper, our attorney, and as we shook hands he explained that he had all the paper work ready and that he had several bank drafts to deposit. Before I could respond the mayor and Boudreau from the bank were shaking hands with Harper and walking him off to the bank. They assured him that they had special rooms ready for him in the Mayors house for his comfort and they were anxious to do business with his investors. Harper sent me his thoughts.

He said he did not anticipate problems and then we both laughed. A crew of twenty men followed a man named Ed off the boat next. Ed introduced himself and explained that he and his men were ready to work as soon as they unloaded the boat and took the material up to the building sight. He also said that they brought a portable steam driven saw mill to cut extra lumber if needed.

Ramon was there so I introduced the two and suggested Ramon and his brothers help with the unloading.

I started to walk away when I heard a familiar voice say, "Hey little brother, aren't you going to wait for us?" I looked back toward the boat and Toby was running down the gang plank, He picked me up and held me in a bear hug, then he turned me around to see Annah coming off the boat. I ran to her and kissed her cheek. Lou was greeting Toby while I fussed over Annah. I asked about the children and she said her parents closed the restaurant for some much needed repairs and they had all the children for the time she and Toby would be away.

I was thrilled to see them again and I explained that we all would be going to New Orleans for a few days as soon as we got the crews in motion. Annah was very excited as she and Lou walked up to the orphanage. Toby and I went down to the local tavern, for want of a better name, so we could talk over a couple of beers. I was so excited that I could hardly believe it. I knew it would take at least a couple of hours for us to catch up. I knew something was wrong and it did not take me long to read what was on his mind. He was trying to find a way to tell me that many of the people in the Point would never change and there was building resentment about me for the changes we had made. I said to Toby," I am sure I will have people to deal with when I get back to the Point." "There will always be people that resist change no matter how positive it is." "Funny you should say that," he said. "I was just going to tell you that." I told him to relax and just enjoy this time together. There will be hell to pay when I return to the Point. The barges may well be full again with those that threaten all we have done.

CHAPTER 38

It was like old times with Toby and me. The ladies stayed busy at the orphanage while Toby and I looked the town over and made plans for all the construction. We decided to build a warehouse by the town dock along with a big hotel with a restaurant and bar. Captain Dave had ordered supplies for the general store and Captain Keys managed to pack them onto the Surprise for the brief trip from St. Louis so the store was now well supplied with everything we would need. Before leaving the bar Toby and I asked the owner where he got his beer and liquor and he explained that he had the same problem everyone else had. He paid high to get it from the freight wagons.

He said, "I hate this business and for fifty dollars, I would sell the whole damn thing, building and all."

The place was a dump, but the location was good and it had potential. I asked him what he would really sell it for and he rubbed the beard stubble on his chin as he looked at the rafters and finally said, "Are you

serious?" I said, "Serious as sin to a preacher." "Well",
he said, "Five hundred dollars would set me up just fine
somewhere else, so what do you think?"

I put out my hand and he took it. While we shook
hands I said, "Done and done." I told him to see my
representative that was working with Boudreau at the
bank and they would give him his money. He said, "In
that case the drinks are on the house".

We were to learn later that we not only got the bar,
but there were several acres of land behind it and a
snug little house that was neat and clean enough for
some of the workers while we were under construction.
I had no idea what to do with the tavern until Ramon
came up to us the next day and asked a favor. He
explained that his youngest brother Pat was the one
with the injured hand and he most likely would not be
much good with an ax or their specialty tools even
when he healed. He wondered if I would be willing to
hire him to run the tavern. He mentioned that there
were often a bad lot of river men that got drunk in the

tavern and with Pat, having four known brothers, it would be much easier to keep the peace. I had been feeling bad about the damage to the hand since I realized that the brothers were nothing like their fat sister. I told him it was a great idea and we could work out something to allow him to buy me out over time. He got a big smile on his face and asked if he could go and tell him. I told him he could if he got him down there to take over right away. He said, "He is with his pregnant wife looking for a place for them to live, but I know he will drop everything to keep his part of this deal." I looked at Toby and he was smiling. I told Ramon that a house came with the tavern so they could stop looking. The old tavern owner had his money and he was long gone. He was afraid I would change my mind. Toby said, "It is interesting how these things always seem to work out for you." I handed Ramon the keys to the tavern and the house and told him to look me up later.

I managed to get Bart back into my mind and I asked him to send twenty barrels of beer along with a barrel of Golden Wedding and one hundred gallons of our whiskey. He let me know that he would take care of it, then he congratulated me on the tavern and wished me well with the coffee. He was always one step ahead of me. Toby and I walked up the hill to the orphanage to check on Annah and Lou. Toby said that there was no way to get Annah away from children. We were both excited about going to New Orleans and happy that the boat was leaving in the morning. We had authorized our construction foreman to hire as many men as he needed to get all of the buildings under way. As it turned out people from all over the area were bringing logs to the saw mill we had set up so lumber was no problem. There was also a brick works not too far away that was anxious to sell us bricks at a very good price. Several of our men were experienced brick layers so I decided that the hotel was to be made of bricks.

Lou and Annah were busy feeding and fussing over the children when we arrived. Others were putting beds together and separating clothing for each of the boys and girls. The preacher was unloading a case of McGuffey Readers and dreaming of beginning school classes. Toby and I decided that we were in the way so we made our way back out the front door and sat down on the two chairs on the porch.

We saw the mayor trudging up the hill and waving at us so we just waited for the poor fellow to reach us. When he finally arrived we were required to wait for several minutes while he sat on the edge of the porch and recovered his wind. He pulled out a great white handkerchief and mopped his face, took a deep breath and let it out before he began.

He told us that he had wonderful news. Because of all we were doing, he was getting requests from business people from other towns to purchase building lots to establish themselves here in River Bend. He said, "The general feeling is that this will be a safe place to live and make a living." "Most of the river towns are infiltrated by crowds of rough men that make them unsafe." I asked him why this town was so special and he said, "The word is out that only the Surprise and your other boats can dock here and everyone knows how you handled the pirates."

Frankly, this was something I had never thought about. I was just looking for a safe place for our people.

I realized that we were going to need more boats if we were going to supply this whole town in addition to our regular shipping. Toby suggested that we look for boats in New Orleans while we were there.

Bart had apparently been listening to my thoughts because he informed me that he would talk to our people there about another boat. Without thinking I said aloud, "Good." Toby said, "What?" I looked at him and started to tell him about Bart before I caught myself and just said, "Your idea about looking for boats in New Orleans is a good one." A moment later Lou entered my mind suggesting that is was time for lunch. When we arrived at River Bend the entire town consisted of one wide street that ran parallel to the river. There was an old warehouse at one end of the street and the path up to the orphanage at the other end. The tavern was tucked in just behind the warehouse. The wood and brick bank was in the center of Main Street with the General store to the right. The rest of the street consisted of empty lots with a few fallen down buildings.

Behind Main Street was a stone path that ran up to the houses belonging to the mayor and the banker. Far back in the heavy growth were shacks occupied by the locals.

Most of them lived off the river or worked periodically on river boats.

Some were hunters and trappers, but they were even deeper back in the swamp. Everything looked as though it had fallen down or it was about to.

Nothing had been painted except a poor attempt to white wash the two big houses had been made not long ago. This was the first time I realized just how bad things were here before our arrival. I was so concentrated on the orphans that I just had not paid attention.

After lunch I had a meeting with Harper and Boudreau at the bank.

When I entered the office the banker was sitting in a chair beside his desk and Harper was sitting at the desk with a stack of ledgers in front of him. I knew what was about to happen because Harper had been sending me his thoughts ever since he arrived. Boudreau hung his head and could not look at me. Harper began the discussion. He said," The bank is in very deep trouble." "The few assets it once had have been spent on keeping the bank open." "A run on the bank would be futile". "There are no cash assets to pay anyone, except for the land that the bank has had to foreclose on." "The bank pretty much has title to the entire town and all the land around it." I asked if Boudreau was responsible and Harper explained that the fault was no ones.

He said that the Banker had used up all of his own money in an attempt to save his bank.

I asked Boudreau what he thought we should do.

He said, "I am a good and honest man." "I spent all of my own money before letting any other assets be used."

"I guess I should have closed the place down when all the businesses were leaving, but I kept hoping that things would change."

I would like you to take over the bank, but the debt you would have to assume is unfair to you." "Hell, the bank even owns my house."

I asked Harper what he recommended even though I already knew. Harper looked at Boudreau and said, "Hold your head up." You bankrupted yourself in an effort to save the bank and what is left of this town."

"We will take over the bank and all the debts if you will stay on to be the President and run it for us. You will get a salary and a bonus each year if we are profitable which I can guarantee you will be the case." "We will forgive the debt on your house and return the deed to you." "There is one additional condition." The smile left the bankers face as his thoughts took him to every possible terrible condition we could force upon him. I spoke up and said, "No one is ever to know what we have decided here." "You may tell your wife if she is aware of your current problem, but we insist that your dignity and your stature in the community remain intact." "You will remain the representative of this bank for any and all purposes." "Crimson Investments will send auditors here periodically to help you and we will be available if you need us. You will forget you ever met Harper and he will never meet you again." "We will begin to look for someone to help you as you grow." If you agree to all of this then we have a deal." The little round banker jumped out of his chair and stuck out his hand. I grabbed it, looked him in the eye and said, "Done and done."

We told the banker to go home and put his wife at ease while we talked things over. When he left Harper said, "You did a very good thing for that poor man, but we will benefit from it to a great extent." "We now own the entire area including the town." The only thing we do not own is the general store and we own a piece of that." When we sell off the building lots to new businesses we will get back our investment plus a huge profit." " I only see a few problems." " We will have to buy or lease more boats if you are going to stop all other boats from coming here." "We need to set up a water and sewage system and as we grow this town, you are going to need some law and order." I agreed and added, "We are now the town so the dock is now our responsibility so I want it big enough to handle several boats at once." "I think the best way to handle the boat traffic is to issue a license to dock to selected boat captains for a small fee." "They will be responsible for their crews and if they cause any trouble we will revoke their license." "If we do that we will probably only need one more boat." Harper wished me a prosperous trip to New Orleans and I left to find Toby. He was just leaving a meeting with the construction company owner when we got together. We owned twenty percent of the company and Toby was like a general adviser to them. As we walked he explained that the crew was working well and they have been hiring men from all over that keep trailing in as the word gets out that there is work here. I told Toby about the big dock and he suggested we build a permanent saw mill a short ways down river. The slabs cut from the logs to make them square can be cut in lengths to feed the boilers on the boats as a supplement to the regular fire wood. He also suggested that since the bricks were so cheap we should use them to pave the street before it becomes a mud and manure infested mess. I asked if we had the men to do it and he said he got the idea from some of the new men that were looking for work. They claimed to have experience with just that kind of work. He also said that they work for half pay because they are black. I asked Toby where they were and he pointed to the warehouse.

We walked over to them and I asked them to tell me about laying brick roads.

A man named Cleve stepped forward and began to explain what a serious process it was to prepare the roadway for the bricks and what kind of bricks he would need.

He sounded like he knew his business. Toby was impressed because he had seen many brick roads laid back in Pittsburgh and he felt confident about this man. I told Cleve that he will be the foreman and that he worked for Crimson Investments. I further explained that he would get full foreman's pay and his men would get full pay also. He would be responsible for getting the first of many streets bricked and they would be paid every week at the bank. I asked if they needed a place to stay and he explained that they lived back in the swamps with their families. He asked if they could spend their money locally and I must have looked puzzled because he said, "There are no blank people stores in the area for them to buy from." I told him to follow me and we went to the general store. We went into the store and I could see the look of surprise on the faces of Tom and Linda. We walked up to them and I introduced them and Tom put out his hand while a very shocked Cleve took it and they shook hands. I said to Tom and Linda, "Cleve is my new foreman for paving the streets with bricks." "He and his men along with their families will be coming here to shop." "They will also need tools to do their work that you can put on my bill." "I assured Cleve and his men that there was no need for me to open up a separate and very low cost store just for them that would compete with you."

If anyone has a problem with that you are to suggest they move on down the river to buy their things since you will remain the only general store I allow in town."

Tom said, "Welcome to River Bend."

As we left the store, I told Cleve that his children would be welcome at the school and any other place in the town. I knew from his thoughts that he was pleased and a little scared. I was sure there would be racial problems along the way, but those things would have to be handled as they happened.

Right now I just wanted to go to New Orleans.

CHAPTER 39

Her scent was all over me and I could feel her heart beat. She was so beautiful and she and I were together in my cabin on the Surprise. The constant drumming of the engines mixed with the sounds of the water escaping the huge paddles on either side of the boat were like a symphony of music to the lyrics of the insects and animals along the bank of the river. Peace was the thought of the moment and love was the scent on our bodies. We were headed for New Orleans and I was as anxious as a child to see this fabled city for the first time. There were several of the People living there and we were offered a house in a very upscale neighborhood to live in during our visit.

We would be met at the dock and transported to the home by friends. Toby and Annah would be staying with us. All in all it looked to be a special visit. I slowly moved away from Lou so as not to disturb her sleep and left the cabin to wash and dress. I then went up to the bridge to meet the day. The wolf light was slowly fading away and I could tell that this would be a beautiful day.

The current was slow and the boat was taking its time through this sand bar infested waters. A sailor was in the front left side of the boat, calling the marks to identify the depth of the water. There were many crocks along the shore and I spoke to them in my mind as we passed by. Suddenly the man calling the marks stumbled and went overboard. I heard the Captain calling for the sailors to grab guns to save him before the crocks got him. The crocks were swimming toward him as fast as they could. I yelled for the sailors to hold their fire and I dove into the water. The sailor was terrified, but I told him to relax as I directed the crocks back to the shore. They complained that it was not fair, so I made them a promise. I helped the man back to the boat that had come to a complete stop and he was hauled onto the deck. Everyone was looking at me and the waiting crocks as I climbed up onto the boat.

Without a thought, I went to the cage in the back of the boat and threw a pig and a goat overboard. The crocks left the shore and swam to their promised breakfast. Keys brought me a blanket. The crazy French gunners were laughing and telling everyone, "We told you so." Keys looked at me and said, "You are getting a reputation as some sort of devil."

I just looked at him and winked my eye and said, "Maybe they are right." Keys shook his head and mumbled something about people calling "HIM" crazy as he walked away. I quickly changed and Toby joined me on the bridge. We each got a large cup of coffee. It was wonderful as the boat picked up speed and the breeze was in our faces. Toby said he and Annah were having a wonderful time and he never imagined that the river trip could be so exciting. He said that this same water had flowed past us in Pittsburgh and he had never thought about how far it traveled. I suggested that we were both about to find out the answer. Soon Lou and Annah came up on deck and we went to the Captains' cabin to eat breakfast. There was fresh bread and butter with cheese and fish. It smelled wonderful and it tasted great.

Captain Keys suggested we enjoy the milk and butter because someone fed the goat to the crocks and there would be no more until we docked. I had a hard time keeping a strait face. We all loved the view as we traveled down the river. Children ran to the water edge to wave to us and we were surprised at the variation in the color of their skin. So many of the children were tall and hansom as they shouted out to us in a wide variety of accents. Sometimes it was impossible to understand what they were saying. Captain Keys explained that they wanted us to throw money for them to dive into the water and retrieve. We all started to throw bright coins to them and it was amazing how they managed to find them in the muddy water. Toby, Annah, Lou and I were having the time of our lives. It was all so peaceful and the day was full of warm sun. As we stood at the railing with the sun in our faces I looked closely at Toby and I could detect the first signs of gray hair at his temples. It made my heart ache to think that he was getting older. This was the first hint of my future without people that I loved. Lou was reading my thoughts as she held me closer and reached up to remove a small tear from my eye. Toby then said, "What is the matter old man?" "Is the wind too hard on your tired eyes?"

I grabbed him in a hug and I said, "I wish we could sail on forever." Annah looked at me and stated, "Well, some of us have children to get back to so don't be talking about sailing on forever." I bowed in submission and we all had a good laugh. The rest of the trip was smooth and uneventful.

We docked in New Orleans and we were met by a small group of the People and several beautiful carriages. After our things were loaded we boarded the coaches and left the water front.

A man named O'Niel rode with us. I thought how strange a first name that was before I remembered that he was one of the People. He looked at me and said, "It is a common first name here in New Orleans, not like Getts." We both agreed to just let it go and I looked in amazement at the beautiful houses and gardens along the streets.

I commented about it and was informed that it was called "The Garden District". " We finally pulled under the portico in front of a huge pink limestone house. It was three stories high with a tower to the right that had to be twenty feet in diameter. There were several acres of lawns and beautiful flower beds surrounding the house. Annah was speechless and Toby was dying to examine every square foot of the building.

We left the coaches and entered the gigantic reception hall. It was at least forty feet square and at the far end was a spiral stair case sixteen feet wide that curled up the twenty five feet to the second floor. A crystal chandelier six feet wide and eight feet long hung from the center of the room. The walls were a mixture of fine oak panels and silk wall paper. The mahogany floors were all but covered with ancient rugs from Persia. I told O'Niel how much I loved the house, as a group of servants came out, bowed and introduced themselves. From cooks to window cleaners they had every task covered. Toby and Annah were ushered up the stairs to a suit of rooms prepared for them. O'Niel introduced Lou and me to the head butler and he explained that the house had thirty six rooms including a ball room on the third floor.

There was also an elevator operated by pulleys and a water tank on the top floor where water was pumped up to provide pressure for the entire house. The butler further explained that he ran the entire estate including the grounds. He said, "My name is Harold and I welcome you to your home."

I quickly turned to O'Niel and he said, "Bart and the People decided that you needed another home for the future and we knew you would love this one." "These people will never pay any attention to how you look no matter how long you live, and when you need to settle here they will all be gone from memory." Lou hugged me and said, "We are going to love this place." "It is so beautiful." We were escorted to our own suit and it was prepared with a sitting room that mirrored my library back in Pittsburgh. There were several marble top tables and on one next to a worn leather chair was a decanter of our ruby scotch and crystal glasses. There were fresh flowers everywhere and an enormous bath in a separate room beside the bedroom. The closets were full of clothes for me and for Lou and at least forty pairs of soft boots. Bart thinks of everything. I fell into the chair and before I knew it a lovely young woman was pouring me a drink and another one was putting out a spread of fruits, cheeses and French breads with several kinds of flavored butters. We were told to just pull the bell cord if we wanted anything else. Lou flopped herself on my lap and said, "I could get used to this." We sat and talked for some time until Lou decided to ring the bell and have a bath prepared.

I took a brief nap before joining her in the tub. We had been assured that Toby and Annah would have a personal staff to explain things and see to their comfort. Dinner tonight would be at six and we would be given time to dress before that.

After a bath and a long time in bed resting we were alerted that it was time to dress. When we left our suit we were taken to the dining room where a table was set for fifty people and it still looked like a small raft in a great lake. The room adjoining was full of the People that I remembered from my time at the Red Gate, and many others that were strangers.

The strangers were all introduced and it seemed they represented the wealthy old families of New Orleans. Everyone was quite cordial and when we were called to dinner I was announced as the new master of the estate. I quickly looked at Toby and Annah and I thought he was going to choke on his drink and Annah was going to faint. There was an appropriate applause and I welcomed them all to my home. Thankfully the servants began to flood the room with serving trays before I had to say anything else. There was course after course and wonderful conversation. At times I abandoned my seat and visited with everyone at the table. There was a harpist playing and the evening passed quickly. When everyone had finally gone Lou and I sat with Toby and Annah in a smaller sitting room with silk covered chairs and a beautiful fire place. It was not cold, but the flames added to the beauty of everything as they reflected off the fine art work on the walls that spoke of the fact that Bart had been here.

Toby finally spoke out and said, "So when were you going to tell us about your new southern mansion?" "Well, the fact is that I just found out about it today," I said. Annah asked me how that could be possible and I told her that I had people all over looking for good investments and when this property came up it must have been too good to pass up. They both just shook their heads and I told them to just enjoy themselves. While Annah and Lou planned their shopping trip for the next day, Toby and I went into the walnut parlor to sit and talk. Toby looked at me and said, "How did all this happen?" "I still remember the first full stomach and the first soft clothes with no critters living in them," I told him that he should never forget those things. I explained that they are the foundation on which we live and build. "I will never enjoy a meal as much as the one you stole and we shared that day," I said. We were both quiet for a moment and I could hear his mind thinking about it all and being afraid that it would all go away. I looked at him and said, "There are powers in this world that you can never be part of that will guarantee your continued success as long as you keep on trying." "It is my goal to protect and help you and your family the way you protected me all those years ago in the Point.

"We will keep growing and keep building for as long as we can."

As long as we can had taken on a whole new meaning for me, but I knew Toby would not be with me forever and it caused me a stab of pain in my heart.

I even considered introducing him to the Red Gate, but I knew that my pain was nothing to what he would suffer watching Annah grow old. This was the first time I realized just how difficult it was to select someone to join the People.

After Toby and Annah went to bed, Lou and I sat and talked about all that had happened. She wondered if my actions with the crocks was a little to obvious, but I just smiled and asked her if she thought anyone would think it was anything but a strange fluke. "I guess talking to crocks is a bit out of their range of reason, but it sure gave the Frenchmen a taste of what they are calling Voodoo," she said. "This is a place of magic to all of the people with in hundreds of miles of the Mississippi Delta." "We are a mixture of French, Indians, whites and slaves." "Even they are a mixture of what ever the circumstances of their berth made them." "It is no wonder that the delta is alive with mystery and people claiming all sort of powers." "Christianity has been diluted with all of the customs and beliefs from our heritage to the point where it finally could be accepted here." "How else could black slaves believe in a white man as the son of god?" "The white slave owners even used the bible to prove that slavery is their right." "I will never figure that one out". "It makes sense that many of the People would migrate here from Europe."

We spoke of many things that night and it was good to become closer to her and understand her background more. When she went to bed I stayed up and thought of Bart and James. They quickly came into my thoughts with questions about the house and if I liked it and if Lou was having a good time. I praised what they had done and explained that I could now understand the lure of this place. They made sure I did not get carried away because there was still much to do at the Point and now River Bend. I told them not to worry and then I too went to bed.

Tomorrow we would see New Orleans and I was anxious to do just that.

CHAPTER 40

The sound was spectacular as it waved around the gigantic room. I felt myself slipping into that euphoria that only came when I sat at a piano, and what a piano it was.

A full size concert grand piano that was tuned to perfection and left calling to me from the tower corner in the ball room. The roof of the mansion was of the gambrel style with eight foot sides soaring to the vaulted ceiling twenty-three feet at the very top. The wooden ceiling was perfectly inlaid with beautiful paintings in oil on silk. The floor was covered in hand carved wooden tiles that shined like they were ceramic. There was a series of ceiling fans that were all connected by leather belts that worked its way down to a hidden crank on the wall in a small adjoining room.

Huge gas lights hung on the walls and a brass chandelier cascaded down from the center of the room with at least four hundred gas lights on it. I was playing with a vigor that I had not felt in a long time.

My fingers danced from Chopin to Bach to every piece I had ever heard. I only stopped once to throw open the windows and let the cool night air in. Next to me I had a piano lamp with a red crystal globe. It splashed just enough light to guide my fingers and turn the entire room into a rose colored pleasure den. I felt the presence of the great Kahn whispering into my brain that the Pleasure Dome of his grandson Kublai should have had such sounds. It was a thousand years ago that he started this whole thing and here I was entertaining him. The sweat was pouring down my face and I had to shut my eyes to keep out the salt. I knew I had been playing for hours and still I could not stop. Music does not please the soul, it controls it.

It is the great equalizer because my beloved Alley Rats were just as entranced as were the great minds of the world. Life should be made up of great meetings of all people around the sounds of music, but we will forever be to busy and too absorbed to find the release that only comes with music. I kissed the heads of some of the most dangerous people in the Point that had stood for hours with tears in their eyes listening to my piano. I would not trade them for an audience full of royalty. And still I played on. The wolf light just before dawn began to creep into the room and my mind became aware of a new day dawning. My fingers slowed down and the Blue Danube, as always, crept out of the piano and settled my brain. I could hear a great many voices in my mind thanking me for the concert. I pulled a handkerchief from my pocket and dried off my face.

When I stood up the staff of the house was watching me. Many of them had tears in their eyes. Harmon stepped to me and said I should look out the window. There was a crowd below on the street just outside the rod iron fence standing under the new electric street lights.

They were all looking up at me. I stood in front of the seventeen foot window and bowed to them all. They began to clap along with my staff and I hurried away with a blush on my face. Moments later I was in my suite and Lou rushed over to hold me. She said, "I never knew that you and the piano were blended like the night becoming day". I have heard you play before, but nothing like the last few hours." "Where does your heart go when you play like that?" I laid my weary head on her shoulder and said, "My heart runs away with my mind to a place that belongs to me and to anyone that wishes to hear." Tonight was a concert for the Great Kahn and I did not even know it." " All of the music belongs to the piano and the composer, and those that would hear, never to me."

I can feel over a thousand years of the People cheering me on because that is why we are here." " We are here to make it better." "We must never forget that."

I collapsed into the bed and after a few hours of sleep Lou woke me up and said it was time to bath and get dressed. I felt wonderful and I was ready to eat a horse. I bathed quickly and got dressed. When I went down to the sun parlor to eat I was greeted by many smiles. Harmon said, "Please forgive me if I am out of line, but the night concert you gave all of us here and on the street was a welcome diversion and greatly appreciated." I thanked him for that and I thanked him for keeping the magnificent piano on tune. He was surprised and said, " Oh no, I had nothing to do with that," " A very quiet man with a cape to the floor that moved like a crab that could float came here and worked on the Piano for hours in anticipation of your arrival."

I smiled and said, "Bart." "Yes, that was his name and he was very mysterious." Toby was there and he and I both laughed as Toby said, "Bart is very mysterious." Annah said, "I like him and I think he is very sweet, not mysterious." Toby and I laughed until I thought my side would split.

I drank coffee and ate a quick breakfast so we all could leave for town. O'Niel was waiting with a coach for Toby and I and two ladies that I recognized from the People at the dinner escorted our ladies to another coach. We agreed to meet at the Maxwell House for lunch in a few hours. I asked O'Neil where we were going first and he said we were going to the boat docks down at the landing. He reminded us that it was a very dangerous section of the city. Toby said to me, "So what else is new." "When we are together it is forever dangerous." I took a good look at Toby and I realized what a massive mountain of muscle he had become. He was no kid, but the hard work had added at least twenty pounds to his six foot six frame. He had to go two hundred seventy five pounds and there was not an ounce of fat on him. I chuckled at the thought that he would die if he knew I could throw him in the river. When we got out of the coach the five Frenchmen from the boat were waiting for us. Ramone said, "Holy mother and all the Saints, we are to protect you, but Keys never said that you travel with a giant." They had been so busy on the boat that they had paid no attention to Toby. We walked along the docks until we came to a big warehouse. We went in and were met by a dozen rough looking long shore men.

Behind them was a big man dressed like a pirate with a long knife in his belt. Six more men stepped up behind him, and they were as big and ugly as the men behind us.

O'Niel was trying as hard as he could not to smile.

The Pirate said to me, "I understand that you want to buy coffee beans to take north. "I own three boats, and the price is double to haul it and double to unload it," I asked him if anyone else sold coffee and he said that they did once upon a time, but now he was the only merchant, so pay the price or get the hell out.

Toby could not hold back any longer. We had negotiated many deals like this and he knew what was coming. He began to laugh like a fool and everyone was looking at him. The blood on my face was crimson when I hit the button on my left wrist and slashed the throat of that obnoxious fool. Toby turned and began crushing heads together as the French men charged the rest and cut them to pieces. O'Niel and I finished off anyone left alive. It was all over in a matter of seconds. O'Niel turned and said to me, "I love the way you negotiate." "We must do this more often." I said, "I think we should have a look at the business we just purchased and check out the boats."

We went and got the three captains of the boats and brought them back to the warehouse. I explained that the negotiations had been concluded and they now worked for Crimson Investments and their salary was doubled and they now owned twenty five percent of all profits. One of them stepped forward and said, "We are all friends with your current captains and we are aware of how fair you are." "We will dispose of this garbage and tomorrow we will talk to Captain Keys about setting up a coffee transport to the north." I thanked him and promised a bright future for us all. We now had two warehouses and three boats. I told the captains to talk to Keys about doing anything the boats needed to make them the best on the river. I said,

"Please tell me anything you think we can do to improve the business." "I am not as skilled as you captains are in this work, so I will listen to your suggestions."

O'Niel said he had people to take care of the paperwork and he had others to run the warehouse.

He explained that there was a real owner out there that the pirates had killed so no one would question what we did. He said, "New Orleans belongs to the strongest." "It has been like that from the beginning because the city has been owned by one country after another and therefore, it has been left to govern itself." "Most business decisions are made by the wealthy people in the better sections up town and carried out by their employees down here on the docks." "The fact that you came down here and took care of business in person will establish your reputation and remove most of your problems." "The mayor and the police chief will expect to be paid, but that has already been arranged." O'Niel looked at the five Frenchmen and laughed.

"Everyone down here knows who you are because of these friends of yours and because even the pirates are all afraid of the man they call "Crazy Keys", they were waiting for us in the warehouse." "They expected to kill us, and that is why there were so many of them." Ramone said, "Mon ami, perhaps now they know why we work for the Getts, no?" "He is always first with the blade and the bullet."

Ramone slapped me on the back and the five of them left, each with an extra hundred dollars in their pocket. I had no doubt they would be clearing out a tavern somewhere before the night was over.

When we got into the coach and were riding to town I apologized to Toby. I told him how I had made a promise to keep him out of this sort of thing and here I am, making him part of a brutal killing of nineteen men. I tried to explain that I did not expect that to happen, but he stopped me by putting up his hand. He said, "Do you really think I run the largest construction crew in the city with smiles and goodwill?"

"I have had to protect our business and myself from disgruntled competitors for years." "The more you isolated me the less your reputation protected me, so I and the Maletic brothers have used the techniques I learned from you many times." "Simon handles the payments to cover us and we keep him from being cheated or harmed." "We have had to fill a few barges ourselves." I asked why no one had told me and he said, "I made it clear that it was my business and you needed to think I was all roses and honey." "I did not want you to know otherwise." "I was with you from the beginning and we did many things to get to where we are." "It was too late for me to change and frankly I did not want to." "I let you handle the problems my father in law had for the sake of my wife, but I was more than prepared to do it myself." The Maletic brothers are wonderful craftsmen, but they are without equal in any kind of a fight, especially Ray." Andy can plan out any kind of operation and Bob is the perfect general to carry it out." "I am sorry to tell you all of this, but now you know that we will never change so let's hope for better for my children."

I did not know what to say. Here I was thinking I was protecting him by keeping him away, and the opposite was the truth. I asked him if Bart knew and he got a good laugh out of that. He said, "Hell, yes, he knew, but I begged him to keep it to himself." "The idea that anything got past Bart was beyond reality." "Bart has been like a father to us both." "He watches our lives and directs our path so long as we do not stray from his advice."

"I run a business and have a family my parents would have been proud of." "You create business and love the comforts of your music and your home surroundings." "I am content in the present while you are always building for the future." "We have both been able to fulfill our dreams because of Bart's direction." "Bart also knows that nothing is free." "Everybody pays and we are no exception to the rule."

What we just did is part of the price we pay to be who we are."

He looked hard at me and said, "Do you think they serve suet pudding at the Maxwell House?" At that we both laughed until our sides hurt. O'Niel looked at us as though we were crazy.

Chapter 41

The waves crashed at our backs and the sounds of fishermen gathering in nets and offloading cargo with good natured teasing were slowly fading away. I was thinking of the revelation given to me by Toby when Bart entered my thoughts and said that he was sorry, but he needed to keep his word to Toby. I explained that I understood, but it would take me some time to realize that we needed to let those that were not of the People, live their lives as they choose.

Toby was looking out the window of the coach and I could see that his mind was clear as though nothing had happened. This was our life and we do whatever it takes to continue on. The city was wonderful to look at and the influence of the Spanish, French, and English was everywhere, especially the French style buildings. I doubted that there was a more alive place on earth with people of every color and accent. I loved the blend of so many beautiful people, but my eyes quickly caught the slight of hands from the pick pockets and the con men on the street. Toby and I just looked at each other and laughed.

Some things were the same all over. There was one man in particular that was extremely fast when stealing from well dressed men. I could swear he was picking up a wallet, emptying the contents and then putting the wallet back.

I could not be sure because he was so fast.

A few yards later our coach slowed to a stop for cross traffic and I had the chance to concentrate on the thief. As I concentrated on watching him I realized that I could regulate time and his actions were in slow motion. Everything around me was also moving very slowly. As he passed his right hand in front of the mans' chest it pulled out the wallet from his coat pocket and dropped it into his left hand. His fingers removed the money and put the wallet back into his right hand that quickly replaced it in his coat. It happened so fast that no one even noticed. Now every time the poor man patted his coat to make sure the wallet was there he would walk on with confidence. By the time he actually opened the wallet he would have no idea where or when he had been robbed.

I was impressed. I blinked my eyes and everything went back to normal.

Well, I guess this is another little advantage given me at the Red Gate.

Thoughts of Lou entered my head and she wanted to know how far from the Maxwell House we were. I told her we would be there very shortly. A little while later we pulled up to the restaurant. It was a beautiful old building with all the charm of the city. As we entered we were greeted by a young man in formal attire who claimed to be waiting for us.

He led us to a table, where we joined the four ladies.

We were barely in our seats before they all began to talk at once about their shopping expedition and all the boxes and bundles that were being delivered to the mansion. The three of us just sat back and let them go on. It was such a pleasure to hear their excitement after our most recent experience.

Toby was all smiles as he listened to Annah and the obvious happiness that poured out of her. I realized just how happy it made me to see my brother and his little wife sharing their joy. The ladies explained that they would be continuing their quest for the perfect whatever after lunch and then returning to the mansion. The meal was wonderful and company was even better. What could surpass fine food and four very happy beautiful women? When the meal was over and the ladies continued their shopping trip the waiter came over and said he was aware that we wanted to see the owner. He suggested we follow him to an office in the back of the building. We followed and were greeted by a short man of about forty years with an excellent shape and beautiful clothes. He had thick black hair and pencil line mustache of the same color on his upper lip. His smile was sincere and his teeth were as white as snow. He greeted us in beautiful English with a hint of French style. He said his name was Steven and he was honored to meet us especially the very infamous Getts. I raised my eye brows and he waved away his comment with a laugh as he continued with, "You are well known for the service your boats have provided all the traffic on the Mississippi and with your recent acquisition of boats and warehouses here in our fair city." "We only wish to welcome you." I thought how fast information traveled here just like the Point.

It appeared that this place was the clearing house for all information. I could tell from his thoughts that he was being cautious, but he wanted to establish himself and his position here with me as soon as possible.

There were several men positioned close enough to us to come to his aid if he were threatened, but I could not blame him for that since he obviously knew what we had done just a few hours ago. I explained that I had no interest in his business unless he was looking to sell, but what I really wanted was to buy his formula for brewing his famous coffee. He appeared greatly relieved. He said, " I am but one of the owners of this particular place." "The original and home restaurant is in San Francisco and they have developed the combination of beans and roasting for all of us." "I have no idea how they do it and I doubt that they would ever disclose the secret." I had to admire them for that and so I just said that I would be grateful if he would just sell me a little for my private home use and promise to tell me if they ever want to sell their coffee to other restaurants. I explained that we would be honored to distribute for them. I think he was surprised and pleased at the complement. He said he would be happy to do both of those things. We stood up and shook hands all around. I gave him several of my cards and said, "I will now think of you as a friend and I hope you feel the same." "Please call on me if you ever need me." He gave me a short bow and said, "You live up to the words spoken about you by my cousins that man your cannons on the Surprise."

Somehow that did not surprise me. It seems like just about everyone from St Louis South is related. I replied, "They are a very important asset to the boat and to me."

As we left the Maxwell House, O'Niel explained that he had to see to other matters and he would meet us later. Toby and I decided we needed a drink and we wanted to find a nice tavern. We walked back down toward the docks and Toby spotted a lively looking place called, "The Silk and Saber," so we decided to check it out. The place was large, loud and smelled like sweat and old beer. Toby looked at me and said, "I think we have come home," and we both started to laugh. We walked up to the bar that was made of a huge tree trunk split in two and sitting on stone blocks. Many years of soap, booze and polish had made the surface smooth and the grain of the wood was beautiful. The bar was at least thirty feet long and the rest of the room was littered with small tables and an assortment of chairs and stools. The floor was planks covered in sawdust and the few lights were close to the ceiling and glowing from their gas flames. The biggest oriental man I had ever seen was standing behind the bar wearing a silk Chinese outfit with a black sash around his waist that held a long curved sword. I said to Toby, "So much for wondering where the name of the place came from."

He came over to us and said with an accent that could only have come from Main, "What can I get for you gents?" When he saw the look of shock on my face he and everyone else in the tavern were laughing. An obvious sailor sitting a little further down the bar got himself under control and said," You may as well tell them the story, George, even though we all have heard it before." The bartender puffed up his chest and explained that his father was a laborer in a factory in Main and he wanted his son to be a real American, so he changed their name to Washington and named him George. At the age of ten he went to sea on a whaler and spent the next twelve years as a sailor. He explained that he was treated like a slave at first until he started to grow and began carrying the sword.

"One day off the coast of South America, we were on our way home with a full cargo of oil when we were attacked by pirates," he explained. "They boarded us and in the ensuing battle most of my mates were killed, but I was still cutting the scum to pieces when they all backed off and offered me a share of the cargo if I joined them." "I knew that I could not fight them off forever and I had few fond memories of the rest of our crew so I agreed." "We sailed up the coast to Boston, where they expected to sell the oil." "When we got into the harbor, I went below and killed the captain and his first mate." "I went up on deck and began killing the rest of the pirates." "When all that was left was me and the members of the crew that they kept to man the ship, I dumped the bodies overboard and we took her into the harbor and lowered the anchor." "I went to the harbor master and told him my story." He took one look at me and decided that I must have stolen the ship myself." "They tried to arrest me so I got back to the ships boat and rowed out to the ship." "We cut anchor and headed for our home port with a skeleton crew." " Good weather prevailed and allowed us to make it home." " When the ship owners saw us returning we were met at the dock by them and all the families." "We had been gone for two years." "It did not take long to tell the story and everyone was glad that we at least saved the whale oil and the families would all get their share of the money." " I was given the captain's share since he had no family and I boarded the next ship headed south."

"I managed to make my way here and opened this tavern where you stand today."

Toby and I were amazed by the story and the room was dead silent after he told it. After a few moments of silence the man next to me said, "If you believe that bullshit he can tell you the one about how he saved the Royal Chinese Princess and her old man rewarded him with the money to buy this dump," and the whole place erupted in screaming laughter. We bought a round of drinks and had a great time with the men and our new friend George. He explained later that everyone knew who we were and they were glad to be rid of the men we disposed of. He said, "Who else would have the guts to walk into a place like this dressed like the two of you?" I guess we had forgotten that we were not back in the Point.

After a short time the five Frenchmen and a few more of our crew from the Surprise wandered in.

I asked them if they knew the story of how George got this place and Ramone said, "Which one?" and the laughter started all over again. We had a very pleasant afternoon and I must admit that I hated to leave, but we were expected back at the mansion.

We bought a final round and hailed a cab in front of the tavern to take us home. Toby was in fine spirits as we made our way through the city. For some reason I did not feel that we were going the right way and when we turned down a dark alley I was sure of it. The cab stopped suddenly and when I looked out the window there were five men standing there each with a club or a knife.

They opened the door and demanded that we get out. I exited first and when Toby followed me they all stepped back after getting a good look at his size. Before they could say a thing Toby was at them with fist and feet and I joined in. Toby kept saying how much he loved a good brawl after a day of drinking. We loaded them into the cab before any of them came. They would all recover, but they would be sore and without several teeth. We managed to turn the cab and drove back to the Silk and Saber. I carried two of them and Toby had the other three as we walked in the door.

We dumped them on the floor and I handed George some money. I told him what happened and they all had a good laugh. I asked him to give them a drink on me and Toby when they came to. I also asked him to tell them to look for a cab somewhere in the garden district where we planned to leave it. Our five French men were curious as to why we did not kill them.

Toby said, "Those little fellows were just trying to pick up a few dollars and it has been so long since I had a good fight that I was kind of grateful to them for the fun." Pat, the youngest Frenchmen of the crew said, "We will explain their good fortune to them when they wake up." Toby and I climbed up onto the drivers' seat of the cab and drove back to the mansion. When we got out Toby slapped the horse on the rump and sent him, cab and all, racing down the street. All in all it had been a very successful day.

Chapter 42

I felt lazy as I lay in bed and listened to the sounds of hammers and saws completing the vast amount of construction here in River Bend. The trip to New Orleans was in the distant past, but the memories would last a long time. Toby and Annah had hitched a ride on one of our new boats taking coffee north to Pittsburgh, and Lou was up fussing over the children. The construction would go on for a long time because we no sooner got one job completed and the demand for another began.

We were selling off lots owned by our bank as soon as the surveys were complete and a real town was forming quickly. The contractor we brought here from Pittsburgh decided to stay and he and his crew sent for their families to join them permanently. In addition to our own boats, we issued a docking license to a dozen other boat captains and the bank and our warehouses were both filling up. The Surprise spent more time on this section of the river and we began to use it to transport goods from St Louis and New Orleans to our warehouses here in River Bend. As I had hoped, the town was becoming a clearing house for all goods on the lower Mississippi. The boats we had given docking permits stopped often to buy products to ship further north or to top off a load they were taking to New Orleans. All in all business was booming and we were constantly looking for talent to run the operations. There was a certain resentment from other towns and rival shippers, but that is why we kept the Surprise in the area. No one wanted to tempt the anger of Captain Keys and his crew. Pat was doing a great job running the tavern and he and his brothers had not only added on to the building, but they were making it into a beautiful place. They enjoyed showing off their talents with wood by doing detailed woodwork around the entire place. My return on the five hundred dollar investment was well paid off so I signed the whole thing over to Pat and his wife.

They now had a son with the middle name of Getts. I told them he would hate them for it but they said they did not care because of what I had done for them. The other four brothers kept peace in the tavern when they were not in their factory turning out wood moldings and intricate trim pieces for the homes of the wealthy all up and down the river. The brick roads were all laid and the crew was working on the hotel. People were drifting in from all over to find work and few of them were turned away.

Cleve added greatly to his brick laying business, and his work went very quickly.

I had a meeting with the Mayor and Boudreau from the bank this morning, so I decided to get dressed and begin the day. I met Lou in the kitchen at the orphanage we looked out at all the children in the half finished school house. I had some coffee and a roll and kissed Lou good-by as I started toward the bank for my meeting.

A large boat had just unloaded at the dock when I heard a loud voice calling to me from the dock.

When I looked that way I could not believe what I was seeing. Angelo, the rolls and hammer guy, was waving and shouting to me from the dock.

His wife and three youngest children were with him. They all ran to me and we met in a confusion of hugs, handshakes and kisses. I said, "What on earth are you doing here?" Angelo explained that they were sick of the cold weather and since their oldest son and his family were running the bakery, they decided to come and start all over down here. He had arranged with our banker to buy property and Ed should have his store and living quarters finished by now, so all the bakery equipment was right here on the dock and he was ready to go to work. I could not believe it; we would now have a bakery right here in town.

As his wife was instructing a crew of men as to where all the furniture and ovens were to go, Angelo pulled me aside and said, "Things in the Point are getting very bad. The street gangs are making it difficult for anyone to do business there and the police are spread to thin to be of much help. "They say you are gone for good and the Point now belongs to them." "They spread stories about how you stole a great deal of money and left to live down here," I told him not to worry because I was returning very soon and I would handle it.

He seemed very relieved. I explained about my meeting and promised to see him later.

As I walked to the bank I thought about Bart and told him about Angelo. He relayed to me that the entire city was having problems with the gangs as more and more immigrants came to find work that either did not exist or paid slave wages. He explained that these things come with too much industrial growth in too short a time. He suggested we develop a plan when I got back, then he asked if Angelo got there safely. I explained that I had just greeted his family at the dock and they were all fine. Then I went to my meeting.

Boudreau and the Mayor were waiting for me in his office. We all sat down at a large meeting table. I told them we had three things that needed to be accomplished. We needed to lay out all the streets and get them bricked right away. We need a police force to control the problems that come with such rapid growth and we need water and sewage in every building of any kind. The whole thing is to be funded by a real estate tax, and docking fees. I explained that I would be leaving soon for Pittsburgh, but that I would stay in touch through the various ship captains that were constantly going up and down the river. Ed, who was the head contractor had informed them of a number of people that had drifted into town that knew how to design and direct the building of a network of sewage and water systems, I told them to have Ed and these men get it done. They further explained that my surveyor was working with a friend that was an engineer from St Louis on laying out the system of roads. I explained that I had some ideas about a police force but I would listen to any they might have. They could not think of any at the time so I suggested we discuss it at a later date.

After the mayor left I asked Boudreau how he was doing. He said, "I cannot tell you how happy my wife and I are." "I love coming to work and being part of all that we are accomplishing, she has even talked her nephew who is a doctor into coming here and opening a clinic." I had forgotten about that particular need. I told Boudreau to give the young man all the money he required to build his clinic at very low interest.

Tell him that I would put him on our payroll as the company doctor to take care of all our workers and everyone at the orphanage to cover the debt.

I suggested he inform Ed about it so he could get busy with the clinic building as soon as possible. I also told him that all of the crew members on our boats will also be his patients. There are so many accidents in the construction and shipping business that there is a great need for a clinic here on the lower Mississippi.

I was happy to hear that we would have one more service available here in River Bend. I now needed to return home and deal with the problems there. It never seemed to end.

Lou decided to stay for a while to finish work at the orphanage so I took the next boat going north and arrived in Pittsburgh a few weeks later. Bart, Sasha, James and I spoke often through mind contact during the trip and by the time we arrived in Pittsburgh I had a very good idea of the situation there. When I asked about Willy she interrupted our thoughts and said that she and, "her Bart", were doing just fine. I could see the red on his face even from the boat. James and Sasha were laughing and I was just happy for the both of them.

When I got off the boat Sasha was waiting for me with the coach. We went directly to Molly's where we met James and Bart. Of course Molly had to fuss over me before I could do anything, but she knew our meeting was important so she surrendered me to them sooner than she normally would have. We were all gathered at the usual table and the place was pretty much empty.

Simon was there a moment after I arrived. Simon had taken on a different roll now that I had passed through the Red Gate. He was an organizer of first rate and he now had a position of leadership in our group. He explained that we could only help with the problems that were now happening in the city.

Before the Red Gate I was easily the leader and the developer of the street programs and it was fine for me to take a leading role in the Point and other sections of the city, but now we must be on the sidelines and only get involved when it is necessary to save our friends.

He said, "All of these people will be dead and the city will constantly change while we will still be alive." We must let them live and evolve as much on their own as we can." "Getts, I know you want to charge in and take over, but you cannot." "What will be a lifetime to them will be a brief moment to us so you must take a secondary role at the most."

"You have trained good people from the time you were a child, but if you think back, Bart only helped and guided you."

"He never interfered with your plans."

"Molly and Billy B were the closest to you during those times."

"Now you must do for others only in the capacity that Bart did for you."

"You need to think about all I have said."

"Now you know why we never told you about your friend Toby."

"You can look out for him and guide him, but he is becoming a very special leader and the only reason he has held back is because of his respect for you." "Move into the shadows the way Bart always has."

"Now, I must announce that Bart and I are leaving for a new life in Paris." James and Sasha will be staying with you for now, but we want to start over again."

Simon turned to Bart and asked, "How long has it been since you lived in Paris?" Bart smiled and said, "Only about ninety years." Simon said, "Perfect."

"Just wait until you see my town home." Bart answered, "Just wait until you see my villa on the Mediterranean." At that they both got up and waked out the door chatting like two old hens. Sasha said, "That is the last we will see of them here in Pittsburgh for at least a century." I was confused. I asked him when they were leaving and he explained that they had just left to get on the train to the coast to go to France.

I said, "No good-by?" Sasha and James explained that time has no meaning to the People so a day is the same as a year and a year is the same as a century so what is the point of a good by?

I guess I will never stop learning. When I asked about Willy, they explained that she already left for

France. Sasha asked if I minded if he move into Bart's rooms and I told him he was more than welcome.

James asked Sasha to take him home and I asked him to come back for me later.

Molly came out to the table after they left and again gave me a hug. I held her tight and looked closely at her pretty face. For the first time I saw the wrinkles around her eyes and the gray hair streaking through the red. Time was calling to her and she was answering it with grace and a beauty that only women that do not try to fight it maintain. She told me that all of my men were coming in two hours for a meeting and Toby and his men would be with them. The tavern would be closed and she was fixing a big meal for all of us. I asked who had arranged all of that and she said, " Bart, who else?"

I decided to visit the various shops and see how they all were doing. Everyone seemed to be happy that I was back and they hinted about the trouble that had been going on in my absence.

When I went into the bakery I could hear two people arguing in the back room. Angelo's daughter in law was holding her hands over her face and crying. I ran to the back room and a filthy thug was threatening her husband with a knife and saying, "I don't care about Getts and his men."

"You will pay me, or your pretty wife will not be so pretty anymore." I lost it. I moved to the man so fast that no one even saw me. I grabbed his arm holding the knife and broke the bone between the elbow and wrist with so much force that the bone came through the skin. I picked him up like a rag doll and carried him out to the alley. I explained to him who I was and then threw him into the back wall. I carried him a block or two up the alley and explained that I would kill him if he ever came back, and then I threw him into the street. There were more than a few people in the area to watch what I had done and when I calmed down I realized that this had to be my last public display. I doubt even Toby could carry a man that size with one hand that distance and then throw him twenty feet into the street.

In time the story would be written off, but I needed to be careful from now on.

I went back to the bakery and made sure they were all right. I explained that their family had arrived in River Bend safe and sound and everyone was happy to have a bakery in town.

They listened, but they were too afraid to talk. I decided to go to the restaurant and have a large glass of scotch. John joined me at the bar and said he heard about the bakery incident and he hoped I was alright. I told him I was fine and I asked about business.

He said there were problems with the street gangs, but he hired a dozen of the off duty police to work weekends to protect the patrons. He also said that the better crowds were decreasing in size do to the problems and the bad publicity.

I thought to myself, was I really gone that long? I got back to Molly's right before all the men began to arrive. In addition to my people, Billy B was there with several of his men and the chief of police was there with two of his captains. I was not aware that all of these people would be represented, but it was just like Bart to drop me into the perfect set up. He was speaking to me in my mind and telling me this was my last interference for awhile.

I greeted everyone and then made sure everyone had a drink and a seat. I started by asking the police chief to give us an appraisal of the situation as he saw it. He explained that mills and mines were getting more labor than they needed from Eastern Europe and so they kept cutting wages.

"Poverty and over crowding with no work for the youth at all were the root causes of the problems," he said.

"We are heading into difficult times and I have no idea how long it will take to correct itself."

"The only good news is that there are pockets of employment especially in mining, outside the city that are attracting specific groups of immigrants. The Polish are moving up river to new mills opening up and many of the Italians are taking jobs in coal mines further north and south."

"There is a community of Croats in Butler County working the limestone mines and all that is beginning to relieve some of the pressure."

"I believe that if we can increase the number of policemen by recruiting many of the young men from these ethnic families, we can better control those that wish to live peacefully, but the gangs are another story.

I told the chief that I would secure the funds he needed from the town council and he thanked me and left with his two captains. At this point I looked at Toby and said,

"You and I have been together controlling these streets since we were kids."

"I will help any way that I can, but we are all deeply involved in this whole area and I must concentrate on all of our investments."

"It is up to you to take over all the problems that the Police cannot or will not handle." I looked at everyone in the room and said, "Toby is in charge of the whole area from our trade partners up and down the rivers including all of Pittsburgh and the North Side."

"We have all gotten rich over the last few years and I will make sure your investments remain safe."

"I recommend that you recruit the young Alley Rats to do all the things we used to do."

"All of us are just a few dollars away from those dirty kids hustling in the back streets just like we did.

"First fill their bellies and then fill their pockets."

CHAPTER 43

I did not even try to go home after the meeting. I decided to stay in my apartment upstairs. I slept for maybe three hours before the piano called to me. So much had happened and so much had changed that I needed to escape and as always, the piano was the conduit to carry me away.

I could feel the warm air whisper over me from the street and I could smell the bodies of the people all around me like a reminder that the air belonged to the earth, but it carried the foul and the wonderful scents of everything that lived.

There was an infusion of sweat and sawdust combined with burned coal and burned wood that clung to the air and smothered the beautiful fragrances of nature. This was a place of men and industry.

My fingers charged the keys of the piano with all the force of the hammers that beat the crust from the hot ingots of steel that were slowly pulled from the furnace. I had no idea what piece I was playing, but the sounds were bouncing off the walls of the room and the buildings out in the street. My head was almost touching the piano keys and my fingers were flying over the key board. I could not hear the music, if that is what it was, because my head was rolling back and forth like an empty jug in the river. My ears were ringing and my fingers were covered in sweat so much so that the moisture was spraying all over everything. I did not care and I maintained the trance for hour after hour while I attacked the piano and allowed it to keep me in its grasp. I needed to run away and my mind hovered somewhere above the sound of the piano where it floated to a place I had never been.

I had spent a long time with Toby after everyone else left the day before. He told me he was turning the day to day decisions of Allegheny Construction over to Andy. He wanted each of our original Alley Rats to put several of their people in charge of cleaning out the Point. He and the Maletic brothers, including Andy, would be available when needed. He had several people in mind to clean out the problems in the Strip District. He, Ray, and Bob would eliminate any trouble on the North Side including the area down the Ohio River. The South Side along the Monongahela River, especially at the railroad concourse, was a problem he had yet to figure out. These thoughts spun around in my head as I played on and on. Finally, I heard someone shouting, "Danube, play the Blue Danube."

I was suddenly released from my trance and I became aware that Dale was sitting next to me, asking me to play our favorite waltz. I smiled at him and began to play his request. The place was crowded and the street was full of listeners also. I guess this will serve notice that I have returned.

Everyone had a smile or an approving nod for me as the crowd went about their routines. Molly came over with a mug of coffee and a hug. She said, "If I had not seen it myself, I would never have believed anyone could move their fingers that fast."

"I do not know what you were playing, but it was beautiful. "

I thanked her and then I realized that my clothes were soaked with sweat. I went up to my rooms to shower and change. When I came back to the bar room Toby was waiting for me and the table was piled high with an assortment of breakfast food. I sat down and Toby was grinning. I asked what was so funny and he said he was thinking about the first meal we had at this very table. It was a million years ago and yet it seemed like yesterday. He told me that after all this time we owed Molly another suet pudding. I just smiled and watched as Toby became very serious. He told me that Bob was an incredible fighter, but Ray was a killer, and anyone that did not know that was a fool. "I plan to gather together at least fifty men who will report to Bob and Ray." Bob will oversee all our actions and Ray will carry them out."

"The Point is in good hands with our old people at least for now, but Billy B needs to stay out of it."

He has enough to do and success has made him a little too soft for this kind of work."

"I got rid of the police protection around the restaurant because I do not want anyone thinking we need to hide behind the Coppers."

Our people can protect it just fine without the patrons seeing uniforms all over the place." "Tomorrow night I am taking fifty men into the Strip District with a list of every gang member operating there."

"We will eliminate all of those problems in one night and the Chief of Police has agreed to keep all of his men out of the area."

"All of our new men are immigrants and a tougher group of fighters does not exist anywhere."

"They are mean and hungry and they hate the gangs that intimidate their people as much as we do."

"I intend to keep them on the payroll of Allegheny Contracting indefinitely."

"We will end up with a small army before it is over, but hopefully we can find honest work for all of them that want it."

When we finish with the Strip District, we will move on to Old Allegheny on the North side and clean up whatever mess we find remaining there."

"After that I will instruct the final clean up in the Point and the downtown area.

"I suggested to the police chief that he wait to do any hiring until we are done because I may have some fine candidates for his police force that will have firsthand experience.

"If you have any suggestions I would greatly appreciate them. "

I told Toby that I thought his approach was simple and effective. I suggested that he cover all escape potentials tomorrow night to prevent any witnesses. We both thought of Bart and the lesson he had taught us.

"Watch for trains and boats leaving the area to be sure no one uses them for escape."

I told him that Sasha and I would be there to help if we were needed, but we would not interfere. He asked me to meet him at the end of Liberty Avenue at eleven P.M. and I agreed. I had never appreciated his talent for organization, but I guess I should have, considering how many crews and projects he kept in motion and on schedule. Toby was not from the Point, but he certainly was of the Point.

After Toby left, I sat there for a while and talked to Molly. She knew what was going to happen and she was worried. I told her that it seemed to me that this battle for the streets was never- ending. She said, "We have nice stores and clean streets, a bank and good schools."

"I thought that would spell the end to the killing, but it looks like I will never quit worrying about you and Toby."

I wished that there was a way for me to explain that she never needed to worry about me, but that was not possible. I gave her a hug and told her to concentrate on her son and I would take care of Toby and me. After that, Sasha showed up and we went home.

Sasha, James and I spent the afternoon discussing how we could help Toby with the enormous task ahead. James explained that he had spent time with Ben at the pawn shop. Ben had a handle on just about everything that happened in and around the city. Ben had given Toby a list of the gang members and where to find them. James explained that it was easy for Ben to gather the information since the thieves all brought their merchandise to his shop for purchase. Ben would just smile and take notes for the day he knew was coming. Ben and Toby have been running the North Side for years and Ben has a crew of some of the hardest men in the area that collect debts for him. Most of the men with Toby tonight will be from that crew.

I just shook my head. I guess a lot had been going on behind my back and I had a suspicion that Bart had orchestrated all of it. Sasha and I met Toby as planned at the end of Liberty Avenue. I explained that we would go in alone first and watch for trains and boats leaving the area. Toby showed us the three buildings that the gangs were using and further explained that all of them should be there tonight for their weekly meetings. Sasha and I climbed to the roofs of the warehouses close to the rails and water. We had a good view of anyone trying to leave on either one. We could see the men spreading out and surrounding the three buildings. When we heard Toby whistle, we were shocked as we watched his men throw dynamite threw the windows and into the buildings from all sides. The explosions were incredible and windows were shattering for a block in each direction. There was nothing left of the three warehouses but smoke and burning wood. There was no way anyone could escape such devastation. The only injuries were to Toby's men from flying glass. Sasha and I were in awe of the devastation caused in a matter of seconds.

All this time, I thought that I was the hard one, but tonight, I understood my best friend for the first time. Toby was thorough in everything he did.

Sasha and I returned to Molly's and waited for Toby. It took him some time to survey the job and then send his people home. He got there around one A.M. and walked into the place as though nothing had happened. Molly was there to greet him and he hugged her and asked if the kitchen was still open because he was starving. Molly explained that the stove was still hot and she would have food for us right away.

We sat and ate the food Molly had brought to us. Toby explained that he felt the first blow to these gangs had to be devastating and quick to serve as a warning to the rest of them. He said, "All of the North Side will be cleaned up by the morning."

"Andy has arranged a design to thoroughly eliminate everyone there that might oppose us."

"Ray and Bob, along with their people, will be rounding them up and making sure that they are never heard from again."

"Ben and I have been compiling a list for quite some time."

"We could have done this earlier, but we chose to lull them into a false sense of security." "That leaves the Point and the South Side."

"I am moving Ray to the South Side along with a few of his men."

"There is nobody in this entire area that is not terrified of him."

"Ray is vicious, but he is also devious."

"He is as cunning as a fox and he will know everything that is happening here in no time at all."

"All of our people here have moved on to better things, so I believe the new blood from the outside will make the difference." Bob and his men are going to the Point to settle any problems there."

"We know that area, so Bob is perfect to take over that entire town." He is smart like Andy and he is a supreme fighter."

"He and Ray will be just a short distance apart so they can help each other if needed."

"Andy will stay with me and run our business."

"I can only do the things I need to do if I know he is handling our investments."

I asked him who would be protecting his back while his best men were scattered all over the area and he replied, "My father-in-law is much more astute than we thought."

"He knew everything about you and me long before he permitted me to marry his daughter."

"It turned out that his family runs a very large Black Market operation in Germany."

"They believe that the Kaiser is preparing for war and they want no part in it."

"His nephews, Bill and John, are here now and they are very capable men."

"They are both almost as big as I am and they were trained over there to take care of any difficult business for the family."

"They are outside right now, and they are never far from me."

"They speak English, but they make a point of acting as though they do not."

"I speak to them in German only to keep up the image."

"Would you like to meet them?"

I told him that I would and he went to get them. When the three of them walked in the door, Molly almost fainted. They were certainly as big as Toby, but somehow, they appeared even bigger. They both had short blonde hair and beards halfway down their chests. Their blue eyes were so deep they were almost black, and they seemed to be looking at nothing and everything at the same time. I could easily read their thoughts and it was obvious that they were devoted to Toby and his safety. When Toby introduced Sasha and me, they both broke into a wide smile that took away any sign of their fierce being. They spoke to us in perfect English as they rushed over to shake our hands.

When they saw Molly, they both took turns picking her up and kissing her cheeks. They kept saying, "You are Toby's mother and we are so happy to meet you."

Toby was grinning and we were all surprised at the change in Bill and John. They turned into two little kids that had just returned from a long trip.

Bill said to Molly, "We are to protect you as though you are our own Mama."

"Can we call you Mama?"

Out came the hanky and Molly said, "Yes" as she ran to the kitchen wiping her eyes'

End of Part Two

PART THREE

Chapter 44

If you have ever watched the clouds roll over the sky on a windy day, then you can understand my life for the last few years. It was as though I was lying on my back in a field of green grass and the world was doing its own thing without me. Oh, Lou did come home and we did help Toby now and again, but my part in the entire drama was quite secondary and usually unnecessary. Sasha stayed busy mostly traveling with the boats and Lou and I attended a great many parties and formal balls. I had to help Herman, the stock broker and Walter at the bank make the transition to a new place to live. I was now doing the job that Bart had done for so many years. I staged a sudden death with the body of some poor unknown soul and then we brought in another of the People to replace them. In some ways, it was great fun to hear about their new life and all the crazy changes they faced. Other things were very sad.

The poor old Mayor died of a worn-out liver and Katherine and I changed our relationship to one of a great friendship. She recognized that she was aging and that I was not, but she never said anything except once. When I escorted her home from the funeral she held my hand very tightly and said,

"The world is full of many mysteries and I have enjoyed reading about them and trying to figure them out."

"I have forever believed that people change with time, both in how they think and in how they look."

"My mother always said that you can never hide your age from your hands."

"She held up my hand as though to inspect it and said, "It appears that she was wrong."

"There were many times that I tried to get pregnant to you and there were many times that I tried to convince myself that the fact that you never got sick or even had a splinter was just good fortune."

"One night I watched you walk from my bed in your bare feet over a broken glass and you not only did not get cut, but you walked on it as though it was not there."

"Please do not try to explain it to me with lies to protect your secret."

"I am content to know that my friend and lover is very blessed."

"Some day when I am dying you can whisper in my ear that I am correct."

"Until then you can be my special young friend."

I never answered her because there was nothing for me to say. Billy B. also passed away and Little Billy, who was much bigger than his father, took over all of Billy B's work. Toby had two sons in the army as we entered World War I and little Dale was a Captain of a merchant marine freighter on the Atlantic Ocean. Rebecca and her husband moved to River Bend where he was the Chief of Police. I had mentioned the job to him and he was very happy to take it and get away from two smothering sets of parents. Lou and I visited James and Bart and Willy many times in France, but the war made it very difficult. They bought an estate in Switzerland and moved there to get away from the war. I had urged them to go to our house in New Orleans, but they refused saying, "What can the Kaiser do to us?" Molly and the Captain were still at the pub although they had hired help to take care of the place. Molly was totally gray, but when she smiled she looked just like the same Molly that saved Toby and me.

Toby was like a machine that never stops running. He held the area in an iron fist and although many tried, no one was ever able to get the best of him. Annah was as round as she was tall and their love affair never ended.

Their nine children were all involved in something, but Toby insisted they get a fine education first. The two boys in the army had both graduated from West Point.

Andy turned out to be a brilliant business man and he totally ran all of our interests. Bob moved to the North Side, but he still controlled all things in the Point. He had a great wife and four sons that knew nothing about his business. He became very involved in professional football and invested a great deal of secret money in it. Ray became Mr. South Side and he had more friends than anyone I ever heard of. It turned out that he was a true politician. After he cleaned out all the trash he found himself elected Mayor even though he did not know he was running. People just normally gravitated to him. He also got married and had one little girl that was way too beautiful, and she was the apple of his eye. John still did well at the restaurant although time was wearing on the Point again and I could see problems for the future.

The best news is that the war ended and both of Toby's boys came home. Dale decided to stay in the shipping business on the ocean so we all got together and bought a beautiful freighter for him to captain. His

Dad often sailed with him, but Molly was never going out into the ocean. She was kept busy because Bill and John were very serious about her being their Mama and they were soon surrounding her with grandchildren.

Bill had three and John had four with one set of twins. The children came one after another and their wives were from Germany, so none of them had any close family here. The little rug rats were at the Pub all the time and Grandma was in her glory. When I visited I noticed that everyone including the kids were jabbering away in a mixture of English, German, and whatever babies make up on their own. I had no idea what they were saying, but Molly and the Captain seemed to get every word. I learned later that the Captain assumed that they were always asking for a cookie which he promptly supplied.

It was wonderful to watch her. It seemed like all of her dreams had come true. It was hard to let them all grow away from me but that was what I had chosen.

A little while later Lou and I decided to visit the people at her old home on the Mississippi. I had been having long thoughts about the old Grandma and it was as though she was asking for me.

We went on board the Surprise and I asked Captain Keys to take us down as soon as he could. He said that he would travel empty just to get us there quickly, but he knew there was a huge supply of sugar and cotton waiting for him at River Bend and the mills were crying for cotton to make clothes for the soldiers and sailors coming home from the war. There would be no loss of profit.

When we arrived at the dock there must have been four hundred people waiting for us and the smells of food cooking were crowding every inch of air for a mile in every direction. I could not remember when I had seen Lou so excited.

When we got to the dock a swarm of people escorted us from the boat and I in particular was taken directly to Grandma.

I could not believe that she looked even older than the last time I had seen her, but she did. She stood and walked to me. When we were facing each other she got on her knees and asked me to do the same. She licked my cheeks and rubbed noses before she held her hands on either side of my head and tipped our foreheads together. She began to hum a song and as she did, we both went into a trance and our souls became one. We talked through our minds about everything she had experienced throughout her very long life. It was as though I was there and I could feel the love and devotion she had for her husband and her step children. I watched as she delivered baby after baby for the people deep in the swamp where her knowledge and her understanding of natural medicines had saved countless lives. We smelled the wild flowers and talked to the gators and snakes. I saw Lou being born and I witnessed her fathers' great love for her. I saw her crying when he was buried and I witnessed his soul leaving his body.

We sat back and the sky was bright blue and above us were thousands of souls circling like the birds that prepare to migrate south for the winter. We laughed and waved good-by to them as they vanished into the heavens. We held each other so tightly that I forgot how old she was and when I looked at her she was a young girl and as beautiful as anyone I had ever seen. She looked up at me and said, "Please listen to what I must tell you." "When we awake there will be a red wolf waiting for you." "I am that wolf and I will stay with you until I must fulfill a promise." "Any time you wish you can enter my thoughts and join me just like you have joined my soul now." "We can be the wolf." "You will exist only as the wolf until you decide to return."

"When we are a wolf we are just as oblivious to injury and death as we are when we are in human form, but I alone will remain a wolf no matter what."

"I am an accomplished violinist and when you come out of this trance, you will be also."

"You must pass this ability on for me."

"Look at me now."

When I looked at her she was no more than four years old. She told me to cradle her in my arms and blow my breath over her little face. With each puff of my breath she got younger until I was holding a fetus with the umbilical cord attached to my chest. I was instructed by a voice in my head to bite it in two. When I did, the baby was no more and I felt myself coming out of the trance.

Grandma was in my arms and she was dead. I closed her eyes and kissed the smile on her face. There was a large crowd around us and every eye was full of tears. Next to us was a beautiful red wolf. Lou came over and picked up grandma and gave her to her family. I asked her how long grandma and I had been kneeling there forehead to forehead and Lou said, "You two have not moved for five days."

No one seemed upset about the wolf. I looked at the wolf and said,'

"Come here G and the wolf curled up in my arms." Lou, G, and I went over to the festivities and I announced that Grandma said good-by and that she would be looking after all of them forever." I said,

"We must all celebrate her life with food, wine and love for each other."

I could feel the gold nugget earring returned to my ear. It felt good. I was so hungry that I wanted to eat forever and G was as hungry as I was. Everyone ate and drank and shared memories of Grandma. When Lou and I finally went to the little hut prepared for us I was ready to fall over. We went inside and G lay down outside the door. When I woke up everyone was very busy preparing a huge bonfire. Grandma was laid out in a beautiful cotton dress and her hair was tied up with ribbons. She looked content and G kept rubbing my side. G said to me in my mind,

"I will miss them, but I know you will bring me back to check on them."

I smiled and said,

"Yes I would."

When the bon fire was finished Grandma's body was placed on top and then the fire was lit. Even I had a tear in my eye even though I knew she was still here, if in another form.

"Well", G said,

"That was the first new dress I had for at least fifty years, and they burned the damn thing."

Some things never change. Well, just when you think the world cannot get any crazier the country decided that everyone should quit drinking. Now, we have been selling illegal whiskey since I was a little alley rat in the Point. I have probably sold enough whiskey to fill the Allegheny River twice. I knew that the workhouse was safe from the crazy government because no one had the guts to even go in there, let alone try to shut it down. I was worried about Hans at the brewery, but I had ideas for him. I figured we could set up a brewery right here where I was standing, only a little further back in the swamps. All we needed to do was bring his equipment down here. The crazy thing was that we would make a fortune with the increase in prices. I had no idea how to help Golden Wedding, but I would try. John would have the fanciest Speak Easy in the city and we would control millions in revenue.

The only problem was me. Everyone I knew was older except me.

I had a long talk with Lou and we decided to move to River Bend for the next fifteen or twenty years and then go to our estate in New Orleans.

Electricity was coming like a tornado. Automobiles were starting to take away the need for horses. The telegraph was everywhere and telephones were coming soon. With all that and our boats, we should be able to keep in constant contact with Pittsburgh. By spending time in St. Louis, River Bend and New Orleans, we should be able to keep people from figuring us out. The first thing I did was lease a suite of rooms at the Grand Hotel in St Louis so we could come and go as we pleased.

Then I started the building of a third floor on our hotel in River Bend just for us.

Ed said he could finish it within a month and I knew the five brothers would make sure the woodwork was spectacular. I loved River Bend, It was perfect to be able to get to St Louis and New Orleans whenever we pleased. One of the People from New York came down to stay in my house and help with the work there. Sasha was there to give him guidance. He, Sasha, Lou and I could converse through our thoughts. His name was Vincent and he had a great many connections.

He knew all about the immigrants from Cicely and their attempts to take over the liquor business, but he also knew how to keep them away from us. He was aware of how big our operation was now and how much we could supply the needs of other cities. There was so much money to make that it boggled the mind.

I frankly did not care about the money, but I knew we had to keep tight control of the city, or someone would do it for us.

Money was pouring into our banks and unlike the rest of the country, we were investing in government bonds and staying out of the stock market. We were very unpopular because we would not lend money to those who gambled on the stock market. We made less, but the money came from illegal whiskey, and we knew it was safe, so who cared. I took huge sums of profit and bought real estate and stock in Bell Tell, Westinghouse, GE, and Ford. When US Steel came on the market, I bought all I could. The thing is, I will live long enough for it to come back, no matter what happens. I loved Ford, he was so damn crazy he had to be a success.

None of these investments mattered because I was financially solid no matter what.

Well, here came the roaring twenties. Lou was a hoot. She was a flappers' flapper and we traveled the country having a ball. Nothing made sense. I bought tons of stock in the morning and sold it at night. I held onto only the stocks I mentioned before, but how could I ignore the stupidity of the market? It was not about money, it was just a way to keep score.

Many groups tried to take over Pittsburgh, but we always knew and Toby was like a lion on a lamb. He worried me because of how vicious he was. The saving grace was Ray, who went absolutely crazy when anyone tried to take over.

Ray had a way of finding out who their family was and sending body parts to them one piece at a time.

One particular pain in the neck made a threat against Ray's daughter and Andy, Bobby and Ray drove to Detroit to throw a case of dynamite into their family living room and blew up half the block. Ray left a sign that said, "Toby was here." I spent very little time in the Point because it would have created too many questions.

Before we knew it the whole world went to hell and the Great Depression landed on the heads of the common man like a sledge hammer.

We had cash deposits everywhere and our two banks were solid. Our stocks fell like all the rest, but they would come back. It seemed like the liquor business just kept on growing, so we started to turn the profit around and opened food stations to feed as many people as we could. We started to get many government contracts for construction projects and we used the profits to hire many more people than we needed to do the work. It was not enough, but we did what we could. The country was in a mess, but our president started many government projects that were slowly getting us out of the depression.

In Europe, where the depression was the worst, the Kaiser was replaced in Germany by a real nut case. A very dangerous nut case. Lou and I had moved to New Orleans permanently. We loved the old house and life there was good. We made a point of keeping to ourselves so no one seemed to notice how we never changed, or perhaps they just did not care. One by one, all of our old friends died off and soon we would be free to go anywhere without notice. G scared the hell out of everyone, but the people at the mansion eventually calmed down and I even saw them scratching her head every so often. All of our contacts with the Point were by delivered notes or telegrams. Ghetts soon became code for the boss and it did not pertain to a real person. Lou, G, and I often visited with the people along the river as I had promised Grandma. They never questioned anything. On many of these visits, I became the wolf and traveled throughout the swamps with G on four legs. It was wild and I loved doing it. We observed all of the people and got to see how they were doing. When there was a problem, we would return to the boat and make arrangements to help if we could. I also got out the beautiful violin and played for them as Grandma had done. Just like at the Point, the people were captivated by the music and I was beginning to love the violin as much as the piano.

It was certainly easier to transport. One day, I was listening to the radio and the President came on. The

Japanese had bombed Pearl Harbor and we were about to join the war. Within days, Hitler declared war on the United States and we entered World War Two. Everyone either went to work or went to war. The Depression was over.

In the history of the world, no country ever switched over to a massive war machine as quickly as the United States did. I became an undiscovered source of information for the Allied countries. The People decided to take sides in the conflict by working as spies. Information was easily transferred to me through our thoughts and no enemy could ever intercept those transmissions. A person I never did learn her true identity was assigned to collect any information I might acquire. We had People in every country without exception and we were happy to assist. Our identities were never to be made public, and we constantly changed and disappeared before even our contacts could decide who we were. It was great fun and I loved helping the Allies against a psycho group of killers.

During one of my visits to River Bed I was approached by a young man of about 12 years. He was tall and very handsome with olive colored skin and soft wavy auburn hair. His eyes were gray and his posture was perfect. He came up to me and asked if we could talk. He showed no fear of G and she rubbed her fur against him as though she knew him. She urged me to listen to him.

We walked over to a bench on the dock and sat down.

"I understand that you were close to Grandma," he said. I said that I was and I could not keep from staring at him. There was something there that I could not put my mind to. G was laughing and telling me to think with my heart for a change. The young man said that his name was Toby and my brain went wild. I thought that my eyes must be playing tricks on me. Toby said,

"My father told me to find you when he died and to give you this note from him."

I thanked him and opened the letter.

The letter said: To my Brother, I do not know how to tell you this, but I am fully aware that you are not like the rest of us humans. You never age and you never get sick. I do not know why, but I am glad it is you, my most beloved friend.

Toby is my very own son. I fell in love with his mother when I was working at River Bend. Believe me, it did not change my love for Annah at all.

I spent as much time with him as I could, but his mother died and Annah and I are old and need each other. Please forgive me for this indiscretion and find it in your heart to love my son as I do. He needs you for all the same reasons that I did and I need you to help him for me. Time has taken a toll on me and I will soon join his mother. Please give him my love and your love. He is an incredible young man and I need the security of knowing you will take my place and finish raising him.

Your loving Brother,

Toby.

I put away the letter and told the young man that it would be my honor to help him. I was trying to digest it all when G entered my thoughts and said, "His mother was a beautiful Creole from my enormous family." "Teach him the violin and piano". I said to her, "Do you know what you are saying?"

"Yes, I do," she said, "He has no blood relations among the People."

Chapter 45

My God, how could something so small project such sound? My hair was almost down to my hips, so it moved with the swaying of my body like a cape hanging down my back. The violin sang the music loud and the range was so that even the very stones of the mansion were vibrating. I was alone in the ballroom and all the windows were open. The staff was new as the old had retired or moved on. No one remembered me or Lou and we kept a very low profile in the city. Lou spent at least six months in Europe, and G was forever hitching a ride on our boats to her old home to check on her huge family. The boat captains loved having her onboard and they loved to spoil her, especially the cooks. She often told me that if she had known how great it was to be a wolf, she would have turned a long time ago. I asked her what stopped her and she explained that she had to have an influx of wolf blood and nothing else for over the last ninety years to get to where she could do it. I asked her why she told me long ago that we could not change into animals and she said, "Why do you believe everything I tell you?" Sometimes, I had no idea what she was talking about.

As I played I ran through a mental inventory of all the people I have loved and lost. I could see my mother as a young and beautiful woman standing next to the huge frame of my father and the violin would take off in high pitched sounds that would come near to shattering the windows. Then I would hear Molly talking to Billy B and the Captain and the violin would escape into tones so mellow that I could feel the tears running down my cheeks. Toby and all my Alley Rat brothers would be laughing and eating on the floor of the old warehouse we lived in and the violin would skip to a lively tune that would set my foot to tapping and a smile would capture my face. Then I would think of Katherine and I would first remember our waltz and the violin would soar into the Blue Danube and I could feel the satisfaction as it spread over my face. And then I was holding her hand and cradling her in my arms. I was whispering into her ear all the secrets of my life.

The violin drifted into the mellow sounds of a gypsy song so sweet and soft that I rocked as I played and moved to the window where I opened my eyes for the first time.

The street was crowded with people and I smiled at them and decided to play on. I continued with a series of classical favorites of mine and I watched the people smile and move with the rhythm of the music. I finally realized how hungry I was and I stopped playing, bowed to their applause and waved good-by.

I went down to my bathroom where I quickly showered, dressed and joined Lou and Toby Jr. in the dining room.

Lou gave me a kiss and said, "So how did the concert go?" Toby asked me how long it took me to learn to play like that and I promised him that he would eventually learn to play as well as I did. Lou entered my thoughts and asked when I would start to introduce the formula to

Toby Jr. Bart and James suddenly entered my thoughts and explained that they would be joining us in a few days and we would all discuss the future for Toby Jr. It took me some time before I realized that these conversations in my mind lasted less than a second so they were never obvious to those around us.

The war was now over and the world was trying to recover from the effects. Millions of military people were mustered out and sent home.

Factories were refitting to build peacetime products again and half of the women were pregnant. Toby Jr. had been going to a private school here in New Orleans and he was now sixteen and as big as his father was, although he was not quite as filled out.

He had become the son I would never have and Lou and I were grateful to his father for giving him to us. I had most of the art work from Pittsburgh moved to the mansion and my library of books.

The North Side was beginning to decay and the old brown stone lost its appeal to the People. The Point had become a slum again and I was glad that Toby was not there to see it. I was satisfied that I had saved as many people as I had and like the wars, I became content to allow the world to turn. I would do what I could for those close to me, but I could not change things forever. James once said to me that after the slaughter at Waterloo and Gettysburg and the mustard gas during WWI, he chose to think past man's inhumanity to his fellow man and look at the world in blocks of one hundred years or more. I once told him that the atomic bomb would change the world forever and he explained that Genghis Kahn once said that steel arrowheads would do the same as he killed hundreds of thousands of people with them. I guess mankind will never stop finding ways to try to dominate one another. If they only knew about us!

God forbid.

After breakfast G asked me to go on a run with her through the swamps just outside of town. We were soon the wolf and we were running wild and free. It is the most wonderful thing to be able to become one with this beautiful animal. G said,

"Let me control our path," and I agreed. We ran and ran for hours until we reached a tall mound in the deep swamp. We lay down on top of the mound and predators of every kind came and joined us. There were bobcats, and gators and snakes of every poisonous kind.

Hawks and owls joined with eagles and raccoons in the trees.

Everything got very quiet. G said to me that we were here for a very special purpose. I was quiet as a pack of wolves came to the mound and sat down, except for a beautiful big male who came to us and said,

"It is time, we have given you our blood all these years and now I want my reward."

A very young female wolf walked up to us and began to lick our face. Suddenly all of the wolves began to howl and in the distance I could hear wolves in the swamp for miles around that were doing the same. I suddenly felt a sharp pain in my heart and I too began to howl as loud as I could.

When we stopped, G was now in the body of the young female wolf. She said to me, "I will now be the Alpha female in this pack and I will have many children of my own."

"I knew this was my destiny all those years ago, but I was waiting for a member of the People that was strong enough to move from a human to a wolf and back without any difficulties."

"When I first met you I knew you were the one and as long as my nugget of gold is in your ear you can be a wolf any time you desire." This is my gift to you and to the People."

The boy Toby will be able to do the same if you take him through the Red Gate."

"You only need to add your blood."

"Now I have a final warning for you."

"Only add your blood to the most deserving."

"You are just coming into all of your powers and until you know what they are, you must only share your blood with those very close and trusted by you."

"Many will seek you out, but few will be worthy."

G said good-by, licked my face and ran off with the pack. I lay on that old Indian burial mound and thought about all that had just happened. I will miss G, but I was so happy to think that she would now have real children of her own. A big Fox came over to me and said, "We are all happy to have her back here where she belongs."

"Remember us and come back to visit."

"You are our only contact with the humans." He licked my face and ran off into the swamp. It was time for me to leave.

I took my time going home and when I went into the mansion I went to my room and instantly returned to my former body. I went over to the mirror to make sure and as I looked on my reflection, I touched the nugget in my ear and noticed that my K-9 teeth began to grow. I started laughing and said," Holly vampire, what is that about?" Grandma entered my mind and said, "How do you think I got all that wolf blood over the years without killing my beloved wolves?" I guess I will never quit learning. She then said, "You can always take a bite out of some dumb human just to keep up the image."

I told her to go play with her friends and I went to find Lou.

I explained to Lou all that had happened. She would miss G, but she was happy for her. We both knew that she would live a normal life span for a wolf and then she would finally die. Many of the People came into my mind and they were all happy that Grandma finally found her destiny.

Bart was especially interested in my ability to become a wolf and he questioned me about it many times after they arrived.

There was little to tell. I just concentrated on it and it happened. I did the same to return. Wolves are fierce predators, but they only hunt to live and they are very close family members. The Alpha male and female mate for life and their children are cared for by the entire pack.

They avoid humans and only extreme starvation would make them attack one. Wolves have an incredible sense of smell. They can tell just by smelling the tracks of an animal if it is sick or not. They can even determine the severity of the illness and remember to return for the animal when it is on its last legs.

It was great to be with James and Bart and of course they had not changed since I was last with them. I played the violin while one or the other of them played the piano. It was great fun. We visited River

Bend and it was now a very large town. I showed Toby where his father and I first started to build, and we visited the orphanage where a whole new staff of people were taking care of the children. None of them knew us, so we were able to enjoy the visit without arousing any suspicion.

They told me that Sasha had joined them in France after the war. He wanted to go back to Russia, but the Russia he knew no longer existed. These were things I was beginning to understand. Great changes would come and go, but we, the People would only get to witness it. We could help along the way like we did with the spying during the war, but we would never be a real part of history because history to us was yesterday.

Young Toby was now almost sixteen years old and I had been giving him very small portions of the formula to protect him from harm. He was filling out quickly and he took his boxing, fencing, shooting, and martial arts instruction very seriously. He was learning the violin and the piano. He commuted to a private school for math and science while Lou and I were teaching him languages. I followed my own experiences while living with Bart and James and insisted that no English be spoken in the house. I did have to keep an eye on him around the ladies that assumed he was much older than he was, but unlike his father, he was not the least bit shy when it came to women.

I had to release more than one of the young maids in the house that took a little too long to tuck him in at night. Lou thought it was a riot to watch me running around like a crazy parent trying to keep him out of trouble.

It turned out that Toby was very adventurous and he loved to be with all kinds of people. He had a very special love for the people down on the water front and he soon got a reputation for fighting with knives or fists. This just added to his appeal with the ladies. Everyone knew about the mansion he lived in, but his personality was such that he fit in anywhere. People of every walk of life stopped him on the street to talk and he treated them all the same. There was not an event that he was not invited to and I often went with him to keep him safe. He was the obvious center of discussions between James, Bart, Lou and I and we were getting a great deal of interested input from all the People.

When Toby was just passed seventeen he had a terrific growth spurt that stopped when he hit six foot six inches tall.

He was a lean 125 pounds but he was all muscle.

We decided it was time to prepare him for the Red Gate. He had gotten into the habit of taking G with him when he went down to the docks which required me to "find him" for Toby. It was the perfect cover for me to be with him and make sure he was safe. Most of the time I stayed out of it, but there were a few times when I got involved.

We were in the "Creole Tavern" when a very attractive bar maid was giving Toby exclusive attention. A large dock worker decided that he was entitled to her time also. This man was about six foot three inches tall and at least two hundred and fifty pounds. The dock worker was called "Tiny" and he had a serious reputation for fighting. Tiny pushed the bar maid to the ground and took a swing at Toby. Tiny missed, but Toby did not when he hit the man with a combination of overhand rights and lefts that put Tiny on his back. Tiny came up off the floor with a knife in his hand.

Toby just smiled at him and warned him to put the knife down. Tiny swung the knife at Toby's head, but he missed and a knife shot out of Toby's left wrist and made a dozen slight cuts on various parts of the big body of Tiny. Toby again told him to put the knife down, but he refused. I noticed a few of the other dock workers starting to move toward Toby so I got in front of them and showed my very large teeth. They decided to back away. Again, the big man charged Toby and this time, Toby had had enough. Toby put a deep slash in his stomach and then hit him with a series of hard punches to his head. Tiny went down and Toby kicked away the knife before helping him up and telling his friends to get him to a doctor. Toby turned to the bar maid and said, "Now, where were we?"

I went over to Toby, grabbed his sleeve in my mouth, and pulled him toward the door. He knew better than to ignore my obvious intentions, so he came along and we went home. I ran to my room and dressed. When I came down to the library, he was reading a book. I said,

"I guess you found my knife."

He smiled and said, "Lou gave it to me a long time ago."

"She said that you did not need it any longer and the time might come when I might."

I asked him why he was fighting over a bar maid and he explained that she was cute and he did not want to give her up to a dock worker. I walked over to him and picked him off of the ground with one hand. I carried him through the house and out into the back garden where I finally put him down on a bench. I wasn't even breathing hard. His face was in shock so I waited for him to settle down before I said,

"You are never to speak down about a person that you do not even know again or you will answer to me."

"That dock worker may be a good man with a family that was just out for a little fun after breaking his back unloading one of our boats all day."

"You need to find him and apologize for what you did and pay him for any expenses he might have, including loss of pay."

"I and your father were raised by some of the toughest people in the Point."

"We did our share of fighting and a whole lot more, but we never got in fights for stupid reasons and we did more to help the poor, we never judged them."

"I can see that I have neglected a big part of your education."

"The first time your father and I had a real meal that filled our bellies was on food we stole from some strangers kitchen."

"We ate it in a dirt hole under a building because we were hiding from the police that had been chasing us."

"We sat on that floor in the filthy clothes that were all we had and we counted the silver pieces we had stolen."

"That is how we met and how we got started." We sold the silver for two weeks of food and clothes that were clean and without lice and fleas in them."

"We felt like kings."

Toby was very quiet. When he finally spoke, he said, "I guess I have been enjoying the fruits of your labor for too long."

"Please tell me all about my father and what he was really like."

"I remember him, but I never got to know him like my step brothers and sisters did."

"When you are through, perhaps you can tell me why you are so strong and why my father got old and died and you did not."

"I love you and Lou, but it has been hard for me not to resent losing my father while his best friend never ages."

"I guess I took to taking out my rage on innocent people when I should have just asked you about it."

I sat down next to him and listened to the voices in my mind telling me to give him the whole truth in detail or forget to take him through the Red Gate. Toby and I talked throughout the whole day and into the night. He asked questions and I answered them truthfully. After I had told him all about his father and me, I suggested that we wait for Lou, Bart, and James before I explain my ageless form and all of the rest through the Red Gate. Toby and I talked throughout the whole day and into the night. He asked questions and I answered them truthfully. After I had told him all about his father and me, I suggested that we wait for Lou, Bart, and James before I explain my ageless form and all of the rest.

CHAPTER 46

The piano in our music room erupted in sound as Toby played with his heart for the first time. His mind ignored his hands and his fingers danced with the keys as his heart served as their guide. I played with him on my violin and the sounds were beyond beautiful. Toby had been getting small portions of the formula the same way James and Bart had given it to me. He was unaware of it. As we played there was a sudden infusion of sound from another source. The sweet sour sounds of a bella ligua joined with the piano and the violin and pushed our hearts into a series of Russian folk music. Sasha had sneaked into the room and he was the third instrument. I had no idea he was coming and Lou, James and Bart were just as surprised as I was. It was wonderful to hear the sounds race around the house and out every open window. We took turns playing a lead solo and when we got to Sasha it was amazing what he could make the instrument do. Before he finished, he jumped up onto the table and started playing an old gypsy tune that got faster and faster as he played. Toby and I joined in and it became a race to keep up with the sounds and the speed of the music. In my head I could envision a hundred Tamburitzens dancing to the music and keeping pace with the sounds. I remembered watching them at Duquesne University in Pittsburgh and thinking then that they would surely collapse from their efforts, but they danced on. Finally, we slowed the song to a mild pace and Toby and I quit playing as Sasha put his instrument through a long series of sad and beautiful sounds. He began to sing in Russian and his voice added more tears to the music he was playing. When he finished we all clapped and suddenly applause erupted from out in the street. We waved Sasha to the front door and he went out onto the porch and gave the crowd a bow. They cheered and he played again just for them. We all smiled because we knew how much Sasha loved to show off.

When he came back in we all hugged him and told him how glad we were that he was there.

Sasha explained that the People had told him to come to represent them. They knew that my blood was all that was needed for Toby to pass through the Red Gate, but they wanted us to know that they were all in favor of Toby joining us. Toby said he had a few things he had to do and asked if he could be excused. When he left we began to discuss the ceremony and when we would do it.

There were several of our People in New Orleans and they would attend also.

Toby went down to the docks by himself and began asking around for the where about of the man called Tiny. He finally located him in a small shack a few blocks back from the water. When he knocked on the door a small woman answered.

She said her husband Tiny was there but he could not come to the door because he was ill. She let Toby in and when he looked around it was obvious that these people were just getting by and if Toby was not working, they were in big trouble. He was very ashamed of what he had done. Poverty and back breaking work often drive men to the taverns for escape and he was never going to judge them again. He went over to the bed and told Tiny he was sorry. Tiny was very weak, but he still said, "I was just as much to blame as you were, so forget about it." Toby said, "No I will not and I will never let something like this happen again." Toby looked at the wound on Tiny' stomach and told his wife to get the doctor. She said they had no money and Toby handed her a roll of money and told her again to get the doctor. When she left Toby noticed two little children huddled against the wall in the next room.

He looked around the shack and there was no food anywhere. He quickly left the house and went to the nearby stalls and bought all the food he could carry. There was also a small grocery store about a block away that he went to after he dropped off the food for the children. He gave the owner of the store some more money and told him that he was to bill him at the mansion for anything these people wanted. When he gave him his address the man almost feinted and began saying, "Yes sir" to everything Toby told him.

When Toby got back to the little shack the doctor was there taking care of Tiny. He explained that he was just in time because there was the beginning of infection in the wound.

Toby told him to bill him for any other services that were needed and when he gave the doctor his address the doctor was just as shocked as the store owner. The two little boys were eating as though they had not seen food in a week. All Toby could think of was his father and Getts in that hole in under the house sharing their stolen food and his heart broke. He would never judge people again, and he would devote himself to helping any time he could. Tinys' wife was named Susan and Toby explained to her about the grocery store. He also asked if he could visit and help with the children. She was very sweet and said he could come whenever he wanted. Toby pulled a chair next to Tiny and said, "Just get well again, I will take care of everything." Tiny thanked him and said he was only worried about losing his job. When Toby asked him where he worked he told him down at the coffee warehouse. Toby smiled and said, "My family owns that warehouse and I can guarantee your job will be waiting for you."

When Toby got home he told them what he had found and what he had done. He explained that he was very sorry for his prior attitude and how he felt so much better to understand the reality of the streets. Over the next few weeks Toby visited the little shack of a house often. He took the boys shopping and saw that they had decent clothes for themselves and their mother. He also found out that Tiny and his wife owned the little house so he sent a crew of carpenters from River Bend to rebuild it into a nice three bedroom house with electricity and plumbing. Tiny recovered and went back to work. When Toby went to check on how he was doing the warehouse supervisor asked if they could talk.

They went to his office and Toby was informed that whatever he had done had made a new man of Tiny. The supervisor further explained that these dock workers were usually impossible to control, but since Tiny returned he made sure everyone did their jobs and never gave anyone a hard time. Toby told him that he was happy for him.

The Supervisor said, "That is not what I wanted to talk to you about." "Tiny is well educated for a dock worker." "I know he finished high school and was taking classes at night in mathematics after that." "He knows how to handle men and he has been helping me with the books and inventory checking since he got back." "I want to make him my assistant and when he is ready I want to retire and give him my job." "It will be a big raise in salary, but I have been trying to replace my old assistant for over a year and I believe he can do the job." Toby told them that he was sure the family would go along with whatever he recommended, so go ahead and tell him.

He brought Tiny in and explained the whole thing to him. He went from this ferocious looking big man to a happy kid with a tear in his eye.

Toby told him that he had nothing to do with this decision, but Tiny picked him up and hugged him anyway. Tiny said that that bar fight was the best thing that ever happened to him, but now that he had a position of respectability he was no longer going to spend time in the taverns. Toby was sure that would be welcome news to all the tavern owners.

Toby and I talked for a long time about what he had done and I was very pleased in the transition in him from the experience. I decided it was time to explain to him all about the Red Gate. That evening Lou, Bart, Sasha, James and I sat him down in the library. We were all drinking the red scotch and we even gave a glass to Toby.

Bart explained the powers he could have. James explained about languages and the ability to play instruments because of the formula we had been giving him. Lou spoke to the fact that he could never have children, and Sasha demonstrated that he could not be killed by shooting himself and watching the bullet bounce off.

I went into depth about watching friends like his father die and knowing there was nothing you can do about it. I spoke about grandma and then shut my eyes and became the wolf. Sasha had never seen it before so he was clapping. Toby was in shock and he just sat there with his mouth open. I turned back and quickly put my clothes on.

I told Toby he had a lot to think about, and I asked him if he had any questions. His first comment was, "I thought our pet wolf was a girl, but I just figured I was mistaken." He had very few questions and we all answered them as completely as we could. When we were done Toby said, "I have been aware that you were all different for a very long time." "The mere fact that none of us ever even gets a cold and I have never been cut or even fell down made it obvious that something was different about this family.

"My recent experience with Tiny has made me realize that I can be happy helping others just as much as I can with a family of my own." "There is no decision to make, please give me the Red Gate."

PART FOUR

CHAPTER 47

New Orleans was and still is magical. I lay in the sun on the grass in our garden surrounded by the scents of magnolias and honeysuckle. It is so powerful that it made my mind fall into a cradle of sweetness like a bee drunk on pollen. The birds carried on a serenade singing in concert with the buzzing of the cloud of insects that floated through the lawn disturbed only when a breeze decided to push them away. So much had changed. So many people had come into my life only to be taken away by time. As always, we the People, remained. I began to feel the closeness of family ties to all of the People more out of love than from necessity. O'Niel and I spent many long hours together talking about our People and how we all came to be part of this family. I asked him to tell me of his past since he knew all about mine. He was there to witness it. One afternoon he relented and began to reveal his story to me.

He was born in the swamp land that bordered the ocean on the western Irish Coast. He and his family lived like all of their friends and relatives, in a thatch covered cottage on one of the thousands of tiny islands scattered through the low coastal country. Their homes were little more than shacks, but the area provided all that they needed to survive with a minimal interference from outsiders. The constant storms from the sea made the land formations appear and disappear as the seasons changed year after year. Only those that lived there were able to navigate through the ever changing channels and this added to their secluded independence. The people lived by fishing and gathering the fruits and berries that grew close by. They also ventured out into the ocean to harvest many different types of sea plants and creatures available to them. All in all, it was a good life and a safe one from everything but the elements. The elements were an accepted part of everyday life and they knew how to live with them. He was the youngest of five children which by Irish standards was a small family. He said he was what they called a "change baby" because his mother had assumed that she was too old to have any more children when she got pregnant with him. There was twelve years between him and his next sibling. By the time he was ten years old his parents were old and all of his brothers and sisters had moved on to families of their own. He became very skilled as a hunter and fisherman early because he had to provide for his aging parents. It was his duty and his pleasure to take care of them.

One morning just as the sun was coming up he heard a voice calling him from outside his tiny house. When he went out to see who it was he was confronted by a tall man in very expensive clothes accompanied by at least a dozen soldiers.

He was told that he had to leave this land because they were going to begin draining this part of the swamp and the land would belong to the Gentleman, Sir Candleman, when it was free of the swamp. O'Niel began to argue that the land had belonged to his family for generations and it was not possible that anyone else had claim to it. The officer in charge said,

"There is a proper claim on file and it is in the name of the gentlemen with them. O'Niel ran to the hut and came out with his rifle, but before he could even lift the barrel he was struck in the back of the head. The last words he heard were those of the officer ordering his men to burn down the house. O'niel was left for dead. Hours later when he came to he realized that his clothes and hair were singed from the heat of the fire and the house was burned to the ground. He crawled to the remains of the house and found what was left of his parents huddled together and burned to death.

He crawled to the swamp and submerged his entire upper body in the water. He could feel the cool sting of the water as it washed over his burned flesh and removed the scale of blood on the back of his head. Somehow he managed to get to his feet and went to what was left of their shed and recovered a shovel. Slowly he began to dig graves for his parents when he heard a shout from the waterway just south of him.

When he looked up he saw his two brothers coming toward him in a small skiff. They were both wet with tears as they called out to him.

When they got to dry land they both ran over and held him tight saying, "Thank God you are safe." When they looked over at the remains of their parents their tears were replaced with anger.

They said that they were told that all three of them were dead.

A friend was heading out to fish when he saw what was happening. By the time he got to the shore he was told that everyone was dead and if he knew what was good for him, he would leave and forget anything he might have seen. He then came to tell the brothers as fast as he could. O'niel asked them how the soldiers were able to find the house in this vast swamp and the brothers became silent. He continued to prod them until the older of the two explained that an old neighbor who had always envied their father led them to the home. They further explained that the man was to get the use of the land to farm when it was drained. O'Niel asked if they were talking about the man known as Kearny and they said that they were. The man that came to them saw Kearny with the soldiers and he was laughing when they burned down the house. He heard Sir Candleman tell him to begin the draining process and all the land would be his to work as he had promised.

O'Niel just sat on the ground as his brothers dug a large grave to bury their parents in and then they dug another smaller one beside it that they threw a large log into. When he questioned them they explained that the large grave was for their parents to rest forever in together and the small one was for everyone to think that they buried O'Niel too. They said he would never be safe if they knew he was alive. ONiel went back to help move his parents when he realized that his old smooth bore long gun was still lying there on the ground where he had dropped it. After they buried the log and his parents, O'Niel went down a long hidden path behind the remains of the house and got into his fishing boat that was safely hidden behind several bushes. In it was all his equipment for hunting and fishing except the long gun. He got in and paddled over to his brothers' skiff. After he fetched the musket he told his brothers to leave and he would get back to them in a day or two. He explained that no one should see him with them so he would hide out on one of the smaller islands for a day or two and then come to them after dark.

He was self sufficient even if he was only thirteen years old. He had been providing for his parents for several years.

O'Niel made his way to an island that he had discovered many years before. He had camped there many times when he stayed out for days hunting and fishing to fill the family larder with food. The next morning early he made his way back to the burned out home.

He hid in the swamp until he heard excited voices talking about how rich they would be when they farmed all of this dry land. He could hear the sucking noise as their shovels dug a soggy trench to begin draining the area. O'Niel got very close to the two men to make sure who they were. Old man Kearny was there with his son. His son was in his twenties and a meaner man never lived.

Without a thought O'Niel lifted the long pole with the three pronged spear head he used for gigging frogs from the floor of his boat and threw it with an arm that had not missed in years, directly at Kearny's son. The spear stuck deep into the throat of his intended target. The man dropped to the ground without a sound. O'Niel walked up to Kearny and when the old man saw his son he charged O'Niel with the shovel. He swung the shovel at the head of O'Niel who just dropped to the ground out of the way and came up with his knife deep into the groin of Mr. Kearny. He held the knife buried to the hilt there as he stood up and looked the old man in the eye and said, "This is more than you did for my parents," as he slowly twisted the blade and Kearny screamed in pain. He then dug up the log and threw both bodies in the hole and did not bother to cover them with dirt.

O'Niel got back in his boat after retrieving his spear and rowed to the Kearny homestead.

When he arrived he got out of the boat and walked up to the house. A woman came out, looked at him, and said, "I thought that you were dead?" He said nothing as he walked into the house and kicked over the stove, setting the whole place on fire. The woman screamed at him that her son and husband would kill him for this, just like they killed his parents. O'Niel went all around the property and destroyed everything of value and anything that could be eaten.

Then he destroyed the only other boat that was there. After that he got in his boat and left her to starve.

Late that night he went to see his older brother. He told him everything, including digging up the grave and leaving the old woman to starve. He said that he had to do it that way so they would know he did it and not his brothers.

He hugged his brother hard and said good-by to his brothers' wife and children before he explained that he would disappear into the swamp for now and decide where to go next. As he rowed away from the little homestead the rain began to fall. He pulled on his oil cloth coat and kept on rowing. Rain was such a part of his life that he paid little attention to it. When he got to his special island he checked his fish traps and took the fish to the small hut he had built for himself over the last few years. While the fish were cooking over a small fire he thought about all that had happened and what he would do next. After his meal of fish and wild vegetables he lay down in the cozy hut and went to sleep.

O'niel spent the next three months fishing, hunting and drying all of the things he had caught. He also planted various vegetables and picked many more from the wild plants in the area. When he got up one morning to a blazing sun he realized that he had enough food prepared to feed an entire family for a year. He decided to take a boat load to his brothers for their families. He waited until the middle of the night to make the trip. He quietly approached the island his oldest brother lived on. It was very quiet and there was no light in the cottage. It was a warm night so there was no fire in the hearth.

When he got a few feet from the door he was stopped by a voice that asked, "Who are you and what do you want." O'Niel smiled when he recognized his brothers' voice and said, "Good evening brother, do you meet everyone in the middle of the night with a gun in your hand?"

His brother relaxed and said, "Are you crazy?" "They have patrols out everywhere looking for you." "There is even a price on your head." "How did you get here without being seen?" O'Niel explained that no one knows these waters the way he does and even if he were spotted he would be long gone before they could catch him.

He told his brother to follow him to the boat and help him unload all the food he had. When his brother saw the volume of food in the boat he was shocked. He said, "What are you going to live on if I take all of this?" O'Niel assured him that he had at least this much back on his island and that he would bring another boat load for him to share with his brothers. When the two went into the cottage his brothers' wife was waiting for them. She ran to her husband and said, "Thank God you are not hurt."

She was afraid because he was gone so long. As the two brought in the baskets of food she could not believe her eyes.

There was always food in the swamps, but to have an abundance for the future was a luxury seldom experienced. It meant that they could concentrate on all the many other chores without having to constantly stop to forage or hunt for food. Her husband could spend more time planting and turning the soil and she could make clothes and repair all the many things about the house. It was a true luxury.

While she prepared something for them to eat O'niel and his brother sat down to talk. The older brother explained that there was no place safe for him here anymore. The military people found the old lady at the Kearny homestead and she told them the whole story. Oddly enough they just left her there to starve as they rowed away. "They ignored her pleas for help." "Now they cannot find anyone willing to go and dig the drainage ditch because everyone is afraid that you will return and kill them." "That is why there is a reward out for you alive or dead." "There are patrols coming here every few days." "It was just luck that you missed them tonight." "When you come back, look for a piece of sail cloth on the big dead oak where we first took you fishing." "If it is safe for you to come the cloth will be there, if it is not there do not come here." They quickly ate and O'Niel rowed back to his island. He stayed there for over a year until a ship got stranded on a sand bar just out from where he was hunting.

He rowed out to the ship and the captain called down to him. The man was speaking French so O'niel hollered back that he only spoke English. The captain quickly changed to English as he said, "We have been blown about by a storm at sea for a very long time." "We need to free ourselves from this sand bar and continue on to France". "We are very much afraid of discovery by the English soldiers." "We are at your mercy mon ami." O'Niel laughed and said, "We are in the same fix." "I have no love of the English and they would love to find me too." The captain then said, "We will buy any food you can sell to us." "We have been out of provisions for a long time." O'Niel asked to come aboard to talk to them. He asked the captain what his ultimate destination was and he was told that they intended to unload in France and the return to New Orleans with a full cargo. O'Niel asked where New Orleans was and he was told it was in the Americas. He replied, "I will trade you three boatloads of food for passage to the Americas with you." "For a little gold I will get your ship off this sand bar also". The captain quickly agreed. O'Niel and two of the ships boats returned to his island and filled up with all the dried food and all of the fresh vegetables from his gardens. The three boats were piled high. When they got back to the ship O'Niel asked for six men to row each of the three boats. The bow of the ship was pointed toward the shore, and buried in the sand. They tied all three boats to the stern of the ship and the men began to pull with all their might toward the shore. After a short time of back breaking labor the ship began to turn so that the port side was facing the ocean. O'Niel then had them continue with the ropes on the stern and again they pulled the oars with all the strength they had. The ship moved backward until the bow was sticking up higher than the rest of the boat. After that O'Niel told all the men to return to the ship. When he was on the deck the captain said, "How is this any better than the way we were stuck before?"

O'Niel told him to wait and watch. In a short time the tide began to come in. Because of the many islands in the area the tide was forced to swirl from left to right as it arrived from the sea. When the motion got stronger the ship began to turn with it in a clockwise pattern. Within a few moments the ship was off the sand bar and headed back out to sea. The pattern of the wind followed the pattern of the sea and the sails soon had them away from the coast back on route to France. O'Niel got a big cheer from the crew, but the cook was happiest of all with the fresh food.

The captain told O'Niel that he would hold his money until they reached New Orleans. He explained that he would not trust even his own crew with the knowledge that a passenger had that much money. He also offered him a job with the crew if he wanted it and then he would pay him for the food and for his work on the ship.

O'Niel was not quite fifteen years old at the time but living alone on the island added even more muscle to his growing frame. He was about five foot ten inches and still growing, but his dark weather worn skin and bulk made him appear significantly older. To preserve his clothing he had taken to wearing as close to nothing as he could while he hunted and fished so even with his torn bottom pants and shirtless top he was sun and sea baked to a dark brown. His skin had endured many cuts and scratches from the swamp so it was now like leather. To conserve powder he had practiced many hours with his three knives so he could use them to hunt. He was happy to accept the offer and he soon took to the ropes and sails as though he were born on a ship. The captain took a special liking to the young man and he was soon teaching him how to use all of the tools of navigation and ship maintenance.

It would have all been perfect except when the sun was going down and O"Niel looked out over the blue water and he realized that he would never be able to return. He would never see his brothers again. He hoped that one day when he was settled he could convince them to visit him where ever he ended up.

When they arrived in France O'Niel was dumb founded. He had never seen so many people and ships and buildings. Just being with the crew on the boat seemed like a crowd so when he saw the hundreds of people and animals moving about the dock area he was fascinated and a bit frightened. The captain had been watching him and he was aware that the boy had never been anywhere outside of the swamps. Captain Boiseau put his hand on O'Niel's shoulder and told him to go with him. While the ship steward saw to the unloading and the subsequent loading of the ship the two went into the city. The first place they stopped was a marine outfitter.

Captain Boiseau ordered a canvas duffle bag with all the clothing and gear a sailor would need to go to sea.

He also got new pants, sox, shoes along with a fine cotton blouse and a heavy jacket and hat for him to change from his rags into. When O'Niel was changing the Captain noticed the three knives hidden in his waistband. He went and got a wide leather belt from a rack and handed it to O'Niel. This is a proper place to hide your knives. The Captain asked if the boy could use the knives and O'Niel said he could. "Show me", the Captain said. O'Niel said, "Right here?" "Yes", said the Captain and the young man turned and in a flash there were three knives sticking in the forehead of a mounted deer head forty feet away on the other side of the room. Captain Boiseau got a big smile on his face and said, "That is very impressive, but what if that was a man and not a deer head?" O"Niel said that the man would be dead and he would not be the first or even the second."

There was a long moment of silence before either of them spoke. Finally O'Niel said, "If that is a problem then you can leave me here and I will understand." The Captain laughed and slapped O'Niel on the shoulder before he said, "The best and the worst of all mankind sail on these ships." "I do not care about your past because I see the makings of a fine sailor in you. "Let's go get something to eat." "You can pay me for the gear when we reach New Orleans." O'Niel put his heavy bag over his shoulder and the two of them left.

Chapter 48

When the Captain realized that his new recruit had never been out of the swamp he decided to show him all the sites. They walked all over the city until they stopped at the home of an old friend. The home belonged to a middle aged woman with a pile of black hair on the top of her head held together with two ivory combs. She was what they call full figured with a little extra. It was obvious that the Captain did not mind as he grabbed her in a great hug and kissed her hard on the mouth. When he settled her back onto the floor he said, "I have been waiting a long time for that Annette and it was worth every second of it." She had a beautiful smile that went well with her flushed face when she said, "I missed you too you old water rat and I think maybe you should settle down and forget trying to out run pirates and foul weather." "I need a man here full time to help me run this place."

"One day," he promised, "One day soon." "This young man is O'Niel, and he is shipping out with me."

Perhaps he will decide to beach me here one day and then you will be stuck with me." She said, "I would like that."

"Good luck to you O'Niel and fair weather." "Now sit down and let me fix you something to eat."

They stayed there a week before leaving to sail west. O'Niel confessed to the Captain that he was worried about the fact that his family would not know if he were alive or dead. The Captain wrote a letter for him and sent it to a friend he had in the closest town to O'Niels' family. He assured the boy that the information would arrive secretly.

After a few weeks at sea O'Niel was speaking French and all the jargon that was exclusive to the handling of the ship, like a true sailor. He had never been happier in his life. The work was hard and dangerous, but he was long used to that type of life. No one knew how old he was and the crew thought it was their duty to test his mettle assuming he was man enough to sail with them.

The first few fights were about even, but the third man was well experienced with his fists and O'Niel found himself being knocked to the deck over and over again. The crew hollered for him to stay down, but he would not. The last time he hit the deck the Captain hollered, "Enough." He told the two to shake hands and then a strange thing happened. The man that had been hitting him grabbed him in a great hug and lifted him off the deck. He said, "I know that you are just a boy even if these fools do not." "I will teach you how to fight with your fists and then I will teach you to use a knife." "We are true ship mates."

The captain started to laugh as he said, "O'Niel, get the bird flying over my head." In a heartbeat one knife hit the bird in flight, the second pinned it to the mast and the third stuck just below it like a perch. The Captain said, "Are you sure you want to teach him how to use a knife?" The whole crew laughed and then cheered their young shipmate. This was his first cross ocean voyage and O'Niel was enjoying every day of it. The long hours and hard physical labor that was required began to but size and muscle on his frame. He was growing quickly toward the natural size of the big Irishmen in his family. While the men taught him everything about sailors and fighting, the Captain spent many hours with him teaching navigation, reading, and mathematics. His name had been shortened to Niel by the men and although he would one day change it back to O'Niel he was content to let them have their way. He was instructed in the use of a short sword common on the ships and he became intrigued with a form of French street fighting called savate. It was all done with your feet and men often put their hands in their pockets or hooked their thumbs in their belts. You were allowed to use your hands, but the feet were the primary weapons. A well trained fighter could do a great deal of damage without getting close enough to the other fighter to get hit back. The crew members loved working out with Niel because he was so young and he picked up their knowledge so quickly. They each bragged about how much they had taught him. His adoption by the crew made for a happy ship and the Captain was content to watch as Niel made each man feel as though he was the most important teacher of all. The Captain would just smile and think to himself that here was a natural leader of men and one day this boy would have his own ship.

A sailing ship is basically a machine and a ships' captain needed a deep sense of weights and pulleys and how they responded to the wind and the waves. The shapes and the sizes of the sails figured into every decision the captain made and there was an infinite number of things that could affect the running of the ship. Knowledge of all of this determined the place of every man aboard. It was not long before everyone was aware that Niel had to do all of the normal work of a sailor while being tutored by all of the men from the Captain on down.

He became a project in which all of the men could take pride. Most ships officers came from wealthy families that purchased their positions. Niel was one of the men and his humble gratitude toward everyone elevated him even higher in their minds.

The trip from France required following the trade winds south along the coast of Africa before turning south and west toward South America.

From there the winds pushed north along the coast and into the Gulf of Mexico. Captain Boudreau was as good a trader as he was a ships' captain. They stopped in ports along the coast of Africa where he traded for coffee and other things. He anchored in a small bay at the mouth of the Niger River to take on fresh water and fruit before they crossed the Atlantic Ocean. Niel saw the slave trade for the first time. He could not believe the indifference of the men as they handled their cargo of humanity. The slaves were sold by other black men and all of the buyers were white men. He was told about the difference between a "loose pack" compared to a "tight pack." Some "slavers" believed in forcing as many bodies as possible into the hold of the ship even though it meant that a large percentage of them would die, while others carried fewer in the hope that they would arrive with just a few dead. The stench and the pathetic depravity of these poor people were beyond anything Niel had ever seen or even heard of. Captain Boiseau loaded and left the port as soon as possible. He announced to his crew that he would never allow a slaver on his ship, not even a man that had sailed on one. Lex, the first mate, put his arm over the shoulder of Niel and said that the world was full of scum like they had just seen, but there are many decent men sailing the world also.

When they finally crossed the ocean, they landed at a place on the coast of Brazil. There were so many Greek sailors there that Spanish and Greek were spoken in equal amounts. Lex explained that the Greek sailors were to be found everywhere because they were among the first and the most daring seamen. They traded many things in Brazil and acquired a fine amount of Spanish gold for their products. They also loaded the ship with beautiful exotic hard wood that would sell well in New Orleans. When they finally were ready to sail north, Niel overheard the Captain and Lex whispering about their cargo of gold and how pirates would be watching for them.

There are no secrets in a port city and there are no secrets on a ship. The crew was well aware that they would be followed by men that would rather risk their lives to steal a cargo than work to earn it. The Captain set a course far to the east and then north. He wanted to stay away from the islands in the Caribbean Sea where pirates thrived. This would add a day or two to the trip, but it was worth it to avoid the pirates. The sailing was uneventful and no other ships were spotted for several days until they heard from the lookout those fateful words, "Sail Ho, off the port side."

Lex and the Captain went to the bow of the ship and used their telescopes to determine what kind of a ship it was. Within a few seconds they both confirmed that she was a pirate, and she was too fast for them to outrun. Captain called for the men to prepare for boarding and make ready all defenses. He asked for Niel to come to the bridge with him. When they were alone and both looking at the pirate ship, he said, "When I first saw you carrying that old musket I wondered." "I watched as we unloaded all the meat and fish from your home." "I figured you must be a pretty good shot to obtain all of that meat." "Are you that good?"

"I hit any target with in the range of that musket," he answered.

Captain Boiseau picked up a long canvas bag that smelled of fine oil and handed it to Niel. He told him to open it up. In the bag was the most beautiful long gun Niel had ever seen. It was much longer than his old musket and every inch of it was beautifully engraved with pictures and scrollwork. The Captain explained that it was a rifle. That meant that groves had been cut inside the barrel to make the ball spin as it left the gun. It was made in Italy by the finest gun smith in the country and it was accurate up to five hundred paces and even further in the right hands. "It takes the young eyes and the steady hands of a born hunter to use it properly."

"Do you think you can be that person even on a rolling ship," asked the Captain? Niel sat down on the deck and began to inspect every inch of the rifle. He thought it was the most beautiful thing he had ever seen. He looked up at the smiling Captain and said, "I guess if I can stand up in a rocking skiff and hit a bird in the wing with an old musket, I can hit whatever you want with this beautiful weapon."

Captain Boiseau pointed toward the pirate ship and said, "I want you to shoot any man that tries to hold the wheel of that ship." "We cannot out run them, but we can sure as hell make catching us as difficult as possible." He showed Niel how to load the rifle using a leather patch to wrap the ball in. He explained that it would add to the accuracy. He also measured out the maximum amount of powder that the barrel could withstand. He explained that a heavy load of powder was used for the farthest targets and that while his old musket would just bounce a ball off a man at sixty paces, this rifle would blow a hole through him at over five hundred paces. Niel was not a killer at heart, but he had to admit to himself that he was very excited to try out the gun.

Captain Boiseau pointed out the pirate ship coming toward them and said, "Time for you to earn your pay my young sailor."

The ship was at least eight hundred paces away when Niel sat on the deck and rested the rifle on the railing. He played the motion of the ship for several moments until he and the ship were one. When his ship began to roll up he pulled the trigger and immediately started to reload. He was in such a hurry to reload that he did not hear the crew cheering his shot. The Captain was holding his telescope as he said, "Your shot was a little high, but you hit him in the forehead, shot the next one." Niel aimed again and fired. This time the man was hit in the chest and there was no one there to grab the wheel.

The pirate ship began move out of control and away from them as a third man tried to grab the wheel and Niel shot him in the head. The pirate ship began to fall away as Captain Boiseau ordered the men aloft to open full sails. The whole crew was cheering Niel as they pulled further and further away from the pirate ship. The Captain told Niel to swab the rifle barrel out with hot water and vinegar and then oil it. As the pirate ship faded away the crew began to relax and talk about the shots that Niel had made and the more they bragged about their young ship mate, the longer the shots became. Niel had not moved from his perch on the deck as he cleaned the rifle and continued to admire every inch of it. When he finally got to his feet and offered the gun back to the Captain, he was surprised when the Captain told him that the gun was now his.

"I cannot accept such a beautiful and expensive gift," said Niel.

The Captain said, "You just earned that rifle and you will continue to earn it when these pirates catch up to us again." "It is not a gift, it is an addition to the safety of our ship and it belongs in the proper hands, your hands." "The pirates will find a way to shield their wheel from you and your rifle, and then they will catch us again." "We cannot outrun them, but now we know they are coming and we will have more time to prepare." "I want you to take your rifle and climb to the crows nest." When they come again they too will have men high in the mast looking for you, but they will not have rifles and I want you to shoot them before we are in range. One of the men made a leather sling for the rifle and Niel was able to carry it over his shoulder as he climbed up to the small platform on the top of the mainmast.

CHAPTER 49

It was the middle of the night and the sound of the violin moved through the mansion like a wave of mist flowing in all directions and covering me like a soft cloud. I got out of bed and pulled on a pair of pants and boots.

In seconds I had climbed the stairs and watched as Toby moved the bow over the strings and his body, eyes closed, swayed to the melody. I crept to the piano and began to play to the music of his strings. Soon I was in the same trance and we moved to the sounds and the emotions that they created. Then Sasha was there and he joined in with what he liked to call his "Croatian Guitar."

The windows were open and we played on and on. Suddenly another instrument was heard as O'Niel joined in with the beautiful deep tones of his cello.

We played on and on as the night rolled into the morning wolf light and we slowed to more soft and dreamy music that calmed us all and we began to look at one another and smile. The session ended when Lou and Bart began to softly clap their approval.

Once again the street was full of the wonderful people of New Orleans that had stopped on their way to or from work to listen to the music. They applauded loudly as we gave a quick bow at the windows and then followed Lou down to the dining room for breakfast.

I told O'Niel that I wanted to meet him in the library after we ate so he could continue his exciting story. He agreed and when we were situated in our respective chairs he began again.

Everyone on the ship was busy doing anything to fortify it for the coming battle. All knives and swords were sharpened to a razors edge. Niel had his special leather belt tight around his waist with the fourteen knives secured in their leather carriers. He also had his new rifle and it was never far from his hands. The cannons and the huge deck gun were cleaned and primed. His new job was to keep anyone from firing or loading their deck canon that projected the feared grapeshot. It was a can filled with musket balls and any other metal scraps and glass available on the ship. There were times when whole crews were put out of action by a single firing of the dreaded canon. Niel hated the canon and he hated anyone that tried to fire it. In his mind he could see the blood as it flew through the air like the spray of an ocean wave. "Sail ho off the stern," called a voice from high in the mast. It was about to begin. When the pirate ship got close, the Captain signaled to Niel that it was time. There was a wooden wall around the ships wheel to protect it but the gunner was standing solid against the deck cannon and Niel put a lead ball right between his eyes. The next man to go to the cannon suffered a ball through his chest. Niel decided to disable the cannon and so he put a lead ball through the firing mechanism that rendered the cannon useless. The pirates were now furious and determined to take the ship at all costs. They guided their ship on a collision course and the two ships hit together with a loud crunch. If there was severe damage, it was too late to care as the crews decided to kill one another.

The pirates swung to the ship on ropes and as soon as the ships were tied together they just jumped from ship to ship with no help needed. Blood flew and men fell to the sea. Our deck cannon roared and a slew of pirates flew into pieces. It was all blood and guts and the stink of bowels being emptied onto the deck as the men died. Captain Boudreau stayed close to Niel.

Niel destroyed the enemy with one knife after another thrown with deadly accuracy into the lifeblood of the enemy. When he was out of knives, he drew his short sword from his belt and screamed something that no man had ever heard before and he jumped into the center of the fight and began to slice people into pieces as he screamed his death song and destroyed anyone in his path. His insane force of destruction was soon noticed by the Pirate hoard and as they died from the blows of his sword they began to back away. Niel was a monster working outside the body of a man and his moves with the sword were so precise and his level of energy was so great that the pirates began to lay down their swords.

The Captain had to jump on top of him to make him stop before he killed them all.

The silence became so harsh that it almost hurt your ears. The Captain held tight to Niel until he was sure he was back in control of his emotions.

There was no sound except the waves against the side of the ship and the occasional bump of the two ships colliding. All of the crew was looking at Niel. He had killed seventeen of the pirates including those he killed with his rifle. Even the remaining pirates were focused on him. Niel held his short sword high above his head and shouted, "I will not abide a pirate or a thief." "Tell all that this is my intention and no man will stop me short of my death."

The entire remaining crew gave a great cheer and the Captain just smiled and patted his shoulder.

The damage to the two ships was quickly gone over and repairs were begun immediately. Lex, the first mate, was given the captainship of the pirate ship until it could be sold and by general agreement Niel was made the first mate. The stories about Niel were now exaggerated beyond belief. The crew loved him and his success was seen as a part of what each man had taught him. He was their pride and his success made each sailor stand just a little taller. When they entered the harbor at New Orleans no one was more in awe than Niel. It was a beautiful harbor and a growing town full of the color of Spain and Africa coated with the spirit of France. Niel believed that the most beautiful people on earth lived there. The Captain told him that they needed to go to the hotel to get rooms before they were all gone. Niel and the Captain went directly to the Hotel Madison and registered. It was the first time Niel had ever read a hotel registry and the first time he had ever signed his name. The Captain knew it and he rubbed his shoulder like a father showing pride in a son. They went to a table and ordered fine Creole food and a bottle of wine.

Captian Boiseau held his glass high and said, "Here is to a fine gentleman and a sailor of the finest canvas. "

"Were you my own son I could be no prouder." They touched glasses and Niel was red faced over the flattery.

"You have a great deal of money coming my young friend between what I owe you for the food, the relief from the sand bar, your wages and a share of the profits and the sale of the pirate ship." "What are you going to do with all that money?"

Niel said, "I want to buy the pirate ship." The Captain pounded his fist on the table and said in a loud voice, "I knew it." "I knew from the start that you had the call and the courage to captain a ship." "I will do you one better." "Sail with me for two years and I will make you the best captain to ever sail an ocean." "Invest your money in our cargo and in two years I will give you my ship and you will be a rich man from the sale of the cargo alone and the owner of a fine merchant ship." The Captain put out his hand and Niel grabbed it. Before he let go Niel said, "I thank you for this fine offer, but I must make two conditions." "One, you let me arm our ship properly so that no one will bother us and two, you retire with that fine woman in France when we return and I will split the profits for four years instead of two." With a tear in his eye Captain Boiseau agreed. He said, "All I ever wanted was a fine ship until I met Annette." "I cannot tell you how I look forward to being able to spend the rest of my life with her." "After we eat we will go to my bank so you can set up an account."

The pirate ship was secured at the dock. All of the prisoners were turned over to the local authorities which turned out to be a joke. New Orleans was a wild city with no real authority except for the men with the most money and most of them were thieves and pirates always in need of sailors.

The pirate crew was released and back at sea the same day. The next day, Captain Boiseau, Niel, and Lex went down to the docks to inspect the pirate ship. Their crew of carpenters was already making all the necessary repairs.

When Niel finally got a chance to tour the ship in detail he was surprised to see what a fine ship it was. She was slightly longer than their ship and not quite as wide which explained the speed difference. She carried twelve twenty pound cannons on each side and a stern pair of thirty pounders which was very rare for a sailing ship. She would put up a fair fight against anything but a military ship of the line. She was much newer than their ship and the cargo hold was designed to carry a considerable amount of tonnage.

The three of them decided to keep the ship and add it to their business. Lex agreed to captain their current ship, The Bonnie, and the Captain and Niel would take the pirate ship now named Annette.

They intended to sail up the coast of North America, trading as they sailed and then followed the trade winds back to France.

While Lex and the Captain sold their cargo and the bounty of cargo found on the Annette, Niel studied every ship that came into the harbor and drove their gunners crazy with questions about arming a ship. At first they were reluctant to speak with him, but when the stories of his fight with the pirates got around he was soon in a world full of friends and fellow sailors. He took this knowledge and applied it to the Bonnie. She would never be as deadly as the Annette, but she would be a handful in a fight and most pirates prefer to fight a ship at anchor so she would be very safe at sea.

When the money was divided up and the crew was given their share Niel was surprised to see how many of the men decided to stay in port and settle there with their families permanently.

Captain Boiseau explained that when the payout is as large as this one the wives realize that their men can sell their talents from their own businesses right here in port. The money is just the start they needed. New Orleans is full of carpenters and smithies from ships. Cooks open restaurants and who better to design and operate ropes and loading cranes then sailors?

Even in the theaters the men who move the scenery and everything else are called by their job titles on a sailing ship. Niel asked what they were going to do for a crew and the Captain explained that there would be plenty of men looking for work on a ship that had the success they had. They stayed in port for three weeks buying cargo, repairing the two ships and hiring on a crew. Much to his delight, many of the gunners Niel had been talking with signed on with the two ships. They liked the idea of a First Mate that came to them for education and they took it as a sign of respect.

They turned out to be very valuable in helping him buy cannons and placing them on the Bonnie.

One of the men named Jean was particularly helpful and he suggested that Niel take a trip with him up the Mississippi to visit his large family and try to recruit some more men for the crews.

They took a keelboat north up the river that was propelled by men with long poles that walked along both sides of the boat pushing their poles into the river bottom and constantly rotating front to back with incredible precision. It took three days of working against the current, but they finally reached a small village on the east side of the river. Their boat pulled in and docked. Like magic people started to come from everywhere.

They were shouting and hugging one another and speaking a strange mixture of French, English and something else. Jean explained that it was called Creole and that all of these people including the boat crew were his relatives. There were hundreds of them and soon big kettles were boiling and bread was baking while men dumped baskets of fish and crawfish into the kettles. The women were running around adding potatoes, onions, and spices to everything. It all smelled so good and everyone was so loving and happy that Niel suddenly remembered his swamp back home and the love most of the people shared. He wondered if he would live long enough to see it again.

Soon the music started and it had a unique sound of its own. Beer and harder stuff was poured freely and it was a very special day.

Later when the dark began to descend and the fires blazed higher there was a great hush as an old woman came and sat on a rocker provided for her. She had long gray hair to her waist and a few teeth missing, but there was something very beautiful about her.

Everyone grew very quiet as she looked at Niel and waved a finger to summon him. Jean whispered to him that she was the grandmother of all of these people and that he should go to her. When Niel was standing in front of her she motioned for him to get down on his knees. He did as she requested and she put her hands on both sides of his face and kissed his forehead and licked his cheeks. She held his face close to hers and said, "You too are special and now the People will know you." She handed him a glass and told him to drink it. He did as he was told and then she said "Go and enjoy all of my grandbabies." She cackled a crazy laugh and the music and the singing began again.

Everyone was smiling at him and shaking their heads as if a great thing had happened as he walked back to Jean. Jean looked at him and said, "Wow, I have heard of it but I never expected to see it happen."

Niel said, "What are you talking about and what is everyone looking at?"

Jean took him to a mirror hanging from a tree and told him to look into it. Niel saw a large gold nugget pierced into his right ear. Jean told him no one knows what it means, but it is very special and everyone in these swamps will now know who you are and that Grandma has chosen you.

Chosen, what does it mean to be chosen, he thought. "How I wish my family were here to enjoy all of this." He and Jean spent three days there and the party never seemed to end. Jean explained that these people wanted little beyond respect and independence and the swamp provided everything else. "This is a very good life," he said but if you have a lust to wonder then you either go to sea or trek west to the mountains. "I love the sea and maybe someday I will return here to live, but I think not." They recruited many good men that knew the water and how to handle any kind of weapon. Together they built a huge raft and floated it back down to New Orleans, but before they left Niel went to see Grandma. She licked her lips and smiled with her remaining teeth as he approached her sitting in her rocker. She said, "You have many questions and I will not answer any of them right now." She gave him a big leather skin and said, "Put a drop of this liquid on your tongue every day." "Never let anyone taste it and never forget to take your drop every day." "When it is almost empty come back to me and I will be waiting."

Niel looked doubtful so she explained that she would not die for a very long time, so she would indeed be waiting. He took the skin and went toward the raft. Before he had gone too far she shouted, "Buy a cello, I love the cello and I know you will learn it easily." He promised that he would and then got on the raft and they pushed off. It was a wonderful, lazy journey as they drifted with the current down the river. He had no idea what he would do with a cello, but a promise is a promise and he would indeed buy a cello and try to play it.

The ships were loaded soon after their return and both crews were anxious to leave.

Niel worked hard with the men every day even though he was the First Mate and soon to be the Captain. The men took to him as one of their own, but his orders were never questioned and when decisions needed to be made, he made them. The day before they weighed anchor a policeman and his five deputies came down the dock to the ship. They explained that several of his men were criminals and that the ship could not leave until the cargo was inspected and each man was questioned. Niel asked them to come aboard and explain themselves again. They did as he asked but the head of the Police group hinted that for several hundred dollars he might forget the whole thing. Niel held his head in his hands as though he were deep in thought, then he asked one of his men to throw his black straw hat in the air. In a blink a knife hit the hat and stuck it to the mast. Two more knives were protruding from the toe of each of the policeman's boots, affixing them to the floor. Niel reached down and pulled the two knives out. He then ordered the six men thrown overboard.

The next day, they left. It seemed the stories about him were just beginning.

CHAPTER 50

Lex took the Bonnie around the Florida peninsula and headed north. He wanted to trade in New York before crossing to France.

The Captain wanted to try trading in the cities along the coast before going to New York to meet Lex. There was no hurry and now both ships were heavily armed so they agreed to travel alone. Niel and the Captain stopped in Miami, Charleston, Savannah, and Trenton before getting to New York. They managed to do some trading, especially for cotton before they headed for New York to meet up with Lex. Trenton and the Port Elizabeth were as wild as any place on earth. While they were in port, Niel went looking for cargo while the Captain visited old friends. After a hard day of negotiating with every warehouse owner in town he headed back toward the ship and a small tavern called the Head of a Dove. A pathetic dead dove was nailed above the entrance, thus the name. Niel walked in and stood at the bar where he ordered a mug of hard cider.

Before he could get the mug to his lips he heard a voice from across the room saying, "I know who you are." "You are that kid that works on the Annette and brags about how tough he is." Niel brought his mug to his lips and began to drink his cider.

Now it is important to know that a man, no matter how young, that commands a ship, survived the elements of the Irish swamp alone, and killed many pirates in hand to hand combat tends to have limited patience with fools. The big sailor was a good head taller than Niel and much heavier. As he walked across the room he continued to berate Niel with any lie he could dream up. When he was about five feet away, Niel put his thumbs in his belt, jumped several feet off the floor and kicked the big sailor in the jaw.

Niel turned and picked up his cider, took a long drink and put the mug down on the bar. When he turned back toward the crowd the big man was on his feet and coming for him again. Niel moved quickly to his left and landed two more kicks to the jaw of the big man and he went down again.

When the man tried to get up again Niel threw two knives that pinned the sleeves of the coat the fellow was wearing to the floor. The poor fellow could not move. Niel explained that he had more knives and he was tired of playing. He suggested, as he retrieved his knives, that it would be more fun if they just stood at the bar while he bought them a drink. The big fellow agreed and as they stood there drinking Niel asked him his name and what he was so upset about, He said, "My name is Stanley and I am upset about my best friend Mica. Niel suggested he tell him about Mica and maybe he could help.

Stanley said that Mica was a free man but slave hunters took him out of a tavern he was in and claimed that he was a runaway. They put him in chains and took him to the block to sell him. They said they had papers and that Mica belonged to them now.

Niel told him to take him to where they were selling him. They left as soon as they could and ran to the auction block. Mica was put up for sale right after they got there. Every time the auctioneer suggested a price everyone in the crowd looked at one man and then looked away quickly. Niel had been to enough auctions to know a set up when he saw one. He also knew that the slavers had no real papers on Mica and by buying him here they would have legitimate papers with which to sell him further south. He slowly made his way through the crowd until he was standing next to the man that everyone was showing so much fear of. When the auctioneer asked if anyone would bid anything the man finally spoke up and said," Five dollars." It was a very ridiculous price.

The auctioneer said, "Are there any more bids?" Niel said, "Six dollars and slid one of his knives under the mans' coat and pressed the tip hard against the lower rib cage.

It would take only a gentle push to slide the razor sharp dagger up and into his heart. Niel had a big smile on his face when the auctioneer said, "Sold." Niel handed Stanley the six dollars and told him to give it to the auctioneer and have him give Mica freedom papers. "Do not ask, tell the bastard you want freedom papers."

Niel waited with his knife still under the coat of the other man as several nasty looking slave hunters came over and asked him what the hell was going on. Niel pushed a little harder on the knife as the man explained that there was nothing wrong and he would tell them all about it later.

When they left Niel said that Mica was one of the ninety seven men in his crew and if the man or any of his friends were around after dark they would be hunted down and hanged. Niel then told the man to give him fifty dollars and the man complained that Niel had only spent six. Niel laughed and said, "My time is valuable so just give me the money." The man paid and ran away. When Stanley returned Niel got a good look at Mica. He was about five foot ten inches tall, but he was built like a fort. He would one day compare him to Captain Keys. Mica began to thank him profusely when Niel held up his hand. He said, "I need good men and I hate slavery with all of my heart." "If you two will join my crew I will consider myself well paid."

Mica stepped forward and said, "I am your man now and always no matter what." Stanley said the same, and Niel said, "Then I am well satisfied." They went back to the tavern for something to eat and a drink to celebrate. When they got there at least thirty of their crew were there having a drink. After about an hour the man from the auction and four slave hunters came into the building. They pointed pistols at Niel and Mica and said we are here to take back our property. Niel said nothing and he motioned for the other men to do the same. The man repeated his demand in an even louder voice and again Niel said nothing. There was a silence that seemed to last forever before Niel spoke.

Finally Niel asked Stanley what he had promised if

these men bothered him again. Stanley said, "You told them you would hang them." Niel looked at the man and said, "If you leave now I will be kind and forget we ever met." "If you do not I will hang all five of you." One of the slavers raised his gun and pointed it at Mica. Before anyone could blink there was a knife sticking through his throat and out the back of his neck. As he dropped to the floor dead, the crew of the Annette jumped the others and held them tight. Niel walked over to the dead man and removed his knife which he cleaned on the dead man's shirt and returned it to his wide belt. Niel told his men to take them out of town and hang them. They asked about the dead man and Niel said, "Hang him too; I keep my word no matter what." His men took the five away and Niel returned to his drink.

The owner of the tavern came over to him and said, "People will want to know what happened here that ended in all those hangings." Niel said, "Tell them that the first mate of the beautiful Annette, riding the waves in their harbor has a crew of the best fighting men on any sea, and the ship we took from pirates is armed to her bilge and looking for a fight." "Leave us be and we will become the best friends you could have." "Bother the first mate or the captain and Niel will deliver his own justice." "Now I think it is time I bought a round for the house, and you my good friend would honor me by drinking with me in a salute to your fine tavern."

As the cheers went up his men returned and everyone celebrated.

The crew celebrated well into the night, but Niel left early followed by Stanley and Mica.

When Niel asked what they were doing they explained that they owed him a life and they would forever watch his back.

They loaded the new trade goods and sailed for New York. The city had changed a great deal since the revolution. Progress and money were pouring in along with many people from across the ocean. Cotton buyers came down from up north to buy cotton for their mills, and the large German farms provided a never ending supply of dried and fresh fruits and meat. It was said that if you could not buy it in New York, then you probably did not need it anyway. They dropped anchor next to the Bonnie in the harbor and enjoyed a great reunion with the crew. Lex, Niel and the Captain went to a fine restaurant to discuss business. Lex explained that he bought a full cargo of cotton in Georgia and rather than sell it here in New York, he took it to Boston where he made a much greater profit.

He used the money to buy Boston Rum to sell in France where it is a favorite in the taverns along the coast. Niel explained that they had a variety of products from cotton to hard liquor from the back woods of the Carolinas. Lex also asked about the hanging of the men back in Port Elizabeth. Niel asked him how he knew about that, and Lex explained that there are faster ships than the Annette and the story has spread among the sailors from ship to ship before they anchored.

Niel just shrugged his shoulders and said, "I was forced to keep my word to a bunch of slavers." "I doubt that your word will be questioned again," added Captain Boiseau. Lex said, "I should think not." And the subject was closed.

The Captain had a good friend that was a tobacco merchant and even if his price was slightly higher than buying further south, the quality of the product was the best. He also had a friend that would pay top price for all the liquor in the hold of the Annette and more than make up any loss on the tobacco.

Trading was their real business and even in the days of sailing ships, millions and millions of tons of cargo were traded all over the world.

You could find Chinese carvings in New York and Boston rum in India.

Sailors came in all sizes and colors as men of the sea signed on to replace lost seamen in every port. Men soon learned to take orders in all the languages to keep the machines that sailed the oceans moving ahead.

A good trader got rich while the wild gamblers were eliminated more often than they were a success. Many pirates started out as honest traders who took too many chances. Niel took to trading like a duck to water, but both Lex and the Captain taught him how to trade smart.

They told him that the single most important thing was to get a reputation for being honest and learn to establish relationships with other honest merchants. "All of us that trade together worldwide make up the backbone of trade and real profit," explained the Captain. "We can go anywhere to trade because a friend here knows a merchant at our next port and he will direct us to him with a letter of introduction." "That merchant will introduce us to others in that port and our group of honest business associates will expand." "If, however, you should cheat anyone of us the word will travel fast and you will be forced to trade in the hell holes of the world."

Niel loved learning from these men and all the members of the crew. He learned that the best sailors would seek out captains that were known for their honesty and all the sailors knew who those men were. Niel realized how lucky he was to have joined this Captain. They spent two weeks trading and loading and unloading cargo from their ships. Many other captains and first mates from other ships came to them and asked if they could inspect the new guns for themselves.

These were good men and they were grateful for the chance to see a merchant ship that had been armed so well for defense. Niel was often asked to inspect their ships and make suggestions for arming them better.

He became well known by all of the ship captains and he was given personal letters of introduction to help him in any port in the world.

There was a very strange and abnormal acceptance of Niel throughout the many ships in the harbor. His own men talked about how open he was to their ideas and opinions that crew members thought of him as one of their own that had been elevated because of their teaching.

They also respected him as their superior on board ship or in a harbor after word got out of his fighting skills and the men he had hanged. Ship Captains liked to think of him as they once were and his quick mind for learning anything impressed all of them. All of this added to his reputation, but nothing impressed them more than when he brought his cello up on deck in the early evening and played it to the waves that carried the notes over the bay and to the ears of sailors throughout the harbor. He had no idea how he had taken to the instrument so easily, but it just became natural that as the bow touched the strings his fingers knew just where to go and his right arm knew just how to move. He was just about sixteen now and he was just under six foot and one hundred and eighty pounds. He never tripped and he never got sick. He often wondered if it was good luck or the daily taste from the wine skin that Grandma had given him.

He figured he would never know.

One time he was hanging upside down repairing a spar high above deck when it snapped and he fell. By the time he hit the deck he had flipped over and he landed softly on his feet. The men rushed over to him, but he just laughed it off and climbed back up to finish the work on the spar. This just added to the mystery that was First Mate, Niel. I believe it is fair to say that there are no men on the face of this planet as superstitious as those that sail the seas. When they had crossed the Atlantic and dropped anchor in France the men were convinced that Niel was the harbinger of very good luck. Not only did they have fair weather, but on two occasions they were approached by pirates that turned and sailed away when they learned they were facing the Annette and the Bonnie was not far away.

All this led up to the Captain announcing that he was going ashore for good and Niel would be the new captain of the ship on all future voyages. The men let out three cheers for good Captain Niel and then they rushed to Captain Boiseau and wished him all the luck in the world.

The next day Niel and Lex attended the wedding of the Captain and Annette. It was a very quiet affair but one filled with joy and good wishes. Lex and Niel had pilfered a large diamond ring from the pirate ship that is now the Annette and decided to keep it for this very occasion. The Captain grinned and shook his head knowingly as he put it on her finger. Lex and Niel found lodging at a nearby hotel and began to make plans for the next voyage. The year was 1812 and the next morning they were informed that England was once again at war with America. They decided to become smugglers running the blockade of English ships guarding the shores of America. Neither Lex, the Frenchman or Niel, the Irishman had any love for the king and crown of England. Throughout the war they carried cargo to and from America at great risk and even greater profit. Their accounts at banks in France and New Orleans grew to enormous sums and Niel was investing heavily in real estate in New Orleans. By the time the war ended Niel had decided to stay permanently in America and so he sold his ship to Lex. He often visited the swamp and the old Grandma during these times and it was the feeling of belonging here with people like his own that made him give up the sea. He had buildings and shipping concerns in the city and the surrounding ports that kept him busy until one day he felt a great need to see Grandma. It was as though the old lady was calling to him in his mind and he knew he must obey.

When he got to the dock there was no one there except the old lady sitting in her rocker smoking a pipe about two feet long. She looked at him and smiled with her few teeth and said, "Good, you are here and we must talk alone." He pulled up an old nail keg to sit on and she began to talk. She told him all about the Red Gate and the People. She gave him the details of her family connections and explained all that he would have from the Red Gate and what he could not have in the way of a family. She then said, "The choice is yours, but you must tell me soon." "I will show you how to regulate the formula to suit your needs, but then you will be on your own."

Niel was very quiet for a very long time and then he said, "All of my blood is still in Ireland if they have not been killed." "I can use the Red Gate to help any that are left." "No one there will recognize me after all this time and all the changes in my appearance." "Yes, please give me the Red Gate and I promise that I will try to never make you sorry for this gift,"

Within moments people began to walk out of the swamp and came to the two of them.

These people were all strangers. Grandma explained that all of them were the People and they came to share their blood with him to allow him to pass through the Red Gate. Niel knelt down before the old lady and she put on the ring with the silver spike and each of the People shed a drop of blood into the vase and when they were all done she pricked her own hand and let several drops fall into the vase. She added the formula and told him to drink. The next day she removed the gold earring the same way she did with Getts.

A few weeks later Niel took a ship to Ireland. He carried with him a small fortune in cash and bank notes. Stanley and Mica traveled with him. The three were dressed as fine gentlemen. They hired a coach and driver and took it to a small village close to where his family lived in the swamp. There was a rooming house there and the three of them got rooms. Niel told the owner that he was a Solicitor and the other two men were his servants. He described his oldest brother by name and gave rather poor directions to his farm. He offered to pay to have the man summoned and explained that there was a death and an inheritance was involved. The owner of the rooming house laughed at the directions and said no one would ever find anyone using those directions, but he knew the man and he would go get him himself. He further explained that the man he wanted was his friend and he would get him as a favor.

The next morning Niel dressed in a dark cloak with a large floppy brim hat to keep off the damp cold. He and Stanley and Mica were sitting in the main room of the building. There was a stone fireplace at one end of the room and the walls were made of mud and waddle. The floors were hard packed dirt and there was a wide board across two barrels at the end opposite the fireplace that served as a bar where hard cider and sometimes rum were served. The ceiling was low and everything was covered with a layer of smoke and soot from the fire. The roof was covered with thatch and the main room also had a series of crude tables and benches of various lengths. Niel was happy that the owner had not recognized him since Niel knew exactly who the man was and he knew his name was Joe.

Niel had visited the place as a child with his father many times to sell fish and produce. Several people came into the tavern during the day, but Stanley and Mica made sure they did not approach Niel. By midafternoon Joe returned with Niels' oldest brother. Niel kept his hat pulled down to cover his face as he explained that he wished to return to his brother Dannys' home and the other members of the family were to attend also because the business involved all of them.

Niel and Danny took the skiff belonging to Danny and Stanley and Mica followed in a borrowed one. When they got to the little homestead it was obvious that they had fallen on difficult times.

The children had grown and gone and his sister in law looked care worn. Her clothes were in bad shape and although the little home was spotlessly clean, there was very little food and everything was old and worn. Niel was ashamed that he had not found a way to help them sooner.

Niel took off his hat and coat and looked at his brother right in the eyes. Danny showed no recognition. Finally, Niels wife gasped and brought her hand to cover her mouth as she exclaimed to her husband, "Don't you see he is your brother Niel?" "I would recognize those eyes anywhere."

Niel grabbed Danny in a hug and said, "She is right, I came home to see you." At first Danny was afraid for his brother until he realized that if he did not know him then no one else would either. They held each other tight until Niel asked about the rest of the family.

Danny told him to sit down and he would explain.

"After you left things began to settle down although Sir Candleman was furious and he swore to find you and kill you." "When the letter came from France explaining that you had escaped and that you would not be returning, we were all very relieved to know that you were safe." "I even went to your island to make sure you were gone." "Someone gave a copy of the letter to Candleman and he was furious. He sent soldiers to kill us all. Everyone fought them, but we were not prepared enough. "They managed to kill all of us except my wife and I and most of the children which we sent away to distant relatives." I stayed but it seemed that the outrage of the people here got to be too much for Candleman so he returned to England and we have not seen him or his men since."

"Most of what we had was used up or ruined during the years of fighting. So what you see is what is left." By this time Mary, his wife, was sobbing.

Niel was so angry that he was having trouble speaking. He took several slow deep breaths and then said, "If money was no object, what would you two like to happen now?"

Mary was first to answer. She said, "Most of our children have settled far from here in Dublin." "I would like a way to go and be near them."

Niel asked her what they were doing there and she said, "They are married and they are saving their money to buy an Inn where we can all live and work." Niel told them to pack whatever they needed and they would all go to Dublin together.

Danny wanted to know what he should do about his little farm and Neal suggested he let the wind and the sea take it back. Niel bought a coach and team of horses and left with Stanley and Mica on top and the three of them in the coach. It was a long trip to Dublin, so it allowed Niel to tell them his story, or at least as much of it as he could. They were shocked, but they made him promise to tell it all to the children so they could have real bed time stories of their uncle that sailed the seas. We had to stop several times during the trip and it gave me a chance to buy them proper clothes and shoes. At first they were afraid, but Mica made sure no one got even close to us and Stanley only had to stare at someone and they were quick to back away. Niel loved spoiling his big brother and his wife and they were all anxious to get to Dublin where the children and grandchildren were.

Danny and Mary looked splendid in their fine new clothes so Niel made sure that they each had a trunk full tied on the back of the coach.

They finally reached Dublin and Niel was surprised to see how large a city it had become. Niel was now familiar with cities from France to Brazil so he was quite comfortable, but when he checked them into a fine hotel Danny and Mary were so ill at ease that all they could do was look around with their mouths open. Niel took care of everything and even escorted them to their suit so he could tip the bellboy. He told them to let the maid unpack their things and they left the rooms with him and returned to the lobby. He took them to the dining room and ordered food and wine which he suggested Mary have a glass of to settle her down. Stanley and Mica took care of the horses and were given rooms of their own in an adjoining building. Niel asked if they could excuse him for a short while and they agreed.

They were anxious to talk about their adventure so far and they still felt as though this was all a dream.

Niel went to the front desk and asked if the owner or manager was available. He was immediately taken to a back office that was as plush as the rest of the hotel. He was introduced to a Mr. Gray and they each took a seat at a table with a crystal bottle of port and two glasses on it. Mr. Gray poured and asked how he could be of service. Niel said he had two requests. "I need a safe place to put the cash and letters of credit I am carrying and I need to find a good investment here in Dublin for my family to run. Mr. Gray got a big smile on his face and said, "How did you like having the nugget in your ear, and I would love to know how the old girl does it."

They both shook hands again and soon they were conversing in their thoughts instead of speaking out loud. Gray explained that there were several of the People here in Dublin and they were all anxious to meet him. He also explained that the owner of the hotel had to finally relocate because his lack of aging was becoming too obvious.

They were looking for another of the People to buy it and start the process all over again. He said, "Grandma said you were coming so we decided you were a perfect fit because you sound like an Irishman and you have a history with this country." "We know all about your family and I will stay on and teach them how to run it." "Gray pulled a pile of papers from his desk drawer and said, "Just start signing and the place is yours, the money has already been transferred to an account for you here in Dublin where you might want to put your other valuables." " I have sent men to fetch the rest of your family and they will join you in the dining room very soon." Again they shook hands and Niel went back to the dining room. He explained that their children would be joining them soon and that they all had much to talk about. Niel began to order from the menu that was all in French and informed the waiter that they would have a large group coming and they were not to be disturbed. Soon the rest arrived. There were three sets of parents and a dozen children. Niel thought, "Oh the Irish, no matter how bad things get we manage to still fill the world with babies." He was answered with loud laughter in his mind as many of the People had heard his thoughts. Everyone was dressed in the best they had and the children were scrubbed to a shine. While he looked at the babies his thoughts were interrupted by Mr. Gray who informed him that three large townhouses also came with the hotel, and a cottage at the shore.

Everyone was very well behaved and the children did their best to act like little ladies and gentlemen. It was a grand reunion and every so often Niel and Danny looked at one another with a tear in their eyes for those that were missing. Niel had decided to attend to that problem at a later date, but for now he would enjoy having a family again. When they were clearing away the dishes the head waiter asked if Niel would be staying at his hotel or would he like any assistance for other plans he might have. Niel explained that he would be staying in his suit for now. Everyone at the table got quiet and they all looked at Niel. "Well", he said, "That brings us to the next order of business." "This is an extremely large hotel and it is now fully owned by me." There were several gasps and more than a few people crossing themselves.

Even the babies seemed to be crossing themselves. Before anyone could say anything, Niel continued. "The staff will stay on to teach all of you how to run the place and there is a townhouse for each of the three couples." "I assume Danny and Mary will live in their suite when they are here, but they also have a cottage at the shore." "We own several horses and coaches that are yours for the asking, and I will be visiting from time to time, but I have other interests in New Orleans and France to take care of also." "I expect each of you to visit me there some day." Each of you will get a salary and two servants come with each town house." "Your father and I will have the final say on everything with

Mary being the tie breaker when we do not agree." "Learn and learn some more." "The staff will tutor you in French and everything else you will need to know."

"It was the sailors on my ships that taught me how to become a Captain and anyone who wants to someday run this or another hotel that we buy will follow my example."

Show them total respect and they will give it back to you." "Anyone that does not want to continue here is welcome to leave with no hard feelings."

"Now, who wants to hear about pirates and battles at sea?" All the children agreed that they wanted to hear the stories.

Soon after he started Mica and Stanley joined them. The two of them soon took over the telling of all of their uncles daring adventures and they had a way of adding a few stories of their own. While the children were busy, their parents were taken to see their new homes. Mary went with them so Niel and Danny were left alone to talk. Danny had a million questions and Niel tried to answer them all.

Finally, Danny asked, "Are you sure you can afford all of this?" Niel hugged him hard and said, "All of this is paid for and I will be putting several hundred pounds into an account for you and Mary before I leave." "Surely you are not going to leave us after we just found you, Danny asked? Niel said that he would be gone a short time and then he would be back to visit and make sure they were all set up. They spent the rest of the evening talking and listening to the young parents rave about their luxurious new homes and how they were all sure this was a dream. Mica said to them, "If the Captain says that this is the way it is to be then you can take it as the honest truth." "I know of no man willing to doubt his word." "One day, I will tell you how he saved me from slavery and what happened to the men that did not believe him when he warned them to stay away." After the children were put to bed, the adults asked Mica to tell them the story. Niel just sat there as

Mica told the story in great detail with Stanley shaking his head in agreement. Mary was shocked into silence, but Danny wanted to know why he hung the dead man.

Niel looked at him with no sign of emotion and said, "I gave them my word that I would hang them all." "After that no one doubted my word."

The family realized then that this blood kin of theirs was a stranger and they would need time to get to know him.

Two days later Niel, Stanley and Mica left for London. The People had tracked down Lord Candleman for Niel and he was staying at a very exclusive club in central London. When the three arrived they booked a suit at a very expensive hotel in Niels' name with the two others listed as his servants. He had a letter of introduction from one of the People that was a very prominent financer in the whole of England. He had it delivered to the club with a request to spend time their relaxing during his visit. It was against club rules to discuss business with anyone while you were there so it was common to use it as a place to escape the stress of every day work. He began spending time there every afternoon. He sat quietly reading a book and sipping scotch while listening to the conversations around him. He noticed that as the time rolled by and Lord Candleman drank more and more, he got louder and more abusive. His favorite topic was what he called the Irish trash and how he intended to see them all in a grave.

Late one afternoon when the Lord was well in his cups as they say, he became louder and more profane in his discussion about the Irish. While he was spouting off Niel whispered, "Bullshit".

Niel continued to pretend to read his book.

At first the Lord ignored it until Niel said just a little louder, "Bullshit." This time the room became very quiet except for a few giggles.

Lord Candleman stood over Niel and shouted at him, "What did you say to me?" Niel answered that he had said nothing directly to him. Candleman said, "I distinctly heard you say something." Niel replied that he did indeed say something.

Candleman was about to lose control when he shouted in a loud voice, "Dammit man." "What did you say?" Niel looked directly at him and said, "I said Bullshit."

"Were you saying that I was bullshit?"

Niel stood up and looked at the fool in the face and said, "I would never say that you were bullshit." "I was referring to everything that comes out of your big mouth."

Lord Candleman got red in the face and pulled back his hand to slap Niel in the face. Niel told him that if he tried that he would return the favor. Niel handed him a soft leather glove and allowed him to lightly strike him on the cheek. Niel was challenged to a duel. They agreed to meet out of the city limits at dawn the next morning. Niel chose sabers as was his right as the one challenged. Everyone in the club planned on attending. Candleman was an obnoxious blow hard, but he was one of them and known to be ruthless with a sword, so everyone assumed he would adjust to the much shorter saber with no problem. The next day Niel introduced Mica as his second which insulted them even further.

The rules were given and they were quite simple. The men would fight until one of them could not continue or one of them was dead. A simple apology by either man would stop the fight at any time.

They stepped apart several feet and then they were instructed to begin. At first Niel only defended as the Lord charged him with vicious blows, one after another. Niel retreated or simply moved to the side of each charge from his opponent. Niel began to smile at the futility of the efforts of Candleman. Niel was a master with a saber after years of life or death fighting on board his ship. He waited for the next charge and sliced the Lords right ear. He said, "Father." As the blood ran Candleman tried again to hack away at him but Niel sliced his left ear. Niel said, "Mother."

They fought back and forth for a little longer but it was obvious that Niel could kill him any time he wanted. Finally, one of the men shouted, "For Gods' sake, Candleman say you are sorry before he has to kill you." Candleman again charged Niel and Niel buried his saber in his stomach. Niel whispered who he was as the Lord sunk to the ground dead.

Niel and Mica returned to the hotel, retrieved Stanley and their luggage and took a boat back to Dublin. Niel had never even broken a sweat. He had kept his word to his parents that he made at their grave. By the next day the news was all over Dublin about the hated Lord Candleman and a blow by blow description of the duel appeared in the newspaper.

No one knew the name of the other duelist since his letter of introduction at the club was missing. Niel smiled when he heard it and thanked the member of the Red Gate that covered his tracks. He was quickly answered by a thought from one of the People in London. "It was our pleasure," it said.

The next day He met with his brother Danny for breakfast. They spoke of many things concerning the hotel and made many decisions about who would be trained to do what.

Finally Danny said, "I will never judge you for anything you have done and I, along with our families, will be forever grateful for this life you have given us." "What happened to you that gave you such strength and such an easy way with dominating some very tough men?" "What will you do next and is there anything I can do to help?" "I know you killed Candleman and I am glad you did, but how do you make it all look so simple?"

"There are many things that I cannot talk about, but I can try to answer some of your questions." "I was alone for so long with our parents to look after that I became more comfortable with the laws of the swamps than the laws the rest of you live by." When I got the chance to go to sea I took it and I fell in love with ships and the men that sail them." "The hard work built muscles and my admiration for the skills of every man on the ship made all the sailors happy to teach their young admirer." After a time, even the Captain began to teach me how to read and the mathematics required to operate the wonderful machine you know as a ship." "My Irish temper and my devotion to the crew combined with the skills I learned hunting threw me into the middle of every fight we had." "There are no secrets on a ship and there are no secrets in port, so my reputation grew quickly." "Never confuse devotion with domination." "I dominate no man, but I give and demand respect in equal amounts from all men." "What you can do for me now is live as I wanted our parents to live." "Surround yourself with children and be the father that I cannot ever be." "I wish to live part of my life through you." "Please do this for me."

CHAPTER 51

Niel sat on the porch of his beautiful hotel and played his cello. It had become an early morning ritual. On that particular morning he was joined by two men with violins that lived in the hotel. It was a reunion of the spirit of Ireland as they played the songs of the hearth and homes of the different parts of the country.

Ireland has always been a country full of magic and music created by the "Little People" and sung to words of sadness created by those that toil to survive.

As the trio played on, several young boys joined them in a choir of tenor voices so much loved by the people. It was as though this whole section of Dublin had become frozen in time as everyone stopped to mouth the words of the sad old songs. Brooms were held still and shovels were idle as memories flooded the minds of the people.

Memories that each held dear to themselves like treasures hidden away to be recovered only when special circumstances called them to the light. They played on and on until school bells signaled their little choir to start their lessons.

Nothing was said while the three put away their instruments. Danny and his wife spent more and more time at their shore house as old age began to take its toll on bodies bent by hard work. Niel visited them often and he and his brother rediscovered their days as children in the little farm buried in the swamp. Sometimes the grandchildren visited and Uncle Niel told them stories of the sea as they watched the waves crashing on the beach.

The boys made little swords of sticks and had mock battles in their make believe ships as they tried to relive the stories that they never tired of hearing. Mica and Stanley only added to their interest in the sea as they provided even more stories that grew in daring each time they told them. These were wonderful times and everyone was grateful to have them.

One morning Niel announced that he would be leaving for a trip back to New Orleans on business. He would take a ship to France and meet Lex who would be docking there on the Bonnie.

He and Lex would then go to New Orleans. He promised to return as soon as possible. He then asked Stanley and Mica to meet him at the tavern down town.

When he got there they were waiting. He sat down and ordered ale for the three of them.

He first turned to Mica and said, "You cannot go with me." Before Mica could respond he stopped him and said, "I have watched you and the pretty widow that runs the laundry." "She is a good woman and you know that America is no place for a black man."

"Slavery is not legal here."

I am an innocent businessman now and I will be much happier knowing you are safe here and happy." "I have established an income for you at my bank that will keep you and the lady for the rest of your lives." "I am asking you to do this for me." "I promise I will call on you if I ever need you."

He then looked at Stanley and said, "I need you and Mica here to look after and protect my family." "The children will see very little of me and I need to know that you will make sure I am remembered." "You promised to protect me for life, so I am asking you now to protect my memory."

"You also have an income for life at our bank." "If you decide to return to the sea I will understand, but all of these children will miss you."

There was a long silence before anyone said anything. Finally, Mica said, "I will never forget all of this." "Now I can ask that lady to marry me because I have been released from my pledge." "I always thought we would leave one day so I held back from her." "I hated the idea of returning to that place full of slavery." "I do not know how to thank you." Niel said, "Just look after my family and I will have been well paid."

Stanley waited a long time to speak. It seemed like he was deep in thought. He finally said, "I have never been happier than I am here with all those children and their parents." "I have no desire to return to the sea."

"I might take a wife, but I promise to protect your

family as though they were my own." "I am

comfortable doing this for one simple reason."

"Although my name is Polish, I was born and raised

in the Carpathian Mountains." "My family was what they

called Gypsies and they knew many things." "My

mother often talked about the "People" and how they

were something beyond the vampires that were used

to scare little children into going to bed." "I may be

wrong, but I have noticed a change in you since you

went to the swamps to see that old lady." "You never

age and you never stumble or fall." During that duel I

saw that man come more than close with his saber."

"His blade seemed to just bounce off." " I have been in

more fights than I can even remember." " I do not miss

the motion of a blade no matter how quick the strike."

"There is a difference between confidence and

knowing." "You knew you would not be hurt."

"Now, I may be entirely wrong about all of this and I know you will neither confirm nor deny it, but let us just say that I no longer fear for your safety." "I will do as you ask and I will do it with great gratitude." "Please know that Mica and I will be here if ever you need us." "Please return as often as you can." "Somehow, I doubt you will change very much."

There was much to do before Niel could leave. There was a wedding to throw for Mica, and a great dinner to say good-by to all the people here. The children now totaled fifteen and each one needed to be supplied with a sufficient trust fund for their future and deposits to cover the never-ending Irish babies to come. It was all quite wonderful and Niel reveled in the doing of it all. Mica and his new wife were a couple made in heaven. Their love was so obvious that only a fool could not see it. One afternoon, Niel sat down with the two of them in their kitchen. He asked them to raise their children with love and strict direction and he would see that the finest universities would be made available to them and paid for. He said, "Mica, you are my friend and a man of great intellect." "Your wife built a business with hard work, courage, and intelligence." "I will see that your children will be the pride of Ireland with the finest educations available if you two direct them toward those goals." "You know that I never lie." "I want to see the day when they argue the most difficult cases in the courts, or heal the worst of the worst in the hospitals."

"I am selfish and I want the things that matter to me so your black children must have every opportunity that money can buy because I hate slavery and I need to prove the worth of your people."

"Forgive me my selfishness but damn the bigots and damn the fools that cannot see past the color of your skin." For one of the few times Niel broke down into tears.

He said, "Not everyone can be as hard as I am." "It has always been easy for me because I see life as a simple set of basic rules that require very little thought."

"Decide what you think is right and do it." "Never let anyone judge you, ever." "Do not look back and second guess a decision that is too late to change," "Deal with it." "Expect nothing from anyone and you will never be disappointed." "Live in your own morality that you are comfortable with." "Do whatever it takes to build a future for your family and never look back." "In two generations no one will know what you did or who had to die to make it happen." "Simple, easy, and for me; comfortable to live with." "If I am a fool, then let the fools rule the earth."

Mica was married to a woman named Pearl. She was extremely black with skin so smooth and beautiful that it looked like the still water of a lake in the moonlight. Her eyes were huge and brown like the shiny mahogany of the finest of furniture. She was tall, about five feet ten inches and she stood like a soldier guarding the gates of heaven. Her figure was thin upon those long legs, and she moved into the kind of curves that make men quiver. To say she was beautiful was to say way too little. She explained to me that she came from a tribe known as the Bushmen of the Kalahari Desert in northwest Africa. They were very tall people and very good hunters. There was no greed among her people and no crime. "Everyone strove to make the finest arrows for the hunt that kept them alive, but everyone gave their arrows away." "The animal killed in the hunt belonged to the man that made the arrow."

"It was his responsibility to share the meat with the whole tribe." "Do the best for others and the rewards will be returned to you." Niel kissed her hard on each cheek and said, "I am pleased to give my dear friend to you." "Please allow me to do whatever I can for the children of two such special people."

Soon Stanley came to him. He said, "Here is my wife Mary Marie, she is as round as a peach and twice a sweet." "I am a man luckier than St. Paul himself to have found her." "She comes to me with six wee ones of her own and a husband as dead as "Kelsey's beer keg". "I love her like the Wales love the sea and she makes the world worth opening your eyes to each morning." There was nothing for Niel to do but laugh and give them both a great hug.

"Somehow Stanley you always say the words that are in my heart before I have the chance to get them out. Your face and hers radiates your happiness and for that I am greatly satisfied. Niel left on the next tide. It would be a very long time before he returned, but he would forever be a guardian angel to his family.

Niel did go to France and leave there on the Bonnie. He spent many years at sea and had many adventures before he once again settled in New Orleans and eventually met Getts and all the rest. He kept in contact with his family in Ireland over all the years and used the People to cover for him and make sure all were safe and prosperous. His brother and all of his immediate family passed away and he became the famous uncle that fought pirates and duels with royalty all over the world. There were many births and deaths from wars and natural causes. The first black member of the Irish Parliament had a familiar last name and a doctor with a Polish last name became a famous scientist all financed by the infamous Uncle O'Niel.

O'Niel, my friend and my brother of the People said that I should write the next words from our experiences together. How could he know that I had already begun

PART FIVE

CHAPTER 52

"I was born in a tall tent on the sands of Persia," explained Bart. "My father was a Lord sent to fight the infidels for the return of the Holy Land". "Instead, he fell in love with a soft skinned Persian woman from a fine family of merchants." "He was a good man, the son of a famous Lord and friend of the king." "He was known for his skill with a sword and for the beautiful wife he left back in England."

"He knew he would return one day to his duties and to that wife, but his heart was captured by the lovely lady from Persia."

Her father had several wives of his own so he did not see the problem and Bartholomew was readily accepted as a son-in-law. They named their little boy after his father, but it was way too difficult to say in their language so it was shortened to Bart. The people of that land seldom had any last name. When asked they would say, "I am Abdul of the tribe of Mohamed."

If the head of their tribe was also named Abdul then they would be Abdul of the tribe of Abdul. People from the West did not understand this so they assumed his full name was Abdul Abdul.

It was very late at night and Bart and I had been talking for a long time. He knew I wanted to know his story and so he had finally relented.

Once he relaxed and began to relate the details to me, he seemed to enjoy the telling of it and as much as I was thrilled to hear it I was also feeling that it was drawing the two of us even closer. It was strange and wonderful at the same time to look at him and picture his life a thousand years ago. He was only three years old when his father was summoned by the king to return to England. Bart would never see him again. His grandfather insisted he call him father because he heard all the Christians use the term to describe their father and their father in heaven which he found confusing, but he liked the respect it seemed to give him. Bart's mother would remain faithful to her husband for the rest of her life which gave her plenty of time to spoil her only child. She spoke to him in English at all times so, "You will be able to speak with your father when he comes back." The rest of the family which was quite large with all the wives and children spoke a perfect Persian dialect, but when they were with people outside the family they spoke Farsi. Farsi was a language spoken by all tradesmen from Persia to Egypt to China. It was the single unifier for everyone even as far away as India. Throughout Europe, the Jewish people spoke Yiddish much the same way.

The head of their tribe was a man named Nasha and all of the Nasha tribes' people were in the business of trade. They would be traveling all the time throughout all of Eastern Europe and Asia. Before he could walk, Bart knew how to ride a camel or a horse. He was also given a knife made of the finest Damascus steel and he was trained every day in the use of it. Bart and Father traded in pearls. They bought them, sold them, and traded them for rare spices especially in China. They were easy to transport, but they were also the most dangerous to carry through the crowded cities and the mountain trails.

They traveled in caravans with other traders, but they were unique in that many of the men and boys that traveled with them were trained warriors and assassins from their families.

All the boys and many of the girls were trained to use a knife and a sword in addition to a garrote and hand to hand skills taught by the Chinese.

Those children that showed an aptitude for it were trained as assassins and those skills were another of their products for sale. Bart was trained to be an assassin from the time he was old enough to understand the work required.

Father insisted on it. By the time he was twelve, he had traveled through all of Asia and the bulk of all the countries with ports on the Mediterranean Sea.

In addition to Farsi, English, and Persian he became fluent in Chinese from a martial arts teacher hired by Father. He worked out with Bart seven days a week from the time he was seven years old and Bart became very close to him.

Father was thrilled to have a son that could negotiate in Chinese for him. This allowed them to travel further north into China, where no one spoke Farsi. Father wanted to buy saffron, which was gathered and pressed into blocks.

The cultivating and gathering of saffron was so difficult that only the Chinese at the time could produce it. It was highly desired throughout the world and the market price per ounce was higher that gold. As they traveled north it became obvious that no one was willing to sell to them until early one morning as they were all sitting around their tents a large group of men on horses rode up to them and stopped. They were as fierce looking a group of warriors as they had ever seen aand there were at least one hundred of them. Chi Low the teacher went down on his needs with his head pressed to the ground and screamed for the others to do the same. Bart and Father alone remained standing when a huge man covered in armor and weapons marched up to face them and said, "You must kneel before me. I am the warlord for all the land as far as you can see and no one will so much as talk to you without my approval."

Bart translated for Father and Father told him to tell the warlord that he is welcome to join them in their tent where he will be treated according to his rank with great respect, but they kneel down to no one. The Warlord got red in the face and said, "If I cut off your legs you will soon bow down to me."

Bart stepped closer to the warlord and said in a very soft voice, "Before anyone touches Father I will have killed you."

The Warlord boomed in laughter and said, "Little boy I think I will have to kill all of these people, but you I will save because you are so fearless." Bart then said in a very loud voice, "Pick out your finest soldier and I will challenge him to fight to the death." By this time, Chi Lo was translating so everyone with Father knew what he was saying. Father was very afraid, but Chi Lo convinced him that Bart was in no danger. He whispered to Father that these men with all their armor were slow and poorly trained so Bart would be too fast for them."

He said, "Bart is a quick and deadly opponent who feels no fear or remorse for what he sees as part of life. Do you want him to kill the man quickly or do you want him to take his time and cut the man to pieces?" Father was so surprised that he could not answer so Chi Lo told Bart to slowly show his skills.

The group of killers parted and a very large man covered in armor walked up to Bart. He had a sword in one hand and a large knife in the other. The warlord backed away, but as he did he instructed his soldier to make it quick. The top of Bart's head did not reach the other mans' shoulder.

Bart stepped back and got in his fighting stance. So far he had shown no weapons. The man charged swinging both his sword and his knife in great loops. At the last moment Bart sat down on the ground and his knife appeared from nowhere and sliced into the right thigh of the man as he past. So far Bart had shown no emotion, but the big soldier was crying out in anger and pain as the blood ran down his leg.

This time he approached Bart with more caution.

When he was close enough he swung his great sword at Bart with all his strength to cut Bart in half.

Bart calmly deflected the blow off to an angle and then kicked it as it went past him.

The sword stuck in the left leg of the great soldier and forced him to fall to the ground. When the man tried to pull the sword from his leg, Bart pulled a long curved sword from over his shoulder and hit the sword stuck in the leg and broke the sword in half.

With two more swift movements he cut off the hands of the man and then he spun around in a circle and cut off his head which flew through the air and landed at the feet of the Warlord.

A great quiet settled over everything as the Warlord stared at the blinking eyes in the severed head of his champion.

A moment later the Warlord and all his men broke out in uncontrolled laughter as the head was kicked about by all the men and the body was carried away. He finally settled down and said to Father, "Sell the boy to me." Father explained that he was not a slave, but a member of his family.

The Warlord threatened to kill them all and just take him, but Chi Lo explained that all of these people including most of the women were as well trained as Bart and trying to kill them all could be very costly especially when Bart would swear to eventually kill the Warlord. Chi Lo, Bart, Father and the Warlord went into the tent where all were fed and treated as royalty.

They negotiated for most of the day and finally came to an agreement suggested by Bart.

They would make a huge trade for saffron now and Father would return in one year with a large supply of weapons made with Damascus steel. They would trade again for the saffron and Father would be given safe passage both ways.

The Warlord turned out to be a Mongol and he gave his daughter to be with them if they would leave Bart with him for one year. He explained that he wanted Bart to teach his sons and he wanted Bart to meet their leaders and open more trade with the south.

His daughter could become an interpreter for all of them in the future. He explained that she was currently skilled in many other languages. Bart's mother would miss him very much, but he was at the age where boys gravitate away from their mothers, and she was very excited about having a daughter if only for a year.

Chapter 53

Bart enjoyed teaching the twelve sons of the Warlord, who turned out to be named Noyan which means simply, prince. The boys ranged in age from three to fifteen and all of them had heard of the fight with their fathers' champion.

They were good children and their father was a most devoted man. As time passed Bart learned that the Mongols were very dutiful to their Kahn and to their families. The sons would die without a question for the family and the entire tribe would do the same for their Kahn. Bart soon fell in love with the sense of devotion that he missed from his real father. One day while he was training the boys to a point of exhaustion their father walked in to watch. After watching for an hour or so he asked Bart how all the stretching and jumping would make better fighters of his sons. Bart called out to his oldest son Moritee and told him to bring over his sword. Bart took a silk scarf and threw it into the air. As the scarf tried to land on the blade of the sword it slowly was cut in two.

Bart turned to Noyan and said, "Is that sharp enough for you?" Noyan just smiled. Bart walked five feet away and turned and said, "Take my sword and try to cut me." Noyan refused, but Bart said, "Listen you fat old fool, you can never hit me." Noyan could not tolerate the insult so he grabbed the sword and went after Bart with a vengeance. Each time he missed with the sword the boys could not suppress a laugh which only infuriated the Noyan more. Finally after poor Noyan was exhausted, he put down the sword and demanded the servants bring him some fermented milk to drink. All his sons ran to him and piled on top of him with hugs and nose rubs until he gave up and joined them in the laughter. Bart could just watch and wonder what it would be like to have a father and brothers. Soon everyone piled off of Noyan and they all, including Noyan, piled onto Bart. Half the boys were older than him, but he soon realized that family love among these people had no bounds.

Loyalty, honor, and steadfast devotion was their credo and it began with their family and spread out to all the Mongols. They were hugging him and licking his cheeks and he had never been happier in his life.

He dismissed the class amongst all the laughter and giggles and went to a chair which he offered to Noyan and then got one for himself.

He said, "I have come to love your family as though it was my own." "You tricked me and it is the best trick I have ever had played on me." You knew that all my moves and all my killer instincts could not hold up to your loving family." "Every day, I am glad for you and for me that this has come to me." "What can I do to repay you?" Noyan was quiet for a very long time and finally he said, "We, the Mongols have conquered much of the world. The sons of Genghis have become Chinese Mongols and they will conquer the what is left, but those of us that that stay here in China must continue on for our families. I want only for my family. I need you to give us an income in addition to the land that we hold." "I want to create a Tong that my family will control, and others will pay for our skills as assassins."

Bart thought for some time and then he finally said, "You will need to control something greater than assassins. You should make an effort to control all of the saffron market. My family can handle all of the marketing of that product you will need.

We can also market your services here in China and be very discreet about it." I will train your sons and anyone else you want, but are you ready for the next six months while I train them?" Noyan said, "Do whatever you feel you need to do."

The sons of the officers in his command were added to the training group along with other young men of promise. At Bart's insistence they were all housed and fed in the same building.

They wore nothing but a small wrap around their waist and between their legs during all the training no matter how cold it was. Bart explained that it was to teach them to concentrate on their training to the exclusion of all else. They were all aware of what Bart had done to the champion so there was no need for him to prove himself. Bart allowed anyone to come and watch them work so there was always a crowd observing. Soon a group of young girls started to mimic their training moves at the other end of the hall. Bart watched with interest as they worked as hard as their male relatives. After about a week he went to them and asked why they were training so hard? One young woman of about fourteen stepped forward and said, "I am Mooti, and we wish to be trained also. We decided to show you how hard we were willing to work before we asked to join your classes." "Chinese women are chained to all the old rules of their society. We wish to remain Mongols, but the longer we remain in China, the more difficult that becomes." Just then several women came over to Bart. They were dressed as

Mongols and they were obviously the mothers of these girls.

"We will guarantee that the Kahn of this tribe will permit the training," the leader said loud enough for everyone to hear. Throughout our history we women have stood beside our men or in front of our children to fight off invaders." We need to know that nothing of this equality will be lost to our daughters." Bart asked how she could be sure the Kahn would approve and all of them laughed. "Noyan is my husband and our Kahn," she answered.

"I have my ways of getting to his inner softness, but the best way is the easiest.

"He loves to reason things out to come to the best decisions." I heard your trainer say that your women were trained as well as your men." "If that is true, why would we give up such potential talent when it is available, and who could become a better assassin than a Mongol woman?" This too caused a great deal of laughter.

A moment later Noran walked into the great hall. He walked up to Bart and said, "I heard all of that discussion and I agree with my wife." "We are a small group in a country of great population." "Our power can only come from the fear and the need we create, and our women can only add to that."

"I have knives and swords made that are exactly like yours in size and weight. The only difference is the quality of the steel and the fact that they are not sharpened." "These will be brought to you when you need them."

"If you want anything else just let it be known and you will have it." With that said, Nolan turned and walked away.

The class was soon grown to four times the original size. Many of the mothers joined their daughters and even many of the soldiers came to be trained. Bart broke them up into smaller groups and placed some of the more talented students in charge. The work time was increased to sixteen hours a day, every day. Bart could not believe how quickly they learned and how devoted they were to the process no matter how grueling it became. Men and women, boys and girls appeared on time every day with smiles and excitement. Bart expected many to drop out but the opposite was true.

More kept coming and the entire tribe got involved in supporting the project. The old women observed every work out and they were the first to chastise any student they thought did not work hard enough. The students just bowed their head to them and said, "Thank- you Mother. I will try harder."

Oddly enough, Bart was getting taller and all of his work outs with all of the classes were putting muscle weight on his frame.

One day Noyan sent for Bart. He immediately left the classes and went to the large hall where Noyan lived. When he entered the hall the guard at the door closed and locked it. The room was empty and there were no sounds.

Bart walked to the center of the room and went to his knees. He stayed in that position and waited. Suddenly a man dressed in all black silk bound out from behind a screen and dove over Bart and into a forward roll before doing a twisted flip in the air and landing on his feet very softly facing Bart. When Bart looked down, he noticed that his clothes had been cut to rags, but his skin was untouched.

The man in black bowed to him and motioned for him to stand up. In an instant the man in black sailed over his erect figure and without a sound cut away the rest of his clothing above his hips and again landed facing him. The next time he was charged, Bart, realizing that the man did not mean to harm him, moved to his right, flipped into the air and cut the long silk pants off the man in black. When they both landed on their feet Bart was bare from the waist up and the man in black was bare from the waist down.

They both started to laugh as Noyan pulled the scarf away from his face and gave Bart a great hug.

Noyan explained that he came from a long line of assassins but he was forbidden to teach it to anyone by the original Great Kahn. He further explained that he was never trained in many of the moves that Bart displayed. "One day the Mongol empire will go away just like all the others before, but I want the Tong of my people to last and change with the times. That can only happen if we establish ourselves as a service provider and we accumulate great wealth." "You arrived as though I had an answer to a prayer." "I never promised that I would not have another train my people." With that Noyan took off his shirt and tied it around his waist. It was the first time Bart saw the incredible amount of muscle and battle scars on Noyan's upper body. "Come with me now my young son and I will teach you to drink vodka."

The next morning Bart woke up with a severe headache. He was in a strange room with thick rugs and pillows covered in colorful silk everywhere.

There were also several young Chinese ladies all tangled up with him and everyone was naked. When he started to get up he was pulled back down by the women and through their giggles he was introduced to a redo of the night before only this time he was sober enough to really enjoy it. It was late morning before he got to the training hall. When he walked in everyone was deep into their work out. When they saw him, the men all saluted and the girls all giggled. His face turned a bright red, but he maintained enough control to get back to work. At the end of the days' work out Noyan showed up. Bart took him aside and spoke to him in private. A few moments later Bart announced that tomorrow there would be a special demonstration during practice. After that all the students left, Bart and Noyan made their plans.

The next day practice started as usual and everyone was working out with great effort. About half way through the work out Bart told them all to form a circle so he could demonstrate some new moves. This was not an uncommon event so everyone formed up very quickly with the taller students in the back rows and the smaller in front so everyone could see.

When they were all formed Bart told them all not to move no matter what happened.

His commands were always serious so there was no danger anyone would disobey. He held his head down for a very long time and then he leaped high into the air and ran at the tallest men in the circle. When he was a few feet away he dove over them with room to spare, made a full flip in the air and landed facing back toward the circle. He then ran around the perimeter of the circle and jumped on an angle over the heads of the next group.

He twisted in the air and landed facing the men he had just jumped over but he now had a sword in each hand. He made a short bow just as a long silk scarf fastened to the ceiling flashed red and black over the circle and a man all in black dropped to the floor behind Bart. Bart turned to face the intruder but he was too late to block his first strike with his long sword. Bart backed up and grabbed his stomach as blood began to flow. He quickly pulled his sash tight to stop the blood and prepared for the next attack. The man in black was covered head to toe in black silk and only his eyes showed. He moved swiftly as a cat as he slashed both blades at Bart. Bart knocked one away and avoided the second while making a swift stab at the intruders' side, which entered deep into the body. Blood squirted out between his fingers as he backed away. Bart ran at him and dove over his head while swiping down with his right hand sword. The intruder parried the blow, but not before it sliced into his left upper arm. The man in black dropped to his knees and plunged his sword up and into Bart's inner thigh. Bart landed on one leg and hobbled backwards. The intruder attacked with what speed he could gather. There was blood everywhere and they were both slipping into it. The students were silent as the shock of the battle set in. Bart dove at the man and buried his knife into his belly, but before he died the man in black made a mortal slash over Bart's kidneys.

The two men fell to their knees and held each other up as their blood drained out and onto the floor.

No one moved and no one spoke as the two kneeled in the throes of death. Finally, the man in black pulled out a small gourd and offered it to Bart. Bart took a long drink of the fiery vodka and handed it back. The man in black pulled the scarf off from his head and began to drink as the crowd gasped in shock to see their beloved leader Noyan covered in blood and drinking with Bart. They both stood up and bowed to the amazement of the crowd. They each pulled off the outer layer of clothing and exposed the now empty bags of blood strapped to their bodies.

They were like two little kids that had just pulled off the greatest prank. All the students rushed up to them with hugs and licks on their cheeks. They were mostly proud of their leader and his ability to make all those moves during the mock battle. Now more than ever they were determined to work hard and learn everything they could.

For the next several months Bart split the training into four sections. They would still train their bodies for four hours each day, but they would also spend four hours on stealth planning and weapon handling including throwing knives. Four more hours would be actual field training where they were supposed to carry out a complete operation up to the point of the kill.

Finally there would be another four hours of body workouts. A local priest was hired from a martial arts monastery to watch over the activity and tend to any injuries. Their ability to heal was amazing and Bart was intrigued by them. He drove them crazy with questions and they kindly responded to him. He had been working with them for eight months when a small caravan approached their land and they went out to meet it.

Bart was allowed to go with them which surprised no one. Since the mock fight, Bart and Noyan have been inseparable. They demonstrated many things to the students and when Bart turned thirteen Noyan gave him a home of his own and the three Chinese ladies to attend him. He also gave him ten horses which was the required amount for a soldier when they took to the field and Mongol bow and arrows for him to practice with. It would be a long time before he could actually pull the bow back the whole way. It always surprised him when he saw the younger boys pull back a bow with ease. The bow required muscles that took years to develop, but Bart still carried the bow with pride where ever he went. When they finally got to the camp of the small caravan Bart was surprised to see Father was with them. There were only about fifty people with him and they were all trained members of the family. There were no women, but there were at least one hundred pack camels. Father ran to him and took him in a great hug. Father stepped back and said, "Allah be praised, you have grown a foot and you are all muscle." Noyan stepped forward and said, "Father, we are pleased to see you again," and he hugged him and licked his cheeks. Father said, "I have much news of great import." Bart translated, but he had been teaching

Farsi to all the people so Noyan finally said in Farsi that he needed no translator.

Father had all his men begin to unload all the camels. There was a wealth of knives and swords all of the finest steel. There were rolls of black silk and fine black rope also made of silk. Noyan and all of his people were amazed. There was also a small wooden keg and thin plates of steel in boxes.

Father explained that people wanted the saffron so badly that half of this load was a gift and the other half was for more saffron. Noyan could not believe his good fortune. Father then told him we needed to talk in private. He explained that he returned early for several reasons.

First he wished to keep the girl a little longer. "She and my daughter have formed a bond and I do not have the heart to break it."

Noyan quickly agreed to a two year extension for both his daughter and for me. I was happy to stay. Next he said that the tribes to the south of us were already jealous of the trade arrangement and threatened to stop any caravan heading north.

There are four leaders that are causing the problem and he gave us their names. Noyan knew all of them. "I suggest you make plans to remove them." I would do it for you but the Great Kahn would not approve." Noyan explained that with Bart to help it would be no problem. "And last of all I bring you a small barrel of poison. If you dip the tip of your blades in the poison, even a scratch will kill your victim.

I suggest you mark any blade with the poison on it. Once the blade is poisoned it cannot be cleaned." There are fifty knives that will hold an edge, but they are, otherwise, of poor quality.

I suggest you use them for the poison," Father explained.

CHAPTER 54

There was a great feast that night, and all the people were invited to the celebration. There were dancing and wrestling matches and wonderful demonstrations of accuracy with a bow and arrow. At one point Father asked Bart to demonstrate the metal gong dance. Bart tried to talk his way out of it but everyone insisted. They had no idea what it was. Father placed a dozen gongs of various sizes around the room in a large circle. Twelve of his men stationed themselves about ten feet from their respective gongs and waited at attention.

Several of the Persians took out instruments and began to play. Bart moved to the center of the room and began to dance and twirl in a circle as he moved around the room.

Every now and then one of the twelve men would run past their gong and hit it with a thick stick and then hold the stick in the air and keep running.

Like a flash a knife would fly from Bart's hand, glance off the gong and become imbedded in the stick the man was carrying. The music got faster and Bart continued to twirl to the beat as one by one his knives hit each gong and then stuck in the stick each man was running away with. Bart never opened his eyes during the entire dance. Everyone was wild with admiration and wanted to know if it was a trick. Father explained that it was not and Bart could do it again and again without a miss.

Noyan ran to Bart and picked him up in a bear hug. He said, "I will never doubt your skills as long as I live." "I have seen Monks perform great mastery with weapons, but nothing is as impressive as this."

"We must have our young ones begin to train as soon as possible." Bart said, "The dance is very entertaining, but there is a purpose in it." Noyan quieted everyone and asked Bart to explain. Bart told them that the vibrations from the gong indicated the bath of the man that hit it and the sound of the running feet gave indication of speed and direction. "You must learn to calculate these things in your mind to determine the exact location." "If you wanted me to stop a runaway thief and you struck a metal object at the angle he was running, I could bring him down with a knife without ever seeing him." "No one can out run the speed of a well thrown dager." Noylan had a big smile and he said to Father, "You have been generous beyond my wildest dreams with this young man and I will repay you in kind."

He called for one of his wives to bring her daughter. The girl was fifteen and considered the right age for marriage. Noylan asked Father if any of his sons were with him.

Father called to his son Abram. Noylan said, "I will give your son this wife who is the child of my first wife and very special to me." If you agree our two tribes will be joined by this union and we will all be one family." Chi Lo the teacher stepped forward and explained that this was more than a great honor. It was something he had never seen before.

Mongols often join families and tribes through a wedding, but only with other Mongols. "If you do this, Noylan and all his people will have to defend you and all of yours." "The two of you will be as brothers and the children from this union will have all the acceptance as members of this Mongol tribe." "He will also expect you to come to his aid in any way you can now and forever." "I believe this union will make you and Noylan very rich and with wealth comes power. There is always a risk, but that is what we all really trade in, is it not?

It turned out that Abram was nineteen and yet unmarried. The girl, Li Bo, was very beautiful and very much desired by all the young men of the tribe. She moved with the grace of the Chinese, but she was raised in the Mongol tradition. Bart also recognized her as one of his most aggressive students.

Father stepped forward and hugged Noylan and they licked cheeks to show their affection and approval.

The ceremony would begin immediately and there would be a great celebration that evening. Abram was shy around women, but at nineteen with thousands of miles behind him he was not without experience.

When he first saw Li Bo, he was instantly taken by her beauty and grace. She would be returning to Persia with Father and her new husband in a few days. Abram was also pleased to find out that she spoke Farsi and he hoped she would teach him Mongol and Chinese. Bart took Father and Noylan aside and told them he would be leaving after the ceremony, but he would return in a few days. They asked why and he said he needed to prepare a wedding gift for them. Hours later Bart was gone. He moved swiftly south along the trade route used by Father and everyone else. Bart traveled swiftly all day and deep into the night. When he finally decided to rest he found a spot well hidden in a grove of trees. He sat down beside the small fire he had built and began to eat the wheat cakes he had taken with him. A moment later he said without lifting his head,

"You may as well come and join me after running behind me all day." A woman in her late thirties appeared at the campfire and sat down. She said, "I should have known that I could not follow you undetected." Bart asked her why she was there and she told him she wanted to learn.

She further stated that all her family had been taken by disease and she was too old to start again. "I have found a new purpose in life now that you are training us all and I want to be the best." My name is Lin and I will do whatever you command, but please do not send me back." "No, I will not send you back, but I will not wait for you either," Bart explained.

They traveled at that grueling pace for two more days until they came to a small village. That was the home of Chi Lo and the first of the leaders that threatened Father. Lin dressed in rags and walked slowly into the village. She tried to beg for some food which quickly made her invisible to the rest of the people. It was an act Bart had used before. She returned to their camp several hours later to tell all that she had learned. She explained that there was to be a banquet that night for all the royal members of the family and officers in the army. About sixty people would attend and the area would be well guarded all around the large hall. While they sat and waited, Lin asked Bart if he had ever killed before and he said that he did. She asked him how old he was at the time and Bart drew in a deep breath and said, "People in the profession never speak of these things except to teach others so I will answer you." He said he was five the first time he was introduced to this business." Lin was shocked. He continued, "There are many men in the lower countries that prefer boys as sex partners and there are even families that train their sons to accommodate that preference. Father was doing a great deal of trading with one such man that was very powerful and a very deadly person to have for an enemy." "He always traveled with a large group of his body guards so he was not an easy man to get to. "One night he became belligerent and insisted Father give Bart to him or he would kill our whole family. Father is a happy merchant who is kind to everyone, but he is also deadly dedicated to his family." "Father told him to return later and Bart would be waiting for him in the back of the tent." All of the women in the tribe were dressed that evening in their most provocative clothing and as the man came into the tent they tried to get his attention, but he just pushed them away as he went to the back of the tent. His men saw this as an opportunity to enjoy the women he refused and began flirting with the women.

The man came into the back tent and began to come at Bart. He told him to remove his clothes. Someone was playing a flute somewhere so Bart began to dance as he slowly removed his clothes. When Bart got very close to him he reached for him and Bart smiled as he slit his throat. He grabbed for him again and Bart slit his eyes. Bart pushed him onto the sand so he would not bleed on the rug and he waited by the side of the doorway. One of his men peeked around the door to get an eyeful and Bart slit his eyes also.

He cried out just before Bart slit his throat. When his men tried to run to help, the women dispatched them quickly and quietly. Any men he had outside were also killed. They dragged the bodies far out into the freezing cold wilderness and left them for the wolves and the howler camels to make short work of them. No one ever asked for them and no one ever questioned, but they were soon offered many contracts to rid the earth of certain unwanted people.

We waited until it was getting dark and the celebration would soon begin. Bart walked up to the guard outside the tent and said he had a gift from Noyan for Chi Lo. He told Bart to wait.

Soon a priest came up and said, "What is it". Bart opened his hand and showed him a magnificent pearl. He explained that Noylan wanted to show his love for his southern neighbors and ask for a meeting to discuss these things. He asked if Bart was an official and he told him that he was just there to give him the gift. Bart returned the pearl to the pouch it was in and put it in his pocket. The priest told him to give it to him and he would deliver the message. Bart insisted that he was to give it to Chi Lo personally. Bart smelled all the cooking food and began to appear faint. The priest asked me when I had last eaten and I told him he did not remember. He put his arm around Bart and took him to the kitchen. He handed him a bowl and chopsticks and told him to eat his fill. He started to leave and then turned and said, "Give me the purse and I will do your bidding." "Chi Lo will never permit you to come to him in person." He hesitated for a few seconds and the handed him the purse, and thanked him for his kindness. Bart knew that purse would never leave the pocket of the priest. He only hoped that the stone he used to replace the pearl would remain hidden until he was far away.

As he inspected all of the food Bart offered to stack the plates and the chopsticks and spoons on the table for the servants. They asked that he just take them out to the dining room and they would arrange them. They explained that these were their finest and everyone would get a set of the matched pieces just like those of Chi Lo. They said that their master wanted them all to see how gracious he was. He took it all out to the main room where he dipped the tips of the spoons and the chopsticks in the poison. He then took a cloth, dipped it in the poison and ran it around the edge of each stack of plates and bowls. He threw the cloth under the table, returned to the kitchen where he loaded a towel with bread and meat and cheese, thanked them, and went out the back of the tent. He moved as quickly as he could without being noticed and into the woods where he broke into a run to go find Lin. When Bart saw her he explained that they must leave as quickly as they were able.

They ran for most of the evening until they were safely away. Three days later they reached the village of Tudor bige, the next warlord.

They found shelter in a small house on the edge of the village. They spent the next few days walking around the village and asking about the trade potential.

Bart had no problem passing as the son of a trader since that was exactly what he was. One morning while they were buying food they heard people talking about how the hand of the devil had killed over a hundred people including Chi Lo and all of his officers and staff.

Even all of the kitchen staff died and the people ransacked the hall and stole all of the valuables. People were still dying and now they believed that the dishes and everything else taken from the hall had a curse on it and they buried all of it. Most of the people left went north to join Noylan.

Tudor was a great fat man that was known for his cruelty. He ruled by fear alone and he was a glutton in all things especially the accumulation of wealth.

It was said that he slept in a room filled with gold and teals of silver. No one would miss him if he were gone except his son that was as fat as he was, but he lacked intelligence and therefore depended on his father.

Bart decided that this death must be simple and quick. It was obvious that the people would rebel as soon as Tudor was gone. Bart did not want to be there when it happened.

One night Bart and Lin dressed completely in black silk including their feet, stole into the hall of Tudor-bige through a small hole they cut in the roof. They dropped a rope down to the floor and climbed down. Without a sound they dispatched the guards inside the hall. When they came to the door to the sleeping quarters of Tudor - bige they could see where he had several large metal bolts locking the door from the inside. He and his son locked themselves in with their wealth every night. To leave their chamber required all the bolts to be released and the door pushed open into the great hall. Bart took out a razor sharp knife and began to slowly cut a small opening between the stone floor and the bottom of the door. Into the hole he began to pour lamp oil from a keg beside one of the lights in the hall.

Every so often he added liquid from a small bottle he had with him to the oil. When he was done he took a small ember from the fireplace in the center of the room and lit the oil. When he was sure it was burning he took the wooden stopper from the keg of lamp oil and forced it into the hole under the door making it impossible to push the door open from the inside without a great force.

They repelled back up the rope and soon were gone into the night. When Lin asked about the contents of the bottle he added to the lamp oil, Bart explained that it was more of the poison and that the fumes from the burning oil would be just as deadly as the poison itself. Lin said nothing.

In two days they reached the home of Lu Shan. It was a very small village settled right on the confluence of two rivers. The people were kind enough to the two strangers but there was little there except the fort and the bridge over the rivers. Bart asked Lin why Lu Shan was so powerfull. She explained that he controlled all the river traffic going both north and south. He also controls the only bridge within a hundred miles so he charges for crossing either way.

His father was a great man in these parts and the people built the fort and the bridge in his honor, but the son is a terrible ruler and he enjoys watching torture. It is said that he pays great sums of money to people who can keep the person alive the longest while keeping them in great pain. Bart was aware that the art of torture was very familiar in his home land of Persia. There were men and women that sold their services to the wealthy for a price and the poor subject of their art could be kept alive for many days in tremendous pain.

For two days Bart searched for an alchemist. When he finally found one he was not surprised to find her to be a fellow Persian. He explained what he needed and offered to pay her with the pearl he carried. She looked at him and said, "If this oil is for Lu Shan then there is no charge today." Bart put the pearl back in his pocket. The woman further explained that she knew of his people and of their special talent. She said, "One day I may have need of you or your people." "I will expect you to return this favor." Bart bowed his head and said, "To be sure. It is a pledge to you before Allah." When they left Bart stopped to buy a cheap copper ring. He took his knife and made several sharp burrs all around the band. He put it in his pocket and they went to the center of the market to wait. Soon Lu Shan appeared as he did every day to walk the market and collect his taxes. Bart took out the ring and put on leather gloves. He sprinkled the powder on his palm and then rolled the ring in it before putting it on his gloved hand. He held up the pearl in his left hand and it caught the attention of Lu Shan. Lu Shan came close to see the pearl and as he did Bart dropped to his knees and said, "Please buy this Pearl from this poor leper. Lu Shan noticed that Bart was covered head to toe in old clothes. He jumped back, but not before Bart ever so lightly rolled the ring up the back of his bare calf. The scratches were tiny and barely noticeable, but they were there. Lu Shan ordered his guards to chase the leper away so Bart got up and ran out of town. Lin soon joined him and asked what happened. "I watched the whole thing, but I saw nothing," she said.

Bart explained the scratches on the back of Lu Shan's leg. He also told her that the skin and eventually his whole leg and body would begin to rot. It would take weeks of excruciating pain for the poison to finally kill him, but he would surely die. He told her that there was only one drug to stop it, but it was known to his family alone. He suggested they move on to the next village.

The last place belonged to a warlord named Andruz.

It was very large and there were many buildings of fine wooden structure. In the center was a small palace with extensive gardens surrounding it and beautiful fish ponds and fountains. When they entered the city people were kind and friendly. There was a feeling of tranquility as the people went about their business.

When Andruz name came up it was spoken with pride and this place was the opposite of the other three. Bart and Lin walked to the center of town and then to the entrance to the palace. When they stood in the opening a man came out to meet them escorted by several guards.

He walked right up to them and gave a slight nod of his head. He was tall and hansom with dark hair and a beard trimmed to a point below his chin. He said, "I welcome you Master Bart, son of my friend from Persia and close confident of Noyan the conqueror of all the northern lands." I am Andruz and I have been watching your exploits since you left Noyan." Andruz took off a magnificent sword and handed it to Bart. He said, "This is a gift from me to show you that there is nothing to fear here." He then turned and discharged his guards. "Please, come with me", he said. They followed him into the palace where a beautiful table had been set with glasses of wine and fine food of every kind.

Andruz picked up a rolled and sealed paper and handed it to Bart.

He opened it and read," My dear son of my beloved daughter, Please believe that Andruz does not lie. He and I have worked together for many years and I needed him to uncover the names of those that would kill us."

I am aware that you have already eliminated those three on the list and I thank you for it.

Their people have already come under the rule of Noyan and he has promised to be fair with all of them.

"You, Noyan, Andruz and I will set up the finest chain of caravans to ever enter this land and they will all be protected by the armies you train for our friends." It is now time for you to return north.

"May Allah guide you ever more," Father.

It was Father's writing and Bart was happy along with Lin to return to Noylan. There was a great feast that night and Andruz provided horses and guards for the trip back. The return trip did not take long because of the horses and the protection provided. At each stop people bowed to Bart and said his name with reverence. He was spoken of as the Persian son of Noylan and the protector of the people. It seemed as though Noylan wanted the people to be aware that he had sent Bart to free them and by sharing the glory Noylan was even more loved by the people.

Lin and Bart continued to work together training all of the soldiers. Lin took on

the role of body guard to Bart and she was always near him. Bart began teaching her all of the secrets he learned from childhood. They were together all the time and they were teased about being brother and sister. Father still made his caravan trips back and forth between Persia and China, but he now controlled several caravans that went all over. The two year deal with Noylan was extended to first four and then six years. Bart was now almost eighteen and he dressed as a Chinese Mongol and he and Lin traveled extensively throughout all of Asia.

Bart carried the sword given to him by Andruz, and he and Lin rode beautiful Arabian horses provided by Father.

As they traveled they set up trade agreements with people all over for Noylan and all of the War Lords in western China. Everything from spices to fine leather and silk cloth was moving into and out of China and Father was taking as much of it south into Persia and Egypt as fast as he could. Bart still trained every day and his skills were vastly improved. Lin remained at his side, but time was catching up with her. While staying with a wealthy Russian, they were surprised to get a message from Noylan asking for their return as soon as possible. They rode hard with their twenty soldiers that traveled with them everywhere. In a matter of days they were back at the palace that had replaced the simple hall that Noylan once occupied. He was now a very wealthy and powerful man thanks in no small way to Bart, and he liked to look the part. Noylan met them at the front gate. His spies had informed him of every mile Bart traveled. He stood with his huge arms extended as Bart left his horse and came to him. Noylan held him tight in an embrace and told him over and over how happy he was to have Bart home. "I miss watching you with the people and seeing how happy you make them. We have not had to worry about enemies for a long time and I must give you part of the credit. "Please come with me to my room where we can talk." Noylan then turned to Lin and said, "You look tired. I am afraid our young friend pushes you too hard. "Please go and rest while we talk."

When they got to his living quarters, Noylan poured them each a large glass of liquid with a red cast to it. He handed a glass to Bart and suggested he try it.

Bart took a large drink and smiled. He said that it was much smoother than the milk vodka they usually drank. Noylan explained that it was called whiskey and it came from very far to the west. Several barrels had arrived by caravan and they were a gift from some tribe near Frankia. It seemed that the Romans were giving them a great deal of trouble and they wanted to trade with us for metal knives and swords since their metal was so inferior to that of the Romans. "I will be keeping all of the whiskey for us and I will demand a great deal more, said Noylan.

Bart said that he had an Idea how to make the trade quick and easy. He said that his father would buy the weapons from the Romans who had stores of such things in great quantity, and then trade them for the whiskey and gold.

They would return here with the whiskey, but use

the gold to buy more weapons from the Romans and return for another load of whiskey. "We can keep what we need and sell the rest of the whiskey here in China at a very high price with ten percent going to the Kahn."

Noylan began to laugh until his sides hurt. He said, "Bart you truly are the devil." "You want to sell Roman weapons to their enemy to use against them and give gold from their enemies to the Romans to pay for it while making a huge profit from both sales that gives us a monopoly on the whiskey business here in China."

"It is so wild an idea that it will probably work." One of your uncles should set the whole thing up." I suggest the one that is married to my daughter." "I do not want you involved in it." They sat for a very long time and spoke of many things. Bart said how happy he was that every time he returned Noylan was in perfect health and seemed to never age.

Noylan brought out a chest that contained twenty small silver flasks. He told Bart that they contained a very special Whiskey just like they were drinking and that he wanted Bart to give him his word that he not only would drink some every day, but he would never share it with anyone. He described it as a health mixture that was added to the whiskey. Bart agreed and for the rest of the evening they talked of good things and happy times.

The next morning they ate together and finally Bart asked why he was summoned. Noylan explained that China has seen many Kahn rulers from the family of the great Genghis over the years. "We have conquered and ruled over vast territories and millions of people" The Kahn is now an educated man of great intellect, but the fire that lived in the heart of the Genghis Kahn has been replaced by political intrigue." Where the people once fought like demons for the spoils of women and horses, we now negotiate for money and position." "I am safe because you have trained the only real army in the empire." No one wants to challenge us and many come from the plains to join us for the training alone."

"For these past years that you have lived with me I have been giving you one of the great secret potions in all of China." "It has been in your food and in your drink." It will help to keep you healthy. "It is now in the flasks of whiskey, but you cannot share it because it takes years to develop a resistance to the poison in it." "It will kill anyone else".

Chapter 55

They spent the entire day talking about the political position the country was now in and the state of all the world powers. Noylan explained that one day Bart would have to leave and find his way in the other cultures of the world. He told him not to worry about China because it will always be protected by its very size. "China need only open its doors to aggression and by the time they reach the center they will be Chinese just like what happened to the Mongols." At that Noylan began to laugh as he stood up and showed off his silk clothing and the Chinese décor all around him. "Even I have succumbed to all that is Chinese". "There is a minister of finance that reports directly to the Kahn. He is a great thief, a coward, and a traitor." "Years ago the Genghis Kahn would have just cut his head off himself, but now the current Kahn fears backlash from the people controlled by this man. "The Kahn has given this problem to me to handle and I have decided that you are the only one that can solve it." "First, you are the most talented assassin in our world and second, you are not Chinese. I am sending you to him for training in finance and management." "He will be flattered because he and I have no connection and everyone is aware of my affection for you." I will also be sending with you a chest of silver as a down payment on your training." "He is rich now, but you will learn that there is never enough for these people and I am sure he will want you to train his home guards for nothing. "Do not be in a hurry." "I want you to know as much as possible before he dies." You may take Lin with you, but be aware that she is getting old and her days are numbered." Learn everything that you can from him and from everyone around him. "When you are satisfied that there is nothing left to gain from being there, find a way to kill him and anyone you think to be dangerous.

Bart thought about it for a very long time and finally began to pack all of the things he thought he might need. He took clothes, his swords and knives and the whiskey. He also took a huge howler camel to carry all of his things.

These camels were very big and strong. They were also hard to handle and they loved meat of all kinds, including Mongol arms and shoulders. During cold winters on the Steppes they were known to attack and eat horses, men and even wolves.

He had this particular camel for many years and they had formed a special bond. He and Lin were the only people that could get near Hannibal, which is the name he had given him. Several men had died or been horribly wounded by Hannibal over the years. You would have to kill him to steal his cargo, and howler camels were known to sense danger and attack a man fifty yards away if they felt threatened. It was best to avoid them.

Hannibal had long hair hanging from his chest and shoulders which was a perfect place to hide a large pouch. Bart typically carried his gold and jewels in it, but it also hid other things. It was impossible to see and only someone with a death wish would ever get close enough to find it. As they left for the trip they were accompanied by the twenty soldiers and they were armed with swords and knives both seen and hidden.

A full day before they reached their destination deep into ancient China they were met by a large group of about sixty soldiers and a carriage pulled by a team of beautiful horses. The small army rode into a formation as if to attack. Bart quietly ordered his ten men to prepare for battle and they formed a horse shoe shape with Bart and Lin in the middle.

As the enemy rode toward them Lin and Bart stood on their saddles as did two men in front of them and one man on each side. When the enemy horses were about four hundred yards away, Bart, Lin and all twenty of his men began to let loose a barrage of arrows that cut down and killed every one of the enemy before they were even close. A strange looking little man jumped down from the carriage and began to jump up and down and clap. He kept yelling "Well done, well done." Bart rode up to him through the mass of dead men and said, "I assume you are Chou Mai from your description given to me and I also assume these are some of your soldiers."

"You are right on both counts and you must be Bart and his famous soldiers." Chou Mai clapped his hands and an army of no less than one thousand soldiers rode out from behind the hills on both sides. "You may send your guards home now unless they would like to stay with you and train my army while you are here." Bart laughed and bowed deeply to Chou Mai. He said, "Master, you take no time living up to your reputation for frugality." "I will gladly trade you my training for the things I can learn from you." "Please train me in the art of numbers and I will make your army the envy of all China.

"You too seem to understand the value of negotiation and trade", said Chou Mai. "I will pretend that I do not know about the chest of silver you carry for me and you can pretend that it is a parting gift of appreciation when you leave." They both smiled and bowed to one another.

After that Chou Mai returned to his carriage and signaled them to follow. It took most of the day, but at last they came to the crest of a hill that looked down on a beautiful city surrounded by deep green water from a river that split and flowed around the city like a diamond in a bed of emeralds. All of the buildings were decorated with red, black green and every color you could think of.

There were beautiful gardens everywhere and all Bart could think of was how much the perfection of it reminded him of home. When he said so to Chou Mai, the older man bowed deeply and said that he was well aware of the beautiful palaces and gardens of the great city of the south. The complement warmed his heart and he would never forget it." He said, "For six generations of my family we have built and designed this city to be a place of peace and beauty for all to appreciate and enjoy."

"You are most gracious with the highest of complements."

"Please treat my city as your own while you are here."

"You are free to go anywhere unguarded that you wish"

Bart expressed his gratitude as they rode down the hill and entered the city. The streets were wide and all of them were paved with stone. There was a series of baked clay pipes that carried fresh water from the mountain springs and other pipes that took away the sewage and dumped it into the river far down stream. Most of the buildings were three stories high with shops on the first floor and living quarters above.

There were hanging gardens cascading down from every window and balcony.The smell of food was everywhere and the people were well dressed and clean. Vendor after vendor came to them with samples of food and then touched their feet as they bowed and backed away. It was so unlike the markets in Persia where every vendor pulled at you until you felt smothered by humanity. When they finally reached the gates of a beautiful palace that Bart assumed was the home of Chou Mai, the whole procession came to a stop. Chou Mai jumped out of his carriage and walked back to Bart.

Chou Mai explained that his soldiers would see to the men with Bart and Bart and Lin should walk with him into the palace. He further explained that no horses or carts were allowed past the gates in front of them.

Chou Mai had a smile of great excitement on his face as he led them through the gates. The palace itself sat a good one hundred paces back from the gates. As they entered they noticed that the wide path that wound its way to the palace door was not only surrounded by the most intricate flower beds and colored stones that Bart had ever seen, but the path itself was made up of a mosaic of small marble tiles that had perfect pictures of everything from ships to small insects and birds.

Every few feet there was a brief story written in perfectly carved black stones that told about the pictures close by. It would take hours to read it all and Bart promised himself that he would do just that before he left. The front doors of the palace were ten feet high and they were made of teak wood highly polished and inlaid with mother of pearl and many semiprecious stones. The door handles were carved ivory and as the servants opened them and bowed deeply Chou Mai, Bart and Lin entered a great hall.

There was a long bench just inside the door where Chou Mai sat down and motioned for them to do the same. As soon as they were seated servants brought each of them beautiful silk slippers with soft thick soles. The servants removed their boots and quickly replaced them with the slippers.

To adequately describe the hall and all of the beautiful rooms that were attached to it would take a life time in itself. There were entire walls made from a giant slab of carved jade. Gold and silver carvings were everywhere and the floors were covered with massive thick hand woven rugs.

Bart and Lin were speechless, as they tried to take it all in. When they thought they had seen it all, Chou Mai took them to a round top door that was covered in tiny bells. Chou Mai clapped his hands and two beautiful young women hurried to open the door. When they swung the door open the bells played a tune that was soft and wonderful to hear. Outside the door was a series of covered bridges that each went to a small house that was a scale model of the palace. Chou Mai told them to each pick a bridge and go to their personal home were they would stay while they were here. "You will each be prepared for dinner after you rest, by your personal servants." With that said he turned and walked away.

Bart and Lin went to their respective houses and they were not surprised to find each house to be as opulent as the rest of the palace, only scaled down in size. Two beautiful young servants followed Bart into the house. The two young women explained that they would be there to take care of his every want and need. There was a bath pool with warm water waiting for him in the next room and before he could say anything they began to remove all of his clothes. Once he was in the water they disrobed and joined him. After being on a horse for several days in the dirt and dust he was more than happy to just lay back and let them clean him. After his bath he went to a large plush bed covered in silk and quickly fell asleep. Several hours later he was awakened by his servants and they quickly dressed him in beautiful silk pants and a tunic that came to his knees. Once his slippers were on he was guided back to the main palace. Lin met him dressed in a beautiful silk dress with a slit up the side. It was bright red with embroidered flowers and her hair was pinned to the top of her head with ivory combs. She looked beautiful.

Both of them had made use of the weapons rack in their new dwellings so neither was carrying a sword or knife. They would not insult their host by being armed, and they knew the servants would tell Chou Mai everything.

They were guided to a large room with a long table and chairs. Like everything else, this room was also beautiful. Soon they were joined by their host and dinner was served. Chou Mai and Bart spoke of many things and Bart heaped praise on him for his beautiful home. Bart asked how long his family had served in the capacity of Treasurer to the Kahn and he was told that this family dated back to a time long before the Kahn rulers.

At the end of dinner Bart suggested that he and Lin begin to organize the army for training. He told Chou Mai that he would need a week to set the whole program up and with his permission they would wait to begin his schooling until after that. Chou Mai was very pleased and he took it as complement. The army was organized in the old Mongol way with ten soldiers reporting to a lieutenant, ten lieutenants reporting to a captain and ten Captains reporting to a Colonel. Above them all was a General and he commanded one thousand soldiers or more. Bart made himself the General and he and Lin began separating the men. The training would be sixteen hours a day seven days a week. Everyone including Lin and Bart took place in the training and Lin did more just by shaming the men then any incentive could have. There were a million things to do and Chou Mai quickly responded to any request that Bart made. Kitchens and adequate healthy food had to be supplied along with cooks and servers had to be established. A code of discipline was written in the old Mongol style and it was read to the troops every day. There was only one punishment, death.

While the troops were being trained the ranks began to swell as new men came to join. Promotions and demotions were constantly happening as the cream rose to the top. The thousand men soon became two thousand and the results were astounding. After just a few months there were archers and swordsmen showing superb talent and even though many of the officers were killed for bulking at commands, the new officers were excellent and the men became devoted to them. Bart spent as much time as he could with Chou Mai learning the difficult job of balancing books, and preparing for any and all kinds of potential disasters. He soon learned that his teacher was a man of great talent and zero compassion.

He was not above selling whole villages into slavery to cover up the money that got lost on its way to the Kahn's treasury and ended up finding its way to Chou Mai. As Bart made it seem like he was having great difficulty understanding the books, he was given more and more access to them. Chou Mai was convinced that his work with Bart was a waste of time and so he played at being the teacher. What he did not know was that Bart was tutored in what to look for by some of the best minds in China before he ever came to Chou Mai. Almost one fourth of the Kahn's taxes never left Chou Mai's hands. It was easy to compile a list of those that were also guilty by just listing the entries in the ledgers that showed payments made for no basic reason at all to them. They had been taking the money for so long that they felt secure.

While the army was kept in training, Lin worked with a very special group of about one hundred women. She trained them in the art of assassination. They learned quickly and they were totally devoted to her and Bart. They women were small and very strong. They could move without being detected just about any place they wanted, but their greatest value came from the fact that they were ruthless. They got their first field training by eliminating any of the soldiers that were not showing total devotion to the general and to Bart. When Bart was satisfied that the women were ready, he sent them out in small groups or alone to eliminate all the thieves on the list. They were given one week to travel through China and find their targets, and one week to make their kill. They were instructed to leave no witnesses. Many of their targets slept in heavily guarded rooms with their wives sleeping with them. The women were very efficient. One wealthy magistrate was killed in a matter of seconds along with his six guards and seven wives. The news traveled fast and it was not long before Chou Mai was aware that someone was killing all of his associates. He went to Bart immediately and instructed him to surround the palace with soldiers to protect him. He especially wanted the new general, Moon, to be with or near him at all times. Bart suggested he also allow Lin and four of her women to guard him at all times. Chou Mai was very grateful and told Bart how having him there was the best move he had ever made.

The next day Noylan came to the front gate with twenty of his soldiers. He was quickly surrounded by the soldiers of Chou Mai. He demanded entry and was finally allowed to come into the compound after several hours had passed. Bart and Chou Mai met him at the door to the palace. Lin and the four assassins stood close by. Chou Mai said, "Why are you here?" "I have not concluded the training of Bart yet." For what appeared to be a long while there was not a sound and then Noylan took a step closer to Chou Mai and said, "The Kahn insists that you pay for all your family has stolen."

Chou Mai said, "My spies tell me that these twenty men are all of your protection." "I have two thousand trained soldiers surrounding you." "You are on the errand of a fool if you think you leave here with your life."

Noylan nodded to Bart and Bart commanded the army to stand at attention. Chou Mai demanded that his army kill the intruders. None of them moved. Noylan told him he should have stuck to keeping books. "More than half of these men are from my army and all of the rest are devoted to my officers and to Bart." In seconds Chou Mai was dispatched in pieces by the four women directed by Lin. Bart and Noylan went into the palace and Bart showed him around. It did not take Noylan long to decide to move his permanent home to this city. General Moon would take half the army and return to govern their northern territories. After a lavish meal for Bart, and Noylan and four strangers Bart had never seen before, Noylan made sure that everyone else was moved far from the room they were in. The six men sat silently until Noylan began to speak. "For quite some time we have been watching you Bart and grooming you to join our very special group." Noylan spoke for a very long time about the Red Gate and what it would require him to give up should he choose to join them. When he was finished Bart stood up to speak. "I realized a very long time ago that I would never marry." ""I have many brothers and sisters and they all are having children enough to satisfy my father" "It will be my honor to join you."

The six men were from all over the known world at that time. One of them held back to introduce himself last. He explained that his name was Sasha and he was the second one to become one of what would eventually be known as the People. He said, "The Great Kahn or what his followers called, the Genghis Kahn, was the first one to be introduced to the formula by the Chinese and I was the first one he brought to the People." I fought against him in many battles and even when we were defeated he could never kill me." "During the last battle I fought in he would not allow any of his men to fight me. "When the fighting was over and I was the last of his enemies alive they formed a circle around me and Genghis Kahn stepped into it." "He drew his sword and challenged me." I fought him for what was left of the daylight and into the dark. "I know I struck him many times with my sword, but he only smiled at me. "We continued until I collapsed from total exhaustion. I could no longer stand let alone lift my sword. He had me carried to his tent where I was fed and my wounds were cleaned and wrapped in soft clean cloth." "He told me of the People and explained why he was not tired and why my sword had no effect on him." "Now I am here to take you through the Red Gate if it is your desire"

Bart became one of the People and then joined his father to travel with him throughout the known world until his father died. He assisted many people through the years and became a very famous assassin. Lin stayed with Noylan and her pupils. Their training and reputation traveled all over, but the Japanese were their finest and the most devoted pupils. Every one hundred years or so he would meet up with Sasha and his new friend James. They would travel together until some new adventure came along that caused them to separate. The discovery of the New World" drew Bart away from Europe and he traveled with the Spanish armies to North America. He had been with Peter the Great and Napoleon. His services and experience were used by kings and conquerers throughout the world up to and until he met a small boy in ragged clothes that just wanted a full belly.